The Lion of the North

A tale of the times of Gustavus Adolphus

G. A. Henty

The Lion of the North: A tale of the times of Gustavus Adolphus Copyright © 2019 Indo-European Publishing

The present edition is a reproduction of previous publication of this classic work. Minor typographical errors may have been corrected without note, however, for an authentic reading experience the spelling, punctuation, and capitalization have been retained from the original text.

ISBN: 978-1-64439-297-3

CONTENTS

PREFACE

MY DEAR LADS,

You are nowadays called upon to acquire so great a mass of learning and information in the period of life between the ages of twelve and eighteen that it is not surprising that but little time can be spared for the study of the history of foreign nations. Most lads are, therefore, lamentably ignorant of the leading events of even the most important epochs of Continental history, although, as many of these events have exercised a marked influence upon the existing state of affairs in Europe, a knowledge of them is far more useful, and, it may be said, far more interesting than that of the comparatively petty affairs of Athens, Sparta, Corinth, and Thebes.

Prominent among such epochs is the Thirty Years' War, which arose from the determination of the Emperor of Austria to crush out Protestantism throughout Germany. Since the invasion of the Huns no struggle which has taken place in Europe has approached this in the obstinacy of the fighting and the terrible sufferings which the war inflicted upon the people at large. During these thirty years the population of Germany decreased by nearly a third, and in some of the states half the towns and two-thirds of the villages absolutely disappeared.

The story of the Thirty Years' War is too long to be treated in one volume. Fortunately it divides itself naturally into two parts. The first begins with the entry of Sweden, under her chivalrous monarch Gustavus Adolphus, upon the struggle, and terminates with his death and that of his great rival Wallenstein. This portion of the war has been treated in the present story. The second period begins at the point when France assumed the leading part in the struggle, and concluded with the peace which secured liberty of conscience to the Protestants of Germany. This period I hope to treat some day in another story, so that you may have a complete picture of the war. The military events of the present tale, the battles, sieges, and operations, are all taken from the best authorities, while for the account of the special doings of Mackay's, afterwards Munro's Scottish Regiment, I am indebted to Mr. J. Grant's Life of Sir John Hepburn.

Yours sincerely,
G. A. HENTY

CHAPTER I

THE INVITATION

It was late in the afternoon in the spring of the year 1630; the hilltops of the south of Scotland were covered with masses of cloud, and a fierce wind swept the driving rain before it with such force that it was not easy to make way against it. It had been raining for three days without intermission. Every little mountain burn had become a boiling torrent, while the rivers had risen above their banks and flooded the low lands in the valleys.

The shades of evening were closing in, when a lad of some sixteen years of age stood gazing across the swollen waters of the Nith rushing past in turbid flood. He scarce seemed conscious of the pouring rain; but with his lowland bonnet pressed down over his eyes, and his plaid wrapped tightly round him, he stood on a rising hummock of ground at the edge of the flood, and looked across the stream.

"If they are not here soon," he said to himself, "they will not get across the Nith tonight. None but bold riders could do so now; but by what uncle says, Captain Hume must be that and more. Ah! here they come."

As he spoke two horsemen rode down the opposite side of the valley and halted at the water's edge. The prospect was not a pleasant one. The river was sixty or seventy feet wide, and in the centre the water swept along in a raging current.

"You cannot cross here," the boy shouted at the top of his voice. "You must go higher up where the water's deeper."

The wind swept his words away, but his gestures were understood.

"The boy is telling us to go higher up," said one of the horsemen.

"I suppose he is," the other replied; "but here is the ford. You see the road we have travelled ends here, and I can see it again on the other side. It is getting dark, and were we to cross higher up we might lose our way and get bogged; it is years since I was here. What's the boy going to do now? Show us a place for crossing?"

The lad, on seeing the hesitation of the horsemen, had run along the bank up the stream, and to their surprise, when he had gone a little more than a hundred yards he dashed into the water.

1

For a time the water was shallow, and he waded out until he reached the edge of the regular bank of the river, and then swam out into the current.

"Go back," the horseman shouted; but his voice did not reach the swimmer, who, in a few strokes, was in the full force of the stream, and was soon lost to the sight of the horsemen among the short foaming waves of the torrent.

"The boy will be drowned," one of the horsemen said, spurring his horse up the valley; but in another minute the lad was seen breasting the calmer water just above the ford.

"You cannot cross here, Captain Hume," he said, as he approached the horsemen. "You must go nigh a mile up the river."

"Why, who are you, lad?" the horseman asked, "and how do you know my name?"

"I'm the nephew of Nigel Graheme. Seeing how deep the floods were I came out to show you the way, for the best horse in the world could not swim the Nith here now."

"But this is the ford," Captain Hume said.

"Yes, this is the ford in dry weather. The bottom here is hard rock and easy to ride over when the river is but waist deep, but below and above this place it is covered with great boulders. The water is six feet deep here now, and the horses would be carried down among the rocks, and would never get across. A mile up the river is always deep, and though the current is strong there is nothing to prevent a bold horseman from swimming across."

"I thank you heartily, young sir," Captain Hume said. "I can see how broken is the surface of the water, and doubt not that it would have fared hard with us had we attempted to swim across here. In faith, Munro, we have had a narrow escape."

"Ay, indeed," the other agreed. "It would have been hard if you and I, after going through all the battlefields of the Low Countries, should have been drowned here together in a Scottish burn. Your young friend is a gallant lad and a good swimmer, for in truth it was no light task to swim that torrent with the water almost as cold as ice."

"Now, sirs, will you please to ride on," the boy said; "it is getting dark fast, and the sooner we are across the better."

So saying he went off at a fast run, the horses trotting behind him. A mile above he reached the spot he had spoken of. The river was narrower here, and the stream was running with great rapidity, swirling and heaving as it went, but with a smooth even surface.

"Two hundred yards farther up," the boy said, "is the

beginning of the deep; if you take the water there you will get across so as to climb up by that sloping bank just opposite."

He led the way to the spot he indicated, and then plunged into the stream, swimming quietly and steadily across, and allowing the stream to drift him down.

The horsemen followed his example. They had swum many a swollen river, and although their horses snorted and plunged at first, they soon quieted down and swam steadily over. They just struck the spot which the boy had indicated. He had already arrived there, and, without a word, trotted forward.

It was soon dark, and the horsemen were obliged to keep close to his heels to see his figure. It was as much as they could do to keep up with him, for the ground was rough and broken, sometimes swampy, sometimes strewn with boulders.

"It is well we have a guide," Colonel Munro said to his companion; "for assuredly, even had we got safely across the stream, we should never have found our way across such a country as this. Scotland is a fine country, Hume, a grand country, and we are all proud of it, you know, but for campaigning, give me the plains of Germany; while, as for your weather here, it is only fit for a water rat."

Hume laughed at this outburst.

"I sha'n't be sorry, Munro, for a change of dry clothes and a corner by a fire; but we must be nearly there now if I remember right. Graheme's hold is about three miles from the Nith."

The boy presently gave a loud shout, and a minute later lights were seen ahead, and in two or three minutes the horsemen drew up at a door beside which two men were standing with torches; another strolled out as they stopped.

"Welcome, Hume! I am glad indeed to see you; and—ah! is it you, Munro? it is long indeed since we met."

"That is it, Graheme; it is twelve years since we were students together at St. Andrews."

"I did not think you would have come on such a night," Graheme said.

"I doubt that we should have come tonight, or any other night, Nigel, if it had not been that that brave boy who calls you uncle swam across the Nith to show us the best way to cross. It was a gallant deed, and I consider we owe him our lives."

"It would have gone hard with you, indeed, had you tried to swim the Nith at the ford; had I not made so sure you would not come I would have sent a man down there. I missed Malcolm after dinner, and wondered what had become of him. But come in and get

3

your wet things off. It is a cold welcome keeping you here. My men will take your horses round to the stable and see that they are well rubbed down and warmly littered."

In a quarter of an hour the party were assembled again in the sitting room. It was a bare room with heavily timbered ceiling and narrow windows high up from the ground; for the house was built for purposes of defence, like most Scottish residences in those days. The floor was thickly strewn with rushes. Arms and trophies of the chase hung on the walls, and a bright fire blazing on the hearth gave it a warm and cheerful aspect. As his guests entered the room Graheme presented them with a large silver cup of steaming liquor.

"Drain this," he said, "to begin with. I will warrant me a draught of spiced wine will drive the cold of the Nith out of your bones."

The travellers drank off the liquor.

"'Tis a famous drink," Hume said, "and there is nowhere I enjoy it so much as in Scotland, for the cold here seems to have a knack of getting into one's very marrow, though I will say there have been times in the Low Countries when we have appreciated such a draught. Well, and how goes it with you, Graheme?"

"Things might be better; in fact, times in Scotland have been getting worse and worse ever since King James went to England, and all the court with him. If it were not for an occasional raid among the wild folks of Galloway, and a few quarrels among ourselves, life would be too dull to bear here."

"But why bear it?" Captain Hume asked. "You used to have plenty of spirit in our old college days, Graheme, and I wonder at your rusting your life out here when there is a fair field and plenty of honour, to say nothing of hard cash, to be won in the Low Country. Why, beside Hepburn's regiment, which has made itself a name throughout all Europe, there are half a score of Scottish regiments in the service of the King of Sweden, and his gracious majesty Gustavus Adolphus does not keep them idle, I warrant you."

"I have thought of going a dozen times," Graheme said, "but you see circumstances have kept me back; but I have all along intended to cross the seas when Malcolm came of an age to take the charge of his father's lands. When my brother James was dying from that sword thrust he got in a fray with the Duffs, I promised him I would be a father to the boy, and see that he got his rights."

"Well, we will talk of the affair after supper, Graheme, for now that I have got rid of the cold I begin to perceive that I am well nigh famished."

As the officer was speaking, the servitors were laying the

4

table, and supper was soon brought in. After ample justice had been done to this, and the board was again cleared, the three men drew their seats round the fire, Malcolm seating himself on a low stool by his uncle.

"And now to business, Nigel," Colonel Munro said. "We have not come back to Scotland to see the country, or to enjoy your weather, or even for the pleasure of swimming your rivers in flood.

"We are commissioned by the King of Sweden to raise some 3000 or 4000 more Scottish troops. I believe that the king intends to take part in the war in Germany, where the Protestants are getting terribly mauled, and where, indeed, it is likely that the Reformed Religion will be stamped out altogether unless the Swedes strike in to their rescue. My chief object is to fill up to its full strength of two thousand men the Mackay Regiment, of which I am lieutenant colonel. The rest of the recruits whom we may get will go as drafts to fill up the vacancies in the other regiments. So you see here we are, and it is our intention to beat up all our friends and relations, and ask them each to raise a company or half a company of recruits, of which, of course, they would have the command.

"We landed at Berwick, and wrote to several of our friends that we were coming. Scott of Jedburgh has engaged to raise a company. Balfour of Lauderdale, who is a cousin of mine, has promised to bring another; they were both at St. Andrew's with us, as you may remember, Graheme. Young Hamilton, who had been an ensign in my regiment, left us on the way. He will raise a company in Douglasdale. Now, Graheme, don't you think you can bring us a band of the men of Nithsdale?"

"I don't know," Graheme said hesitatingly. "I should like it of all things, for I am sick of doing nothing here, and my blood often runs hot when I read of the persecutions of the Protestants in Germany; but I don't think I can manage it."

"Oh, nonsense, Nigel!" said Hume; "you can manage it easily enough if you have the will. Are you thinking of the lad there? Why not bring him with you? He is young, certainly, but he could carry a colour; and as for his spirit and bravery, Munro and I will vouch for it."

"Oh, do, uncle," the lad exclaimed, leaping to his feet in his excitement. "I promise you I would not give you any trouble; and as for marching, there isn't a man in Nithsdale who can tire me out across the mountains."

"But what's to become of the house, Malcolm, and the land and the herds?"

5

"Oh, they will be all right," the boy said. "Leave old Duncan in charge, and he will look after them."

"But I had intended you to go to St. Andrews next year, Malcolm, and I think the best plan will be for you to go there at once. As you say, Duncan can look after the place."

Malcolm's face fell.

"Take the lad with you, Graheme," Colonel Munro said. "Three years under Gustavus will do him vastly more good than will St. Andrews. You know it never did us any good to speak of. We learned a little more Latin than we knew when we went there, but I don't know that that has been of any use to us; whereas for the dry tomes of divinity we waded through, I am happy to say that not a single word of the musty stuff remains in my brains. The boy will see life and service, he will have opportunities of distinguishing himself under the eye of the most chivalrous king in Europe, he will have entered a noble profession, and have a fair chance of bettering his fortune, all of which is a thousand times better than settling down here in this corner of Scotland."

"I must think it over," Graheme said; "it is a serious step to take. I had thought of his going to the court at London after he left the university, and of using our family interest to push his way there."

"What is he to do in London?" Munro said. "The old pedant James, who wouldn't spend a shilling or raise a dozen men to aid the cause of his own daughter, and who thought more of musty dogmatic treatises than of the glory and credit of the country he ruled over, or the sufferings of his co-religionists in Germany, has left no career open to a lad of spirit."

"Well, I will think it over by the morning," Graheme said. "And now tell me a little more about the merits of this quarrel in Germany. If I am going to fight, I should like at least to know exactly what I am fighting about."

"My dear fellow," Hume laughed, "you will never make a soldier if you always want to know the ins and outs of every quarrel you have to fight about; but for once the tenderest conscience may be satisfied as to the justice of the contention. But Munro is much better versed in the history of the affair than I am; for, to tell you the truth, beyond the fact that it is a general row between the Protestants and Catholics, I have not troubled myself much in the matter."

"You must know," Colonel Munro began, "that some twenty years ago the Protestant princes of Germany formed a league for mutual protection and support, which they called the Protestant Union; and a year later the Catholics, on their side, constituted what they called the Holy League. At that time the condition of the Protestants was not unbearable. In Bohemia, where they constituted two-thirds of the population, Rudolph II, and after him Mathias, gave conditions of religious freedom.

"Gradually, however, the Catholic party about the emperor gained the upper hand; then various acts in breach of the conditions granted to the Protestants were committed, and public spirit on both sides became much embittered. On the 23d of May, 1618, the Estates of Bohemia met at Prague, and the Protestant nobles, headed by Count Thurn, came there armed, and demanded from the Imperial councillors an account of the high handed proceedings. A violent quarrel ensued, and finally the Protestant deputies seized the councillors Martinitz and Slavata, and their secretary, and hurled them from the window into the dry ditch, fifty feet below. Fortunately for the councillors the ditch contained a quantity of light rubbish, and they and their secretary escaped without serious damage. The incident, however, was the commencement of war. Bohemia was almost independent of Austria, administering its own internal affairs. The Estates invested Count Thurn with the command of the army. The Protestant Union supported Bohemia in its action. Mathias, who was himself a tolerant and well meaning man, tried to allay the storm; but, failing to do so, marched an army into Bohemia.

"Had Mathias lived matters would probably have arranged themselves, but he died the following spring, and was succeeded by Ferdinand II. Ferdinand is one of the most bigoted Catholics living, and is at the same time a bold and resolute man; and he had taken a solemn vow at the shrine of Loretto that, if ever he came to the throne, he would re-establish Catholicism throughout his dominions. Both parties prepared for the strife; the Bohemians renounced their allegiance to him and nominated the Elector Palatine Frederick V, the husband of our Scotch princess, their king.

"The first blow was struck at Zablati. There a Union army, led by Mansfeldt, was defeated by the Imperial general Bucquoi. A few days later, however, Count Thurn, marching through Moravia and Upper Austria, laid siege to Vienna. Ferdinand's own subjects were estranged from him, and the cry of the Protestant army, 'Equal rights for all Christian churches,' was approved by the whole population—for even in Austria itself there were a very large number of Protestants. Ferdinand had but a few soldiers, the population of the city were hostile, and had Thurn only entered the town he could have seized the emperor without any resistance.

"Thurn hesitated, and endeavoured instead to obtain the conditions of toleration which the Protestants required; and sixteen Austrian barons in the city were in the act of insisting upon Ferdinand signing these when the head of the relieving army entered the city. Thurn retired hastily. The Catholic princes and representatives met at Frankfort and elected Ferdinand Emperor of Germany. He at once entered into a strict agreement with Maximilian of Bavaria to crush Protestantism throughout Germany. The Bohemians, however, in concert with Bethlem Gabor, king of Hungary, again besieged Vienna; but as the winter set in they were obliged to retire. From that moment the Protestant cause was lost; Saxony and Hesse-Darmstadt left the Union and joined Ferdinand. Denmark, which had promised its assistance to the Protestants, was persuaded to remain quiet. Sweden was engaged in a war with the Poles.

"The Protestant army was assembled at Ulm; the army of the League, under the order of Maximilian of Bavaria, was at Donauworth. Maximilian worked upon the fears of the Protestant princes, who, frightened at the contest they had undertaken, agreed to a peace, by which they bound themselves to offer no aid to Frederick V.

"The Imperial forces then marched to Bohemia and attacked Frederick's army outside Prague, and in less than an hour completely defeated it. Frederick escaped with his family to Holland. Ferdinand then took steps to carry out his oath. The religious freedom granted by Mathias was abolished. In Bohemia, Moravia, Silesia, and Austria proper. Many of the promoters of the rebellion were punished in life and property. The year following all members of the Calvinistic sect were forced to leave their country, a few months afterwards the Lutherans were also expelled, and in 1627 the exercise of all religious forms except those of the Catholic Church was forbidden; 200 of the noble, and 30,000 of the wealthier and industrial classes, were driven into exile; and lands and property to the amount of 5,000,000 or 6,000,000 pounds were confiscated.

"The hereditary dominions of Frederick V were invaded, the Protestants were defeated, the Palatinate entirely subdued, and the electorate was conferred upon Maximilian of Bavaria; and the rigid laws against the Protestants were carried into effect in the Palatinate also. It had now become evident to all Europe that the

Emperor of Austria was determined to stamp out Protestantism throughout Germany; and the Protestant princes, now thoroughly alarmed, besought aid from the Protestant countries, England, Holland, and Denmark. King James, who had seen unmoved the misfortunes which had befallen his daughter and her husband, and who had been dead to the general feeling of the country, could no longer resist, and England agreed to supply an annual subsidy; Holland consented to supply troops; and the King of Denmark joined the League, and was to take command of the army.

"In Germany the Protestants of lower Saxony and Brunswick, and the partisan leader Mansfeldt, were still in arms. The army under the king of Denmark advanced into Brunswick, and was there confronted by that of the league under Tilly, while an Austrian army, raised by Wallenstein, also marched against it. Mansfeldt endeavoured to prevent Wallenstein from joining Tilly, but was met and defeated by the former general. Mansfeldt was, however, an enterprising leader, and falling back into Brandenburg, recruited his army, joined the force under the Duke of Saxe-Weimar, and started by forced marches to Silesia and Moravia, to join Bethlem Gabor in Hungary. Wallenstein was therefore obliged to abandon his campaign against the Danes and to follow him. Mansfeldt joined the Hungarian army, but so rapid were his marches that his force had dwindled away to a mere skeleton, and the assistance which it would be to the Hungarians was so small that Bethlem Gabor refused to cooperate with it against Austria.

"Mansfeldt disbanded his remaining soldiers, and two months afterwards died. Wallenstein then marched north. In the meantime Tilly had attacked King Christian at Lutter, and completely defeated him. I will tell you about that battle some other time. When Wallenstein came north it was decided that Tilly should carry the war into Holland, and that Wallenstein should deal with the King of Denmark and the Protestant princes. In the course of two years he drove the Danes from Silesia, subdued Brandenburg and Mecklenburg, and, advancing into Pomerania, besieged Stralsund.

"What a siege that was to be sure! Wallenstein had sworn to capture the place, but he didn't reckon upon the Scots. After the siege had begun Lieutenant General Sir Alexander Leslie, with 5000 Scots and Swedes, fought his way into the town; and though Wallenstein raised fire upon it, though we were half starved and ravaged by plague, we held out for three months, repulsing every assault, till at last the Imperialists were obliged to draw off; having lost 12,200 men.

"This, however, was the solitary success on our side, and a few

9

months since, Christian signed a peace, binding himself to interfere no more in the affairs of Germany. When Ferdinand considered himself free to carry out his plans, he issued an edict by which the Protestants throughout Germany were required to restore to the Catholics all the monasteries and land which had formerly belonged to the Catholic Church. The Catholic service was alone to be performed, and the Catholic princes of the empire were ordered to constrain their subjects, by force if necessary, to conform to the Catholic faith; and it was intimated to the Protestant princes that they would be equally forced to carry the edict into effect. But this was too much. Even France disapproved, not from any feeling of pity on the part of Richelieu for the Protestants, but because it did not suit the interests of France that Ferdinand should become the absolute monarch of all Germany.

"In these circumstances Gustavus of Sweden at once resolved to assist the Protestants in arms, and ere long will take the field. That is what has brought us here. Already in the Swedish army there are 10,000 Scotchmen, and in Denmark they also form the backbone of the force; and both in the Swedish and Danish armies the greater part of the native troops are officered and commanded by Scotchmen.

"Hitherto I myself have been in the Danish service, but my regiment is about to take service with the Swedes. It has been quietly intimated to us that there will be no objection to our doing so, although Christian intends to remain neutral, at any rate for a time. We suffered very heavily at Lutter, and I need 500 men to fill up my ranks to the full strength.

"Now, Graheme, I quite rely upon you. You were at college with Hepburn, Hume, and myself, and it will be a pleasure for us all to fight side by side; and if I know anything of your disposition I am sure you cannot be contented to be remaining here at the age of nine-and-twenty, rusting out your life as a Scotch laird, while Hepburn has already won a name which is known through Europe."

CHAPTER II

SHIPWRECKED

Upon the following morning Nigel Graheme told his visitors that he had determined to accept their offer, and would at once set to work to raise a company.

"I have," he said, "as you know, a small patrimony of my own, and as for the last eight years I have been living here looking after Malcolm I have been laying by any rents, and can now furnish the arms and accoutrements for a hundred men without difficulty. When Malcolm comes of age he must act for himself, and can raise two or three hundred men if he chooses; but at present he will march in my company. I understand that I have the appointment of my own officers."

"Yes, until you join the regiment," Munro said. "You have the first appointments. Afterwards the colonel will fill up vacancies. You must decide how you will arm your men, for you must know that Gustavus' regiments have their right and left wings composed of musketeers, while the centre is formed of pikemen, so you must decide to which branch your company shall belong."

"I would choose the pike," Nigel said, "for after all it must be by the pike that the battle is decided."

"Quite right, Nigel. I have here with me a drawing of the armour in use with us. You see they have helmets of an acorn shape, with a rim turning up in front; gauntlets, buff coats well padded in front, and large breast plates. The pikes vary from fourteen to eighteen feet long according to the taste of the commander. We generally use about sixteen. If your company is a hundred strong you will have two lieutenants and three ensigns. Be careful in choosing your officers. I will fill in the king's commission to you as captain of the company, authorizing you to enlist men for his service and to appoint officers thereto."

An hour or two later Colonel Munro and Captain Hume proceeded on their way. The news speedily spread through Nithsdale that Nigel Graheme had received a commission from the King of Sweden to raise a company in his service, and very speedily men began to pour in. The disbandment of the Scottish army had left but few careers open at home to the youth of that country, and very large numbers had consequently flocked to the Continent and taken service in one or other of the armies there, any opening of the sort, therefore, had only to be known to be freely embraced.

Consequently, in eight-and-forty hours Nigel Graheme had applications from a far larger number than he could accept, and he was enabled to pick and choose among the applicants. Many young men of good family were among them, for in those days service in the ranks was regarded as honourable, and great numbers of young men of good family and education trailed a pike in the Scotch regiments in the service of the various powers of Europe. Two young men whose property adjoined his own, Herries and Farquhar, each of whom brought twenty of his own tenants with him, were appointed lieutenants, while two others, Leslie and Jamieson, were with Malcolm named as ensigns. The noncommissioned officers were appointed from men who had served before. Many of the men already possessed armour which was suitable, for in those day's there was no strict uniformity of military attire, and the armies of the various nationalities differed very slightly from each other. Colonel Munro returned in the course of a fortnight, Nigel Graheme's company completing the number of men required to fill up the ranks of his regiment.

Captain Hume had proceeded further north. Colonel Munro stopped for a week in Nithsdale, giving instructions to the officers and noncommissioned officers as to the drill in use in the Swedish army. Military manoeuvres were in these days very different to what they have now become. The movements were few and simple, and easily acquired. Gustavus had, however, introduced an entirely new formation into his army. Hitherto troops had fought in solid masses, twenty or more deep. Gustavus taught his men to fight six deep, maintaining that if troops were steady this depth of formation should be able to sustain any assault upon it, and that with a greater depth the men behind were useless in the fight. His cavalry fought only three deep. The recruits acquired the new tactics with little difficulty. In Scotland for generations every man and boy had received a certain military training, and all were instructed in the use of the pike; consequently, at the end of a week Colonel Munro pronounced Nigel Graheme's company capable of taking their place in the regiment without discredit, and so went forward to see to the training of the companies of Hamilton, Balfour, and Scott, having arranged with Graheme to march his company to Dunbar in three weeks' time, when he would be joined by the other three companies. Malcolm was delighted with the stir and bustle of his new life. Accustomed to hard exercise, to climbing and swimming, he was a strong and well grown lad, and was in appearance fully a year beyond his age. He felt but little fatigued by the incessant drill in which the days were passed, though he was glad enough of an evening to lay aside his armour, of which the officers wore in those days considerably more than the soldiers, the mounted officers being still clad in full armour, while those on foot wore back and arm pieces, and often leg pieces, in addition to the helmet and breastplate. They were armed with swords and pistols, and carried besides what were called half pikes, or pikes some 7 feet long. They wore feathers in their helmets, and the armour was of fine quality, and often richly damascened, or inlaid with gold.

Very proud did Malcolm feel as on the appointed day he marched with the company from Nithsdale, with the sun glittering on their arms and a drummer beating the march at their head. They arrived in due course at Dunbar, and were in a few hours joined by the other three companies under Munro himself. The regiment which was now commanded by Lieutenant Colonel Munro had been raised in 1626 by Sir Donald Mackay of Farre and Strathnaver, 1500 strong, for the service of the King of Denmark. Munro was his cousin, and when Sir Donald went home shortly before, he succeeded to the command of the regiment. They embarked at once on board a ship which Munro had chartered, and were landed in Denmark and marched to Flensberg, where the rest of the regiment was lying.

A fortnight was spent in severe drill, and then orders were received from Oxenstiern, the chancellor of Sweden, to embark the regiment on board two Swedish vessels, the Lillynichol and the Hound. On board the former were the companies of Captains Robert Munro, Hector Munro, Bullion, Nigel Graheme, and Hamilton. Colonel Munro sailed in this ship, while Major Sennot commanded the wing of the regiment on board the Hound. The baggage horses and ammunition were in a smaller vessel.

The orders were that they were to land at Wolgast on the southern shore of the Baltic. Scarcely had they set sail than the weather changed, and a sudden tempest burst upon them. Higher and higher grew the wind, and the vessels were separated in the night. The Lillynichol laboured heavily in the waves, and the discomfort of the troops, crowded together between decks, was very great. Presently it was discovered that she had made a leak, and that the water was entering fast. Munro at once called forty-eight soldiers to the pumps. They were relieved every quarter of an hour, and by dint of the greatest exertions barely succeeded in keeping down the water. So heavily did the vessel labour that Munro bore away for Dantzig; but when night came on the storm increased in fury. They were now in shoal water, and the vessel, already half waterlogged, became quite unmanageable in the furious waves. Beyond the fact that they were fast driving on to the Pomeranian coast, they were ignorant of their position.

"This is a rough beginning," Nigel said to his nephew. "We bargained to run the risk of being killed by the Germans, but we did not expect to run the hazard of being drowned. I doubt if the vessel can live till morning. It is only eleven o'clock yet, and in spite of the pumps she is getting lower and lower in the water."

Before Malcolm had time to answer him there was a tremendous crash which threw them off their feet. All below struggled on deck, but nothing could be seen in the darkness save masses of foam as the waves broke on the rock on which they had struck. There were two more crashes, and then another, even louder and more terrible, and the vessel broke in two parts.

"Come aft all," Colonel Munro shouted; "this part of the wreck is fixed."

With great efforts all on board managed to reach the after portion of the vessel, which was wedged among the rocks, and soon afterwards the forepart broke up and disappeared. For two hours the sea broke wildly over the ship, and all had to hold on for life.

Malcolm, even in this time of danger, could not but admire the calmness and coolness of his young colonel. He at once set men to work with ropes to drag towards the vessel the floating pieces of wreck which were tossing about in the boiling surf. The masts and yards were hauled alongside, and the colonel instructed the men to make themselves fast to these in case the vessel should go to pieces.

Hour after hour passed, and at last, to the joy of all, daylight appeared. The boats had all been broken to pieces, and Munro now set the men to work to bind the spars and timbers together into a raft. One of the soldiers and a sailor volunteered to try to swim to shore with lines, but both were dashed to pieces.

At one o'clock in the day some natives were seen collecting on the shore, and these presently dragged down a boat and launched it, and with great difficulty rowed out to the ship. A line was thrown to them, and with this they returned to shore, where they made the line fast. The storm was now abating somewhat, and Munro ordered the debarkation to commence.

As many of the troops as could find a place on the raft, or could cling to the ropes fastened on its sides, started first, and by means of the line hauled the raft ashore. A small party then brought it back to the ship, while others manned the boat; and so after a number of trips the whole of the troops and crew were landed, together with all the weapons and armour that could be saved.

From the peasantry Munro now learned that they had been wrecked upon the coast of Rugenwalde, a low lying tract of country in the north of Pomerania. The forts upon it were all in the

14

possession of the Imperialists, while the nearest post of the Swedes was eighty miles away.

The position was not a pleasant one. Many of the arms had been lost, and the gunpowder was of course destroyed. The men were exhausted and worn out with their long struggle with the tempest. They were without food, and might at any moment be attacked by their enemies.

"Something must be done, and that quickly," Munro said, "or our fate will be well nigh as bad as that of the Sinclairs; but before night we can do nothing, and we must hope that the Germans will not discover us till then."

Thereupon he ordered all the men to lie down under shelter of the bushes on the slopes facing the shore, and on no account to show themselves on the higher ground. Then he sent a Walloon officer of the regiment to the Pomeranian seneschal of the old castle of Rugenwalde which belonged to Bogislaus IV, Duke of Pomerania, to inform him that a body of Scotch troops in the service of the Swedish king had been cast on the coast, and begging him to supply them with a few muskets, some dry powder, and bullets, promising if he would do so that the Scotch would clear the town of its Imperial garrison.

The castle itself, which was a very old feudal building, was held only by the retainers of the duke, and the seneschal at once complied with Munro's request, for the Duke of Pomerania, his master, although nominally an ally of the Imperialists, had been deprived of all authority by them, and the feelings of his subjects were entirely with the Swedes.

Fifty old muskets, some ammunition, and some food were sent out by a secret passage to the Scots. There was great satisfaction among the men when these supplies arrived. The muskets which had been brought ashore were cleaned up and loaded, and the feeling that they were no longer in a position to fall helplessly into the hands of any foe who might discover them restored the spirits of the troops, and fatigue and hunger were forgotten as they looked forward to striking a blow at the enemy.

"What did the colonel mean by saying that our position was well nigh as bad as that of the Sinclairs?" Malcolm asked Captain Hector Munro, who with two or three other officers was sheltering under a thick clump of bushes.

"That was a bad business," Captain Munro replied. "It happened now nigh twenty years ago. Colonel Monkhoven, a Swedish officer, had enlisted 2300 men in Scotland for service with Gustavus, and sailed with them and with a regiment 900 strong raised by Sinclair entirely of his own clan and name. Sweden was at

15

war with Denmark, and Stockholm was invested by the Danish fleet when Monkhoven arrived with his ships. Finding that he was unable to land, he sailed north, landed at Trondheim, and marching over the Norwegian Alps reached Stockholm in safety, where the appearance of his reinforcements discouraged the Danes and enabled Gustavus to raise the siege.

"Unfortunately Colonel Sinclair's regiment had not kept with Monkhoven, it being thought better that they should march by different routes so as to distract the attention of the Norwegians, who were bitterly hostile. The Sinclairs were attacked several times, but beat off their assailants; when passing, however, through the tremendous gorge of Kringellen, the peasantry of the whole surrounding country gathered in the mountains. The road wound along on one side of the gorge. So steep was the hill that the path was cut in solid rock which rose almost precipitously on one side, while far below at their feet rushed a rapid torrent. As the Sinclairs were marching along through this rocky gorge a tremendous fire was opened upon them from the pine forests above, while huge rocks and stones came bounding down the precipice.

"The Sinclairs strove in vain to climb the mountainside and get at their foes. It was impossible, and they were simply slaughtered where they stood, only one man of the whole regiment escaping to tell the story."

"That was a terrible massacre indeed," Malcolm said. "I have read of a good many surprises and slaughters in our Scottish history, but never of such complete destruction as that only one man out of 900 should escape. And was the slaughter never avenged?"

"No," Munro replied. "We Scots would gladly march north and repay these savage peasants for the massacre of our countrymen, but the King of Sweden has had plenty of occupation for his Scotchmen in his own wars. What with the Russians and the Poles and the Danes his hands have been pretty full from that day to this, and indeed an expedition against the Norsemen is one which would bring more fatigue and labour than profit. The peasants would seek shelter in their forests and mountains, and march as we would we should never see them, save when they fell upon us with advantage in some defile."

At nightfall the troops were mustered, and, led by the men who had brought the arms, they passed by the secret passage into the castle, and thence sallied suddenly into the town below. There they fell upon a patrol of Imperial cavalry, who were all shot down before they had time to draw their swords. Then scattering through the town, the whole squadron of cuirassiers who garrisoned it were either killed or taken prisoners. This easy conquest achieved, the first care of Munro was to feed his troops. These were then armed from the stores in the town, and a strong guard being placed lest they should be attacked by the Austrian force, which was, they learned, lying but seven miles away, on the other side of the river, the troops lay down to snatch a few hours of needed rest.

In the morning the country was scoured, and a few detached posts of the Austrians captured. The main body then advanced and blew up the bridge across the river. Five days later an order came from Oxenstiern, to whom Munro had at once despatched the news of his capture of Rugenwalde, ordering him to hold it to the last, the position being a very valuable one, as opening an entrance into Pomerania.

The passage of the river was protected by entrenchments, strong redoubts were thrown up round Rugenwalde, and parties crossing the river in boats collected provisions and stores from the country to the very gates of Dantzig. The Austrians rapidly closed in upon all sides, and for nine weeks a constant series of skirmishes were maintained with them.

At the end of that time Sir John Hepburn arrived from Spruce, having pushed forward by order of Oxenstiern by forced marches to their relief. Loud and hearty was the cheering when the two Scotch regiments united, and the friends, Munro and Hepburn, clasped hands. Not only had they been at college together, but they had, after leaving St. Andrews, travelled in companionship on the Continent for two or three years before taking service, Munro entering that of France, while Hepburn joined Sir Andrew Gray as a volunteer when he led a band to succour the Prince Palatine at the commencement of the war.

"I have another old friend in my regiment, Hepburn," the colonel said after the first greeting was over—"Nigel Graheme, of course you remember him."

"Certainly I do," Hepburn exclaimed cordially, "and right glad will I be to see him again; but I thought your regiment was entirely from the north."

"It was originally," Munro said; "but I have filled up the gaps with men from Nithsdale and the south. I was pressed for time, and our glens of Farre and Strathnaver had already been cleared of all their best men. The other companies are all commanded by men who were with us at St. Andrews—Balfour, George Hamilton, and James Scott."

"That is well," Hepburn said. "Whether from the north or the south Scots fight equally well; and with Gustavus 'tis like being in our own country, so large a proportion are we of his majesty's army.

17

And now, Munro, I fear that I must supersede you in command, being senior to you in the service, and having, moreover, his majesty's commission as governor of the town and district."

"There is no one to whom I would more willingly resign the command. I have seen some hard fighting, but have yet my name to win; while you, though still only a colonel, are famous throughout Europe."

"Thanks to my men rather than to myself," Hepburn said, "though, indeed, mine is no better than the other Scottish regiments in the king's service; but we have had luck, and in war, you know, luck is everything."

There were many officers in both regiments who were old friends and acquaintances, and there was much feasting that night in the Scotch camp. In the morning work began again. The peasants of the district, 8000 strong, were mustered and divided into companies, armed and disciplined, and with these and the two Scotch regiments Hepburn advanced through Pomerania to the gates of Colberg, fifty miles away, clearing the country of the Austrians, who offered, indeed, but a faint resistance.

The Lord of Kniphausen, a general in the Swedish service, now arrived with some Swedish troops, and prepared to besiege the town. The rest of Munro's regiment accompanied him, having arrived safely at their destination, and the whole were ordered to aid in the investment of Colberg, while Hepburn was to seize the town and castle of Schiefelbrune, five miles distant, and there to check the advance of the Imperialists, who were moving forward in strength towards it.

Hepburn performed his mission with a party of cavalry, and reported that although the castle was dilapidated it was a place of strength, and that it could be held by a resolute garrison; whereupon Munro with 500 men of his regiment was ordered to occupy it. Nigel Graheme's company was one of those which marched forward on the 6th of November, and entering the town, which was almost deserted by its inhabitants, set to work to prepare it for defence. Ramparts of earth and stockades were hastily thrown up, and the gates were backed by piles of rubbish to prevent them being blown in by petards.

Scarcely were the preparations completed before the enemy were seen moving down the hillside.

"How many are there of them, think you?" Malcolm asked Lieutenant Farquhar.

"I am not skilled in judging numbers, Malcolm, but I should say that there must be fully five thousand."

There were indeed eight thousand Imperialists approaching,

led by the Count of Montecuculi, a distinguished Italian officer, who had with him the regiments of Coloredo, Isslani, Goetz, Sparre, and Charles Wallenstein, with a large force of mounted Croats.

Munro's orders were to hold the town as long as he could, and afterwards to defend the castle to the last man. The Imperial general sent in a message requesting him to treat for the surrender of the place; but Munro replied simply, that as no allusion to the word treaty was contained in his instructions he should defend the place to the last. The first advance of the Imperialists was made by the cavalry covered by 1000 musketeers, but these were repulsed without much difficulty by the Scottish fire.

The whole force then advanced to the attack with great resolution. Desperately the Highlanders defended the town, again and again the Imperialists were repulsed from the slight rampart, and when at last they won their way into the place by dint of numbers, every street, lane, alley, and house was defended to the last. Malcolm was almost bewildered at the din, the incessant roll of musketry, the hoarse shouts of the contending troops, the rattling of the guns, and the shrieks of pain.

Every time the Imperialists tried to force their way in heavy columns up the streets the Scots poured out from the houses to resist them, and meeting them pike to pike hurled them backwards. Malcolm tried to keep cool, and to imitate the behaviour of his senior officers, repeating their orders, and seeing that they were carried out.

Time after time the Austrians attempted to carry the place, and were always hurled back, although outnumbering the Scots by nigh twenty to one. At last the town was in ruins, and was on fire in a score of places. Its streets and lanes were heaped with dead, and it was no longer tenable. Munro therefore gave orders that the houses should everywhere be set on fire, and the troops fall back to the castle.

Steadily and in good order his commands were carried out, and with levelled pikes, still facing the enemy, the troops retired into the castle. The Imperial general, seeing how heavy had been his losses in carrying the open town, shrank from the prospect of assaulting a castle defended by such troops, and when night fell he quietly marched away with the force under his command.

CHAPTER III

SIR JOHN HEPBURN

Munro's first care, when he found that the Imperialists had retreated in the direction of Colberg, was to send out some horsemen to discover whether the Swedes were in a position to cover that town. The men returned in two hours with the report that Field Marshal Horn, with the Swedish troops from Stettin, had joined Kniphausen and Hepburn, and were guarding the passage between the enemy and Colberg.

Two days later a message arrived to the effect that Sir Donald Mackay, who had now been created Lord Reay, had arrived to take the command of his regiment, and that Nigel Graheme's company was to march and join him; while Munro with the rest of his command was to continue to hold the Castle of Schiefelbrune.

Shortly afterwards General Bauditzen arrived with 4000 men and 18 pieces of cannon to press the siege of Colberg, which was one of the strongest fortresses in North Germany. On the 13th of November the news arrived that Montecuculi was again advancing to raise the siege; and Lord Reay with his half regiment, Hepburn with half his regiment, and a regiment of Swedish infantry marched out to meet him, Kniphausen being in command. They took up a position in a little village a few miles from the town; and here, at four o'clock in the morning, they were attacked by the Imperialists, 7000 strong. The Swedish infantry fled almost without firing a shot, but the Scottish musketeers of Hepburn and Reay stood their ground.

For a time a desperate conflict raged. In the darkness it was utterly impossible to distinguish friend from foe, and numbers on both sides were mown down by the volleys of their own party. In the streets and gardens of the little village men fought desperately with pikes and clubbed muskets. Unable to act in the darkness, and losing many men from the storm of bullets which swept over the village, the Swedish cavalry who had accompanied the column turned and fled; and being unable to resist so vast a superiority of force, Kniphausen gave the word, and the Scotch fell slowly back under cover of the heavy mist which rose with the first breath of day, leaving 500 men, nearly half their force, dead behind them.

Nigel Graheme's company had suffered severely; he himself

was badly wounded. A lieutenant and one of the ensigns were killed, with thirty of the men, and many others were wounded with pike or bullet. Malcolm had had his share of the fighting. Several times he and the men immediately round him had been charged by the Imperialists, but their long pikes had each time repulsed the assaults.

Malcolm had before this come to the conclusion, from the anecdotes he heard from the officers who had served through several campaigns, that the first quality of an officer is coolness, and that this is even more valuable than is reckless bravery. He had therefore set before himself that his first duty in action was to be perfectly calm, to speak without hurry or excitement in a quiet and natural tone.

In his first fight at Schiefelbrune he had endeavoured to carry this out, but although he gained much commendation from Nigel and the other officers of the company for his coolness on that occasion, he had by no means satisfied himself; but upon the present occasion he succeeded much better in keeping his natural feelings in check, forcing himself to speak in a quiet and deliberate way without flurry or excitement, and in a tone of voice in no way raised above the ordinary. The effect had been excellent, and the soldiers, in talking over the affair next day, were loud in their praise of the conduct of the young ensign.

"The lad was as cool as an old soldier," one of the sergeants said, "and cooler. Just as the Austrian column was coming on for the third time, shouting, and cheering, and sending their bullets in a hail, he said to me as quietly as if he was giving an order about his dinner, 'I think, Donald, it would be as well to keep the men out of fire until the last moment. Some one might get hurt, you see, before the enemy get close enough to use the pikes.' And then when they came close he said, 'Now, sergeant, I think it is time to move out and stop them.' When they came upon us he was fighting with his half pike with the best of us. And when the Austrians fell back and began to fire again, and we took shelter behind the houses, he walked about on the road, stooping down over those who had fallen, to see if all were killed, and finding two were alive he called out, 'Will one of you just come and help me carry these men under shelter? They may get hit again if they remain here.' I went out to him, but I can tell you I didn't like it, for the bullets were coming along the road in a shower. His helmet was knocked off by one, and one of the men we were carrying in was struck by two more bullets and killed, and the lad seemed to mind it no more than if it had been a rainstorm in the hills at home. I thought when we left Nithsdale that the captain

21

was in the wrong to make so young a boy an officer, but I don't think so now. Munro himself could not have been cooler. If he lives he will make a great soldier."

The defence of the Scots had been so stubborn that Montecuculi abandoned his attempt to relieve Colberg that day, and so vigilant was the watch which the besiegers kept that he was obliged at last to draw off his troops and leave Colberg to its fate. The place held out to the 26th of February, when the garrison surrendered and were allowed to march out with the honours of war, with pikes carried, colours flying, drums beating, matches lighted, with their baggage, and with two pieces of cannon loaded and ready for action. They were saluted by the army as they marched away to the nearest town held by the Austrians, and as they passed by Schiefelbrune Munro's command were drawn up and presented arms to the 1500 men who had for three months resisted every attempt to capture Colberg by assault.

Nigel Graheme's wound was so severe that he was obliged for a time to relinquish the command of his company, which he handed over to Herries.

As there had been two vacancies among the officers Malcolm would naturally have been promoted to the duties of lieutenant, but at his urgent request his uncle chose for the purpose a young gentleman of good family who had fought in the ranks, and had much distinguished himself in both the contests. Two others were also promoted to fill up the vacancies as ensigns.

The troops after the capture of Colberg marched to Stettin, around which town they encamped for a time, while Gustavus completed his preparations for his march into Germany. While a portion of his army had been besieging Colberg, Gustavus had been driving the Imperialists out of the whole of Pomerania. Landing on the 24th of June with an army in all of 15,000 infantry, 2000 cavalry, and about 3000 artillery, he had, after despatching troops to aid Munro and besiege Colberg, marched against the Imperialists under Conti. These, however, retreated in great disorder and with much loss of men, guns, and baggage, into Brandenburg; and in a few weeks after the Swedish landing only Colberg, Greifswald, and Demming held out. In January Gustavus concluded a treaty with France, who agreed to pay him an annual subsidy of 400,000 thalers on the condition that Gustavus maintained in the field an army of 30,000 infantry and 6000 cavalry, and assured to the princes and peoples whose territory he might occupy the free exercise of their religion. England also promised a subsidy, and the Marquis of Hamilton was to bring over 6000 infantry; but as the king did not wish openly to take part in the war this force was not to appear as an English contingent. Another regiment of Highlanders was brought over by Colonel John Munro of Obstell, and also a regiment recruited in the Lowlands by Colonel Sir James Lumsden.

Many other parties of Scotch were brought over by gentlemen of rank. Four chosen Scottish regiments, Hepburn's regiment, Lord Reay's regiment, Sir James Lumsden's musketeers, and Stargate's corps, were formed into one brigade under the command of Hepburn. It was called the Green Brigade, and the doublets, scarfs, feathers, and standards were of that colour. The rest of the infantry were divided into the Yellow, Blue, and White Brigades.

One evening when the officers of Reay's regiment were sitting round the campfire Lieutenant Farquhar said to Colonel Munro:

"How is it that Sir John Hepburn has, although still so young, risen to such high honour in the counsel of the king; how did he first make his way?"

"He first entered the force raised by Sir Andrew Gray, who crossed from Leith to Holland, and then uniting with a body of English troops under Sir Horace Vere marched to join the troops of the Elector Palatine. It was a work of danger and difficulty for so small a body of men to march through Germany, and Spinola with a powerful force tried to intercept them. They managed, however, to avoid him, and reached their destination in safety.

"Vere's force consisted of 2200 men, and when he and Sir Andrew Gray joined the Margrave of Anspach the latter had but 4000 horse and 4000 foot with him. There was a good deal of fighting, and Hepburn so distinguished himself that although then but twenty years old he obtained command of a company of pikemen in Sir Andrew Gray's band, and this company was specially selected as a bodyguard for the king.

"There was one Scotchman in the band who vied even with Hepburn in the gallantry of his deeds. He was the son of a burgess of Stirling named Edmund, and on one occasion, laying aside his armour, he swam the Danube at night in front of the Austrian lines, and penetrated to the very heart of the Imperial camp. There he managed to enter the tent of the Imperialist general, the Count de Bucquoi, gagged and bound him, carried him to the river, swam across with him and presented him as a prisoner to the Prince of Orange, under whose command he was then serving.

"It was well for Hepburn that at the battle of Prague he was guarding the king, or he also might have fallen among the hosts who died on that disastrous day. When the elector had fled the country Sir Andrew Gray's bands formed part of Mansfeldt's force, under whom they gained great glory. When driven out of the Palatinate they still kept up the war in various parts of Germany and Alsace. With the Scotch companies of Colonel Henderson they defended Bergen when the Marquis of Spinola besieged it. Morgan with an English brigade was with them, and right steadily they fought. Again and again the Spaniards attempted to storm the place, but after losing 12,000 men they were forced to withdraw on the approach of Prince Maurice.

"The elector now made peace with the emperor, and Mansfeldt's bands found themselves without employment. Mansfeldt in vain endeavoured to obtain employment under one of the powers, but failing, marched into Lorraine. There, it must be owned, they plundered and ravaged till they were a terror to the country. At last the Dutch, being sorely pressed by the Spaniards, offered to take them into their pay, and the bands marched out from Lorraine in high spirits.

"They were in sore plight for fighting, for most of them had been obliged to sell even their arms and armour to procure food. Spinola, hearing of their approach pushed forward with a strong force to intercept them, and so came upon them at Fleurus, eight miles from Namur, on the 30th of August, 1622.

"The Scots were led by Hepburn, Hume, and Sir James Ramsay; the English by Sir Charles Rich, brother to the Earl of Warwick, Sir James Hayes, and others. The odds seemed all in favour of the Spaniards who were much superior in numbers, and were splendidly accoutred and well disciplined, and what was more, were well fed, while Mansfeldt's bands were but half armed and almost wholly starving.

"It was a desperate battle, and the Spaniards in the end remained masters of the field, but Mansfeldt with his bands had burst their way through them, and succeeded in crossing into Holland. Here their position was bettered; for, though there was little fighting for them to do, and they could get no pay, they lived and grew fat in free quarters among the Dutch. At last the force broke up altogether; the Germans scattered to their homes, the English crossed the seas, and Hepburn led what remained of Sir Andrew Gray's bands to Sweden, where he offered their services to Gustavus. The Swedish king had already a large number of Scotch in his service, and Hepburn was made a colonel, having a strong regiment composed of his old followers inured to war and hardship, and strengthened by a number of new arrivals. When in 1625 hostilities were renewed with Poland Hepburn's regiment formed part of the army which invaded Polish Prussia. The first feat in which he distinguished himself in the service of Sweden was at the relief of Mewe, a town in Eastern Prussia, which was blockaded by King Sigismund at the head of 30,000 Poles. The town is situated at the confluence of the Bersa with the Vistula, which washes two sides of its walls.

"In front of the other face is a steep green eminence which the Poles had very strongly entrenched, and had erected upon it ten batteries of heavy cannon. As the town could only be approached on this side the difficulties of the relieving force were enormous; but as the relief of the town was a necessity in order to enable Gustavus to carry out the campaign he intended, the king determined to make a desperate effort to effect it.

"He selected 3000 of his best Scottish infantry, among whom was Hepburn's own regiment, and 500 horse under Colonel Thurn. When they were drawn up he gave them a short address on the desperate nature of the service they were about to perform, namely, to cut a passage over a strongly fortified hill defended by 30,000 men. The column, commanded by Hepburn, started at dusk, and, unseen by the enemy, approached their position, and working round it began to ascend the hill by a narrow and winding path encumbered by rocks and stones, thick underwood, and overhanging trees.

"The difficulty for troops with heavy muskets, cartridges, breastplates, and helmets, to make their way up such a place was enormous, and the mountain side was so steep that they were frequently obliged to haul themselves up by the branches of the trees; nevertheless, they managed to make their way through the enemy's outposts unobserved, and reached the summit, where the ground was smooth and level.

"Here they fell at once upon the Poles, who were working busily at their trenches, and for a time gained a footing there; but a deadly fire of musketry with showers of arrows and stones, opened upon them from all points, compelled the Scots to recoil from the trenches, when they were instantly attacked by crowds of horsemen in mail shirts and steel caps. Hepburn drew off his men till they reached a rock on the plateau, and here they made their stand, the musketeers occupying the rock, the pikemen forming in a wall around it.

"They had brought with them the portable chevaux-de-frise carried by the infantry in the Swedish service. They fixed this along in front, and it aided the spearmen greatly in resisting the desperate charges of the Polish horsemen. Hepburn was joined by Colonel Mostyn, an Englishman, and Count Brahe, with 200 German arquebusiers, and this force for two days withstood the incessant attacks of the whole of the Polish army.

"While this desperate strife was going on, and the attention of the enemy entirely occupied, Gustavus managed to pass a strong force of men and a store of ammunition into the town, and the Poles, seeing that he had achieved his purpose, retired unmolested. In every battle which Gustavus fought Hepburn bore a prominent part. He distinguished himself at the storming of Kesmark and the defeat of the Poles who were marching to its relief.

"He took part in the siege and capture of Marienburg and in the defeat of the Poles at Dirschau. He was with Leslie when last year he defended Stralsund against Wallenstein, and inflicted upon the haughty general the first reverse he had ever met with. Truly Hepburn has won his honours by the edge of the sword."

"Wallenstein is the greatest of the Imperial commanders, is he not?" Farquhar asked.

"He and Tilly," Munro replied. "'Tis a question which is the greatest. They are men of a very different stamp. Tilly is a soldier, and nothing but a soldier, save that he is a fanatic in religion. He is as cruel as he is brave, and as portentously ugly as he is cruel.

"Wallenstein is a very different man. He has enormous ambition and great talent, and his possessions are so vast that he is a dangerous subject for any potentate, even the most powerful. Curiously enough, he was born of Protestant parents, but when they died, while he was yet a child, he was committed to the care of his uncle, Albert Slavata, a Jesuit, and was by him brought up a strict Catholic. When he had finished the course of his study at Metz he spent some time at the University of Altdorf, and afterwards studied at Bologna and Padua. He then travelled in Italy, Germany, France, Spain, England, and Holland, studying the military forces and tactics of each country.

"On his return to Bohemia he took service under the Emperor Rudolph and joined the army of General Basta in Hungary, where he distinguished himself greatly at the siege of Grau. When peace was made in 1606 Wallenstein returned to Bohemia, and though he was but twenty-three years old he married a wealthy old widow, all of whose large properties came to him at her death eight years afterwards.

"Five years later he raised at his own cost two hundred dragoons to support Ferdinand of Gratz in his war against the Venetians. Here he greatly distinguished himself, and was promoted to a colonelcy. He married a second time, and again to one of the richest heiresses of Austria. On the outbreak of the religious war of

1618 he raised a regiment of Cuirassiers, and fought at its head. Two years later he was made quartermaster general of the army, and marched at the head of an independent force into Moravia, and there re-established the Imperial authority.

"The next year he bought from the Emperor Ferdinand, for a little over 7,000,000 florins, sixty properties which the emperor had confiscated from Protestants whom he had either executed or banished. He had been made a count at the time of his second marriage; he was now named a prince, which title was changed into that of the Duke of Friedland. They say that his wealth is so vast that he obtains two millions and a half sterling a year from his various estates.

"When in 1625 King Christian of Denmark joined in the war against the emperor, Wallenstein raised at his own cost an army of 50,000 men and defeated Mansfeldt's army. After that he cleared the Danes out of Silesia, conquered Brandenburg and Mecklenburg, and laid siege to Stralsund, and there broke his teeth against our Scottish pikes. For his services in that war Wallenstein received the duchy of Mecklenburg.

"At present he is in retirement. The conquests which his army have made for the emperor aroused the suspicion and jealousy of the German princes, and it may be that the emperor himself was glad enough of an excuse to humble his too powerful subject. At any rate, Wallenstein's army was disbanded, and he retired to one of his castles. You may be sure we shall hear of him again. Tilly, you know, is the Bavarian commander, and we shall probably encounter him before long."

New Brandenburg and several other towns were captured and strongly garrisoned, 600 of Reay's regiment under Lieutenant Colonel Lindsay being left in New Brandenburg. Nigel Graheme was still laid up, but his company formed part of the force.

"This is ill fortune indeed," Malcolm said to Lieutenant Farquhar, "thus to be shut up here while the army are marching away to win victories in the field."

"It is indeed, Malcolm, but I suppose that the king thinks that Tilly is likely to try and retake these places, and so to threaten his rear as he marches forward. He would never have placed as strong a force of his best soldiers here if he had not thought the position a very important one."

The troops were quartered in the larger buildings of New Brandenburg; the officers were billeted upon the burghers. The position of the country people and the inhabitants of the towns of Germany during this long and desolating war was terrible; no matter which side won, they suffered. There were in those days no commissariat wagons bringing up stores from depots and magazines to the armies. The troops lived entirely upon the country through which they marched. In exceptional cases, when the military chest happened to be well filled, the provisions acquired might be paid for, but as a rule armies upon the march lived by foraging. The cavalry swept in the flocks and herds from the country round. Flour, forage, and everything else required was seized wherever found, and the unhappy peasants and villagers thought themselves lucky if they escaped with the loss of all they possessed, without violence, insult, and ill treatment. The slightest resistance to the exactions of the lawless foragers excited their fury, and indiscriminate slaughter took place. The march of an army could be followed by burned villages, demolished houses, crops destroyed, and general ruin, havoc, and desolation.

In the cases of towns these generally escaped indiscriminate plunder by sending deputies forward to meet advancing armies, when an offer would be made to the general to supply so much food and to pay so much money on condition that private property was respected. In these cases the main body of the troops was generally encamped outside the town. Along the routes frequently followed by armies the country became a desert, the hapless people forsook their ruined homes, and took refuge in the forests or in the heart of the hills, carrying with them their portable property, and driving before them a cow or two and a few goats.

How great was the general slaughter and destruction may be judged by the fact that the population of Germany decreased by half during the war, and in Bohemia the slaughter was even greater. At the commencement of the war the population of Bohemia consisted of 3,000,000 of people, inhabiting 738 towns and 34,700 villages. At the end of the war there were but 780,000 inhabitants, 230 towns, and 6000 villages. Thus three out of four of the whole population had been slaughtered during the struggle.

Malcolm was, with Lieutenant Farquhar, quartered upon one of the principal burghers of New Brandenburg, and syndic of the weavers. He received them cordially.

"I am glad," he said, "to entertain two Scottish officers, and, to speak frankly, your presence will be of no slight advantage, for it is only the houses where officers are quartered which can hope to escape from the plunder and exactions of the soldiers. My wife and I will do our best to make you comfortable, but we cannot entertain you as we could have done before this war began, for trade is altogether ruined. None have money wherewith to buy goods. Even when free from the presence of contending armies, the country is infested with parties of deserters or disbanded soldiers, who plunder and murder all whom they meet, so that none dare travel along the roads save in strong parties. I believe that there is scarce a village standing within twenty miles, and many parts have suffered much more than we have. If this war goes on, God help the people, for I know not what will become of them. This is my house, will you please to enter."

Entering a wide hall, he led them into a low sitting room where his wife and three daughters were at work. They started up with looks of alarm at the clatter of steel in the hall.

"Wife," the syndic said as he entered, "these are two gentlemen, officers of the Scottish regiment; they will stay with us during the occupation of the town. I know that you and the girls will do your best to make their stay pleasant to them."

As the officers removed their helmets the apprehensions of the women calmed down on perceiving that one of their guests was a young man of three or four and twenty, while the other was a lad, and that both had bright pleasant faces in no way answering the terrible reputation gained by the invincible soldiers of the Swedish king.

"I hope," Farquhar said pleasantly, "that you will not put yourselves out of your way for us. We are soldiers of fortune accustomed to sleep on the ground and to live on the roughest fare, and since leaving Scotland we have scarcely slept beneath a roof. We will be as little trouble to you as we can, and our two soldier servants will do all that we need."

Farquhar spoke in German, for so large a number of Germans were serving among the Swedes that the Scottish officers had all learned to speak that language and Swedish, German being absolutely necessary for their intercourse with the country people. This was the more easy as the two languages were akin to each other, and were less broadly separated from English in those days than they are now.

It was nearly a year since Farquhar and Malcolm had landed on the shores of the Baltic, and living as they had done among Swedes and Germans, they had had no difficulty in learning to speak both languages fluently.

CHAPTER IV

NEW BRANDENBURG

Farquhar and Malcolm Graheme were soon at home with their hosts. The syndic had offered to have their meals prepared for them in a separate chamber, but they begged to be allowed to take them with the family, with whom they speedily became intimate.

Three weeks after the capture of New Brandenburg the news came that Tilly with a large army was rapidly approaching.

Every effort was made to place the town in a position of defence. Day after day messengers came in with the news that the other places which had been garrisoned by the Swedes had been captured, and very shortly the Imperialist army was seen approaching. The garrison knew that they could expect no relief from Gustavus, who had ten days before marched northward, and all prepared for a desperate resistance. The townsfolk looked on with trembling apprehension, their sympathies were with the defenders, and, moreover, they knew that in any case they might expect pillage and rapine should the city be taken, for the property of the townspeople when a city was captured was regarded by the soldiery as their lawful prize, whether friendly to the conquerors or the reverse. The town was at once summoned to surrender, and upon Lindsay's refusal the guns were placed in position, and the siege began.

As Tilly was anxious to march away to the north to oppose Gustavus he spared no effort to reduce New Brandenburg as speedily as possible, and his artillery fired night and day to effect breaches in the walls. The Scotch officers saw little of their hosts now, for they were almost continually upon the walls.

At the first news of the approach of the Imperialists the syndic had sent away his daughters to the house of a relative at Stralsund, where his son was settled in business. When Farquhar and Malcolm returned to eat a meal or to throw themselves on their beds to snatch a short sleep, the syndic anxiously questioned them as to the progress of the siege. The reports were not hopeful. In several places the walls were crumbling, and it was probable that a storm would shortly be attempted. The town itself was suffering heavily, for the balls of the besiegers frequently flew high, and came crashing among the houses. Few of the inhabitants were to be seen in the streets; all had buried their most valuable property, and with scared faces awaited the issue of the conflict.

After six days' cannonade the walls were breached in many places, and the Imperialists advanced to the assault. The Scotch defended them with great resolution, and again and again the Imperialists recoiled, unable to burst their way through the lines of pikes or to withstand the heavy musketry fire poured upon them from the walls and buildings.

But Tilly's army was so strong that he was able continually to bring up fresh troops to the attack, while the Scotch were incessantly engaged. For eight-and-forty hours the defenders resisted successfully, but at last, worn out by fatigue, they were unable to withstand the onslaught of the enemy, and the latter forced their way into the town. Still the Scots fought on. Falling back from the breaches, they contested every foot of the ground, holding the streets and lanes with desperate tenacity, and inflicting terrible losses upon the enemy.

At last, twelve hours later, they were gathered in the marketplace, nearly in the centre of the town, surrounded on all sides by the enemy. Several times the Scottish bugles had sounded a parley, but Tilly, furious at the resistance, and at the loss which the capture of the town had entailed, had issued orders that no quarter should be given, and his troops pressed the now diminished band of Scotchmen on all sides.

Even now they could not break through the circle of spears, but from every window and roof commanding them a deadly fire was poured in. Colonel Lindsay was shot dead. Captain Moncrieff, Lieutenant Keith, and Farquhar fell close to Malcolm. The shouts of "Kill, kill, no quarter," rose from the masses of Imperialists. Parties of the Scotch, preferring to die sword in hand rather than be shot down, flung themselves into the midst of the enemy and died fighting.

At last, when but fifty men remained standing, these in a close body rushed at the enemy and drove them by the fury of their attack some distance down the principal street. Then numbers told. The band was broken up, and a desperate hand-to-hand conflict raged for a time.

Two of the Scottish officers alone, Captain Innes and Lieutenant Lumsden, succeeded in breaking their way down a side lane, and thence, rushing to the wall, leapt down into the moat, and swimming across, succeeded in making their escape, and in carrying the news of the massacre to the camp of Gustavus, where the tale filled all with indignation and fury. Among the Scotch regiments deep vows of vengeance were interchanged, and in after battles the Imperialists had cause bitterly to rue having refused quarter to the Scots at New Brandenburg.

When the last melee was at its thickest, and all hope was at an end, Malcolm, who had been fighting desperately with his half pike, found himself for a moment in a doorway. He turned the handle, and it opened at once. The house, like all the others, was full of Imperialists, who had thrown themselves into it when the Scots made their charge, and were now keeping up a fire at them from the upper windows. Closing the door behind him, Malcolm stood for a moment to recover his breath. He had passed unscathed through the three days' fighting, though his armour and helmet were deeply dinted in many places.

The din without and above was tremendous. The stroke of sword on armour, the sharp crack of the pistols, the rattle of musketry, the shouts of the Imperialists, and the wild defiant cries of the Highlanders mingled together.

As Malcolm stood panting he recalled the situation, and, remembering that the syndic's house was in the street behind, he determined to gain it, feeling sure that his host would shelter him if he could. Passing through the house he issued into a courtyard, quickly stripped off his armour and accoutrements, and threw them into an outhouse. Climbing on the roof of this he got upon the wall, and ran along it until behind the house of the syndic. He had no fear of being observed, for the attention of all in the houses in the street he had left would be directed to the conflict below.

The sound of musketry had already ceased, telling that the work of slaughter was well nigh over, when Malcolm dropped into the courtyard of the syndic; the latter and his wife gave a cry of astonishment as the lad entered the house, breathless and pale as death.

"Can you shelter me awhile?" he said. "I believe that all my countrymen are killed."

"We will do our best, my lad," the syndic said at once. "But the houses will be ransacked presently from top to bottom."

"Let him have one of the servant's disguises," the wife said; "they can all be trusted."

One of the serving men was at once called in, and he hurried off with Malcolm.

The young Scotchmen had made themselves very popular with the servants by their courtesy and care to avoid giving unnecessary trouble, and in a few minutes Malcolm was attired as a serving man, and joined the servants who were busy in spreading the tables with provisions, and in broaching a large cask of wine to allay the passions of the Imperialists.

It was not long before they came. Soon there was a thundering knocking at the door, and upon its being opened a number of soldiers burst in. Many were bleeding from wounds. All bore signs of the desperate strife in which they had been engaged.

"You are welcome," the host said, advancing towards them. "I have made preparations for your coming; eat and drink as it pleases you."

Rushing to the wine casks, the soldiers appeased their thirst with long draughts of wine, and then fell upon the eatables. Other bands followed, and the house was soon filled from top to bottom with soldiers, who ransacked the cupboards, loaded themselves with such things as they deemed worth carrying away, and wantonly broke and destroyed what they could not. The servants were all kept busy bringing up wine from the cellars. This was of good quality, and the soldiers, well satisfied, abstained from personal violence.

All night long pandemonium reigned in the town. Shrieks and cries, oaths and sounds of conflict arose from all quarters, as citizens or their wives were slaughtered by drunken soldiers, or the latter quarrelled and fought among themselves for some article of plunder. Flames broke out in many places, and whole streets were burned, many of the drunken soldiers losing their lives in the burning houses; but in the morning the bugles rang out, the soldiers desisted from their orgies, and such as were able to stand staggered away to join their colours.

A fresh party marched into the town; these collected the stragglers, and seized all the horses and carts for the carriage of the baggage and plunder. The burgomaster had been taken before Tilly and commanded to find a considerable sum of money the first thing in the morning, under threat that the whole town would be burned down, and the inhabitants massacred if it was not forthcoming.

A council of the principal inhabitants was hastily summoned at daybreak. The syndics of the various guilds between them contributed the necessary sum either in money or in drafts, and at noon Tilly marched away with his troops, leaving the smoking and ruined town behind him. Many of the inhabitants were forced as drivers to accompany the horses and carts taken away. Among these were three of the syndic's serving men, Malcolm being one of the number.

33

It was well that the Pomeranian dialect differed so widely from the Bavarian, so Malcolm's German had consequently passed muster without suspicion. The Imperialist army, although dragging with them an immense train of carts laden with plunder, marched rapidly. The baggage was guarded by horsemen who kept the train in motion, galloping up and down the line, and freely administering blows among their captives whenever a delay or stoppage occurred.

The whole country through which they passed was desolated and wasted, and the army would have fared badly had it not been for the herds of captured cattle they drove along with them, and the wagons laden with flour and wine taken at New Brandenburg and the other towns they had stormed. The marches were long, for Tilly was anxious to accomplish his object before Gustavus should be aware of the direction he was taking.

This object was the capture of the town of Magdeburg, a large and important city, and one of the strongholds of Protestantism. Here he was resolved to strike a blow which would, he believed, terrify Germany into submission.

When Gustavus heard that Tilly had marched west, he moved against Frankfort-on-the-Oder, where the Imperialists were commanded by Count Schomberg. The latter had taken every measure for the defence of the town, destroying all the suburbs, burning the country houses and mills, and cutting down the orchards and vineyards.

Gustavus, accompanied by Sir John Hepburn, at once reconnoitred the place and posted his troops. The Blue and Yellow Brigades were posted among the vineyards on the road to Custrin; the White Brigade took post opposite one of the two gates of the town. Hepburn and the Green Brigade were stationed opposite the other.

As the Swedes advanced the Imperialist garrison, who were 10,000 strong, opened fire with musketry and cannon from the walls. The weakest point in the defence was assigned by Schomberg to Colonel Walter Butler, who commanded a regiment of Irish musketeers in the Imperialist service. In the evening Hepburn and some other officers accompanied the king to reconnoitre near the walls. A party of Imperialists, seeing some officers approaching, and judging by their waving plumes they were of importance, sallied quietly out of a postern gate unperceived and suddenly opened fire. Lieutenant Munro, of Munro's regiment, was shot in the leg, and Count Teuffel, a colonel of the Life Guards, in the arm. A body of Hepburn's regiment, under Major Sinclair, rushed forward and

34

drove in the Imperialists, a lieutenant colonel and a captain being captured.

So hotly did they press the Imperialists that they were able to make a lodgment, on some high ground near the rampart, on which stood an old churchyard surrounded by a wall, and whence their fire could sweep the enemy's works. Some cannon were at once brought up and placed in position here, and opened fire on the Guben gate. Captain Gunter, of Hepburn's regiment, went forward with twelve men, and in spite of a very heavy fire from the walls reconnoitred the ditch and approaches to the walls.

The next day all was ready for the assault. It was Palm Sunday, the 3d of April, and the attack was to take place at five o'clock in the afternoon. Before advancing, Hepburn and several of the other officers wished to lay aside their armour, as its weight was great, and would impede their movements. The king, however, forbade them to do so.

"No," he said; "he who loves my service will not risk life lightly. If my officers are killed, who is to command my soldiers?"

Fascines and scaling ladders were prepared. The Green Brigade were to head the assault, and Gustavus, addressing them, bade them remember New Brandenburg.

At five o'clock a tremendous cannonade was opened on the walls from all the Swedish batteries, and under cover of the smoke the Green Brigade advanced to the assault. From the circle of the walls a cloud of smoke and fire broke out from cannon and arquebus, muskets, and wall pieces. Sir John Hepburn and Colonel Lumsden, side by side, led on their regiments against the Guben gate; both carried petards.

In spite of the tremendous fire poured upon them from the wall they reached the gate, and the two colonels fixed the petards to it and retired a few paces. In a minute there was a tremendous explosion, and the gate fell scattered in fragments. Then the Scottish pikemen rushed forward. As they did so there was a roar of cannon, and a storm of bullets ploughed lanes through the close ranks of the pikemen, for the Imperialists, expecting the attack, had placed cannon, loaded to the muzzle with bullets, behind the gates.

Munro's regiment now leapt into the moat, waded across, and planting their ladders under a murderous fire, stormed the works flanking the gate, and then joined their comrades, who were striving to make an entrance. Hepburn, leading on the pikemen, was hit on the knee, where he had in a former battle been badly wounded.

"Go on, bully Munro," he said jocularly to his old schoolfellow, "for I am wounded."

A major who advanced to take his place at the head of the regiment was shot dead, and so terrible was the fire that even the pikemen of Hepburn's regiment wavered for a moment; but Munro and Lumsden, with their vizors down and half pikes in their hands, cheered on their men, and, side by side, led the way.

"My hearts!" shouted Lumsden, waving his pike—"my brave hearts, let's enter."

"Forward!" shouted Munro; "advance pikes!"

With a wild cheer the Scots burst forward; the gates were stormed, and in a moment the cannon, being seized, were turned, and volleys of bullets poured upon the dense masses of the Imperialists. The pikemen pressed forward in close column, shoulder to shoulder, the pikes levelled in front, the musketeers behind firing on the Imperialists in the houses.

In the meantime Gustavus, with the Blue and Yellow Swedish Brigades, stormed that part of the wall defended by Butler with his Irishmen. These fought with extreme bravery, and continued their resistance until almost every man was killed, when the two brigades burst into the town, the White Brigade storming the wall in another quarter. Twice the Imperialist drums beat a parley, but their sound was deadened by the roar of musketry and the boom of cannon from wall and battery, and the uproar and shouting in every street and house. The Green Brigade, under its commander, maintained its regular order, pressing forward with resistless strength. In vain the Austrians shouted for quarter. They were met by shouts of— "Remember New Brandenburg!"

Even now, when all was lost, Tilly's veterans fought with extreme bravery and resolution; but at last, when Butler had fallen, and Schomberg and Montecuculi, and a few other officers had succeeded in escaping, all resistance ceased. Four colonels, 36 officers, and 3000 men were killed. Fifty colours and ten baggage wagons, laden with gold and silver plate, were captured.

Many were taken prisoners, and hundreds were drowned in the Oder, across which the survivors of the garrison made their escape. Plundering at once began, and several houses were set on fire; but Gustavus ordered the drums to beat, and the soldiers to repair to their colours outside the town, which was committed to the charge of Sir John Hepburn, with his regiment.

The rumour that Magdeburg was the next object of attack circulated among Tilly's troops the day after they marched west from New Brandenburg. It originated in some chance word dropped by a superior officer, and seemed confirmed by the direction which they were taking which was directly away from the Swedish army.

There was a report, too, that Count Pappenheim, who commanded a separate army, would meet Tilly there, and that every effort would be made to capture the town before Gustavus could march to its assistance.

Malcolm could easily have made his escape the first night after leaving New Brandenburg; but the distance to be traversed to join the Swedish army was great, confusion and disorder reigned everywhere, and he had decided that it would be safer to remain with the Imperialist army until Gustavus should approach within striking distance. On the road he kept with the other two men who had been taken with the horses from the syndic of the weavers, and, chatting with them when the convoy halted, he had not the least fear of being questioned by others. Indeed, none of those in the long train of carts and wagons paid much attention to their fellows, all had been alike forced to accompany the Imperialists, and each was too much occupied by the hardships of his own lot, and by thoughts of the home from which he had been torn, to seek for the companionship of his comrades in misfortune.

As soon, however, as Malcolm heard the report of Tilly's intentions, he saw that it was of the utmost importance that the King of Sweden should be informed of the Imperialist plans as early as possible, and he determined at once to start and endeavour to make his way across the country. At nightfall the train with the baggage and plunder was as usual so placed that it was surrounded by the camps of the various brigades of the army in order to prevent desertion. The previous night an escape would have been comparatively easy, for the soldiers were worn out by their exertions at the siege of New Brandenburg, and were still heavy from the drink they had obtained there; but discipline was now restored, and the sentries were on the alert. A close cordon of these was placed around the baggage train; and when this was passed, there would still be the difficulty of escaping through the camps of soldiery, and of passing the outposts. Malcolm waited until the camp became quiet, or rather comparatively quiet, for the supplies of wine were far from exhausted, and revelling was still going on in various parts of the camp, for the rigid discipline in use in modern armies was at that time unknown, and except when on duty in the ranks a wide amount of license was permitted to the soldiers. The night was fine and bright, and Malcolm saw that it would be difficult to get through the line of sentries who were stationed some thirty or forty yards apart.

After thinking for some time he went up to a group of eight or ten horses which were fastened by their bridles to a large store wagon on the outside of the baggage camp. Malcolm unfastened the bridles and turned the horses heads outwards. Then he gave two of them a sharp prick with his dagger, and the startled animals dashed forward in affright, followed by their companions. They passed close to one of the sentries, who tried in vain to stop them, and then burst into the camp beyond, where their rush startled the horses picketed there. These began to kick and struggle desperately to free themselves from their fastenings. The soldiers, startled at the sudden noise, sprang to their feet, and much confusion reigned until the runaway horses were secured and driven back to their lines.

The instant he had thus diverted the attention of the whole line of sentries along that side of the baggage camp, Malcolm crept quietly up and passed between them. Turning from the direction in which the horses had disturbed the camp, he made his way cautiously along. Only the officers had tents, the men sleeping on the ground around their fires. He had to move with the greatest caution to avoid treading upon the sleepers, and was constantly compelled to make detours to get beyond the range of the fires, round which groups of men were sitting and carousing.

At last he reached the outside of the camp, and taking advantage of every clump of bushes he had no difficulty in making his way through the outposts, for as the enemy was known to be far away, no great vigilance was observed by the sentries. He had still to be watchful, for fires were blazing in a score of places over the country round, showing that the foragers of the army were at their usual work of rapine, and he might at any moment meet one of these returning laden with spoil.

Once or twice, indeed, he heard the galloping of bodies of horse, and the sound of distant pistol shots and the shrieks of women came faintly to his ears. He passed on, however, without meeting with any of the foraging parties, and by morning was fifteen miles away from Tilly's camp. Entering a wood he threw himself down and slept soundly for some hours. It was nearly noon before he started again. After an hour's walking he came upon the ruins of a village. Smoke was still curling up from the charred beams and rafters of the cottages, and the destruction had evidently taken place but the day before. The bodies of several men and women lay scattered among the houses; two or three dogs were prowling about, and these growled angrily at the intruder, and would have attacked him had he not flourished a club which he had cut in the woods for self defence.

Moving about through the village he heard a sound of wild laughter, and going in that direction saw a woman sitting on the ground. In her lap was a dead child pierced through with a lance. The woman was talking and laughing to it, her clothes were torn, and her hair fell in wild disorder over her shoulders. It needed but a glance to tell Malcolm that the poor creature was mad, distraught by the horrors of the previous day.

A peasant stood by leaning on a stick, mournfully regarding her. He turned suddenly round with the weapon uplifted at the sound of Malcolm's approach, but lowered it on seeing that the newcomer was a lad.

"I hoped you were a soldier," the peasant said, as he lowered his stick. "I should like to kill one, and then to be killed myself. My God, what is life worth living for in this unhappy country? Three times since the war began has our village been burned, but each time we were warned of the approach of the plunderers, and escaped in time. Yesterday they came when I was away, and see what they have done;" and he pointed to his wife and child, and to the corpses scattered about.

"It is terrible," Malcolm replied. "I was taken a prisoner but two days since at the sack of New Brandenburg, but I have managed to escape. I am a Scot, and am on my way now to join the army of the Swedes, which will, I hope, soon punish the villains who have done this damage."

"I shall take my wife to her mother," the peasant said, "and leave her there. I hope God will take her soon, and then I will go and take service under the Swedish king, and will slay till I am slain. I would kill myself now, but that I would fain avenge my wife and child on some of these murderers of Tilly's before I die."

Malcolm felt that the case was far beyond any attempt at consolation.

"If you come to the Swedish army ask for Ensign Malcolm Graheme of Reay's Scottish regiment, and I will take you to one of the German corps, where you will understand the language of your comrades." So saying he turned from the bloodstained village and continued his way.

CHAPTER V

MARAUDERS

Malcolm had brought with him from Tilly's camp a supply of provisions sufficient for three or four days, and a flask of wine. Before he started from New Brandenburg the syndic had slipped into his band a purse containing ten gold pieces, and whenever he came to a village which had escaped the ravages of the war he had no difficulty in obtaining provisions.

It was pitiable at each place to see the anxiety with which the villagers crowded round him upon his arrival and questioned him as to the position of the armies and whether he had met with any parties of raiders on the way. Everywhere the cattle had been driven into the woods; boys were posted as lookouts on eminences at a distance to bring in word should any body of men be seen moving in that direction; and the inhabitants were prepared to fly instantly at the approach of danger.

The news that Tilly's army was marching in the opposite direction was received with a deep sense of thankfulness and relief, for they were now assured of a respite from his plunderers, although still exposed to danger from the arrival of some of the numerous bands. These, nominally fighting for one or other of the parties, were in truth nothing but marauders, being composed of deserters and desperadoes of all kinds, who lived upon the misfortunes of the country, and were even more cruel and pitiless than were the regular troops.

At one of these villages Malcolm exchanged his attire as a serving man of a rich burgher for that of a peasant lad. He was in ignorance of the present position of the Swedish army, and was making for the intrenched camp of Schwedt, on the Oder, which Gustavus had not left when he had last heard of him.

On the fourth day after leaving the camp of Tilly, as Malcolm was proceeding across a bare and desolate country he heard a sound of galloping behind him, and saw a party of six rough looking horsemen coming along the road. As flight would have been useless he continued his way until they overtook him. They reined up when they reached him.

"Where are you going, boy, and where do you belong to?" the leader of the party asked.

"I am going in search of work," Malcolm answered. "My village is destroyed and my parents killed."

40

"Don't tell me that tale," the man said, drawing a pistol from his holster. "I can tell by your speech that you are not a native of these parts."

There was nothing in the appointments of the men to indicate which party they favoured, and Malcolm thought it better to state exactly who he was, for a doubtful answer might be followed by a pistol shot, which would have brought his career to a close.

"You are right," he said quietly; "but in these times it is not safe always to state one's errand to all comers. I am a Scotch officer in the army of the King of Sweden. I was in New Brandenburg when it was stormed by Tilly. I disguised myself, and, passing unnoticed, was forced to accompany his army as a teamster. The second night I escaped, and am now making my way to Schwedt, where I hope to find the army."

The man replaced his pistol.

"You are an outspoken lad," he said laughing, "and a fearless one. I believe that your story is true, for no German boor would have looked me in the face and answered so quietly; but I have heard that the Scotch scarce know what danger is, though they will find Tilly and Pappenheim very different customers to the Poles."

"Which side do you fight on?" Malcolm asked.

"A frank question and a bold one!" the leader laughed. "What say you, men? Whom are we for just at present? We were for the Imperialists the other day, but now they have marched away, and as it may be the Swedes will be coming in this direction, I fancy that we shall soon find ourselves on the side of the new religion."

The men laughed. "What shall we do with this boy? To begin with, if he is what he says, no doubt he has some money with him."

Malcolm at once drew out his purse. "Here are nine gold pieces," he said. "They are all I have, save some small change."

"That is better than nothing," the leader said, pocketing the purse. "And now what shall we do with him?"

"He is a Protestant," one of the men replied; "best shoot him."

"I should say," another said, "that we had best make him our cook. Old Rollo is always grumbling at being kept at the work, and his cooking gets worse and worse. I could not get my jaws into the meat this morning."

A murmur of agreement was raised by the other horsemen.

"So be it," the leader said. "Dost hear, lad? You have the choice whether you will be cook to a band of honourable gentlemen or be shot at once."

"The choice pleases me not," Malcolm replied. "Still, if it must needs be, I would prefer for a time the post of cook to the other alternative."

"And mind you," the leader said sharply, "at the first attempt to escape we string you up to the nearest bough. Carl, do you lead him back and set him to work, and tell the men there to keep a sharp watch upon him."

One of the men turned his horse, and, with Malcolm walking by his side, left the party. They soon turned aside from the road, and after a ride of five miles across a rough and broken country entered a wood. Another half mile and they reached the foot of an eminence, on the summit of which stood a ruined castle. Several horses were picketed among the trees at the foot of the hill, and two men were sitting near them cleaning their arms. The sight of these deterred Malcolm from carrying into execution the plan which he had formed—namely, to strike down his guard with his club as he dismounted, to leap on his horse, and ride off.

"Who have you there, Carl?" one of the men asked as they rose and approached the newcomers.

"A prisoner," Carl said, "whom the captain has appointed to the honourable office of cook instead of old Rollo, whose food gets harder and tougher every day. You are to keep a sharp eye over the lad, who says he is a Scotch officer of the Swedes, and to shoot him down if he attempts to escape."

"Why, I thought those Scots were very devils to fight," one of the men said, "and this is but a boy. How comes he here?"

"He told the captain his story, and he believed it," Carl said carelessly, "and the captain is not easily taken in. He was captured by Tilly at New Brandenburg, which town we heard yesterday he assaulted and sacked, killing every man of the garrison; but it seems this boy put on a disguise, and being but a boy I suppose passed unnoticed, and was taken off as a teamster with Tilly's army. He gave them the slip, but as he has managed to fall into our hands I don't know that he has gained much by the exchange. Now, youngster, go up to the castle."

Having picketed his horse the man led the way up the steep hill. When they reached the castle Malcolm saw that it was less ruined than it had appeared to be from below. The battlements had indeed crumbled away, and there were cracks and fissures in the upper parts of the walls, but below the walls were still solid and unbroken, and as the rock was almost precipitous, save at the point at which a narrow path wound up to the entrance, it was still capable of making a stout defence against attack.

A strong but roughly made gate, evidently of quite recent make, hung on the hinges, and passing through it Malcolm found himself in the courtyard of the castle. Crossing this he entered with his guide what had once been the principal room of the castle. A good fire blazed in the centre; around this half a dozen men were lying on a thick couch of straw. Malcolm's guide repeated the history of the newcomer, and then passed through with him into a smaller apartment, where a man was attending to several sauce pans over a fire.

"Rollo," he said, "I bring you a substitute. You have been always grumbling about being told off for the cooking, just because you happened to be the oldest of the band. Here is a lad who will take your place, and tomorrow you can mount your horse and ride with the rest of us."

"And be poisoned, I suppose, with bad food when I return," the man grumbled—"a nice lookout truly."

"There's one thing, you old grumbler, it is quite certain he cannot do worse than you do. My jaws ache now with trying to eat the food you gave us this morning. Another week and you would have starved the whole band to death."

"Very well," the man said surlily; "we will see whether you have gained by the exchange. What does this boy know about cooking?"

"Very little, I am afraid," Malcolm said cheerfully; "but at least I can try. If I must be a cook I will at least do my best to be a good one. Now, what have you got in these pots?"

Rollo grumblingly enumerated their contents, and then putting on his doublet went out to join his comrades in the hall, leaving Malcolm to his new duties.

The latter set to work with a will. He saw that it was best to appear contented with the situation, and to gain as far as possible the goodwill of the band by his attention to their wants. In this way their vigilance would become relaxed, and some mode of escape might open itself to him. At dusk the rest of the band returned, and Malcolm found that those who had met him with the captain were but a portion of the party, as three other companies of equal strength arrived at about the same time, the total number mounting up to over thirty.

Malcolm was conscious that the supper was far from being a success; but for this he was not responsible, as the cooking was well advanced when he undertook it; however the band were not dissatisfied, for it was much better than they had been accustomed to, as Malcolm had procured woodwork from the disused part of the castle, and had kept the fire briskly going; whereas his predecessor in the office had been too indolent to get sufficient wood to keep the water on the boil.

In the year which Malcolm had spent in camp he had learned a good deal of rough cookery, for when on active duty the officers

43

had often to shift for themselves, and consequently next day he was able to produce a dinner so far in advance of that to which the band was accustomed that their approbation was warmly and loudly expressed.

The stew was juicy and tender, the roast done to a turn, and the bread, baked on an iron plate, was pronounced to be excellent. The band declared that their new cook was a treasure. Malcolm had already found that though he could move about the castle as he chose, one of the band was now always stationed at the gate with pike and pistols, while at night the door between the room in which he cooked and the hall was closed, and two or three heavy logs thrown against it.

Under the pretence of getting wood Malcolm soon explored the castle. The upper rooms were all roofless and open to the air. There were no windows on the side upon which the path ascended, and by which alone an attack upon the castle was possible. Here the walls were pierced only by narrow loopholes for arrows or musketry. On the other sides the windows were large, for here the steepness of the rock protected the castle from attack.

The kitchen in which he cooked and slept had no other entrance save that into the hall, the doorway into the courtyard being closed by a heap of fallen stones from above. Two or three narrow slits in the wall allowed light and air to enter. Malcolm saw that escape at night, after he had once been shut in, was impossible, and that in the daytime he could not pass out by the gate; for even if by a sudden surprise he overpowered the sentry there, he would be met at the bottom of the path by the two men who were always stationed as guards to the horses, and to give notice of the approach of strangers.

The only chance of escape, therefore, was by lowering himself from one of the windows behind, down the steep rock. To do this a rope of some seventy feet long was necessary, and after a careful search through the ruins he failed to discover even the shortest piece of rope.

That afternoon some of the band on their return from foraging drove in half a dozen cattle, and one of these was with much difficulty compelled to climb up the path to the castle, and was slaughtered in the yard.

"There, Scot, are victuals for the next week; cut it up, and throw the head and offal down the rock behind."

As Malcolm commenced his unpleasant task a thought suddenly struck him, and he laboured away cheerfully and hopefully. After cutting up the animal into quarters he threw the head, the lower joints of the legs, and the offal, from the window. The hide he carried, with the four quarters, into his kitchen, and there concealed it under the pile of straw which served for his bed.

When the dinner was over, and the usual carousal had begun, and he knew there was no chance of any of the freebooters coming into the room, he spread out the hide on the floor, cut off the edges, and trimmed it up till it was nearly circular in form, and then began to cut a strip two inches wide round and round till he reached the centre. This gave him a thong of over a hundred feet long. Tying one end to a ring in the wall he twisted the long strip until it assumed the form of a rope, which was, he was sure, strong enough to bear many times his weight.

This part of the work was done after the freebooters had retired to rest. When he had finished cutting the hide he went in as usual and sat down with them as they drank, as he wished to appear contented with his position. The freebooters were discussing an attack upon a village some thirty miles away. It lay in a secluded position, and had so far escaped pillage either by the armies or wandering bands. The captain said he had learned that the principal farmer was a well-to-do man with a large herd of cattle, some good horses, and a well stocked house. It was finally agreed that the band should the next day carry out another raid which had already been decided upon, and that they should on the day following that sack and burn Glogau.

As soon as the majority of the band had started in the morning Malcolm made his way with his rope to the back of the castle, fastened it to the window, and launched himself over the rock, which, although too steep to climb, was not perpendicular; and holding by the rope Malcolm had no difficulty in lowering himself down. He had before starting taken a brace of pistols and a sword from the heap of weapons which the freebooters had collected in their raids, and as soon as he reached the ground he struck off through the wood.

Enough had been said during the conversation the night before to indicate the direction in which Glogau lay, and he determined, in the first place, to warn the inhabitants of the village of the fate which the freebooters intended for them.

He walked miles before seeing a single person in the deserted fields. He had long since left the wood, and was now traversing the open country, frequently turning round to examine the country around him, for at any moment after he had left, his absence from the castle might be discovered, and the pursuit begun. He hoped, however, that two or three hours at least would elapse before the discovery was made.

He had, before starting, piled high the fire in the hall, and had placed plenty of logs for the purpose of replenishing it close at hand. He put tankards on the board, and with them a large jug full of wine, so that the freebooters would have no occasion to call for him, and unless they wanted him they would be unlikely to look into the kitchen. Except when occasionally breaking into a walk to get breath, he ran steadily on. It was not until he had gone nearly ten miles that he saw a goatherd tending a few goats, and from him he learned the direction of Glogau, and was glad to find he had not gone very far out of the direct line. At last, after asking the way several times, he arrived within a short distance of the village. The ground had now become undulating, and the slopes were covered with trees. The village lay up a valley, and it was evident that the road he was travelling was but little frequented, ending probably at the village itself. Proceeding for nearly two miles through a wood he came suddenly upon Glogau.

It stood near the head of the valley, which was here free of trees, and some cultivated fields lay around it. The houses were surrounded by fruit trees, and an air of peace and tranquillity prevailed such as Malcolm had not seen before since he left his native country. One house was much larger than the rest; several stacks stood in the rick yard, and the large stables and barns gave a proof of the prosperity of its owner. The war which had already devastated a great part of Germany had passed by this secluded hamlet.

No signs of work were to be seen, the village was as still and quiet as if it was deserted. Suddenly Malcolm remembered that it was the Sabbath, which, though always kept strictly by the Scotch and Swedish soldiers when in camp, for the most part passed unobserved when they were engaged in active service. Malcolm turned his steps towards the house; as he neared it he heard the sound of singing within. The door was open, and he entered and found himself on the threshold of a large apartment in which some twenty men and twice as many women and children were standing singing a hymn which was led by a venerable pastor who stood at the head of the room, with a powerfully built elderly man, evidently the master of the house, near him.

The singing was not interrupted by the entrance of the newcomer. Many eyes were cast in his direction, but seeing that their leaders went on unmoved, the little congregation continued their hymn with great fervour and force. When they had done the pastor prayed for some time, and then dismissed the congregation with his blessing. They filed out in a quiet and orderly way, but not until the last had left did the master of the house show any sign of observing Malcolm, who had taken his place near the door.

Then he said gravely, "Strangers do not often find their way to Glogau, and in truth we can do without them, for a stranger in these times too often means a foe; but you are young, my lad, though strong enough to bear weapons, and can mean us no ill. What is it that brings you to our quiet village?"

"I have, sir, but this morning escaped from the hands of the freebooters at Wolfsburg, and I come to warn you that last night I heard them agree to attack and sack your village tomorrow; therefore, before pursuing my own way, which is to the camp of the Swedish king, in whose service I am, I came hither to warn you of their intention."

Exclamations of alarm arose from the females of the farmer's family, who were sitting at the end of the room. The farmer waved his hand and the women were instantly silent.

"This is bad news, truly," he said gravely; "hitherto God has protected our village and suffered us to worship Him in our own way in peace and in quiet in spite of the decrees of emperors and princes. This gang of Wolfsburg have long been a scourge to the country around it, and terrible are the tales we have heard of their violence and cruelty. I have for weeks feared that sooner or later they would extend their ravages even to this secluded spot."

"And, indeed, I thank you, brave youth, for the warning you have given us, which will enable us to send our womenkind, our cattle and horses, to a place of safety before these scourges of God arrive here. Gretchen, place food and wine before this youth who has done us so great a service; doubtless he is hungry and thirsty, for 'tis a long journey from Wolfsburg hither."

"What think you, father, shall I warn the men at once of the coming danger, or shall I let them sleep quietly this Sabbath night for the last time in their old homes?"

"What time, think you, will these marauders leave their hold?" the pastor asked Malcolm.

"They will probably start by daybreak," Malcolm said, "seeing that the journey is a long one; but this is not certain, as they may intend to remain here for the night, and to return with their plunder on the following day to the castle."

"But, sir," he went on, turning to the farmer, "surely you will not abandon your home and goods thus tamely to these freebooters. You have here, unless I am mistaken, fully twenty stout men capable

47

of bearing arms; the marauders number but thirty in all, and they always leave at least five to guard the castle and two as sentries over the horses; thus you will not have more than twenty-three to cope with. Had they, as they expected, taken you by surprise, this force would have been ample to put down all resistance here; but as you will be prepared for them, and will, therefore, take them by surprise, it seems to me that you should be able to make a good fight of it, stout men-at-arms though the villains be."

"You speak boldly, sir, for one but a boy in years," the pastor said; "it is lawful, nay it is right to defend one's home against these lawless pillagers and murderers, but as you say, evil though their ways are, these freebooters are stout men-at-arms, and we have heard that they have taken a terrible vengeance on the villages which have ventured to oppose them."

"I am a Scottish officer in the King of Sweden's army," Malcolm said, "and fought at Schiefelbrune and New Brandenburg, and in the fight when the Imperialists tried to relieve Colberg, and having, I hope, done my duty in three such desperate struggles against the Imperialist veterans, I need not shrink from an encounter with these freebooters. If you decide to defend the village I am ready to strike a blow at them, for they have held me captive for five days, and have degraded me by making me cook for them."

A slight titter was heard among the younger females at the indignant tone in which Malcolm spoke of his enforced culinary work.

"And you are truly one of those Scottish soldiers of the Swedish hero who fight so stoutly for the Faith and of whose deeds we have heard so much!" the pastor said. "Truly we are glad to see you. Our prayers have not been wanting night and morning for the success of the champions of the Reformed Faith. What say you, my friend? Shall we take the advice of this young soldier and venture our lives for the defence of our homes?"

"That will we," the farmer said warmly. "He is used to war, and can give us good advice. As far as strength goes, our men are not wanting. Each has his sword and pike, and there are four or five arquebuses in the village. Yes, if there be a chance of success, even of the slightest, we will do our best as men in defence of our homes."

CHAPTER VI

THE ATTACK ON THE VILLAGE

"And now," the farmer said to Malcolm, "what is your advice? That we will fight is settled. When, where, and how? This house is strongly built, and we could so strengthen its doors and windows with beams that we might hold out for a long time against them."

"No," Malcolm said, "that would not be my advice. Assuredly we might defend the house; but in that case the rest of the village, the herds and granaries, would fall into their hands. To do any good, we must fight them in the wood on their way hither. But although I hope for a favourable issue, I should strongly advise that you should have the herds and horses driven away. Send off all your more valuable goods in the wagons, with your women and children, to a distance. We shall fight all the better if we know that they are all in safety. Some of the old men and boys will suffice for this work. And now, methinks, you had best summon the men, for there will be work for them tonight."

The bell which was used to call the hands from their work in the fields and woods at sunset soon sounded, and the men in surprise came trooping in at the summons. When they were assembled the farmer told them the news he had heard, and the determination which had been arrived at to defend the village.

After the first movement of alarm caused by the name of the dreaded band of the Wolfsburg had subsided Malcolm was glad to see an expression of stout determination come over the faces of the assemblage, and all declared themselves ready to fight to the last. Four of the elder men were told off at once to superintend the placing of the more movable household goods of the village in wagons, which were to set out at daybreak with the cattle and families.

"Now," Malcolm said, "I want the rest to bring mattocks and shovels and to accompany me along the road. There is one spot which I marked as I came along as being specially suited for defence."

This was about half a mile away, and as darkness had now set in the men lighted torches, and with their implements followed him. At the spot which he had selected there was for the distance of a hundred yards a thick growth of underwood bordering the track on

49

either side. Across the road, at the end of the passage nearest to the farm, Malcolm directed ten of the men to dig a pit twelve feet wide and eight feet deep. The rest of the men he set to work to cut nearly through the trunks of the trees standing nearest the road until they were ready to fall.

Ten trees were so treated, five on either side of the road. Standing, as they did, among the undergrowth, the operation which had been performed on them was invisible to any one passing by. Ropes were now fastened to the upper part of the trees and carried across the road, almost hidden from sight by the foliage which met over the path. When the pit was completed the earth which had been taken from it was scattered in the wood out of sight. Light boughs were then placed over the hole. These were covered with earth and sods trampled down until the break in the road was not perceptible to a casual eye.

This was done by Malcolm himself, as the lightest of the party, the boughs sufficing to bear his weight, although they would give way at once beneath that of a horse. The men all worked with vigour and alacrity as soon as they understood Malcolm's plans. Daylight was breaking when the preparations were completed. Malcolm now divided the party, and told them off to their respective posts. They were sixteen in all, excluding the pastor.

Eight were placed on each side of the road. Those on one side were gathered near the pit which had been dug, those on the other were opposite to the tree which was farthest down the valley. The freebooters were to be allowed to pass along until the foremost fell into the pit. The men stationed there were at once to haul upon the rope attached to the tree near it and to bring it down. Its fall would bar the road and prevent the horsemen from leaping the pit. Those in the rear were, if they heard the crash before the last of the marauders had passed through, to wait until they had closed up, which they were sure to do when the obstacle was reached, and then to fell the tree to bar their retreat.

The instant this was done both parties were to run to other ropes and to bring down the trees upon the horsemen gathered on the road, and were then to fall upon them with axe, pike, and arquebus.

"If it works as well as I expect," Malcolm said, "not one of them will escape from the trap."

Soon after daybreak bowls of milk and trays of bread and meat were brought down to the workers by some of the women. As there was no immediate expectation of attack, the farmer himself, with the pastor, went back to the village to cheer the women before their departure.

"You need not be afraid, wife," the farmer said. "I shall keep to my plans, because when you have once made a plan it is foolish to change it; but I deem not that there is any real need for sending you and the wagons and beasts away. This young Scotch lad seems made for a commander, and truly, if all his countrymen are like himself, I wonder no longer that the Poles and Imperialists have been unable to withstand them. Truly he has constructed a trap from which this band of villains will have but little chance of escape, and I trust that we may slay them without much loss to ourselves. What rejoicings will there not be in the fifty villages when the news comes that their oppressors have been killed! The good God has assuredly sent this youth hither as His instrument in defeating the oppressors, even as He chose the shepherd boy David out of Israel to be the scourge of the Philistines."

By this time all was ready for a start, and having seen the wagons fairly on their way the farmer returned to the wood, the pastor accompanying the women. Three hours passed before there were any signs of the marauders, and Malcolm began to think that the idea might have occurred to them that he had gone to Glogau, and that they might therefore have postponed their raid upon that village until they could make sure of taking it by surprise, and so capturing all the horses and valuables before the villagers had time to remove them. Glogau was, however, quite out of Malcolm's direct line for the Swedish camp, and it was hardly likely that the freebooters would think that their late captive would go out of his way to warn the village, in which he had no interest whatever; indeed they would scarcely be likely to recall the fact that he had been present when they were discussing their proposed expedition against it.

All doubts were, however, set at rest when a boy who had been stationed in a high tree near the edge of the wood ran in with the news that a band of horsemen were riding across the plain, and would be there in a few minutes. Every one fell into his appointed place. The farmer himself took the command of the party on one side of the road, Malcolm of that on the other. Matches were blown, and the priming of the arquebuses looked to; then they gathered round the ropes, and listened for the tramp of horses.

Although it was but a few minutes before it came, the time seemed long to those waiting; but at last a vague sound was heard, which rapidly rose into a loud trampling of horses. The marauders had been riding quietly until they neared the wood, as speed was no object; but as they wished to take the village by surprise—and it was just possible that they might have been seen approaching—they were now riding rapidly.

Suddenly the earth gave way under the feet of the horses of the captain and his lieutenant, who were riding at the head of the troop, and men and animals disappeared from the sight of those who followed. The two men behind them pulled their horses back on their haunches, and checked them at the edge of the pit into which their leaders had fallen.

As they did so a loud crack was heard, and a great tree came crashing down, falling directly upon them, striking them and their horses to the ground. A loud cry of astonishment and alarm rose from those behind, followed by curses and exclamations of rage. A few seconds after the fall of the tree there was a crash in the rear of the party, and to their astonishment the freebooters saw that another tree had fallen there, and that a barricade of boughs and leaves closed their way behind as in front. Deprived of their leaders, bewildered and alarmed at this strange and unexpected occurrence, the marauders remained irresolute. Two or three of those in front got off their horses and tried to make their way to the assistance of their comrades who were lying crushed under the mass of foliage, and of their leaders in the pit beyond.

But now almost simultaneously two more crashes were heard, and a tree from each side fell upon them. Panic stricken now the horsemen strove to dash through the underwood, but their progress was arrested, for among the bushes ropes had been fastened from tree to tree; stakes had been driven in, and the bushes interlaced with cords. The trees continued to fall till the portion of the road occupied by the troop was covered by a heap of fallen wood and leaf. Then for the first time the silence in the wood beyond them was broken, the flashes of firearms darted out from the brushwood, and then with a shout a number of men armed with pikes and axes sprang forward to the attack.

A few only of the marauders were in a position to offer any resistance whatever. The greater portion were buried under the mass of foliage. Many had been struck down by the trunks or heavy arms of the trees. All were hampered and confused by the situation in which they found themselves. Under such circumstances it was a massacre rather than a fight. Malcolm, seeing the inability of the freebooters to oppose any formidable resistance, sheathed his sword, and left it to the peasants to avenge the countless murders which the band had committed, and the ruin and misery which they had inflicted upon the country.

In a few minutes all was over. The brigands were shot down, piked, or slain by the heavy axes through the openings in their leafy prison. Quarter was neither asked for nor given. The freebooters knew that it would be useless, and died cursing their foes and their own fate in being thus slaughtered like rats in a trap. Two or three of the peasants were wounded by pistol shots, but this was all the injury that their success cost them.

"The wicked have digged a pit, and they have fallen into it themselves," the farmer said as he approached the spot where Malcolm was standing, some little distance from the scene of slaughter. "Verily the Lord hath delivered them into our hands. I understand, my young friend, why you as a soldier did not aid in the slaughter of these villains. It is your trade to fight in open battle, and you care not to slay your enemies when helpless; but with us it is different. We regard them as wild beasts, without heart or pity, as scourges to be annihilated when we have the chance; just as in winter we slay the wolves who come down to attack our herds."

"I blame you not," Malcolm said. "When men take to the life of wild beasts they must be slain as such. Now my task is done, and I will journey on at once to join my countrymen; but I will give you one piece of advice before I go.

"In the course of a day or two the party left at Wolfsburg will grow uneasy, and two of their number are sure to ride hither to inquire as to the tarrying of the band. Let your men with arquebuses keep watch night and day and shoot them down when they arrive. Were I in your place I would then mount a dozen of your men and let them put on the armour of these dead robbers and ride to Wolfsburg, arriving there about daybreak. If they see you coming they will take you to be the band returning. The two men below you will cut down without difficulty, and there will then be but three or four to deal with in the castle.

"I recommend you to make a complete end of them; and for this reason: if any of the band survive they will join themselves with some other party and will be sure to endeavour to get them to avenge this slaughter; for although these bands have no love for each other, yet they would be ready enough to take up each other's quarrel as against country folk, especially when there is a hope of plunder. Exterminate them, then, and advise your men to keep their secret. Few can have seen the brigands riding hither today. When it is found that the band have disappeared the country around will

53

thank God, and will have little curiosity as to how they have gone. You will of course clear the path again and bury their bodies; and were I you I would prepare at once another ambush like that into which they have fallen, and when a second band of marauders comes into this part of the country set a watch night and day. Your men will in future be better armed than hitherto, as each of those freebooters carries a brace of pistols. And now, as I would fain be off as soon as possible, I would ask you to let your men set to work with their axes and cut away the boughs and to get me out a horse. Several of them must have been killed by the falling trees, and some by the fire of the arquebuses; but no doubt there are some uninjured."

In a quarter of an hour a horse was brought up, together with the helmet and armour worn by the late captain of the band.

As Malcolm mounted, the men crowded round him and loaded him with thanks and blessings for the danger from which he had delivered them, their wives and families.

When the fugitives had left the village a store of cooked provisions had been left behind for the use of the defenders during the day. As the women could not be fetched back before nightfall, the farmer had despatched a man for some of this food and the wallets on the saddle were filled with sufficient to last Malcolm for three or four days.

A brace of pistols were placed in the holsters, and with a last farewell to the farmer Malcolm gave the rein to his horse and rode away from the village. He travelled fast now and without fear of interruption. The sight of armed men riding to join one or other of the armies was too common to attract any attention, and avoiding large towns Malcolm rode unmolested across the plain.

He presently heard the report that the Swedes had captured Frankfort-on-the-Oder, and as he approached that town, after four days' riding, heard that they had moved towards Landsberg. Thither he followed them, and came up to them outside the walls of that place six days after leaving Glogau. The main body of the Swedish army had remained in and around Frankfort, Gustavus having marched against Landsberg with only 3200 musketeers, 12 pieces of cannon, and a strong body of horse. Hepburn and Reay's Scotch regiments formed part of the column, and Malcolm with delight again saw the green scarves and banners.

As he rode into the camp of his regiment he was unnoticed by the soldiers until he reached the tents of the officers, before which Colonel Munro was standing talking with several others. On seeing an officer approach in full armour they looked up, and a cry of astonishment broke from them on recognizing Malcolm.

"Is it you, Malcolm Graheme, or your wraith?" Munro exclaimed.

"It is I in the flesh, colonel, sound and hearty."

"Why, my dear lad," Munro exclaimed, holding out his hand, "we thought you had fallen at the sack of New Brandenburg. Innes and Lumsden were believed to be the only ones who had escaped."

"I have come through it, nevertheless," Malcolm said; "but it is a long story, colonel, and I would ask you first if the king has learned what Tilly is doing."

"No, he has received no news whatever of him since he heard of the affair at New Brandenburg, and is most anxious lest he should fall upon the army at Frankfort while we are away. Do you know aught about him?"

"Tilly marched west from New Brandenburg," Malcolm said, "and is now besieging Magdeburg."

"This is news indeed," Munro said; "you must come with me at once to the king."

Malcolm followed Colonel Munro to the royal tent, which was but a few hundred yards away. Gustavus had just returned after visiting the advanced lines round the city. On being told that Colonel Munro wished to speak to him on important business, he at once came to the entrance of his tent.

"Allow me to present to you, sire, Malcolm Graheme, a very gallant young officer of my regiment. He was at New Brandenburg, and I deemed that he had fallen there; how he escaped I have not yet had time to learn, seeing that he has but now ridden into the camp; but as he is bearer of news of the whereabouts of Tilly and his army, I thought it best to bring him immediately to you."

"Well, sir," Gustavus said anxiously to Malcolm, "what is your news?"

"Tilly is besieging Magdeburg, sire, with his whole strength."

"Magdeburg!" Gustavus exclaimed incredulously. "Are you sure of your news? I deemed him advancing upon Frankfort."

"Quite sure, sire, for I accompanied his column to within two marches of the city, and there was no secret of his intentions. He started for that town on the very day after he had captured New Brandenburg."

"This is important, indeed," Gustavus said; "follow me," and he turned and entered the tent. Spread out on the table was a large map, which the king at once consulted.

"You see, Colonel Munro, that to relieve Magdeburg I must march through Kustrin, Berlin, and Spandau, and the first and last are strong fortresses. I can do nothing until the Elector of Brandenburg declares for us, and gives us leave to pass those places, for I dare not march round and leave them in my rear until sure that this weak prince will not take sides with the Imperialists. I will despatch a messenger tonight to him at Berlin demanding leave to march through his territory to relieve Magdeburg. In the meantime we will finish off with this place, and so be in readiness to march west when his answer arrives. And now, sir," he went on, turning to Malcolm, "please to give me the account of how you escaped first from New Brandenburg, and then from Tilly."

Malcolm related briefly the manner of his escape from the massacre at New Brandenburg, and how, after accompanying Tilly's army as a teamster for two days, he had made his escape. He then still more briefly related how he had been taken prisoner by a band of freebooters, but had managed to get away from them, and had drawn them into an ambush by peasants, where they had been slain, by which means he had obtained a horse and ridden straight to the army.

Gustavus asked many questions, and elicited many more details than Malcolm had deemed it necessary to give in his first recital.

"You have shown great prudence and forethought," the king said when he had finished, "such as would not be looked for in so young a soldier."

"And he behaved, sire, with distinguished gallantry and coolness at Schiefelbrune, and in the destructive fight outside Colberg," Colonel Munro put in. "By the slaughter on the latter day he would naturally have obtained his promotion, but he begged to be passed over, asserting that it was best that at his age he should remain for a time an ensign."

"Such modesty is unusual," the king said, "and pleases me; see the next time a step is vacant, colonel, that he has it. Whatever his age, he has shown himself fit to do man's work, and years are of no great value in a soldier; why, among all my Scottish regiments I have scarcely a colonel who is yet thirty years old."

Malcolm now returned with Colonel Munro to the regiment, and there had to give a full and minute account of his adventures, and was warmly congratulated by his fellow officers on his good fortune in escaping from the dangers which had beset him. The suit of armour was a handsome one, and had been doubtless stripped off from the body of some knight or noble murdered by the freebooters. The leg pieces Malcolm laid aside, retaining only a cuirass, back piece, and helmet, as the full armour was too heavy for service on foot.

Two days later the king gave orders that the assault upon Landsberg was to be made that night. The place was extremely strong, and Gustavus had in his previous campaign twice failed in attempts to capture it. Since that time the Imperialists had been busy in strengthening the fortification, and all the peasantry for ten miles round had been employed in throwing up earthworks; but its principal defence was in the marsh which surrounded it, and which rendered the construction of approaches by besiegers almost impossible. Its importance consisted in the fact that from its great strength its garrison dominated the whole district known as the Marc of Brandenburg. It was the key to Silesia, and guarded the approaches to Pomerania, and its possession was therefore of supreme importance to Gustavus. The garrison consisted of five thousand Imperialist infantry and twelve troops of horse, the whole commanded by Count Gratz. The principal approach to the town was guarded by a strong redoubt armed with numerous artillery.

Colonel Munro had advanced his trenches to within a short distance of this redoubt, and had mounted the twelve pieces of cannon to play upon it, but so solid was the masonry of the fort that their fire produced but little visible effect. Gustavus had brought from Frankfort as guide on the march a blacksmith who was a native of Landsberg, and this man had informed him of a postern gate into the town which would not be likely to be defended, as to reach it it would be necessary to cross a swamp flanked by the advanced redoubt and covered with water.

For two days previous to the assault the troops had been at work cutting bushes and trees, and preparing the materials for constructing a floating causeway across the mud and water. As soon as night fell the men were set to work laying down the causeway, and when this was finished the column advanced to the attack. It consisted of 250 pikemen under Colonel Munro, and the same number of the dragoons under Colonel Deubattel. Hepburn with 1000 musketeers followed a short distance behind them.

The pikemen led the way, and passed along the floating causeway without difficulty, but the causeway swayed and often sank under the feet of the cavalry behind them. These, however, also managed to get across. Their approach was entirely unobserved, and they effected an entrance into the town.

Scarcely had they done so when they came upon a body of three hundred Imperialists who were about to make a sally under Colonel Gratz, son of the governor. The pikemen at once fell upon them. Taken by surprise the Imperialists fought nevertheless stoutly, and eighty of the Scots fell under the fire of their musketry. But the pikemen charged home; Colonel Gratz was killed, with many of his men, and the rest taken prisoners. Hepburn marching on behind heard the din of musketry and pressed forward; before reaching the town he found a place in the swamp sufficiently firm to enable his men to march across it, and, turning off, he led his troops between the town and the redoubt, and then attacked the latter in the rear where its defences were weak, and after three minutes' fighting with its surprised and disheartened garrison the latter surrendered.

The redoubt having fallen, and Munro's men having effected a lodgment in the town, while the retreat on one side was cut off by the force of Gustavus, and on the other by a strong body of cavalry under Marshal Horn, the governor sent a drummer to Colonel Munro to say that he was ready to surrender, and to ask for terms. The drummer was sent to Gustavus, who agreed that the garrison should be allowed to march away with the honours of war, taking their baggage and effects with them. Accordingly at eight o'clock the Count of Gratz at the head of his soldiers marched out with colours flying and drums beating, and retired into Silesia. A garrison was placed in Landsberg, and the blacksmith appointed burgomaster of the town. Landsberg fell on the 15th of April, and on the 18th the force marched back to Frankfort.

CHAPTER VII

A QUIET TIME

In spite of the urgent entreaties of Gustavus and the pressing peril of Magdeburg, the wavering Duke of Brandenburg could not bring himself to join the Swedes. He delivered Spandau over to them, but would do no more. The Swedish army accordingly marched to Berlin and invested his capital. The duke sent his wife to Gustavus to beseech him to draw off his army and allow him to remain neutral; but Gustavus would not listen to his entreaties, and insisted, as the only condition upon which he would raise the siege, that the duke should ally himself with him, and that the troops of Brandenburg should join his army.

These conditions the duke was obliged to accept, but in the meantime his long hesitation and delay had caused the loss of Magdeburg, which after a gallant defence was stormed by the troops of Pappenheim and Tilly on the 10th of May. The ferocious Tilly had determined upon a deed which would, he believed, frighten Germany into submission; he ordered that no quarter should be given, and for five days the city was handed over to the troops.

History has no record since the days of Attila of so frightful a massacre. Neither age nor sex was spared, and 30,000 men, women, and children were ruthlessly massacred. The result for a time justified the anticipations of the ferocious leader. The terrible deed sent a shudder of horror and terror through Protestant Germany. It seemed, too, as if the catastrophe might have been averted had the Swedes shown diligence and marched to the relief of the city; for in such a time men were not inclined to discuss how much of the blame rested upon the shoulders of the Duke of Brandenburg, who was, in fact, alone responsible for the delay of the Swedes.

Many of the princes and free towns which had hitherto been staunch to the cause of Protestantism at once hastened to make their peace with the emperor. For a time the sack of Magdeburg greatly strengthened the Imperialist cause. No sooner did the news reach the ears of the Duke of Brandenburg than his fears overcame him, and he wrote to Gustavus withdrawing from the treaty he had made, and saying that as Spandau had only been delivered to him in order that he might march to the relief of Magdeburg he was now bound in honour to restore it.

Gustavus at once ordered Spandau to be evacuated by his

troops, and again marched with the army against Berlin, which he had but a few days before left. Here he again dictated terms, which the duke was forced to agree to.

The Swedish army now marched to Old Brandenburg, thirty-four miles west of Berlin, and there remained for some time waiting until some expected reinforcements should reach it.

The place was extremely unhealthy, and great numbers died from malaria and fever, thirty of Munro's musketeers dying in a single week. During this time the king was negotiating with the Elector of Saxony and the Landgrave of Hesse. These were the two most powerful of the Protestant princes in that part of Germany, and Tilly resolved to reduce them to obedience before the army of Gustavus was in a position to move forward, for at present his force was too small to enable him to take the field against the united armies of Tilly and Pappenheim.

He first fell upon the Landgrave of Hesse, and laid Thuringen waste with fire and sword. Frankenhausen was plundered and burned to the ground. Erfurt saved itself from a similar fate by the payment of a large sum of money, and by engaging to supply great stores of provisions for the use of the Imperial army. The Landgrave of Hesse-Cassel was next summoned by Tilly, who threatened to carry fire and sword through his dominions unless he would immediately disband his troops, pay a heavy contribution and receive the Imperial troops into his cities and fortresses; but the landgrave refused to accept the terms.

Owing to the unhealthiness of the district round Old Brandenburg, Gustavus raised his camp there, and marched forward to Werben near the junction of the Elbe with the Havel. He was joined there by his young queen, Maria Eleonora, with a reinforcement of 8000 men, and by the Marquis of Hamilton with 6200, for the most part Scotch, who had been raised by him with the consent of Charles I, to whom the marquis was master of the horse.

Werben was distant but a few miles from Magdeburg, and Pappenheim, who commanded the troops in that neighbourhood, seeing that Gustavus was now in a position to take the field against him, sent an urgent message to Tilly for assistance; and the Imperial general, who was on the point of attacking the Landgrave of Hesse-Cassel, at once marched with his army and effected a junction with Pappenheim, their combined force being greatly superior to that of Gustavus even after the latter had received his reinforcements.

Malcolm had not accompanied the army in its march from Old Brandenburg. He had been prostrated by fever, and although he shook off the attack it left him so weak and feeble that he was altogether unfit for duty. The army was still lying in its swampy quarters, and the leech who had attended him declared that he could never recover his strength in such an unhealthy air. Nigel Graheme, who had now rejoined the regiment cured of his wound, reported the surgeon's opinion to Munro.

"I am not surprised," the colonel said, "and there are many others in the same state; but whither can I send them? The Elector of Brandenburg is so fickle and treacherous that he may at any moment turn against us."

"I was speaking to Malcolm," Nigel replied, "and he said that he would he could go for a time to recruit his health in that village among the hills where he had the fight with the freebooters who made him captive. He said he was sure of a cordial welcome there, and it is but three days' march from here."

"'Tis an out-of-the-way place," Munro said, "and if we move west we shall be still further removed from it. There are Imperial bands everywhere harrying the country unguarded by us, and one of these might at any moment swoop down into that neighbourhood."

"That is true; but, after all, it would be better that he should run that risk than sink from weakness as so many have done here after getting through the first attack of fever."

"That is so, Nigel, and if you and Malcolm prefer that risk to the other I will not say you nay; but what is good for him is good for others, and I will ask the surgeon to make me a list of twenty men who are strong enough to journey by easy stages, and who yet absolutely require to get out of this poisonous air to enable them to effect their recovery. We will furnish them with one of the baggage wagons of the regiment, so that they can ride when they choose. Tell the paymaster to give each man in advance a month's pay, that they may have money to pay what they need. Horses are scarce, so we can give them but two with the wagon, but that will be sufficient as they will journey slowly. See that a steady and experienced driver is told off with them. They had best start at daybreak tomorrow morning."

At the appointed time the wagon was in readiness, and those who had to accompany Malcolm gathered round, together with many of their comrades who had assembled to wish them Godspeed. The pikes and muskets, helmets and breast pieces were placed in the wagon, and then the fever stricken band formed up before it.

Munro, Nigel, and most of the officers came down to bid farewell to Malcolm, and to wish him a speedy return in good health. Then he placed himself at the head of the band and marched off, the wagon following in the rear. Before they had been gone a mile several of the men had been compelled to take their places in the wagon, and by the time three miles had been passed the rest had one by one been forced to give in.

Malcolm was one of the last. He took his seat by the driver, and the now heavily freighted wagon moved slowly across the country. A store of provisions sufficient for several days had been placed in the wagon, and after proceeding fifteen miles a halt was made at a deserted village, and two of the houses in the best condition were taken possession of, Malcolm and the sergeant of the party, a young fellow named Sinclair, occupying the one, and the men taking up their quarters in another.

The next morning the benefit of the change and the removal from the fever tainted air made itself already apparent. The distance performed on foot was somewhat longer than on the preceding day; the men were in better spirits, and marched with a brisker step than that with which they had left the camp. At the end of the fourth day they approached the wood in which the village was situated.

"I will go on ahead," Malcolm said. "Our approach will probably have been seen, and unless they know who we are we may meet with but a rough welcome. Halt the wagon here until one returns with news that you may proceed, for there may be pitfalls in the road."

Malcolm had kept the horse on which he had ridden to Landsberg, and it had been tied behind the wagon. During the last day's march he had been strong enough to ride it. He now dismounted, and taking the bridle over his arm he entered the wood. He examined the road cautiously as he went along. He had gone about half way when the farmer with four of his men armed with pikes suddenly appeared in the road before him.

"Who are you," the farmer asked, "and what would you here?"

"Do you not remember me?" Malcolm said. "It is but three months since I was here."

"Bless me, it is our Scottish friend! Why, lad, I knew you not again, so changed are you. Why, what has happened to you?"

"I have had the fever," Malcolm said, "and have been like to die; but I thought that a change to the pure air of your hills and woods here would set me up. So I have travelled here to ask your hospitality."

By this time the farmer had come up and had grasped Malcolm's hand.

"All that I have is yours," he said warmly. "The lookout saw a wagon coming across the plain with three or four men walking beside it, and he thought that many more were seated in it; so thinking that this might be a ruse of some freebooting band, I had the alarm bell rung, and prepared to give them a hot reception."

"I have brought some sick comrades with me," Malcolm said. "I have no thought of quartering them on you. That would be nigh as bad as the arrival of a party of marauders, for they are getting strength, and will, I warrant you, have keen appetites ere long; but we have brought tents, and will pay for all we have."

"Do not talk of payment," the farmer said heartily. "As long as there is flour in the storehouse and bacon on the beams, any Scottish soldier of Gustavus is welcome to it, still more if they be comrades of thine."

"Thanks, indeed," Malcolm replied. "I left them at the edge of the wood, for I knew not what welcome you might have prepared here; and seeing so many men you might have shot at them before waiting to ask a question."

"That is possible enough," the farmer said, "for indeed we could hardly look for friends. The men are all posted a hundred yards further on."

The farmer ordered one of his men to go on and bring up the wagon, and then with Malcolm walked on to the village. A call that all was right brought out the defenders of the ambush. It had been arranged similarly to that which had been so successful before, except that instead of the pit, several strong ropes had been laid across the road, to be tightened breast high as soon as an enemy came close to them.

"These are not as good as the pit," the farmer said as they passed them; "but as we have to use the road sometimes we could not keep a pit here, which, moreover, might have given way and injured any one from a neighbouring village who might be riding hither. We have made a strong stockade of beams among the underwood on either side, so that none could break through into the wood from the path."

"That is good," Malcolm said; "but were I you I would dig a pit across the road some twelve feet wide, and would cover it with a stout door with a catch, so that it would bear wagons crossing, but when the catch is drawn it should rest only on some light supports below, and would give way at once if a weight came on it. It would, of course, be covered over with turf. It will take some time to make, but it will add greatly to your safety."

"It shall be done," the farmer said. "Wood is in plenty, and some of my men are good carpenters. I will set about it at once."

On arriving at the village Malcolm was cordially welcomed by the farmer's wife and daughters. The guest chamber was instantly prepared for him and refreshments laid on the table, while the maids, under the direction of the farmer's wife, at once began to cook a bounteous meal in readiness for the arrival of the soldiers. A spot was chosen on some smooth turf under the shade of trees for the erection of the tents, and trusses of clean straw carried there for bedding.

Malcolm as he sat in the cool chamber in the farm house felt the change delightful after the hot dusty journey across the plain. There was quite an excitement in the little village when the wagon drove up. The men lifted the arms and baggage from the wagon. The women offered fruit and flagons of wine, and fresh cool water, to the soldiers. There was not only general pleasure throughout the village caused by the novelty of the arrival of the party from the outer world, but a real satisfaction in receiving these men who had fought so bravely against the oppressors of the Protestants of Germany. There was also the feeling that so long as this body of soldiers might remain in the village they would be able to sleep in peace and security, safe from the attacks of any marauding band. The tents were soon pitched by the peasants under the direction of Sergeant Sinclair, straw was laid down in them, and the canvas raised to allow the air to sweep through them.

Very grateful were the weary men for the kindness with which they were received, and even the weakest felt that they should soon recover their strength.

In an hour two men came up from the farm house carrying a huge pot filled with strong soup. Another brought a great dish of stew. Women carried wooden platters, bowls of stewed fruit, and loaves of bread; and the soldiers, seated upon the grass, fell to with an appetite such as they had not experienced for weeks. With the meal was an abundant supply of the rough but wholesome wine of the country.

To the Scottish soldiers after the hardships they had passed through, this secluded valley seemed a perfect paradise. They had nought to do save to eat their meals, to sleep on the turf in the shade, or to wander in the woods and gardens free to pick what fruit they fancied. Under these circumstances they rapidly picked up strength, and in a week after their arrival would hardly have been recognized as the feeble band who had left the Swedish camp at Old Brandenburg.

On Sunday the pastor arrived. He did not live permanently at the village, but ministered to the inhabitants of several villages scattered among the hills, holding services in them by turns, and remaining a few days in each. As the congregation was too large for the room in the farm house the service was held in the open air. The Scotch soldiers were all present, and joined heartily in the singing, although many of them were ignorant of the language, and sang the words of Scotch hymns to the German tunes.

Even the roughest of them, and those who had been longest away from their native country, were much moved by the service. The hush and stillness, the air of quiet and peace which prevailed, the fervour with which all joined in the simple service, took them back in thought to the days of their youth in quiet Scottish glens, and many a hand was passed hastily across eyes which had not been moistened for many a year.

The armour and arms were now cleaned and polished, and for a short time each day Malcolm exercised them. The martial appearance and perfect discipline of the Scots struck the villagers with admiration the first time they saw them under arms, and they earnestly begged Malcolm that they might receive from him and Sergeant Sinclair some instruction in drill.

Accordingly every evening when work was done the men of the village were formed up and drilled. Several of the soldiers took their places with them in the ranks in order to aid them by their example. After the drill there was sword and pike exercise, and as most of the men had already some knowledge of the use of arms they made rapid progress, and felt an increased confidence in their power to defend the village against the attacks of any small bands of plunderers. To Malcolm the time passed delightfully. His kind hosts vied with each other in their efforts to make him comfortable, and it was in vain that he assured them that he no longer needed attention and care. A seat was always placed for him in the coolest nook in the room, fresh grapes and other fruit stood in readiness on a table hard by. The farmer's daughters, busy as they were in their household avocations, were always ready to sit and talk with him when he was indoors, and of an evening to sing him the country melodies.

At the end of a fortnight the men were all fit for duty again, but the hospitable farmer would not hear of their leaving, and as news from time to time reached them from the outer world, and Malcolm learned that there was no chance of any engagement for a time between the hostile armies, he was only too glad to remain.

Another fortnight passed, and Malcolm reluctantly gave the word that on the morrow the march must be recommenced. A general feeling of sorrow reigned in the village when it was known that their guests were about to depart, for the Scottish soldiers had made themselves extremely popular. They were ever ready to assist in the labours of the village. They helped to pick the apples from the heavily laden trees, they assisted to thrash out the corn, and in every way strove to repay their entertainers for the kindness they had shown them.

Of an evening their camp had been the rendezvous of the whole village. There alternately the soldiers and the peasants sang their national songs, and joined in hearty choruses. Sometimes there were dances, for many of the villagers played on various instruments; and altogether Glogau had never known such a time of festivity and cheerfulness before.

Late in the evening of the day before they had fixed for their departure the pastor rode into the village.

"I have bad news," he said. "A party of Pappenheim's dragoons, three hundred strong, are raiding in the district on the other side of the hills. A man came in just as I mounted my horse, saying that it was expected they would attack Mansfeld, whose count is a sturdy Protestant. The people were determined to resist to the last, in spite of the fate of Magdeburg and Frankenhausen, but I fear that their chance of success is a small one; but they say they may as well die fighting as be slaughtered in cold blood."

"Is Mansfeld fortified?" Malcolm asked.

"It has a wall," the pastor replied, "but of no great strength. The count's castle, which stands on a rock adjoining it, might defend itself for some time, but I question whether it can withstand Pappenheim's veterans.

"Mansfeld itself is little more than a village. I should not say it had more than a thousand inhabitants, and can muster at best about two hundred and fifty men capable of bearing arms."

"How far is it from here?" Malcolm asked after a pause.

"Twenty-four miles by the bridle path across the hills."

"When were the Imperialists expected to arrive?"

"They were ten miles away this morning," the pastor replied; "but as they were plundering and burning as they went they will not probably arrive before Mansfeld before the morning. Some of the more timid citizens were leaving, and many were sending away their wives and families."

"Then," Malcolm said, "I will march thither at once. Twenty good soldiers may make all the difference, and although I have, of course, no orders for such an emergency, the king can hardly blame me even if the worst happens for striking a blow against the Imperialists here. Will you give me a man," he asked the farmer, "to guide us across the hills?"

"That will I right willingly," the farmer said; "but it seems to me a desperate service to embark in. These townspeople are of little good for fighting, and probably intend only to make a show of resistance in order to procure better terms. The count himself is a brave nobleman, but I fear that the enterprise is a hopeless one."

"Hopeless or not," Malcolm said, "I will undertake it, and will

66

at once put the men under arms. The wagon and horses with the baggage I will leave here till I return, that is if we should ever come back again."

A tap of the drum and the soldiers came running in hastily from various cottages where they were spending their last evening with their village friends, wondering at the sudden summons to arms. As soon as they had fallen in, Malcolm joined them.

"Men," he said, "I am sorry to disturb you on your last evening here, but there is business on hand. A party of Pappenheim's dragoons are about to attack the town of Mansfeld, where the people are of the Reformed Religion. The siege will begin in the morning, and ere that time we must be there. We have all got fat and lazy, and a little fighting will do us good."

The thought of a coming fray reconciled the men to their departure from their quiet and happy resting place. Armour was donned, buckles fastened, and arms inspected, and in half an hour, after a cordial adieu from their kind hosts, the detachment marched off, their guide with a lighted torch leading the way. The men were in light marching order, having left everything superfluous behind them in the wagon; and they marched briskly along over hill and through forest without a halt, till at three o'clock in the morning the little town of Mansfeld, with its castle rising above it, was visible before them in the first light of morning.

As they approached the walls a musketoon was fired, and the alarm bell of the church instantly rang out. Soon armed men made their appearance on the walls. Fearing that the burghers might fire before waiting to ascertain who were the newcomers, Malcolm halted his band, and advanced alone towards the walls.

"Who are you who come in arms to the peaceful town of Mansfeld?" an officer asked from the wall.

"I am an officer of his Swedish Majesty, Gustavus, and hearing that the town was threatened with attack by the Imperialists, I have marched hither with my detachment to aid in the defence."

A loud cheer broke from the walls. Not only was the reinforcement a most welcome one, small as it was, for the valour of the Scottish soldiers of the King of Sweden was at that time the talk of all Germany, but the fact that a detachment of these redoubted troops had arrived seemed a proof that the main army of the Swedish king could not be far away. The gates were at once opened, and Malcolm with his band marched into Mansfield.

CHAPTER VIII

THE SIEGE OF MANSFELD

"Will it please your worship at once to repair to the castle?" the leader of the townspeople said. "The count has just sent down to inquire into the reason of the alarm."

"Yes," Malcolm replied, "I will go at once. In the meantime, sir, I pray you to see to the wants of my soldiers, who have taken a long night march and will be none the worse for some refreshment. Hast seen aught of the Imperialists?"

"They are at a village but a mile distant on the other side of the town," the citizen said. "Yesterday we counted eighteen villages in flames, and the peasants who have come in say that numbers have been slain by them."

"There is little mercy to be expected from the butchers of Magdeburg," Malcolm replied; "the only arguments they will listen to are steel and lead, and we will not be sparing of these."

A murmur of assent rang through the townsfolk who had gathered round, and then the burgomaster himself led Malcolm up the ascent to the castle. The news that the newcomers were a party of Scots had already been sent up to the castle, and as Malcolm entered the gateway the count came forward to welcome him.

"You are welcome indeed, fair sir," he said. "It seems almost as if you had arrived from the clouds to our assistance, for we had heard that the Swedish king and his army were encamped around Old Brandenburg.

"His majesty has moved west, I hear," Malcolm said; "but we have been a month away from the camp. My detachment consisted of a body of invalids who came up among the hills to get rid of the fever which was playing such havoc among our ranks. I am glad to say that all are restored, and fit as ever for a meeting with the Imperialists. I heard but yestereven that you were expecting an attack, and have marched all night to be here in time. My party is a small one, but each man can be relied upon; and when it comes to hard fighting twenty in good soldiers may turn the day."

"You are heartily welcome, sir, and I thank you much for coming to our aid. The townspeople are determined to do their best, but most of them have little skill in arms. I have a score or two of old soldiers here in the castle, and had hoped to be able to hold this to the end; but truly I despaired of a successful defence of the town. But enter, I pray you; the countess will be glad to welcome you."

68

Malcolm accompanied the count to the banquet hall of the castle. The countess, a gentle and graceful woman, was already there; for indeed but few in Mansfeld had closed an eye that night, for it was possible that the Imperialists might attack without delay. By her side stood her daughter, a girl of about fourteen years old. Malcolm had already stated his name to the count, and the latter now presented him to his wife.

"We have heard so much of the Scottish soldiers," she said as she held out her hand, over which Malcolm bent deeply, "that we have all been curious to see them, little dreaming that a band of them would appear here like good angels in our hour of danger."

"It was a fortunate accident which found me within reach when I heard of the approach of the Imperialists. The names of the Count and Countess of Mansfeld are so well known and so highly esteemed through Protestant Germany that I was sure that the king would approve of my hastening to lend what aid I might to you without orders from him."

"I see you have learned to flatter," the countess said smiling. "This is my daughter Thekla."

"I am glad to see you," the girl said; "but I am a little disappointed. I had thought that the Scots were such big fierce soldiers, and you are not very big—not so tall as papa; and you do not look fierce at all—not half so fierce as my cousin Caspar, who is but a boy."

"That is very rude, Thekla," her mother said reprovingly, while Malcolm laughed gaily.

"You are quite right, Fraulein Thekla. I know I do not look very fierce, but I hope when my moustache grows I shall come up more nearly to your expectations. As to my height, I have some years to grow yet, seeing that I am scarce eighteen, and perhaps no older than your cousin."

"Have you recently joined, sir?" the countess asked.

"I have served through the campaign," Malcolm replied, "and have seen some hard knocks given, as you may imagine when I tell you that I was at the siege of New Brandenburg."

"When your soldiers fought like heroes, and, as I heard, all died sword in hand save two or three officers who managed to escape."

"I was one of the three, countess; but the tale is a long one, and can be told after we have done with the Imperialists. Now, sir," he went on, turning to the count, "I am at your orders, and will take post with my men at any point that you may think fit."

"Before doing that," the count said, "you must join us at breakfast. You must be hungry after your long march, and as I have

69

been all night in my armour I shall do justice to it myself. You will, of course, take up your abode here. As to other matters I have done my best, and the townspeople were yesterday all told off to their places on the walls. I should think it were best that your band were stationed in the marketplace as a reserve, they could then move to any point which might be seriously threatened. Should the Imperialists enter the town the citizens have orders to fall back here fighting. All their most valuable goods were sent up here yesterday, together with such of their wives and families as have not taken flight, so that there will be nothing to distract them from their duty."

"That is good," Malcolm said. "The thought that one is fighting for home and family must nerve a man in the defence, but when the enemy once breaks in he would naturally think of home first and hasten away to defend it to the last, instead of obeying orders and falling back with his comrades in good order and discipline."

The meal was a cheerful one. Malcolm related more in detail how he and his detachment happened to be so far removed from the army.

Just as the meal came to an end a drum beat in the town and the alarm bells began to ring. The count and Malcolm sallied out at once to the outer wall, and saw a small party of officers riding from the village occupied by the Imperialists towards the town.

"Let us descend," the count said. "I presume they are going to demand our surrender."

They reached the wall of the town just as the Imperialist officers approached the gate.

"In the name of his majesty the emperor," one of them cried out, "I command you to open the gate and to surrender to his good will and pleasure."

"The smoking villages which I see around me," Count Mansfeld replied, "are no hopeful sign of any good will or pleasure on the part of his majesty towards us. As to surrendering, we will rather die. But I am willing to pay a fair ransom for the town if you will draw off your troops and march away."

"Beware, sir!" the officer said. "I have a force here sufficient to compel obedience, and I warn you of the fate which will befall all within these walls if you persist in refusing to admit us."

"I doubt not as to their fate," the count replied; "there are plenty of examples before us of the tender mercy which your master's troops show towards the towns you capture.

"Once again I offer you a ransom for the town. Name the sum, and if it be in reason such as I and the townspeople can pay, it shall be yours; but open the gates to you we will not."

"Very well," the officer said; "then your blood be on your own heads." And turning his horse he rode with his companions back towards the village.

On their arrival there a bustle was seen to prevail. A hundred horsemen rode off and took post on an eminence near the town, ready to cut off the retreat of any who might try to escape, and to enter the town when the gates were forced open. The other two hundred men advanced on foot in a close body towards the principal gate.

"They will try and blow it open with petards," Malcolm said. "Half of my men are musketeers and good shots, and I will, with your permission, place them on the wall to aid the townsfolk there, for if the gate is blown open and the enemy force their way in it will go hard with us."

The count assented, and Malcolm posted his musketeers on the wall, ordering Sergeant Sinclair with the remainder to set to work to erect barricades across the street leading from the gate, so that, in case this were blown in, such a stand might be made against the Imperialists as would give the townspeople time to rally from the walls and to gather there.

The Imperialists heralded their advance by opening fire with pistols and musketoons against the wall, and the defenders at once replied. So heavy was the fire that the head of the column wavered, many of the leading files being at once shot down, but, encouraged by their officers, they rallied, and pushed forward at a run. The fire of the townspeople at once became hurried and irregular, but the Scots picked off their men with steady aim. The leader of the Imperialists, who carried a petard, advanced boldly to the edge of the ditch. The fosse was shallow and contained but little water, and he at once dashed into it and waded across, for the drawbridge had, of course, been raised. He climbed up the bank, and was close to the gate, when Malcolm, leaning far over the wall, discharged his pistol at him. The ball glanced from the steel armour.

Malcolm drew his other pistol and again fired, this time more effectually, for the ball struck between the shoulder and the neck at the junction of the breast and back pieces, and passed down into the body of the Austrian, who, dropping the petard, fell dead; but a number of his men were close behind him.

"Quick, lads!" Malcolm cried. "Put your strength to this parapet. It is old and rotten. Now, all together! Shove!"

The soldiers bent their strength against the parapet, while some of the townspeople, thrusting their pikes into the rotten

71

mortar between the stones, prised them up with all their strength. The parapet tottered, and then with a tremendous crash fell, burying five or six of the Imperialists and the petard beneath the ruins.

A shout of exultation rose from the defenders, and the Imperialists at once withdrew at full speed. They halted out of gunshot, and then a number of men were sent back to the village, whence they returned carrying ladders, some of which had been collected the day before from the neighbouring villages and others manufactured during the night. The enemy now divided into three parties, which advanced simultaneously against different points of the wall.

Notwithstanding the storm of shot poured upon them as they advanced, they pressed forward until they reached the wall and planted their ladders, and then essayed to climb; but at each point the stormers were stoutly met with pike and sword, while the musketeers from the flanking towers poured their bullets into them.

The troops proved themselves worthy of their reputation, for it was not until more than fifty had fallen that they desisted from the attempt and drew off.

"Now we shall have a respite," Malcolm said. "If there are no more of them in the neighbourhood methinks they will retire altogether, but if they have any friends with cannon anywhere within reach they will probably send for them and renew the attack."

The day passed quietly. Parties of horsemen were seen leaving the village to forage and plunder the surrounding country, but the main body remained quietly there. The next day there was still no renewal of the attack, but as the enemy remained in occupation of the village Malcolm guessed that they must be waiting for the arrival of reinforcements. The following afternoon a cloud of dust was seen upon the plain, and presently a column of infantry some four hundred strong, with three cannon, could be made out. The townspeople now wavered in their determination. A few were still for resistance, but the majority held that they could not attempt to withstand an assault by so strong a force, and that it was better to make the best terms they could with the enemy.

A parlementaire was accordingly despatched to the Imperialists asking what terms would be granted should the place surrender.

"We will grant no terms whatever," the colonel in command of the Imperialists said. "The town is at our mercy, and we will do as we will with it and all within it; but tell Count Mansfeld that if he will surrender the castle as well as the town at once, and without striking another blow, his case shall receive favourable consideration."

"That will not do," the count said. "They either guarantee our lives or they do not. I give not up my castle on terms like these, but I will exercise no pressure on the townspeople. If they choose to defend themselves till the last I will fight here with them; if they choose to surrender they can do so; and those who differ from their fellows and put no faith in Tilly's wolves can enter the castle with me."

The principal inhabitants of the town debated the question hotly. Malcolm lost patience with them, and said: "Are you mad as well as stupid? Do you not see the smoking villages round you? Do you not remember the fate of Magdeburg, New Brandenburg, and the other towns which have made a resistance? You have chosen to resist. It was open to you to have fled when you heard the Imperialists were coming. You could have opened the gates then with some hope at least of your lives; but you decided to resist. You have killed some fifty or sixty of their soldiers. You have repulsed them from a place which they thought to take with scarce an effort. You have compelled them to send for reinforcements and guns. And now you are talking of opening the gates without even obtaining a promise that your lives shall be spared. This is the extremity of folly, and all I can say is, if you take such a step you will well deserve your fate."

Malcolm's indignant address had its effect, and after a short discussion the townspeople again placed themselves at the count's disposal, and said that they would obey his orders.

"I will give no orders," the count said. "My Scottish friend here agrees with me that it is useless to try to defend the town. We might repulse several attacks, but in the end they would surely break in, for the walls are old and weak, and will crumble before their cannon. Were there any hope of relief one would defend them to the last, but as it is it would be but a waste of blood, for many would be slain both in the defence and before they could retreat to the castle; therefore we propose at once to withdraw. We doubt not that we can hold the castle. Any who like to remain in their houses and trust to the tender mercy of Tilly's wolves can do so."

There was no more hesitation, and a cannonball, the first which the Imperialists had fired, at that moment crashed into a house hard by, and sharpened their decision wonderfully.

"I have no great store of provisions in the castle," the count said, "and although I deem it not likely that we shall have to stand a long siege we must be prepared for it. There are already more than 700 of your wives and children there, therefore while half of the force continue to show themselves upon the walls, and so deter the enemy from attempting an assault until they have opened some breaches, let the rest carry up provisions to the castle. Any houses from which the women have fled are at once to be broken open. All that we leave behind the enemy will take, and the less we leave for them the better; therefore all stores and magazines of food and wine must be considered as public property. Let the men at once be divided into two bodies—the one to guard the walls, the other to search for and carry up provisions. They can be changed every three or four hours."

The resolution was taken and carried into effect without delay. Most of the horses and carts in the town had left with the fugitives, those that remained were at once set to work. The carts were laden with large barrels of wine and sacks of flour, while the men carried sides of bacon, kegs of butter, and other portable articles on their heads. The Imperialists, seeing the movement up the steep road to the castle gate, opened fire with their arquebuses, but the defenders of the wall replied so hotly that they were forced to retire out of range. The cannon played steadily all day, and by nightfall two breaches had been effected in the wall and the gate had been battered down.

But by this time an ample store of provisions had been collected in the castle and as the Imperialists were seen to form up for the assault the trumpet was sounded, and at the signal the whole of the defenders of the walls left their posts and fell back to the castle, leaving the deserted town at the mercy of the enemy. The Imperialists raised a shout of triumph as they entered the breaches and found them undefended, and when once assured that the town was deserted they broke their ranks and scattered to plunder.

It was now quite dark, and many of them dragging articles of furniture into the streets made great bonfires to light them at their work of plunder. But they had soon reason to repent having done so, for immediately the flames sprang up and lighted the streets, flashes ran round the battlements of the castle, and a heavy fire was opened into the streets, killing many of the soldiers. Seeing the danger of thus exposing the men to the fire from the castle, the Imperialist commander issued orders at once that all fires should be extinguished, that anyone setting fire to a house should be instantly hung, and that no lights were to be lit in the houses whose windows faced the castle.

Foreseeing the possibility of an attack from the castle, the Austrians placed a hundred men at the foot of the road leading up to it, and laid their three cannon loaded to the muzzle to command it.

"Have you not," Malcolm asked the count, "some means of exit from the castle besides the way into the town?"

"Yes," the count said, "there is a footpath down the rock on the other side."

"Then," Malcolm said, "as soon as they are fairly drunk, which will be before midnight, let us fall upon them from the other side. Leave fifty of your oldest men with half a dozen veteran soldiers to defend the gateway against a sudden attack; with the rest we can issue out, and marching round, enter by the gate and breaches, sweeping the streets as we go, and then uniting, burst through any guard they may have placed to prevent a sortie, and so regain the castle."

The count at once assented. In a short time shouts, songs, the sound of rioting and quarrels, arose from the town, showing that revelry was general. At eleven o'clock the men in the castle were mustered, fifty were told off to the defence with five experienced soldiers, an officer of the count being left in command. The rest sallied through a little door at the back of the castle and noiselessly descended the steep path. On arriving at the bottom they were divided into three bodies. Malcolm with his Scots and fifty of the townspeople formed one. Count Mansfeld took the command of another, composed of his own soldiers and fifty more of the townspeople. The third consisted of eighty of the best fighting men of the town under their own leaders. These were to enter by the gate, while the other two parties came in by the breaches. The moment the attack began the defenders of the castle were to open as rapid a fire as they could upon the foot of the road so as to occupy the attention of the enemy's force there, and to lead them to anticipate a sortie.

The breach by which Malcolm was to enter was the farthest from the castle, and his command would, therefore, be the last in arriving at its station. When he reached it he ordered the trumpeters who accompanied him to sound, and at the signal the three columns rushed into the town uttering shouts of "Gustavus! Gustavus!"

The Imperialists in the houses near were slaughtered with scarcely any resistance. They were for the most part intoxicated, and such as retained their senses were paralysed at the sudden attack, and panic stricken at the shouts, which portended the arrival of a relieving force from the army of the King of Sweden. As the bands pressed forward, slaying all whom they came upon, the resistance became stronger; but the three columns were all headed by parties of pikemen who advanced steadily and in good order, bearing down all opposition, and leaving to those behind them the task of slaying all found in the houses.

Lights flashed from the windows and partly lit up the streets, and the Imperialist officers attempted to rally their men; but the Scottish shouts, "A Hepburn! A Hepburn!" and the sight of their green scarves added to the terror of the soldiers, who were convinced that the terrible Green Brigade of the King of Sweden was upon them.

Hundreds were cut down after striking scarce a blow in their defence, numbers fled to the walls and leapt over. The panic communicated itself to the party drawn up to repel a sortie. Hearing the yells, screams, and shouts, accompanied by the musketry approaching from three different quarters of the town, while a steady fire from the castle indicated that the defenders there might, at any moment, sally out upon them, they stood for a time irresolute; but as the heads of the three columns approached they lost heart, quitted their station, and withdrew in a body by a street by which they avoided the approaching columns. On arriving at the spot Malcolm found the guns deserted.

"The town is won now," he said. "I will take my post here with my men in case the Austrians should rally; do you with the rest scatter over the town and complete the work, but bid them keep together in parties of twenty."

The force broke up and scattered through the town in their work of vengeance. House after house was entered and searched, and all who were found there put to the sword; but by this time most of those who were not too drunk to fly had already made for the gates.

In half an hour not an Imperialist was left alive in the town. Then guards were placed at the gate and breaches, and they waited till morning. Not a sign of an Imperialist was to be seen on the plain, and parties sallying out found that they had fled in the utmost disorder. Arms, accoutrements, and portions of plunder lay scattered thickly about, and it was clear that in the belief that the Swedish army was on them, the Imperialists had fled panic stricken, and were now far away. Upwards of two hundred bodies were found in the streets and houses.

A huge grave was dug outside the walls, and here the fallen foes were buried. Only three or four of the defenders of the town were killed and a score or so wounded in the whole affair. Although there was little fear of a return, as the Imperialists would probably continue their headlong flight for a long distance, and would then march with all haste to rejoin their main army with the news that a strong Swedish force was at Mansfeld, the count set the townspeople at once to repair the breaches.

The people were overjoyed with their success, and delighted at having preserved their homes from destruction, for they knew that the Imperialists would, if unsuccessful against the castle, have given the town to the flames before retiring. The women and children flocked down to their homes again, and although much furniture had been destroyed and damage done, this was little heeded when so much was saved.

All vied in the expression of gratitude towards Malcolm and his Scots, but Malcolm modestly disclaimed all merit, saying that he and his men had scarcely struck a blow.

"It is not so much the fighting," the count said, "as the example which you set the townsmen, and the spirit which the presence of you and your men diffused among them. Besides, your counsel and support to me have been invaluable; had it not been for you the place would probably have been carried at the first attack, and if not the townspeople would have surrendered when the enemy's reinforcements arrived; and in that case, with so small a force at my command I could not have hoped to defend the castle successfully. Moreover, the idea of the sortie which has freed us of them and saved the town from destruction was entirely yours. No, my friend, say what you will I feel that I am indebted to you for the safety of my wife and child, and so long as I live I shall be deeply your debtor."

The following day Malcolm with his party marched away. The count had presented him with a suit of magnificent armour, and the countess with a gold chain of great value. Handsome presents were also made to Sergeant Sinclair, who was a cadet of good family, and a purse of gold was given to each of the soldiers, so in high spirits the band marched away over the mountains on their return to the village.

CHAPTER IX

THE BATTLE OF BREITENFELD

Great joy was manifested as Malcolm's band marched into the village and it was found that they had accomplished the mission on which they went, had saved Mansfeld, and utterly defeated the Imperialists, and had returned in undiminished numbers, although two or three had received wounds more or less serious, principally in the first day's fighting. They only remained one night in the village.

On the following morning the baggage was placed in the wagons with a store of fruit and provisions for their march, and after another hearty adieu the detachment set out in high spirits. After marching for two days they learned that the Swedish army had marched to Werben, and that Tilly's army had followed it there.

After the receipt of this news there was no more loitering; the marches were long and severe, and after making a detour to avoid the Imperialists the detachment entered the royal camp without having met with any adventure on the way. His fellow officers flocked round Malcolm to congratulate him on his safe return and on his restored health.

"The change has done wonders for you, Malcolm," Nigel Graheme said. "Why, when you marched out you were a band of tottering scarecrows, and now your detachment looks as healthy and fresh as if they had but yesterday left Scotland; but come in, the bugle has just sounded to supper, and we are only waiting for the colonel to arrive. He is at present in council with the king with Hepburn and some more. Ah! here he comes."

Munro rode up and leapt from his horse, and after heartily greeting Malcolm led the way into the tent where supper was laid out. Malcolm was glad to see by the faces of his comrades that all had shaken off the disease which had played such havoc among them at Old Brandenburg.

"Is there any chance of a general engagement?" he asked Nigel.

"Not at present," Nigel said. "We are expecting the reinforcements up in a few days. As you see we have fortified the camp too strongly for Tilly to venture to attack us here. Only yesterday he drew up his army and offered us battle; but the odds were too great, and the king will not fight till his reinforcements arrive. Some of the hotter spirits were sorry that he would not accept Tilly's invitation, and I own that I rather gnashed my teeth myself; but I knew that the king was right in not risking the whole cause rashly when a few days will put us in a position to meet the Imperialists on something like equal terms. Is there any news, colonel?" he asked, turning to Munro.

"No news of importance," the colonel replied; "but the king is rather puzzled. A prisoner was taken today—one of Pappenheim's horsemen—and he declares that a force of horse and foot have been defeated at Mansfeld by a Swedish army with heavy loss. He avers that he was present at the affair, and arrived in camp with the rest of the beaten force only yesterday. We cannot make it out, as we know that there are no Swedish troops anywhere in that direction."

Malcolm burst into a hearty laugh, to the surprise of his fellow officers.

"I can explain the matter, colonel," he said. "It was my detachment that had the honour of representing the Swedish army at Mansfeld."

"What on earth do you mean, Malcolm?" the colonel asked.

"Well, sir, as you know I went with a detachment to the village where I had before been well treated, and had earned the gratitude of the people by teaching them how to destroy a party of marauders. After having been there for a month I was on the point of marching, for the men were all perfectly restored to health; and indeed I know I ought to have returned sooner, seeing that the men were fit for service; but as I thought you were still at Old Brandenburg, and could well dispense with our services, I lingered on to the last. But just as I was about to march the news came that a party of Imperialist horse, three hundred strong, was about to attack Mansfeld, a place of whose existence I had never heard; but hearing that its count was a staunch Protestant, and that the inhabitants intended to make a stout defence, I thought that I could not be doing wrong in the service of the king by marching to aid them, the place being but twenty-four miles away across the hills. We got there in time, and aided the townspeople to repulse the first assault. After two days they brought up a reinforcement of four hundred infantry and some cannon. As the place is a small one, with but about two hundred and fifty fighting men of all ages, we deemed it impossible to defend the town, and while they were breaching the walls fell back to the castle. The Imperialists occupied it at sunset, and at night, leaving a party to hold the castle, we sallied out from the other side, and marching round, entered by the breaches, and, raising the Swedish war cry fell upon the enemy, who were for the most part too drunk to offer any serious resistance. We killed two hundred and fifty of them, and the rest fled in terror, thinking they had the whole Swedish army upon them. The next day I started on my march back here, and though we have not spared speed, it seems that the Imperialists have arrived before us."

A burst of laughter and applause greeted the solution of the mystery.

"You have done well, sir," Munro said cordially, "and have rendered a great service not only in the defeat of the Imperialists, but in its consequences here, for the prisoner said that last night five thousand men were marched away from Tilly's army to observe and make head against this supposed Swedish force advancing from the east. When I have done my meal I will go over to the king with the news, for his majesty is greatly puzzled, especially as the prisoner declared that he himself had seen the Scots of the Green Brigade in the van of the column, and had heard the war cry, 'A Hepburn! A Hepburn!'

"Hepburn himself could make neither head nor tail of it, and was half inclined to believe that this avenging force was led by the ghosts of those who had been slain at New Brandenburg. Whenever we can't account for a thing, we Scots are inclined to believe it's supernatural.

"Now tell me more about the affair, Malcolm. By the way do you know that you are a lieutenant now? Poor Foulis died of the fever a few days after you left us, and as the king had himself ordered that you were to have the next vacancy, I of course appointed you at once. We must drink tonight to your promotion."

Malcolm now related fully the incidents of the siege.

"By my faith, Malcolm Graheme," Munro said when he had finished, "you are as lucky as you are brave. Mansfeld is a powerful nobleman, and has large possessions in various parts of Germany and much influence, and the king will be grateful that you have thus rendered him such effective assistance and so bound him to our cause. I believe he has no children."

"He has a daughter," Malcolm said, "a pretty little maid some fourteen years old."

"In faith, Malcolm, 'tis a pity that you and she are not some four or five years older. What a match it would be for you, the heiress of Mansfeld; she would be a catch indeed! Well, there's time enough yet, my lad, for there is no saying how long this war will last."

There was a general laugh, and the colonel continued:

"Malcolm has the grace to colour, which I am afraid the rest of us have lost long ago. Never mind, Malcolm, there are plenty of Scotch cadets have mended their fortune by means of a rich heiress before now, and I hope there will be many more. I am on the lookout for a wealthy young countess myself, and I don't think there is one here who would not lay aside his armour and sword on such inducement. And now, gentlemen, as we have all finished, I will leave you to your wine while I go across with our young lieutenant to the king. I must tell him tonight, or he will not sleep with wondering over the mystery. We will be back anon and will broach a cask of that famous wine we picked up the other day, in honour of Malcolm Graheme's promotion."

Sir John Hepburn was dining with Gustavus, and the meal was just concluded when Colonel Munro was announced.

"Well, my brave Munro, what is it?" the king said heartily, "and whom have you here? The young officer who escaped from New Brandenburg and Tilly, unless I am mistaken."

"It is, sir, but I have to introduce him in a new character tonight, as the leader of your majesty's army who have defeated the Imperialists at Mansfeld."

"Say you so?" exclaimed the king. "Then, though I understand you not, we shall hear a solution of the mystery which has been puzzling us. Sit down, young sir; fill yourself a flagon of wine, and expound this riddle to us."

Malcolm repeated the narrative as he had told it to his colonel, and the king expressed his warm satisfaction.

"You will make a great leader some day if you do not get killed in one of these adventures, young sir. Bravery seems to be a common gift of the men of your nation; but you seem to unite with it a surprising prudence and sagacity, and, moreover, this march of yours to Mansfeld shows that you do not fear taking responsibility, which is a high and rare quality. You have done good service to the cause, and I thank you, and shall keep my eye upon you in the future."

The next day Malcolm went round the camp, and was surprised at the extensive works which had been erected. Strong ramparts and redoubts had been thrown up round it, faced with stone, and mounted with 150 pieces of cannon. In the centre stood an inner entrenchment with earthworks and a deep fosse. In this stood the tents of the king and those of his principal officers. The Marquis of Hamilton had, Malcolm heard, arrived and gone. He had lost on the march many of the soldiers he had enlisted in England, who had died from eating German bread, which was heavier, darker coloured, and more sour than that of their own country. This, however, did not disagree with the Scotch, who were accustomed to black bread.

"I wonder," Malcolm said to Nigel Graheme, "that when the king has in face of him a force so superior to his own he should have sent away on detached service the four splendid regiments which they say the marquis brought."

"Well, the fact was," Nigel said laughing, "Hamilton was altogether too grand for us here. We all felt small and mean so long as he remained. Gustavus himself, who is as simple in his tastes as any officer in the army, and who keeps up no ostentatious show, was thrown into the shade by his visitor. Why, had he been the Emperor of Germany or the King of France he could not have made a braver show. His table was equipped and furnished with magnificence; his carriages would have created a sensation in Paris; the liveries of his attendants were more splendid than the uniforms of generals; he had forty gentlemen as esquires and pages, and 200 yeomen, splendidly mounted and armed, rode with him as his bodyguard.

"Altogether he was oppressive; but the Hamiltons have ever been fond of show and finery. So Gustavus has sent him and his troops away to guard the passages of the Oder and to cover our retreat should we be forced to fall back."

Tilly, finding that the position of Gustavus was too strong to be forced, retired to Wolmirstadt, whence he summoned the Elector of Saxony to admit his army into his country, and either to disband the Saxon army or to unite it to his own. Hitherto the elector had held aloof from Gustavus, whom he regarded with jealousy and dislike, and had stood by inactive although the slightest movement of his army would have saved Magdeburg. To disband his troops, however, and to hand over his fortresses to Tilly, would be equivalent to giving up his dominions to the enemy; rather than do this he determined to join Gustavus, and having despatched Arnheim to treat with the King of Sweden for alliance, he sent a point blank refusal to Tilly.

The Imperialist general at once marched towards Leipzig, devastating the country as he advanced. Terms were soon arranged between the elector and Gustavus, and on the 3d of September, 1631, the Swedish army crossed the Elbe, and the next day joined the Saxon army at Torgau. By this time Tilly was in front of Leipzig, and immediately on his arrival burned to the ground Halle, a suburb lying beyond the wall, and then summoned the city to surrender.

Alarmed at the sight of the conflagration of Halle, and with the fate of Magdeburg in their minds, the citizens of Leipzig opened their gates at once on promise of fair treatment. The news of this speedy surrender was a heavy blow to the allies, who, however, after a council of war, determined at once to march forward against the city, and to give battle to the Imperialists on the plain around it.

Leipzig stands on a wide plain which is called the plain of Breitenfeld, and the battle which was about to commence there has been called by the Germans the battle of Breitenfeld, to distinguish it from the even greater struggles which have since taken place under the walls of Leipzig.

The baggage had all been left behind, and the Swedish army lay down as they stood. The king occupied his travelling coach, and passed the night chatting with Sir John Hepburn, Marshal Horn, Sir John Banner, Baron Teuffel, who commanded the guards, and other leaders. The lines of red fires which marked Tilly's position on the slope of a gentle eminence to the southwest were plainly to be seen. The day broke dull and misty on the 7th of September, and as the light fog gradually rose the troops formed up for battle. Prayers were said in front of every regiment, and the army then moved forward. Two Scottish brigades had the places of honour in the van, where the regiments of Sir James Ramsay, the Laird of Foulis, and Sir John Hamilton were posted, while Hepburn's Green Brigade formed part of the reserve—a force composed of the best troops of the army, as on them the fate of the battle frequently depends. The Swedish cavalry were commanded by Field Marshal Horn, General Banner, and Lieutenant General Bauditzen.

The king and Baron Teuffel led the main body of infantry; the King of Saxony commanded the Saxons, who were on the Swedish left. The armies were not very unequal in numbers, the allies numbering 35,000, of whom the Swedes and Scots counted 20,000, the Saxons 15,000. The Imperialists numbered about 40,000. Tilly was fighting unwillingly, for he had wished to await the arrival from Italy of 12,000 veterans under General Altringer, and who were within a few days' march; but he had been induced, against his own better judgment, by the urgency of Pappenheim, Furstenberg, and the younger generals, to quit the unassailable post he had taken up in front of Leipzig, and to move out on to the plain of Breitenfeld to accept the battle which the Swedes offered.

A short distance in his front was the village of Podelwitz. Behind his position were two elevations, on which he placed his guns, forty in number. In rear of these elevations was a very thick wood. The Imperialist right was commanded by Furstenberg, the left by Pappenheim, the centre by Tilly himself. Although he had yielded to his generals so far as to take up a position on the plain, Tilly was resolved, if possible, not to fight until the arrival of the reinforcements; but the rashness of Pappenheim brought on a battle. To approach the Austrian position the Swedes had to cross the little river Loder, and Pappenheim asked permission of Tilly to charge them as they did so. Tilly consented on condition that he only charged with two thousand horse and did not bring on a general engagement. Accordingly, as the Scottish brigade under Sir James Ramsay crossed the Loder, Pappenheim swept down upon them.

The Scots stood firm, and with pike and musket repelled the attack; and after hard fighting Pappenheim was obliged to fall back, setting fire as he retired to the village of Podelwitz. The smoke of the burning village drifted across the plain, and was useful to the Swedes, as under its cover the entire army passed the Loder, and formed up ready for battle facing the Imperialists position, the movement being executed under a heavy fire from the Austrian batteries on the hills.

The Swedish order of battle was different from that of the Imperialists. The latter had their cavalry massed together in one heavy, compact body, while the Swedish regiments of horse were placed alternately with the various regiments or brigades of infantry. The Swedish centre was composed of four brigades of pikemen. Guns were behind the first line, as were the cavalry supporting the pikemen. The regiments of musketeers were placed at intervals among the brigades of pikemen.

Pappenheim on his return to the camp ordered up the whole of his cavalry, and charged down with fury upon the Swedes, while at the same moment Furstenberg dashed with seven regiments of cavalry on the Saxons. Between these and the Swedes there was a slight interval, for Gustavus had doubts of the steadiness of his allies, and was anxious that in case of their defeat his own troops should not be thrown into confusion. The result justified his anticipations.

Attacked with fury on their flank by Furstenberg's horse, while his infantry and artillery poured a direct fire into their front, the Saxons at once gave way. Their elector was the first to set the example of flight, and, turning his horse, galloped without drawing rein to Torgau, and in twenty minutes after the commencement of the fight the whole of the Saxons were in utter rout, hotly pursued by Furstenberg's cavalry.

Tilly now deemed the victory certain, for nearly half of his opponents were disposed of, and he outnumbered the remainder by two to one; but while Furstenberg had gained so complete a victory over the Saxons, Pappenheim, who had charged the Swedish centre, had met with a very different reception.

In vain he tried to break through the Swedish spears. The wind was blowing full in the faces of the pikemen, and the clouds of smoke and dust which rolled down upon them rendered it impossible for them to see the heavy columns of horse until they fell upon them like an avalanche, yet with perfect steadiness they withstood the attacks.

Seven times Pappenheim renewed his charge; seven times he fell back broken and disordered.

As he drew off for the last time Gustavus, seeing the rout of the Saxons, and knowing that he would have the whole of Tilly's force upon him in a few minutes, determined to rid himself altogether of Pappenheim, and launched the whole of his cavalry upon the retreating squadrons with overwhelming effect. Thus at the end of half an hour's fighting Tilly had disposed of the Saxons, and Gustavus had driven Pappenheim's horse from the field.

Three of the Scottish regiments were sent from the centre to strengthen Horn on the left flank, which was now exposed by the flight of the Saxons. Scarcely had the Scottish musketeers taken their position when Furstenberg's horse returned triumphant from their pursuit of the Saxons, and at once fell upon Horn's pikemen. These, however, stood as firmly as their comrades in the centre had done; and the Scottish musketeers, six deep, the three front ranks kneeling, the three in rear standing, poured such heavy volleys into the horsemen that these fell back in disorder; the more confused perhaps, since volley firing was at that time peculiar to the Swedish army, and the crashes of musketry were new to the Imperialists.

As the cavalry fell back in disorder, Gustavus led his horse, who had just returned from the pursuit of Pappenheim, against them. The shock was irresistible, and Furstenberg's horse were driven headlong from the field. But the Imperialist infantry, led by Tilly himself, were now close at hand, and the roar of musketry along the whole line was tremendous, while the artillery on both sides played unceasingly.

85

Just as the battle was at the hottest the Swedish reserve came up to the assistance of the first line, and Sir John Hepburn led the Green Brigade through the intervals of the Swedish regiments into action. Lord Reay's regiment was in front, and Munro, leading it on, advanced against the solid Imperialist columns, pouring heavy volleys into them. When close at hand the pikemen passed through the intervals of the musketeers and charged furiously with levelled pikes, the musketeers following them with clubbed weapons.

The gaps formed by the losses of the regiment at New Brandenburg and the other engagements had been filled up, and two thousand strong they fell upon the Imperialists. For a few minutes there was a tremendous hand-to-hand conflict, but the valour and strength of the Scotch prevailed, and the regiment was the first to burst its way through the ranks of the Imperialists, and then pressed on to attack the trenches behind, held by the Walloon infantry. While the battle was raging in the plain the Swedish cavalry, after driving away Furstenberg's horse, swept round and charged the eminence in the rear of the Imperialists, cutting down the artillerymen and capturing the cannon there.

These were at once turned upon the masses of Imperialist infantry, who thus, taken between two fires—pressed hotly by the pikemen in front, mown down by the cannon in their rear—lost heart and fled precipitately, four regiments alone, the veterans of Furstenberg's infantry, holding together and cutting their way through to the woods in the rear of their position.

The slaughter would have been even greater than it was, had not the cloud of dust and smoke been so thick that the Swedes were unable to see ten yards in front of them. The pursuit was taken up by their cavalry, who pressed the flying Imperialists until nightfall. So complete was the defeat that Tilly, who was badly wounded, could only muster 600 men to accompany him in his retreat, and Pappenheim could get together but 1400 of his horsemen. Seven thousand of the Imperialists were killed, 5000 were wounded or taken prisoners. The Swedes lost but 700 men, the Saxons about 2000.

The Swedes that night occupied the Imperial tents, making great bonfires of the broken wagons, pikes, and stockades. A hundred standards were taken. Tilly had fought throughout the battle with desperate valour. He was ever in the van of his infantry, and three times was wounded by bullets and once taken prisoner, and only rescued after a desperate conflict.

At the conclusion of the day Cronenberg with 600 Walloon

cavalry threw themselves around him and bore him from the field. The fierce old soldier is said to have burst into a passion of tears on beholding the slaughter and defeat of his infantry. Hitherto he had been invincible, this being the first defeat he had suffered in the course of his long military career. Great stores of provision and wine had been captured, and the night was spent in feasting in the Swedish camp.

The next morning the Elector of Saxony rode on to the field to congratulate Gustavus on his victory. The latter was politic enough to receive him with great courtesy and to thank him for the services the Saxons had rendered. He intrusted to the elector the task of recapturing Leipzig, while he marched against Merseburg, which he captured with its garrison of five hundred men.

After two or three assaults had been made on Leipzig the garrison capitulated to the Saxons, and on the 11th of September the army was drawn up and reviewed by Gustavus. When the king arrived opposite the Green Brigade he dismounted and made the soldiers an address, thanking them for their great share in winning the battle of Leipzig.

Many of the Scottish officers were promoted, Munro being made a full colonel, and many others advanced a step in rank. The Scottish brigade responded to the address of the gallant king with hearty cheers. Gustavus was indeed beloved as well as admired by his soldiers. Fearless himself of danger, he ever recognized bravery in others, and was ready to take his full share of every hardship as well as every peril.

He had ever a word of commendation and encouragement for his troops, and was regarded by them as a comrade as well as a leader. In person he was tall and rather stout, his face was handsome, his complexion fair, his forehead lofty, his hair auburn, his eyes large and penetrating, his cheeks ruddy and healthy. He had an air of majesty which enabled him to address his soldiers in terms of cheerful familiarity without in the slightest degree diminishing their respect and reverence for him as their monarch.

CHAPTER X

THE PASSAGE OF THE RHINE

"I suppose," Nigel Graheme said, as the officers of the regiment assembled in one of the Imperialist tents on the night after the battle of Leipzig, "we shall at once press forward to Vienna;" and such was the general opinion throughout the Swedish army; but such was not the intention of Gustavus. Undoubtedly the temptation to press forward and dictate peace in Vienna was strong, but the difficulties and disadvantages of such a step were many. He had but 20,000 men, for the Saxons could not be reckoned upon; and indeed it was probable that their elector, whose jealousy and dislike of Gustavus would undoubtedly be heightened by the events of the battle of Breitenfeld, would prove himself to be a more than a doubtful ally were the Swedish army to remove to a distance.

Tilly would soon rally his fugitives, and, reinforced by the numerous Imperialist garrisons from the towns, would be able to overrun North Germany in his absence, and to force the Saxons to join him even if the elector were unwilling to do so. Thus the little Swedish force would be isolated in the heart of Germany; and should Ferdinand abandon Vienna at his approach and altogether refuse to treat with him—which his obstinacy upon a former occasion when in the very hands of his enemy rendered probable—the Swedes would find themselves in a desperate position, isolated and alone in the midst of enemies.

There was another consideration. An Imperialist diet was at that moment sitting at Frankfort, and Ferdinand was using all his influence to compel the various princes and representatives of the free cities to submit to him. It was of the utmost importance that Gustavus should strengthen his friends and overawe the waverers by the approach of his army. Hitherto Franconia and the Rhine provinces had been entirely in the hands of the Imperialists, and it was needful that a counterbalancing influence should be exerted. These considerations induced Gustavus to abandon the tempting idea of a march upon Vienna. The Elector of Saxony was charged with carrying the war into Silesia and Bohemia, the Electors of Hesse and Hesse-Cassel were to maintain Lower Saxony and Westphalia, and the Swedish army turned its face towards the Rhine.

On the 20th of September it arrived before Erfurt, an important fortified town on the Gera, which surrendered at discretion. Gustavus granted the inhabitants, who were for the most part Catholics, the free exercise of their religion, and nominated the Duke of Saxe-Weimar to be governor of the district and of the province of Thuringen, and the Count of Lowenstein to be commander of the garrison, which consisted of Colonel Foulis's Scottish regiment, 1500 strong.

Travelling by different routes in two columns the army marched to Wurtzburg, the capital of Franconia, a rich and populous city, the Imperialist garrison having withdrawn to the strong castle of Marienburg, on a lofty eminence overlooking the town, and only separated from it by the river Maine. The cathedral at Wurtzburg is dedicated to a Scottish saint, St. Kilian, a bishop who with two priests came from Scotland in the year 688 to convert the heathen of Franconia. They baptized many at Wurtzburg, among them Gospert, the duke of that country. This leader was married to Geilana, the widow of his brother; and Kilian urging upon him that such a marriage was contrary to the laws of the Christian church, the duke promised to separate from her. Geilana had not, like her lord, accepted Christianity, and, furious at this interference of Kilian, she seized the opportunity when the latter had gone with his followers on an expedition against the pagan Saxons to have Kilian and his two companions murdered.

The cathedral was naturally an object of interest to the Scotch soldiers in the time of Gustavus, and there was an animated argument in the quarters of the officers of Munro's regiment on the night of their arrival as to whether St. Kilian had done well or otherwise in insisting upon his new convert repudiating his wife. The general opinion, however, was against the saint, the colonel summing up the question.

"In my opinion," he said, "Kilian was a fool. Here was no less a matter at stake than the conversion of a whole nation, or at least of a great tribe of heathens, and Kilian imperilled it all on a question of minor importance; for in the first place, the Church of Rome has always held that the pope could grant permission for marriage within interdicted degrees; in the second place, the marriage had taken place before the conversion of the duke to Christianity, and they were therefore innocently and without thought of harm bona fide man and wife. Lastly, the Church of Rome is opposed to divorce; and Kilian might in any case have put up with this small sin, if sin it were, for the sake of saving the souls of thousands of pagans. My opinion is that St. Kilian richly deserved the fate which befell him. And now to a subject much more interesting to us—viz, the capture of Marienburg.

"I tell you, my friends, it is going to be a warm business; the castle is considered impregnable, and is strong by nature as well as art, and Captain Keller is said to be a stout and brave soldier. He has 1000 men in the garrison, and all the monks who were in the town have gone up and turned soldiers. But if the task is a hard one the reward will be rich; for as the Imperialists believe the place cannot be taken, the treasures of all the country round are stored up there. And I can tell you more, in the cellars are sixty gigantic tuns of stone, the smallest of which holds twenty-five wagon loads of wine, and they say some of it is a hundred years old. With glory and treasure and good wine to be won we will outdo ourselves tomorrow; and you may be sure that the brunt of the affair will fall upon the Scots."

"Well, there is one satisfaction," said Nigel Graheme—who after Leipzig had been promoted to the rank of major—"if we get the lion's share of the fighting, we shall have the lion's share of the plunder and wine."

"For shame, Graheme! You say nothing of the glory."

"Ah! well," Graheme laughed, "we have already had so large share of that, that I for one could do without winning any more just at present. It's a dear commodity to purchase, and neither fills our belly nor our pockets."

"For shame, Graheme! for shame!" Munro said laughing. "It is a scandal that such sentiments should be whispered in the Scottish brigade; and now to bed, gentlemen, for we shall have, methinks, a busy day tomorrow."

Sir James Ramsay was appointed to command the assault. The river Maine had to be crossed, and he sent off Lieutenant Robert Ramsay of his own regiment to obtain boats from the peasantry. The disguise in which he went was seen through, and he was taken prisoner and carried to the castle. A few boats were, however, obtained by the Swedes.

The river is here 300 yards wide, and the central arch of the bridge had been blown up by the Imperialists, a single plank remaining across the chasm over the river 48 feet below. The bridge was swept by the heaviest cannon in the fortress, and a passage appeared well nigh hopeless. On the afternoon of the 5th of October the party prepared to pass, some in boats, others by the bridge. A tremendous fire was opened by the Imperialists from cannon and musketry, sweeping the bridge with a storm of missiles and lashing the river to foam around the boats. The soldiers in these returned the fire with their muskets, and the smoke served as a cover to conceal them from the enemy.

In the meantime Major Bothwell of Ramsay's regiment led a company across the bridge. These, in spite of the fire, crossed the plank over the broken arch and reached the head of the bridge, from whence they kept up so heavy a fire upon the gunners and musketeers in the lower works by the river that they forced them to quit their posts, and so enabled Sir James Ramsay and Sir John Hamilton to effect a landing.

Major Bothwell, his brother, and the greater part of his followers were, however, slain by the Imperialists' fire from above. The commandant of the castle now sallied out and endeavoured to recapture the works by the water, but the Scotch repelled the attack and drove the enemy up the hill to the castle again. The Scottish troops having thus effected a lodgment across the river, and being protected by the rocks from the enemy's fire, lay down for the night in the position they had won.

Gustavus during the night caused planks to be thrown across the broken bridge and prepared to assault at daybreak. Just as morning was breaking, a Swedish officer with seven men climbed up the hill to reconnoitre the castle, and found to his surprise that the drawbridge was down, but a guard of 200 men were stationed at the gate. He was at once challenged, and, shouting "Sweden!" sprang with his men on to the end of the drawbridge. The Imperialists tried in vain to raise it; before they could succeed some companions of the Swedes ran up, and, driving in the guard, took possession of the outer court.

Almost at the same moment Ramsay's and Hamilton's regiments commenced their assault on a strong outwork of the castle, which, after two hours' desperate fighting, they succeeded in gaining. They then turned its guns upon the gate of the keep, which they battered down, and were about to charge in when they received orders from the king to halt and retire, while the Swedish regiment of Axel-Lilly and the Blue Brigade advanced to the storm.

The Scottish regiments retired in the deepest discontent, deeming themselves affronted by others being ordered to the post of honour after they had by their bravery cleared the way. The Swedish troops forced their way in after hard fighting; and the Castle of Marienburg, so long deemed impregnable, was captured after a few hours' fighting. The quantity of treasure found in it was enormous, and there were sufficient provisions to have lasted its garrison for twenty years.

Immediately the place was taken, Colonel Sir John Hamilton advanced to Gustavus and resigned his commission on the spot; nor did the assurances of the king that he intended no insult to the Scotch soldiers mollify his wrath, and quitting the Swedish service he returned at once to Scotland. Munro's regiment had taken no part in the storming of Marienburg, but was formed up on the north side of the river in readiness to advance should the first attack be repelled, and many were wounded by the shot of the enemy while thus inactive.

Malcolm while binding up the arm of his sergeant who stood next to him felt a sharp pain shoot through his leg, and at once fell to the ground. He was lifted up and carried to the rear, where his wound was examined by the doctor to the regiment.

"Your luck has not deserted you," he said after probing the wound. "The bullet has missed the bone by half an inch, and a short rest will soon put you right again."

Fortunately for a short time the army remained around Wurtzburg. Columns scoured the surrounding country, capturing the various towns and fortresses held by the Imperialists, and collecting large quantities of provisions and stores. Tilly's army lay within a few days' march; but although superior in numbers to that of Gustavus, Tilly had received strict orders not to risk a general engagement as his army was now almost the only one that remained to the Imperialists, and should it suffer another defeat the country would lie at the mercy of the Swedes.

One evening when Malcolm had so far recovered as to be able to walk for a short distance, he was at supper with Colonel Munro and some other officers, when the door opened and Gustavus himself entered. All leapt to their feet.

"Munro," he said, "get the musketeers of your brigade under arms with all haste, form them up in the square before the town hall, and desire Sir John Hepburn to meet me there."

The drum was at once beaten, and the troops came pouring from their lodgings, and in three or four minutes the musketeers, 800 strong, were formed up with Hepburn and Munro at their head. Malcolm had prepared to take his arms on the summons, but Munro said at once:

"No, Malcolm, so sudden a summons augurs desperate duty, maybe a long night march; you would break down before you got half a mile; besides, as only the musketeers have to go, half the officers must remain here."

Without a word the king placed himself at the head of the men, and through the dark and stormy night the troops started on their unknown mission. Hepburn and Munro were, like their men, on foot, for they had not had time to have their horses saddled.

After marching two hours along the right bank of the Maine the tramp of horses was heard behind them, and they were reinforced by eighty troopers whom Gustavus before starting had ordered to mount and follow. Hitherto the king had remained lost in abstraction, but he now roused himself.

"I have just received the most serious news, Hepburn. Tilly has been reinforced by 17,000 men under the Duke of Lorraine, and is marching with all speed against me. Were my whole army collected here he would outnumber us by two to one, but many columns are away, and the position is well nigh desperate.

"I have resolved to hold Ochsenfurt. The place is not strong, but it lies in a sharp bend of the river and may be defended for a time. If any can do so it is surely you and your Scots. Tilly is already close to the town; indeed the man who brought me the news said that when he left it his advanced pickets were just entering, hence the need for this haste.

"You must hold it to the last, Hepburn, and then, if you can, fall back to Wurtzburg; even a day's delay will enable me to call in some of the detachments and to prepare to receive Tilly."

Without halting, the little column marched sixteen miles, and then, crossing the bridge over the Maine, entered Ochsenfurt.

It was occupied by a party of fifty Imperialist arquebusiers, but these were driven headlong from it. The night was extremely dark, all were ignorant of the locality, and the troops were formed up in the marketplace to await either morning or the attack of Tilly. Fifty troopers were sent half a mile in advance to give warning of the approach of the enemy. They had scarcely taken their place when they were attacked by the Imperialists, who had been roused by the firing in the town. The incessant flash of fire and the heavy rattle of musketry told Gustavus that they were in force, and a lieutenant of Lumsden's regiment with fifty musketeers was sent off to reinforce the cavalry. The Imperialists were, however, too strong to be checked, and horse and foot were being driven in when Colonel Munro sallied out with a hundred of his own regiment, and the Imperialists after a brisk skirmish, not knowing what force they had to deal with, fell back.

As soon as day broke the king and Hepburn made a tour of the walls, which were found to be in a very bad condition and ill calculated to resist an assault. The Imperialists were not to be seen, and the king, fearing they might have marched by some other route against Wurtzburg, determined to return at once, telling Hepburn to mine the bridge, and to blow it up if forced to abandon the town.

Hepburn at once set to work to strengthen the position, to demolish all the houses and walls outside the defences, cut down and destroy all trees and hedges which might shelter an enemy, and to strengthen the walls with banks of earth and platforms of wood. For three days the troops laboured incessantly; on the third night the enemy were heard approaching. The advanced troopers and a half company of infantry were driven in, contesting every foot of the way. When they reached the walls heavy volleys were poured in by the musketeers who lined them upon the approaching enemy, and Tilly, supposing that Gustavus must have moved forward a considerable portion of his army, called off his troops and marched away to Nuremberg. Two days later Hepburn was ordered to return with his force to Wurtzburg.

The king now broke up his camp near Wurtzburg, and leaving a garrison in the castle of Marienburg and appointing Marshal Horn to hold Franconia with 8000 men, he marched against Frankfort-on-the-Maine, his troops capturing all the towns and castles on the way, levying contributions, and collecting great booty. Frankfort opened its gates without resistance, and for a short time the army had rest in pleasant quarters.

The regiments were reorganized, in some cases two of those which had suffered most being joined into one. Gustavus had lately been strengthened by two more Scottish regiments under Sir Frederick Hamilton and Alexander Master of Forbes, and an English regiment under Captain Austin. He had now thirteen regiments of Scottish infantry, and the other corps of the army were almost entirely officered by Scotchmen. He had five regiments of English and Irish, and had thus eighteen regiments of British infantry.

At Frankfort he was joined by the Marquis of Hamilton, who had done splendid service with the troops under his command. He had driven the Imperialists out of Silesia, and marching south, struck such fear into them that Tilly was obliged to weaken his army to send reinforcements to that quarter. By the order of Gustavus he left Silesia and marched to Magdeburg. He had now but 3500 men with him, 2700 having died from pestilence, famine, and disease. He assisted General Banner in blockading the Imperialist garrison of Magdeburg, and his losses by fever and pestilence thinned his troops down to two small regiments; these were incorporated with the force of the Duke of Saxe-Weimar, and the Marquis of Hamilton joined the staff of Gustavus as a simple volunteer.

The king now determined to conquer the Palatinate, which was held by a Spanish army. He drove them before him until he reached the Rhine, where they endeavoured to defend the passage by burning every vessel and boat they could find, and for a time the advance of the Swedes was checked. It was now the end of November, the snow lay thick over the whole country, and the troops, without tents or covering, were bivouacked along the side of the river, two miles below Oppenheim. The opposite bank was covered with bushes to the water's edge, and on an eminence a short distance back could be seen the tents of the Spaniards.

"If it were summer we might swim across," Nigel Graheme said to Malcolm; "the river is broad, but a good swimmer could cross it easily enough."

"Yes," Malcolm agreed, "there would be no difficulty in swimming if unencumbered with arms and armour, but there would be no advantage in getting across without these; if we could but get hold of a boat or two, we would soon wake yonder Spaniards up."

The next morning Malcolm wandered along the bank closely examining the bushes as he went, to see if any boats might be concealed among them, for the fishermen and boatmen would naturally try to save their craft when they heard that the Imperialists were destroying them. He walked three miles up the river without success. As he returned he kept his eyes fixed on the bushes on the opposite bank. When within half a mile of the camp he suddenly stopped, for his eye caught something dark among them. He went to the water's edge and stooped, the better to see under the bushes, and saw what he doubted not to be the stern of a boat hauled up and sheltered beneath them. He leapt to his feet with a joyful exclamation. Here was the means of crossing the river; but the boat had to be brought over. Once afloat this would be easy enough, but he was sure that his own strength would be insufficient to launch her, and that he should need the aid of at least one man. On returning to camp he called aside the sergeant of his company, James Grant, who was from his own estate in Nithsdale, and whom he knew to be a good swimmer.

"Sergeant," he said, "I want you to join me in an enterprise tonight. I have found a boat hauled up under the bushes on the opposite shore, and we must bring her across. I cannot make out her size; but from the look of her stern I should say she was a large

95

boat. You had better therefore borrow from the artillerymen one of their wooden levers, and get a stout pole two or three inches across, and cut half a dozen two foot lengths from it to put under her as rollers. Get also a plank of four inches wide from one of the deserted houses in the village behind us, and cut out two paddles; we may find oars on board, but it is as well to be prepared in case the owner should have removed them."

"Shall I take my weapons, sir?"

"We can take our dirks in our belts, sergeant, and lash our swords to the wooden lever, but I do not think we shall have any fighting. The night will be dark, and the Spaniards, believing that we have no boats, will not keep a very strict watch. The worst part of the business is the swim across the river, the water will be bitterly cold; but as you and I have often swum Scotch burns when they were swollen by the melting snow I think that we may well manage to get across this sluggish stream."

"At what time will we be starting, sir?"

"Be here at the edge of the river at six o'clock, sergeant. I can get away at that time without exciting comment, and we will say nothing about it unless we succeed."

Thinking it over, however, it occurred to Malcolm that by this means a day would be lost—and he knew how anxious the king was to press forward. He therefore abandoned his idea of keeping his discovery secret, and going to his colonel reported that he had found a boat, and could bring it across from the other side by seven o'clock.

The news was so important that Munro at once went to the king. Gustavus ordered three hundred Swedes and a hundred Scots of each of the regiments of Ramsay, Munro, and the Laird of Wormiston, the whole under the command of Count Brahe, to form up after dark on the river bank and prepare to cross, and he himself came down to superintend the passage. By six it was perfectly dark. During the day Malcolm had placed two stones on the edge of the water, one exactly opposite the boat, the other twenty feet behind it in an exact line. When Gustavus arrived at the spot where the troops were drawn up, Malcolm was taken up to him by his colonel.

"Well, my brave young Graheme," the king said, "so you are going to do us another service; but how will you find the boat in this darkness? Even were there no stream you would find it very difficult to strike the exact spot on a dark night like this."

"I have provided against that, sir, by placing two marks on the bank. When we start lanterns will be placed on these. We shall cross higher up so as to strike the bank a little above where I believe the boat to be, then we shall float along under the bushes until the lanterns are in a line one with another, and we shall know then that we are exactly opposite the boat."

"Well thought of!" the king exclaimed. "Munro, this lieutenant of yours is a treasure. And now God speed you, my friend, in your cold swim across the stream!"

Malcolm and the sergeant now walked half a mile up the river, a distance which, judging from the strength of the current and the speed at which they could swim, would, they thought, take them to the opposite bank at about the point where the boat was lying. Shaking hands with Colonel Munro, who had accompanied them, Malcolm entered the icy cold water without delay. Knowing that it was possible that their strength might give out before they reached the opposite side, Malcolm had had two pairs of small casks lashed two feet apart. These they fastened securely, so that as they began to swim the casks floated a short distance behind each shoulder, giving them perfect support. The lever and paddles were towed behind them. The lights in the two camps afforded them a means of directing their way. The water was intensely cold, and before they were halfway across Malcolm congratulated himself upon having thought of the casks. Had it not been for them he would have begun to doubt his ability to reach the further shore, for although he would have thought nothing of the swim at other times his limbs were fast becoming numbed with the extreme cold. The sergeant kept close to him, and a word or two was occasionally exchanged.

"I think it is colder than our mountain streams, Grant?"

"It's no colder, your honour, but the water is smooth and still, and we do not have to wrestle with it as with a brook in spate. It's the stillness which makes it feel so cold. The harder we swim the less we will feel it."

It was with a deep feeling of relief that Malcolm saw something loom just in front of him from the darkness, and knew that he was close to the land. A few more strokes and he touched the bushes. Looking back he saw that the two lights were nearly in a line. Stopping swimming he let the stream drift him down. Two or three minutes more and one of the tiny lights seemed exactly above the other.

"This is the spot, Grant," he said in a low voice; "land here as quietly as you can."

CHAPTER XI

THE CAPTURE OF OPPENHEIM

The two swimmers dragged themselves on shore, but for a minute or two could scarce stand, so numbed were their limbs by the cold. Malcolm took from his belt a flask of brandy, took a long draught, and handed it to his companion, who followed his example.

The spirit sent a glow of warmth through their veins, and they began to search among the bushes for the boat, one proceeding each way along the bank. They had not removed their leathern doublets before entering the water, as these, buoyed up as they were, would not affect their swimming, and would be a necessary protection when they landed not only against the cold of the night air but against the bushes.

Malcolm's beacon proved an accurate guide, for he had not proceeded twenty yards before he came against a solid object which he at once felt to be the boat. A low whistle called the sergeant to his side, bringing with him the rollers and paddles from the spot where they had landed. They soon felt that the boat was a large one, and that their strength would have been wholly insufficient to get her into the water without the aid of the lever and rollers. Taking the former they placed its end under the stern post, and placing a roller under its heel to serve as a pivot they threw their weight on the other end of the lever and at once raised the boat some inches in the air.

Grant held the lever down and Malcolm slid a roller as far up under the keel as it would go; the lever was then shifted and the boat again raised, and the process was continued until her weight rested upon three rollers. She was now ready to be launched, and as the bank was steep they had no doubt of their ability to run her down. An examination had already shown that their paddles would be needless, as the oars were inside her. They took their places one on each side of the bow, and applying their strength the boat glided rapidly down.

"Gently, Grant," Malcolm said, "don't let her go in with a splash. There may be some sentries within hearing."

They continued their work cautiously, and the boat noiselessly entered the water. Getting out the oars they gave her a push, and she was soon floating down the stream. The rowlocks were in their places, and rowing with extreme care so as to avoid making the slightest sound they made their way across the river. They were below the camp when they landed, but there were many men on the lookout, for the news of the attempt had spread rapidly.

Leaping ashore amidst a low cheer from a group of soldiers, Malcolm directed them to tow the boat up at once to the place where the troops were formed ready for crossing, while he and the sergeant, who were both chilled to the bone, for their clothes had frozen stiff upon them, hurried to the spot where the regiment was bivouacked. Here by the side of a blazing fire they stripped, and were rubbed with cloths by their comrades till a glow of warmth again began to be felt, the external heat and friction being aided by the administration of two steaming flagons of spiced wine. Dry clothes were taken from their knapsacks and warmed before the fire, and when these were put on they again felt warm and comfortable.

Hurrying off now to the spot where the troops were drawn up, they found that the boat had already made two passages. She rowed four oars, and would, laden down to the water's edge, carry twenty-five men. The oars had been muffled with cloths so as to make no sound in the rowlocks. A party of Munro's Scots had first crossed, then a party of Swedes. Malcolm and the sergeant joined their company unnoticed in the darkness. Each detachment sent over a boat load in turns, and when six loads had crossed it was again the turn of the men of Munro's regiment, and Malcolm entered the boat with the men. The lights still burned as a signal, enabling the boat to land each party almost at the same spot. Malcolm wondered what was going on. A perfect stillness reigned on the other side, and it was certain that the alarm had not yet been given.

On ascending the bank he saw in front of him some dark figures actively engaged, and heard dull sounds. On reaching the spot he found the parties who had preceded him hard at work with shovels throwing up an intrenchment. In the darkness he had not perceived that each of the soldiers carried a spade in addition to his arms. The soil was deep and soft, and the operations were carried on with scarce a sound. As each party landed they fell to work under the direction of their officers. All night the labour continued, and when the dull light of the winter morning began to dispel the darkness a solid rampart of earth breast high rose in a semicircle, with its two extremities resting on the riverbank.

The last boat load had but just arrived across, and the 600

men were now gathered in the work, which was about 150 feet across, the base formed by the river. The earth forming the ramparts had been taken from the outside, and a ditch 3 feet deep and 6 feet wide had been thus formed.

The men, who, in spite of the cold were hot and perspiring from their night's work, now entered the intrenched space, and sat down to take a meal, each man having brought two days' rations in his havresack. It grew rapidly lighter, and suddenly the sound of a trumpet, followed by the rapid beating of drums, showed that the Spaniards had, from their camp on the eminence half a mile away, discovered the work which had sprung up during the night as if by magic on their side of the river.

In a few minutes a great body of cavalry was seen issuing from the Spanish camp, and fourteen squadrons of cuirassiers trotted down towards the intrenchments. Soon the word was given to charge, and, like a torrent, the mass of cavalry swept down upon it.

Two-thirds of those who had crossed were musketeers, the remainder pikemen. The latter formed the front line behind the rampart, their spears forming a close hedge around it, while the musketeers prepared to fire between them. By the order of Count Brahe not a trigger was pulled until the cavalry were within fifty yards, then a flash of flame swept round the rampart, and horses and men in the front line of the cavalry tumbled to the ground. But half the musketeers had fired, and a few seconds later another volley was poured into the horsemen. The latter, however, although many had fallen, did not check their speed, but rode up close to the rampart, and flung themselves upon the hedge of spears.

Nothing could exceed the gallantry with which the Spaniards fought. Some dismounted, and, leaping into the ditch, tried to climb the rampart; others leapt the horses into it, and standing up in their saddles, cut at the spearmen with their swords, and fired their pistols among them. Many, again, tried to leap their horses over ditch and rampart, but the pikemen stood firm, while at short intervals withering volleys tore into the struggling mass.

For half an hour the desperate fight continued, and then, finding that the position could not be carried by horsemen, the Spanish commander drew off his men, leaving no less than 600 lying dead around the rampart of earth. There were no Spanish infantry within some miles of the spot, and the cavalry rode away, some to Maintz, but the greater part to Oppenheim, where there was a strong garrison of 1000 men.

A careful search among the bushes brought three more boats

100

to light, and a force was soon taken across the river sufficient to maintain itself against any attack. Gustavus himself was in one of the first boats that crossed.

"Well done, my brave hearts!" he said as he landed, just as the Spanish horsemen had ridden away. "You have fought stoutly and well, and our way is now open to us. Where are Lieutenant Graheme and the sergeant who swam across with him?"

Malcolm and his companion soon presented themselves.

"I sent for you to your camp," the king said, "but found that you but waited to change your clothes, and had then joined the force crossing. You had no orders to do so."

"We had no orders not to do so, sire, but having begun the affair it was only natural that we should see the end of it."

"You had done your share and more," the king said, "and I thank you both heartily for it, and promote you, Graheme, at once to the rank of captain, and will request Colonel Munro to give you the first company which may fall vacant in his regiment. If a vacancy should not occur shortly I will place you in another regiment until one may happen in your own corps. To you, sergeant, I give a commission as officer. You will take that rank at once, and will be a supernumerary in your regiment till a vacancy occurs. Such promotion has been well and worthily won by you both."

Without delay an advance was ordered against Oppenheim. It lay on the Imperialist side of the Rhine. Behind the town stood a strong and well fortified castle upon a lofty eminence. Its guns swept not only the country around it, but the ground upon the opposite side of the river. There, facing it, stood a strong fort surrounded by double ditches, which were deep and broad and full of water. They were crossed only by a drawbridge on the side facing the river, and the garrison could therefore obtain by boats supplies or reinforcements as needed from the town.

The Green and Blue Brigades at once commenced opening trenches against this fort, and would have assaulted the place without delay had not a number of boats been brought over by a Protestant well wisher of the Swedes from the other side of the river. The assault was therefore delayed in order that the attack might be delivered simultaneously against the positions on both sides of the river. The brigade of guards and the White Brigade crossed in the boats at Gernsheim, five miles from the town, and marched against it during the night.

The Spaniards from their lofty position in the castle of Oppenheim saw the campfires of the Scots around their fort on the

101

other side of the river, and opened a heavy cannonade upon them. The fire was destructive, and many of the Scots were killed, Hepburn and Munro having a narrow escape, a cannonball passing just over their heads as they were sitting together by a fire.

The defenders of the fort determined to take advantage of the fire poured upon their assailants, and two hundred musketeers made a gallant sortie upon them; but Hepburn led on his pikemen who were nearest at hand, and, without firing a shot, drove them back again into the fort. At daybreak the roar of cannon on the opposite side of the river commenced, and showed that the king with the divisions which had crossed had arrived at their posts. The governor of the fort, seeing that if, as was certain, the lower town were captured by the Swedes, he should be cut off from all communication with the castle and completely isolated, surrendered to Sir John Hepburn.

The town had, indeed, at once opened its gates, and two hundred men of Sir James Ramsay's regiment were placed there. Hepburn prepared to cross the river with the Blue and Green Brigades to aid the king in reducing the castle—a place of vast size and strength—whose garrison composed of Spaniards and Italians were replying to the fire of Gustavus. A boat was lying at the gate of the fort.

"Captain Graheme," Hepburn said to Malcolm, "take with you two lieutenants and twenty men in the boat and cross the river; then send word by an officer to the king that the fort here has surrendered, and that I am about to cross, and let the men bring over that flotilla of boats which is lying under the town wall."

Malcolm crossed at once. After despatching the message to the king and sending the officer back with the boats he had for the moment nothing to do, and made his way into the town to inquire from the officers of Ramsay's detachment how things were going. He found the men drawn up.

"Ah! Malcolm Graheme," the major in command said, "you have arrived in the very nick of time to take part in a gallant enterprise."

"I am ready," Malcolm said; "what is to be done?"

"We are going to take the castle, that is all," the major said.

"You are joking," Malcolm laughed, looking at the great castle and the little band of two hundred men.

"That am I not," the major answered; "my men have just discovered a private passage from the governor's quarters here up to the very gate of the outer wall. As you see we have collected some ladders, and as we shall take them by surprise, while they are occupied with the king, we shall give a good account of them."

"I will go with you right willingly," Malcolm said; but he could not but feel that the enterprise was a desperate one, and wished that the major had waited until a few hundred more men had crossed. Placing himself behind the Scottish officer, he advanced up the passage which had been discovered. Ascending flight after flight of stone stairs, the column issued from the passage at the very foot of the outer wall before the garrison stationed there were aware of their approach. The ladders were just placed when the Italians caught sight of them and rushed to the defence, but it was too late. The Scotch swarmed up and gained a footing on the wall.

Driving the enemy before them they cleared the outer works, and pressed so hotly upon the retiring Imperialists that they entered with them into the inner works of the castle, crossing the drawbridge over the moat which separated it from its outer works before the garrison had time to raise it.

Now in the very heart of the castle a terrible encounter took place. The garrison, twelve hundred strong, ran down from their places on the wall, and seeing how small was the force that had entered fell upon them with fury. It was a hand to hand fight. Loud rose the war cries of the Italian and Spanish soldiers, and the answering cheers of the Scots mingled with the clash of sword on steel armour and the cries of the wounded, while without the walls the cannon of Gustavus thundered incessantly.

Not since the dreadful struggle in the streets of New Brandenburg had Malcolm been engaged in so desperate a strife. All order and regularity was lost, and man to man they fought with pike, sword, and clubbed musket. There was no giving of orders, for no word could be heard in such a din, and the officers with their swords and half pikes fought desperately in the melee with the rest.

Gradually, however, the strength and endurance of Ramsay's veterans prevailed over numbers. Most of the officers of the Imperialists had been slain, as well as their bravest men, and the rest began to draw off and to scatter through the castle, some to look for hiding places, many to jump over the walls rather than fall into the hands of the terrible Scots.

The astonishment of Gustavus and of Hepburn, who was now marching with his men towards the castle, at hearing the rattle of musketry and the din of battle within the very heart of the fortress was great indeed, and this was heightened when, a few minutes later, the soldiers were seen leaping desperately from the walls, and a great shout arose from the troops as the Imperial banner was seen to descend from its flagstaff on the keep. Gustavus with his staff rode at once to the gate, which was opened for him; and on entering he found Ramsay's little force drawn up to salute him as he entered. It was reduced nearly half in strength, and not a man but was bleeding from several wounds, while cleft helms and dinted armour showed how severe had been the fray.

"My brave Scots," he exclaimed, "why were you too quick for me?"

The courtyard of the castle was piled with slain, who were also scattered in every room throughout it, five hundred having been slain there before the rest threw down their arms and were given quarter. This exploit was one of the most valiant which was performed during the course of the whole war. Four colours were taken, one of which was that of the Spanish regiment, this being the first of that nationality which had ever been captured by Gustavus.

After going over the castle, whose capture would have tasked his resources and the valour of his troops to the utmost had he been compelled to attack it in the usual way, Gustavus sent for the officers of Ramsay's companies and thanked them individually for their capture.

"What! you here, Malcolm Graheme!" Gustavus said as he came in at the rear of Ramsay's officers. "Why, what had you to do with this business?"

"I was only a volunteer, sire," Malcolm said. "I crossed with the parties who fetched the boats; but as my instructions ended there I had nought to do, and finding that Ramsay's men were about to march up to the attack of the castle, I thought it best to join them, being somewhat afraid to stop in the town alone."

"And he did valiant service, sire," the major said. "I marked him in the thick of the fight, and saw more than one Imperialist go down before his sword."

"You know the story of the pitcher and the well, Captain Graheme," the king said, smiling. "Some day you will go once too often, and I shall have to mourn the loss of one of the bravest young officers in my army."

There was no rest for the soldiers of Gustavus, and no sooner had Oppenheim fallen than the army marched against Maintz. This was defended by two thousand Spanish troops under Don Philip de Sylvia, and was a place of immense strength. It was at once invested, and trenches commenced on all sides, the Green Brigade as usual having the post of danger and honour facing the citadel.

The investment began in the evening, but so vigorously did the Scotch work all night in spite of the heavy musketry and artillery fire with which the garrison swept the ground that by morning the first parallel was completed, and the soldiers were under shelter behind a thick bank of earth.

All day the Imperialists kept up their fire, the Scots gradually pushing forward their trenches. In the evening Colonel Axel Lily, one of the bravest of the Swedish officers, came into the trenches to pay a visit to Hepburn. He found him just sitting down to dinner with Munro by the side of a fire in the trench. They invited him to join them, and the party were chatting gaily when a heavy cannonball crashed through the earthen rampart behind them, and, passing between Hepburn and Munro, carried off the leg of the Swedish officer.

Upon the following day the governor, seeing that the Swedes had erected several strong batteries, and that the Green Brigade, whose name was a terror to the Imperialists, was preparing to storm, capitulated, and his soldiers were allowed to march out with all their baggage, flying colours, and two pieces of cannon. Eighty pieces of cannon fell into the hands of the Swedes. The citizens paid 220,000 dollars as the ransom of their city from pillage, and the Jews 180,000 for the protection of their quarters and of their gorgeous synagogue, whose wealth and magnificence were celebrated; and on the 14th of December, 1631, on which day Gustavus completed his thirty-seventh year, he entered the city as conqueror.

Here he kept Christmas with great festivity, and his court was attended by princes and nobles from all parts of Germany. Among them were six of the chief princes of the empire and twelve ambassadors from foreign powers. Among the nobles was the Count of Mansfeld, who brought with him his wife and daughter. Three days before Christmas Hepburn's brigade had been moved in from their bivouac in the snow covered trenches, and assigned quarters in the town, and the count, who arrived on the following day, at once repaired to the mansion inhabited by the colonel and officers of Munro's regiment, and inquired for Malcolm Graheme.

"You will find Captain Graheme within," the Scottish soldier on sentry said.

"It is not Captain Graheme I wish to see," the count said, "but Malcolm Graheme, a very young officer."

"I reckon that it is the captain," the soldier said; "he is but a boy; but in all the regiment there is not a braver soldier; not even the colonel himself. Donald," he said, turning to a comrade, "tell Captain Graheme that he is wanted here."

In a short time Malcolm appeared at the door.

"Ah! it is you, my young friend!" the count exclaimed; "and you have won the rank of captain already by your brave deeds! Right glad am I to see you again. I have come with my wife, to attend the court of this noble king of yours. Can you come with me at once? The countess is longing to see you, and will be delighted to hear that you have passed unscathed through all the terrible contests in which you have been engaged. My daughter is here too; she is never tired of talking about her young Scottish soldier; but now that you are a captain she will have to be grave and respectful."

Malcolm at once accompanied the count to his house, and was most kindly received by the countess.

"It is difficult to believe," she said, "that 'tis but four months since we met, so many have been the events which have been crowded into that time. Scarce a day has passed but we have received news of some success gained, of some town or castle captured, and your Green Brigade has always been in the van. We have been constantly in fear for you, and after that terrible battle before Leipzig Thekla scarcely slept a wink until we obtained a copy of the Gazette with the names of the officers killed."

"You are kind indeed to bear me so in remembrance," Malcolm said, "and I am indeed grateful for it. I have often wondered whether any fresh danger threatened you; but I hoped that the advance of the Marquis of Hamilton's force would have given the Imperialists too much to do for them to disturb you."

"Yes, we have had no more trouble," the countess replied. "The villages which the Imperialists destroyed are rising again; and as after the flight of the enemy the cattle and booty they had captured were all left behind, the people are recovering from their visit. What terrible havoc has the war caused! Our way here led through ruined towns and villages, the country is infested by marauders, and all law and order is at an end save where there are strong bodies of troops. We rode with an escort of twenty men; but even then we did not feel very safe until we were fairly through Franconia. And so you have passed unwounded through the strife?"

"Yes, countess," Malcolm replied. "I had indeed a ball through my leg at Wurtzburg; but as it missed the bone, a trifle like that is scarcely worth counting. I have been most fortunate indeed."

"He is a captain now," the count said, "and to obtain such promotion he must have greatly distinguished himself. I do not suppose that he will himself tell us his exploits; but I shall soon learn all about them from others. I am to meet his colonel this evening at a dinner at the palace, and shall be able to give you the whole history tomorrow."

"But I want the history now," Thekla said. "It is much nicer to hear a thing straight from some one who has done it, than from any one else."

"There is no story to tell," Malcolm said. "I had been promised my lieutenancy at the first vacancy before I was at Mansfeld, and on my return found that the vacancy had already occurred, and I was appointed. I got my company the other day for a very simple matter, namely, for swimming across the Rhine with a barrel fixed on each side of me to prevent my sinking. Nothing very heroic about that, you see, young lady."

"For swimming across the Rhine!" the count said. "Then you must have been the Scottish officer who with a sergeant swam and fetched the boat across which enabled the Swedes to pass a body of troops over, and so open the way into the Palatinate. I heard it spoken of as a most gallant action."

"I can assure you," Malcolm said earnestly, "that there was no gallantry about it. It was exceedingly cold, I grant, but that was all."

"Then why should the king have made you a captain for it? You can't get over that."

"That was a reward for my luck," Malcolm laughed. "'Tis better to be lucky than to be rich, it is said, and I had the good luck to discover a boat concealed among the bushes just at the time when a boat was worth its weight in gold."

For an hour Malcolm sat chatting, and then took his leave, as he was going on duty, promising to return the next day, and to spend as much of his time as possible with them while they remained in the city.

CHAPTER XII

THE PASSAGE OF THE LECH

For the next two months the Green Brigade remained quietly at Maintz, a welcome rest after their arduous labours. The town was very gay, and every house was occupied either by troops or by the nobles and visitors from all parts of Northern Europe. Banquets and balls were of nightly occurrence; and a stranger who arrived in the gay city would not have dreamt that a terrible campaign had just been concluded, and that another to the full as arduous was about to commence.

During this interval of rest the damages which the campaign had effected in the armour and accoutrements of men and officers were repaired, the deep dents effected by sword, pike, and bullet were hammered out, the rust removed, and the stains of blood and bivouac obliterated; fresh doublets and jerkins were served out from the ample stores captured from the enemy, and the army looked as gay and brilliant as when it first landed in North Germany.

Malcolm spent much of his spare time with the Count and Countess of Mansfeld, who, irrespective of their gratitude for the assistance he had rendered them in time of need, had taken a strong liking to the young Scotchman.

"You are becoming quite a court gallant, Graheme," one of his comrades said at a court ball where Malcolm had been enjoying himself greatly, having, thanks to the Countess of Mansfeld, no lack of partners, while many of the officers were forced to look on without taking part in the dancing, the number of ladies being altogether insufficient to furnish partners to the throng of officers, Swedish, German, and Scottish. Beyond the scarf and feathers which showed the brigade to which officers belonged, there was, even when in arms, but slight attempt at uniformity in their attire, still less so when off duty. The scene at these balls was therefore gay in the extreme, the gallants being all attired in silk, satin, or velvet of brilliant colours slashed with white or some contrasting hue. The tailors at Maintz had had a busy time of it, for in so rapid a campaign much baggage had been necessarily lost, and many of the officers required an entirely new outfit before they could take part in the court festivities.

There was, however, no lack of money, for the booty and

treasure captured had been immense, and each officer having received a fixed share, they were well able to renew their wardrobes. Some fresh reinforcements arrived during their stay here, and the vacancies which battle and disease had made in the ranks were filled up.

But although the Green Brigade did not march from Maintz till the 5th of March, 1632, the whole army did not enjoy so long a rest. In February Gustavus despatched three hundred of Ramsay's regiment under Lieutenant Colonel George Douglas against the town of Creutzenach, together with a small party of English volunteers under Lord Craven. Forty-seven of the men were killed while opening the trenches, but the next day they stormed one of the gates and drove the garrison, which was composed of six hundred Walloons and Burgundians, out of the town into the castle of Kausemberg, which commanded it. Its position was extremely strong, its walls and bastions rising one behind another, and their aspect was so formidable that they were popularly known as the "Devil's Works." From these the garrison opened a very heavy fire into the town, killing many of the Scots. Douglas, however, gave them but short respite, for gathering his men he attacked the castle and carried bastion after bastion by storm until the whole were taken.

About the same time the important town of Ulm on the Danube opened its gates to the Swedes, and Sir Patrick Ruthven was appointed commandant with 1200 Swedes as garrison, Colonel Munro with two companies of musketeers marched to Coblentz and aided Otto Louis the Rhinegrave, who with a brigade of twenty troops of horse was expecting to be attacked by 10,000 Spaniards and Walloons from Spires. Four regiments of Spanish horse attacked the Rhinegrave's quarters, but were charged so furiously by four troops of Swedish dragoons under Captain Hume that 300 of them were killed and the Elector of Nassau taken prisoner; after this the Spaniards retired beyond the Moselle.

In other parts of Germany the generals of Gustavus were equally successful. General Horn defeated the Imperialists at Heidelberg and Heilbronn. General Lowenhausen scoured all the shores of the Baltic, and compelled Colonel Graham, a Scotch soldier in the Imperial service, to surrender the Hanse town of Wismar. Graham marched out with his garrison, 3000 strong, with the honours of war en route for Silesia, but having, contrary to terms, spiked the cannon, plundered the shipping, and slain a Swedish lieutenant, Lowenhausen pursued him, and in the battle which ensued 500 of Graham's men were slain and the colonel himself with 2000 taken prisoner.

General Ottentodt was moving up the Elbe carrying all before him with a force of 14,000 men, among whom were five battalions of Scots and one of English. This force cleared the whole duchy of Mecklenburg, capturing all the towns and fortresses in rapid succession. Sir Patrick Ruthven advanced along the shores of Lake Constance, driving the Imperialists before him into the Tyrol. Magdeburg was captured by General Banner, the Landgrave of Hesse-Cassel reduced all Fulda-Paderborn and the adjacent districts, the Elector of Saxony overran Bohemia, and Sir Alexander Leslie threatened the Imperialists in Lower Saxony.

Thus the campaign of 1632 opened under the most favourable auspices. The Green Brigade marched on the 5th of March to Aschaffenburg, a distance of more than thirty miles, a fact which speaks volumes for the physique and endurance of the troops, for this would in the present day be considered an extremely long march for troops, and the weight of the helmet and armour, musket and accoutrements, of the troops of those days was fully double that now carried by European soldiers. Here they were reviewed by the king.

By the 10th the whole army, 23,000 strong, were collected at Weinsheim and advanced towards Bavaria, driving before them the Imperialists under the Count de Bucquio. The Chancellor Oxenstiern had been left by the king with a strong force to guard his conquests on the Rhine.

No sooner had the king marched than the Spaniards again crossed the Moselle. The chancellor and the Duke of Weimar advanced against them. The Dutch troops, who formed the first line of the chancellor's army, were unable to stand the charge of the Spanish and fled in utter confusion; but the Scottish regiment of Sir Roderick Leslie, who had succeeded Sir John Hamilton on his resignation, and the battalion of Sir John Ruthven, charged the Spaniards with levelled pikes so furiously that these in turn were broken and driven off the field.

On the 26th of March Gustavus arrived before the important town and fortress of Donauworth, being joined on the same day by the Laird of Foulis with his two regiments of horse and foot. Donauworth is the key to Swabia; it stands on the Danube, and was a strongly fortified place, its defences being further covered by fortifications upon a lofty eminence close by, named the Schellemberg. It was held by the Duke of Saxe-Lauenburg with two thousand five hundred men. The country round Donauworth is fertile and hilly, and Gustavus at once seized a height which commanded the place. The Bavarians were at work upon entrenchments here as the Swedes advanced, but were forced to fall back into the town. From the foot of the hill a suburb extended to the gates of the city. This was at once occupied by five hundred musketeers, who took up their post in the houses along the main road in readiness to repel a sortie should the garrison attempt one; while the force on the hillside worked all night, and by daybreak on the 27th had completed and armed a twenty gun battery.

In this was placed a strong body of infantry under Captain Semple, a Scotchman. As this battery commanded the walls of the town, and flanked the bridge across the Danube, the position of the defenders was now seriously menaced, but the Duke of Saxe-Lauenburg refused the demand of Gustavus to surrender. The battery now opened fire, first demolishing a large stone building by the river occupied by a force of Imperialists, and then directing its fire upon the city gates.

The cannonade continued after nightfall, but in the darkness a body of Imperialist horsemen under Colonel Cronenberg dashed out at full speed through the gate, cut a passage through the musketeers in the suburb, galloped up the hill, and fell upon the infantry and artillery in the battery. So furious was their charge that the greater part of the defenders of the battery were cut down. The guns were spiked, and the cavalry, having accomplished their purpose, charged down the hill, cut their way through the suburb, and regained the town.

This gallant exploit deranged the plans of the Swedes. Gustavus reconnoitred the town accompanied by Sir John Hepburn, and by the advice of that officer decided upon a fresh plan of operations. Hepburn pointed out to him that by taking possession of the angle formed by the confluence of the Wermitz and Danube to the west of the town the bridge crossing from Donauworth into Bavaria would be completely commanded, and the garrison would be cut off from all hope of escape and of receiving relief from Bavaria.

The plan being approved, Hepburn drew off his brigade with its artillery, and marching five miles up the Danube crossed the river at the bridge of Hassfurt, and descended the opposite bank until he faced Donauworth. He reached his position at midnight, and placed his cannon so as to command the whole length of the bridge, and then posted his musketeers in the gardens and houses of a suburb on the river, so that their crossfire also swept it.

The pikemen were drawn up close to the artillery at the head of the bridge. Quietly as these movements were performed the garrison took the alarm, and towards morning the duke, finding his retreat intercepted, sallied out at the head of eight hundred musketeers to cut his way through; but as the column advanced upon the bridge the Green Brigade opened fire, the leaden hail of their musketeers smote the column on both sides, while the cannon ploughed lanes through it from end to end. So great was the destruction that the Bavarians retreated in confusion back into the town again, leaving the bridge strewn with their dead.

Alone the gallant Duke of Saxe-Lauenburg charged through the hail of fire across the bridge, fell upon the pikemen sword in hand, and cutting his way through them rode away, leaving his garrison to their fate. The roar of artillery informed Gustavus what was going on, and he immediately opened fire against the other side of the town and led his men to the assault of the gate.

The instant the Scotch had recovered from their surprise at the desperate feat performed by the duke, Hepburn, calling them together, placed himself at their head and led them across the bridge. The panic stricken fugitives had omitted to close the gate, and the Scotch at once entered the town. Here the garrison resisted desperately; their pikemen barred the streets, and from every window and roof their musketeers poured their fire upon the advancing column.

The day was breaking now, and the roar of battle in the city mingled with that at the gates, where the Swedes were in vain striving to effect an entrance. Gradually the Scotch won their way forward; 500 of the Bavarians were killed, in addition to 400 who had fallen on the bridge. The rest now attempted to fly. Great numbers were drowned in the Danube, and the remainder were taken prisoners. The streets were encumbered by the heavily laden baggage wagons, and a vast amount of booty fell into the hands of the Scotch, who thus became masters of the town before Gustavus and his Swedes had succeeded in carrying the gate.

The king now entered the town, and as soon as order was restored Hepburn's brigade recrossed the Danube and threw up a strong work on the other side of the bridge; for Tilly was on the Lech, but seven miles distant, and might at any moment return. He had just struck a severe blow at Marshal Horn, who had recently taken Bamberg. His force, 9000 strong, had been scattered to put down a rising of the country people, when Tilly with 16,000 fell upon them.

A column under Bauditzen was attacked and defeated, and

Tilly's horsemen pursued them hotly to the bridge leading to the town. Marshal Horn threw a barricade across this and defended it until nightfall. Tilly had then fallen back before the advance of Gustavus to a very strong position on the Lech. This was an extremely rapid river, difficult to cross and easily defensible. Tilly had broken down the bridges, and was prepared to dispute till the last the further advance of the Swedes. He placed his army between Rain, where the Lech falls into the Danube, and Augsburg, a distance of sixteen miles—all the assailable points being strongly occupied, with small bodies of cavalry in the intervals to give warning of the approach of the enemy. He had been joined by Maximilian of Bavaria, and his force amounted to 40,000 men.

Gustavus gave his army four days' rest at Donauworth, and then advanced with 32,000 men against the Lech. His dragoons, who had been pushed forward, had found the bridges destroyed. He first attempted to repair that at Rain, but the fire of the artillery and musketry was so heavy that he was forced to abandon the idea. He then made a careful reconnaissance of the river, whose course was winding and erratic.

Finding that at every point at which a crossing could be easily effected Tilly's batteries and troops commanded the position, he determined to make his attack at a point where the river made a sharp bend in the form of a semicircle, of which he occupied the outer edge. He encamped the bulk of his army at the village of Nordheim, a short distance in the rear, and erected three powerful batteries mounting seventy-two guns. One of these faced the centre of the loop, the others were placed opposite the sides.

The ground on the Swedish bank of the river was higher than that facing it; and when the Swedish batteries opened they so completely swept the ground inclosed by the curve of the river that the Imperialists could not advance across it, and were compelled to remain behind a rivulet called the Ach, a short distance in the rear of the Lech. They brought up their artillery, however, and replied to the cannonade of the Swedes.

For four days the artillery duel continued, and while it was going on a considerable number of troops were at work in the village of Oberndorf, which lay in a declivity near the river, hidden from the sight of the Imperialists, constructing a bridge. For that purpose a number of strong wooden trestles of various heights and with feet of unequal length for standing in the bed of the river were prepared, together with a quantity of piles to be driven in among and beside them to enable them to resist the force of the current.

113

On the night of the fourth day the king caused a number of fires to be lighted near the river, fed with green wood and damp straw. A favourable wind blew the smoke towards the enemy, and thus concealed the ground from them. At daybreak on the 5th of April, a thousand picked men crossed the river in two boats, and having reached the other side at once proceeded to throw up intrenchments to cover the head of the bridge, while at the same time the workmen began to place the trestles in position.

As soon as day broke Tilly became aware of what was being done, and two batteries opened fire upon the work at the head of the bridge and against the bridge itself; but the low and swampy nature of the ground on the Imperialist side of the river prevented his placing the batteries in a position from which they could command the works, and their fire proved ineffective in preventing the construction of the bridge. Seeing this, Tilly at once commenced preparations for arresting the further advance of the Swedes.

To reach his position they would be obliged to cross the swampy ground exposed to the fire of his troops, and to render their progress still more difficult he proceeded to cut down large trees, lopping and sharpening their branches to form a chevaux-de-frise before his troops. All the morning a heavy cannonade was kept up on both sides, but by noon the bridge was completed and the advance guard of the Swedes, led by Colonels Wrandel and Gassion, advanced across it. As the other brigades were following, Tilly directed General Altringer to lead his cavalry against them.

Altringer led his troops round the end of the marsh and charged with great bravery down upon the Swedes. These, however, had time to form up, and a tremendous fire of musketry was poured into the Imperialist horse, while the round shot from the three Swedish batteries ploughed their ranks in front and on both flanks. Under such circumstances, although fighting with reckless bravery, the Imperialist cavalry were repulsed. Altringer, however, rallied them and led them back again to the charge, but a cannonball grazed his temple and he was carried senseless from the field. His men, shaken by the tremendous fire and deprived of their leader, fell back in confusion.

Tilly at once placed himself at the head of a chosen body of troops and advanced to the attack, fighting with the ardour and bravery which always distinguished him. He was short in stature and remarkable for his ugliness as well as his bravery. Lean and spare in figure, he had hollow cheeks, a long nose, a broad wrinkled forehead, heavy moustaches, and a sharp pointed chin. He had from his boyhood been fighting against the Protestants. He had learned the art of war under the cruel and pitiless Spanish general Alva in the Netherlands, of which country he was a native, and had afterwards fought against them in Bavaria, in Bohemia, and the Palatinate, and had served in Hungary against the Turks.

Until he met Gustavus at Breitenfeld he had never known a reverse. A bigoted Catholic, he had never hesitated at any act of cruelty which might benefit the cause for which he fought, or strike terror into the Protestants; and the singularity of his costume and the ugliness of his appearance heightened the terror which his deeds inspired among them. When not in armour his costume was modelled upon that of the Duke of Alva, consisting of a slashed doublet of green silk, with an enormously wide-brimmed and high conical hat adorned with a large red ostrich feather. In his girdle he carried a long dagger and a Toledo sword of immense length. His personal bravery was famous, and never did he fight more gallantly than when he led his veterans to the attack of the Swedes.

For twenty minutes a furious hand to hand conflict raged, and the result was still uncertain when a shot from a falconet struck Tilly on the knee and shattered the bone, and the old general fell insensible to the ground. He was carried off the field, and his troops, now without a leader, gave way, the movement being hastened by two bodies of Swedish horse, who, eager for action, swam their horses across the river and threatened to cut off the retreat. By this time evening was at hand. The Swedes had secured the passage of the river, but the Imperialist army still held its intrenched position in the wood behind the Lech. Gustavus brought the rest of his army across and halted for the night.

The Imperialist position was tremendously strong, being unassailable on the right and covered in the front by the marshy ground. It could still have been defended with every prospect of success by a determined general, but the two best Imperialist commanders were hors de combat, and Maximilian of Bavaria, the nominal generalissimo, had no military experience. The army, too, was disheartened by the first success of the Swedes and by the loss of the general whom they regarded as well nigh invincible.

Tilly had now recovered his senses, but was suffering intense agony from his wound, and on being consulted by Maximilian he advised him to fall back, as the destruction of his army would leave the whole country open to the Swedes.

The Imperialists accordingly evacuated their position and fell back in good order during the night on Neuberg, and then to

Ingolstadt. Rain and Neuberg were occupied the next day by the Swedes. Gustavus despatched Marshal Horn to follow the retreating enemy to Ingolstadt, and he himself with the rest of his army marched up the Lech to Augsburg, which was held by Colonel Breda with four thousand five hundred men.

The Imperialists had broken down the bridge, but Gustavus immediately built two others, one above and the other below the city, and summoned it to surrender. Breda, hearing that Tilly was dying, Altringer severely wounded, and that no help was to be expected from Maximilian, considered it hopeless to resist, and surrendered the town, which Gustavus, attended by the titular King of Bohemia and many other princes, entered in triumph on the following day, April 14th. The capture of Augsburg was hailed with peculiar satisfaction, as the city was regarded as the birthplace of the Reformation in Germany. Leaving a garrison there the king retraced his steps along the Lech to Neuberg, and marched thence to join Marshal Horn in front of Ingolstadt.

This town was one of the strongest places in Germany and had never been captured. It was now held by a formidable garrison, and the Imperialist army covered it on the north. Tilly had implored Maximilian to defend it and Ratisbon at all hazards, as their possession was a bar to the further advance of Gustavus.

The king arrived before it on the 19th, and on the following day advanced to reconnoitre it closely. The gunners of the town, seeing a number of officers approaching, fired, and with so good an aim that a cannonball carried off the hindquarters of the horse the king was riding. A cry of alarm and consternation burst from the officers, but their delight was great when the king rose to his feet, covered with dust and blood indeed, but otherwise unhurt.

On the following day a cannonball carried off the head of the Margrave of Baden-Durlach, and on the same day Tilly expired. With his last breath he urged Maximilian never to break his alliance with the emperor, and to appoint Colonel Cratz, an officer of great courage and ability, to the command of his army.

Gustavus remained eight days before Ingolstadt, and then, finding that the reduction of the place could not be effected without the loss of much valuable time, he raised the siege. On his march he took possession of Landshut and forced it to pay a ransom of 100,000 thalers and to receive a garrison, and then continued his way to Munich.

The Bavarian capital surrendered without a blow on the 17th of May. Gustavus made a triumphal entry into the town, where he

116

obtained possession of a vast quantity of treasure and stores. Here he remained some little time reducing the country round and capturing many cities and fortresses. The Green Brigade had suffered severely at Ingolstadt. On the evening of the 19th of April the king, expecting a sally, had ordered Hepburn to post the brigade on some high ground near the gate and the soldiers remained under arms the whole night.

The glow of their matches enabled the enemy to fire with precision, and a heavy cannonade was poured upon them throughout the whole night. Three hundred men were killed as they stood, Munro losing twelve men by one shot; but the brigade stood their ground unflinchingly, and remained until morning in steady line in readiness to repel any sortie of the enemy.

The army suffered greatly on the march from the Lech to Ingolstadt, and thence to Munich, from the attacks of the country people, who were excited against them by the priests. Every straggler who fell into their hands was murdered with horrible cruelty, the hands and feet being cut off, and other savage mutilations being performed upon them, in revenge for which the Swedes and Scots shot all the Bavarians who fell into their hands, and burned two hundred towns and villages.

CHAPTER XIII

CAPTURED BY THE PEASANTS

Malcolm Graheme was not present at the siege of Ingolstadt. The orders after crossing the Lech had been very strict against straggling, so soon as the disposition of the country people was seen; but it is not easy to keep a large column of troops in a solid body. The regiments in the march indeed, under the eye of the officers, can be kept in column, but a considerable number of troops are scattered along the great convoy of wagons containing the tents, stores, and ammunition of the army, and which often extends some miles in length. Even if the desire for plunder does not draw men away, many are forced to fall behind either from sickness, sore feet, or other causes.

The number of these was comparatively small in the army of Gustavus, for discipline was strict and the spirit of the troops good. As soon, however, as it was found that every straggler who fell into the hands of the peasantry was murdered under circumstances of horrible atrocity it became very difficult for the officers to keep the men together, so intense was their fury and desire for vengeance against the savage peasantry, and on every possible occasion when a village was seen near the line of march men would slip away and slay, plunder, and burn.

Gustavus endeavoured to repress these proceedings. He shared the indignation of his troops at the barbarous conduct of the peasantry, but throughout the war he always tried to carry on hostilities so as to inflict as little loss and suffering as possible upon noncombatants. This state of warfare too between his troops and the country people added to his difficulties, for the peasantry drove off their cattle and burned their stacks, and rendered it necessary for provisions and forage to be carried with the army. Parties were therefore sent out on the flanks of the column for the double purpose of preventing soldiers stealing off to plunder and burn, and of picking up stragglers and saving them from the fury of the peasants.

A strong rear guard followed a short distance behind the army. It was accompanied by some empty wagons, in which those who fell out and were unable to keep up with the march were placed. Two days after the advance from the Lech, Malcolm was in charge of a small party on the right flank of the column. There was no fear of an attack from the enemy, for the Swedish horsemen were out scouring the country, and the Imperialists were known to have fallen back to Ingolstadt. The villages were found deserted by the male inhabitants, the younger women too had all left, but a few old crones generally remained in charge. These scowled at the invaders, and crossing themselves muttered curses beneath their breath upon those whom their priests had taught them to regard as devils. There was nothing to tempt the cupidity of the soldiers in these villages. Malcolm's duty was confined to a casual inspection, to see that no stragglers had entered for the purpose of procuring wine.

The day's march was nearly over when he saw some flames rise from a village a short distance away. Hurrying forward with his men he found a party of ten of the Swedish soldiers who had stolen away from the baggage guard engaged in plundering. Two peasants lay dead in the street, and a house was in flames.

Malcolm at once ordered his detachment, who were twenty strong, to arrest the Swedes and to march them back to the columns. While they were doing this he went from house to house to see that none of the party were lurking there. At the door of the last house of the village three women were standing.

"Are any of the soldiers here?" he asked.

The women gave him an unintelligible answer in the country patois, and passing between them he entered the cottage. On the table stood a large jug of water, and lifting it he took a long draught. There was a sudden crash, and he fell heavily, struck down from behind with a heavy mallet by one of the women. He was stunned by the blow, and when he recovered his senses he found that he was bound hand and foot, a cloth had been stuffed tightly into his mouth, and he was covered thickly with a heap of straw and rubbish. He struggled desperately to free himself, but so tightly were the cords bound that they did not give in the slightest.

A cold perspiration broke out on his forehead as he reflected that he was helpless in the power of these savage peasants, and that he should probably be put to death by torture. Presently he could hear the shouts of his men, who, on finding that he did not return, had scattered through the village in search of him. He heard the voice of his sergeant.

"These old hags say they saw an officer walk across to the left. The captain may have meant us to march the prisoners at once to the column, and be waiting just outside the village for us, but it is not likely. At any rate, lads, we will search every house from top to bottom before we leave. So set to work at once; search every room, cupboard, and shed. There may be foul play; though we see no men about, some may be in hiding."

Malcolm heard the sound of footsteps, and the crashing of planks as the men searched the cottages, wrenched off the doors of cupboards, and ransacked the whole place. Gradually the sound ceased, and everything became quiet. Presently he heard the sound of drums, and knew that the regiment which formed the rear guard was passing.

It was bitterness indeed to know that his friends were within sound of a call for aid, and that he was bound and helpless. The halting place for the night was, he knew, but a mile or two in advance, and his only hope was that some band of plunderers might in the night visit the village; but even then his chances of being discovered were small indeed, for even should they sack and burn it he would pass unnoticed lying hidden in the straw yard. His captors were no doubt aware of the possibility of such a visit, for it was not until broad daylight, when the army would again be on its forward march, that they uncovered him.

Brave as Malcolm was he could scarce repress a shudder as he looked at the band of women who surrounded him. All were past middle age, some were old and toothless, but all were animated by a spirit of ferocious triumph. Raising him into a sitting position, they clustered round him, some shook their skinny hands in his face, others heaped curses upon him, some of the most furious assailed him with heavy sticks, and had he not still been clothed in his armour, would then and there have killed him.

This, however, was not their intention, for they intended to put him to death by slow torture. He was lifted and carried into the cottage. There the lacings of his armour were cut, the cords loosened one by one, sufficient to enable them to remove the various pieces of which it was composed, then he was left to himself, as the hags intended to postpone the final tragedy until the men returned from the hills.

This might be some hours yet, as the Swedish cavalry would still be scouring the country, and other bodies of troops might be marching up. From the conversation of the women, which he understood but imperfectly, Malcolm gathered that they thought the men would return that night. Some of the women were in favour of executing the vengeance themselves, but the majority were of opinion that the men should have their share of the pleasure.

All sorts of fiendish propositions were made as to the manner in which his execution should be carried out, but even the mildest caused Malcolm to shudder in anticipation. His arms were bound tightly to his side at the elbows, and the wrists were fastened in front of him, his legs were tied at the knees and ankles. Sometimes he was left alone as the women went about their various avocations in the village, but he was so securely bound that to him as to them his escape appeared altogether impossible. The day passed heavily and slowly. The cloth had been removed from his mouth, but he was parched with thirst, while the tightly bound cords cut deeply into his flesh.

He had once asked for water, but his request had been answered with such jeers and mockery that he resolved to suffer silently until the last. At length the darkness of the winter evening began to fall when a thought suddenly struck him. On the hearth a fire was burning; he waited until the women had again left the hut. He could hear their voices without as they talked with those in the next cottage. They might at any moment return, and it was improbable that they would again go out, for the cold was bitter, and they would most likely wait indoors for the return of the men.

This then was his last opportunity. He rolled himself to the fire, and with his teeth seized the end of one of the burning sticks. He raised himself into a sitting position, and with the greatest difficulty laid the burning end of the stick across the cords which bound his wrists. It seemed to him that they would never catch fire. The flesh scorched and frizzled, and the smoke rose up with that of the burning rope. The agony was intense, but it was for life, and Malcolm unflinchingly held the burning brand in its place until the cords flew asunder and his hands were free. Although almost mad with the pain, Malcolm set to work instantly to undo the other ropes. As soon as one of his arms was free he seized a hatchet, which lay near him, and rapidly cut the rest. He was not a moment too soon, for as he cut the last knot he heard the sound of steps, and two women appeared at the door.

On seeing their prisoner standing erect with an axe in his hand they turned and fled shrieking loudly. It was well for Malcolm that they did so, for so stiff and numbed were his limbs that he could scarcely hold the axe, and the slightest push would have thrown him to the ground.

Some minutes passed before, by stamping his feet and rubbing his legs he restored circulation sufficiently to totter across the room. Then he seized a brand and thrust it into the thatch of the house, having first put on his helmet and placed his sword and pistols in his belt. His hands were too crippled and powerless to enable him to fasten on the rest of his armour. He knew that he had no time to lose. Fortunately the women would not know how weak and helpless he was, for had they returned in a body they could easily have overpowered him; but at any moment the men might arrive, and if he was found there by them his fate was sealed.

Accordingly as soon as he had fired the hut he made his way from the village as quickly as he could crawl along. He saw behind him the flames rising higher and higher. The wind was blowing keenly, and the fire spread rapidly from house to house, and by the time he reached the road along which the army had travelled the whole village was in flames. He felt that he could not travel far, for the intense sufferings which he had endured for twenty-four hours without food or water had exhausted his strength.

His limbs were swollen and bruised from the tightness of the cords, the agony of his burned wrists was terrible, and after proceeding slowly for about a mile he drew off from the broad trampled track which the army had made in passing, and dragging himself to a clump of trees a short distance from the road, made his way through some thick undergrowth and flung himself down. The night was intensely cold, but this was a relief to him rather than otherwise, for it alleviated the burning pain of his limbs while he kept handfuls of snow applied to his wrists.

Two hours after he had taken refuge he heard a number of men come along the road at a run. Looking through the bushes he could see by their figures against the snow that they were peasants, and had no doubt that they were the men of the village who had returned and at once started in pursuit of him.

An hour later, feeling somewhat relieved, he left his hiding place and moved a mile away from the road, as he feared that the peasants, failing to overtake him, might, as they returned, search every possible hiding place near it. He had no fear of the track being noticed, for the surface of the snow was everywhere marked by parties going and returning to the main body. He kept on until he saw a small shed. The door was unfastened; opening it he found that the place was empty, though there were signs that it was usually used as a shelter for cattle.

A rough ladder led to a loft. This was nearly full of hay. Malcolm threw himself down on this, and covering himself up thickly, felt the blood again begin to circulate in his limbs. It brought, however, such a renewal of his pain, that it was not until morning that fatigue overpowered his sufferings and he fell asleep.

It was late in the afternoon when he woke at the sound of

shouts and holloaing. Springing to his feet he looked out between the cracks in the boards and saw a party of forty or fifty peasants passing close by the shed. They were armed with hatchets, scythes, and pikes. On the heads of four of the pikes were stuck gory heads, and in the centre of the party were three prisoners, two Swedes and a Scot. These were covered with blood, and were scarcely able to walk, but were being urged forward with blows and pike thrusts amid the brutal laughter of their captors.

Malcolm retired to his bed full of rage and sorrow. It would have been madness to have followed his first impulse to sally out sword in hand and fall upon the ruffians, as such a step would only have ensured his own death without assisting the captives.

"Hitherto," he said to himself, "I have ever restrained my men, and have endeavoured to protect the peasants from violence; henceforward, so long as we remain in Bavaria, no word of mine shall be uttered to save one of these murderous peasants. However, I am not with my company yet. The army is two marches ahead, and must by this time be in front of Ingolstadt. I have been two days without food, and see but little chance of getting any until I rejoin them, and the whole country between us is swarming with an infuriated peasantry. The prospect is certainly not a bright one. I would give a year's pay to hear the sound of a Swedish trumpet."

When darkness had fairly set in Malcolm started on his way again. Although his limbs still smarted from the weals and sores left by the cords they had now recovered their lissomeness; but he was weak from want of food, and no longer walked with the free elastic stride which distinguished the Scottish infantry. His wrists gave him great pain, being both terribly burned, and every movement of the hand sent a thrill of agony up the arm. He persisted, however, in frequently opening and clenching his hands, regardless of the pain, for he feared that did he not do so they would stiffen and he would be unable to grasp a sword. Fortunately the wounds were principally on the upper side of the thumbs, where the flesh was burned away to the bone, but the sinews and muscles of the wrists had to a great extent escaped.

He had not journeyed very far when he saw a light ahead and presently perceived the houses of a village. A fire was lit in the centre, and a number of figures were gathered round it.

"Something is going on," Malcolm said to himself; "as likely as not they have got some unfortunate prisoner. Whatever it be, I will steal in and try to get some food. I cannot go much further without it; and as their attention is occupied, I may find a cottage empty."

Making his way round to the back of the houses, he approached one of the cottages in the rear. He lifted the latch of the door and opened it a little. All was still. With his drawn sword he entered. The room was empty; a fire burned on the hearth, and on the table were some loaves which had evidently been just baked. Malcolm fell upon one of them and speedily devoured it, and, taking a long draught of rough country wine from a skin hanging against the wall, he felt another man.

He broke another loaf in two and thrust the pieces into his doublet, and then sallied out from the cottage again. Still keeping behind the houses he made his way until he got within view of the fire. Here he saw a sight which thrilled him with horror. Some eight or ten peasants and forty or fifty women were yelling and shouting. Fastened against a post in front of the fire were the remains of a prisoner. He had been stripped, his ears, nose, hands, and feet cut off, and he was slowly bleeding to death.

Four other men, bound hand and foot, lay close to the fire. By its flames Malcolm saw the green scarves that told they were Scotchmen of his own brigade, and he determined at once to rescue them or die in the attempt. He crept forward until he reached the edge of the road; then he raised a pistol and with a steady aim fired at one of the natives, who fell dead across the fire.

Another shot laid another beside him before the peasants recovered from their first surprise. Then with a loud shout in German, "Kill—kill! and spare none!" Malcolm dashed forward. The peasants, believing that they were attacked by a strong body, fled precipitately in all directions. Malcolm, on reaching the prisoners, instantly severed their bonds.

"Quick, my lads!" he exclaimed; "we shall have them upon us again in a minute."

The men in vain tried to struggle to their feet—their limbs were too numbed to bear them.

"Crawl to the nearest cottage!" Malcolm exclaimed; "we can hold it until your limbs are recovered."

He caught up from the ground some pikes and scythes which the peasants had dropped in their flight, and aided the men to make their way to the nearest cottage. They were but just in time; for the peasants, finding they were not pursued, had looked round, and seeing but one opponent had gained courage and were beginning to approach again. Malcolm barred the door, and then taking down a skin of wine bade his companions take a drink. There were loaves on the shelves, and these he cut up and handed to them.

"Quick, lads!" he said; "stamp your legs and swing your arms, and get the blood in motion. I will keep these fellows at bay a few minutes longer."

He reloaded his pistols and fired through the door, at which the peasants were now hewing with axes. A cry and a heavy fall told him that one of the shots had taken effect. Suddenly there was a smell of smoke.

"They have fired the roof," Malcolm said. "Now, lads, each of you put a loaf of bread under his jerkin. There is no saying when we may get more. Now get ready and sally out with me. There are but six or eight men in the village, and they are no match for us. They only dared to attack us because they saw that you couldn't walk."

The door was opened, and headed by Malcolm the four Scotchmen dashed out. They were assailed by a shower of missiles by the crowd as they appeared, but as soon as it was seen that the men were on foot again the peasants gave way. Malcolm shot one and cut down another, and the rest scattered in all directions.

"Now, lads, follow me while we may," and Malcolm again took to the fields. The peasants followed for some distance, but when the soldiers had quite recovered the use of their limbs Malcolm suddenly turned on his pursuers, overtaking and killing two of them. Then he and his men again continued their journey, the peasants no longer following. When at some distance from the village he said:

"We must turn and make for the Lech again. It is no farther than it is to Ingolstadt, and we shall find friends there. These peasants will go on ahead and raise all the villagers against us, and we should never get through. What regiment do you belong to, lads?" for in the darkness he had been unable to see their faces.

"Your own, Captain Graheme. We were in charge of one of the wagons with sick. The wheel came off, and we were left behind the convoy while we were mending it. As we were at work, our weapons laid on the ground, some twenty men sprang out from some bushes hard by and fell upon us. We killed five or six of them, but were beaten down and ten of our number were slain. They murdered all the sick in the wagons and marched us away, bound, to this village where you found us. Sandy McAlister they had murdered just as you came up, and we should have had a like horrible fate had you been a few minutes later. Eh, sir! but it's an awful death to be cut in pieces by these devils incarnate!"

"Well, lads," Malcolm said, "we will determine that they shall not take us alive again. If we are overtaken or met by any of these gangs of peasants we will fight till we die. None of us, I hope, are afraid of death in fair strife, but the bravest might well shrink from such a death as that of your poor comrade. Now let us see what arms we have between us."

Malcolm had his sword and pistols, two of the men had pikes, the other two scythes fastened to long handles.

"These are clumsy weapons," Malcolm said. "You had best fit short handles to them, so as to make them into double handed swords."

They were unable to travel far, for all were exhausted with the sufferings they had gone through, but they kept on until they came upon a village which had been fired when the troops marched through. The walls of a little church were alone standing. It had, like the rest of the village, been burned, but the shell still remained.

"So far as I can see," Malcolm said, "the tower has escaped. Had it been burned we should see through the windows. We may find shelter in the belfry."

On reaching the church they found that the entrance to the belfry tower was outside the church, and to this, no doubt, it owed its escape from the fire which had destroyed the main edifice. The door was strong and defied their efforts to break it in.

"I must fire my pistol through the lock," Malcolm said. "I do not like doing so, for the sound may reach the ears of any peasants in the neighbourhood; but we must risk it, for the cold is extreme, and to lie down in the snow would be well nigh certain death."

He placed his pistol to the keyhole and fired. The lock at once yielded and the party entered the door.

"Before we mount," Malcolm said, "let each pick up one of these blocks of stone which have fallen from the wall. We will wedge the door from behind, and can then sleep secure against a surprise."

When the door was closed one of the men, who was a musketeer, struck some sparks from a flint and steel on to a slow match which he carried in his jerkin, and by its glow they were enabled to look around them. The stone steps began to ascend close to the door, and by laying the stones between the bottom step and the door they wedged the latter firmly in its place. They then ascended the stairs, and found themselves in a room some ten feet square, in which hung the bell which had called the village to prayers. It hung from some beams which were covered with a boarded floor, and a rough ladder led to a trapdoor, showing that there was another room above. The floor of the room in which they stood was of stone.

"Now, lads," Malcolm said, "two of you make your way up that ladder and rip up some of the planks of the flooring. See if there are any windows or loopholes in the chamber above, and if so stuff your jerkins into them; we will close up those here. In a few minutes we will have a roaring fire; but we must beware lest a gleam of light be visible without, for this belfry can be seen for miles round."

Some of the boards were soon split up into fragments; but before the light was applied to them Malcolm carefully examined each window and loophole to be sure that they were perfectly stopped. Then the slow match was placed in the centre of a number of pieces of dry and rotten wood. One of the men kneeling down blew lustily, and in a few seconds a flame sprang up. The wood was now heaped on, and a bright fire was soon blazing high.

A trapdoor leading out on to the flat top of the tower was opened for the escape of the smoke, and the party then seated themselves round the fire, under whose genial warmth their spirits speedily rose. They now took from their wallets the bread which they had brought away with them.

"If we had," one of the soldiers said, "but a few flasks of Rhine wine with us we need not envy a king."

"No," Malcolm replied, "we are better off at present than our comrades who are sleeping in the snow round the watchfires; but for all that I would that we were with them, for we have a long and dangerous march before us. And now, lads, you can sleep soundly. There will be no occasion to place a watch, for the door is securely fastened; but at the first dawn of light we must be on our feet; for although I do not mean to march until nightfall, we must remove the stoppings from the windows, for should the eye of any passing peasant fall upon them, he will guess at once that some one is sheltering here, and may proceed to find out whether it be friend or foe."

Having finished half their bread, for Malcolm had warned them to save the other half for the next day, the men lay down round the fire, and soon all were sound asleep.

CHAPTER XIV

IN THE CHURCHTOWER

Malcolm was the first to awake, and was vexed to find by a stream of light pouring down through the half open trapdoor above that it was broad day. He roused the men, and the stoppings were at once removed from the loopholes. The sun was already high, for the party, overpowered with fatigue, had slept long and soundly.

Malcolm looked cautiously from the window; no one was in sight, and the ruins of the village below lay black and deserted. The men resumed the clothes which had been used for blocking the loopholes, and sat down to pass the long hours which would elapse before the time for action arrived. It was exceedingly cold, for there were loopholes on each side of the chamber, and the wind blew keenly through.

"Sergeant," Malcolm said, "we will risk a bit of fire again, for the cold pierces to the bone; only be sure that you use perfectly dry wood. Examine each piece to see that no drip from the roof has penetrated it. If it is dry it will give but little smoke, and a slight vapour is not likely to be observed rising from the top of the tower."

The fire was again lighted, and the smoke was so slight that Malcolm had little fear of its being observed.

An hour later, as the men were talking, Malcolm suddenly held up his hand for silence, and the murmur of voices was heard without. Malcolm rose to his feet to reconnoitre, standing far back from the loophole as he did so. A group of some eight or ten peasants were standing looking at the tower, while a woman was pointing to it and talking eagerly.

It was towards the windows that she was pointing, and Malcolm guessed at once that, having returned in the early morning to see what remained of her home, she had happened to notice the garments stuffed in the windows, and had carried the news to some of her companions. Malcolm regretted bitterly now that he had not set a watch, so that at the first gleam of daylight the windows might have been unblocked; but it was now too late.

"We shall have to fight for it, lads," he said, turning round. "Our clothes must have been seen early this morning, and there is a party of peasants watching the tower. Of course they cannot know at present whether we are friends or foes; but no doubt the news of last evening's doings has travelled through the country, and the peasants are on the lookout for us, so they may well guess that we are here. However, we shall soon see. Sergeant, place one of your men on sentry at the foot of the stairs, but do not let him speak or give any signs of his presence if the door is tried."

One of the soldiers was placed on guard. Scarcely had he taken his station when there was a knocking at the door, and shouts were heard outside from the peasants calling on those within, if they were friends, to come out. No answer was returned.

"It's fortunate for you," Malcolm muttered, "that we don't come out, or we should make short work of you; but I know you would fly like hares if you saw us, and would bring the whole country down on us. No; we must hold out here. Our only hope is to escape at night, or to hold this place till some of our troops come along. At any moment some regiments from the Lech may be marching forward to join the king.

"We must make our bread last, lads," he said cheerfully to the men, "for we may have to stand a long siege. Methinks we can hold this stone staircase against all the peasants of this part of Bavaria; and we must do so until we hear the sound of the Swedish drums; they may come along at any time. If the worst comes to the worst one of us must start at night and carry news of our peril to the Lech. We made a good supper last night, and can fast for a bit. If we cut our bread up into small portions we can hold out for days. There should be snow enough on the tower top to furnish us with drink."

After hammering at the door for some time, the peasants retired convinced that there were none of their own people within the tower, and that those who had slept there were the fugitives of whom they had been in search during the night. These might, indeed, have departed in the interval between the time when the woman first saw the traces of their presence and her return with them; but they did not think that this was so, for in that case they could not have fastened the door behind them. The peasants accordingly withdrew a short distance from the church, and three of their number were sent off in different directions to bring up reinforcements. As soon as Malcolm saw this movement he knew that concealment was useless, and began to make preparations for the defence. First, he with the sergeant ascended to the roof of the tower. To his disappointment he saw that the heat of the flames had melted the snow, and that most of the water had run away. Some, however, stood in the hollows and inequalities of the stone platform, where it had again frozen into ice.

As the supply would be very precious, Malcolm directed that before any moved about on the platform every piece of ice should be carefully taken up and carried below. Here it was melted over the fire in one of the iron caps, and was found to furnish three quarts of water. The appearance of Malcolm and his companion on the tower had been hailed by a shout of hatred and exultation by the peasants; but the defenders had paid no attention to the demonstration, and had continued their work as if regardless of the presence of their enemies.

On his return to the platform Malcolm found, looking over the low parapet, that on the side farthest from the church great icicles hung down from the mouth of the gutter, the water having frozen again as it trickled from the platform. These icicles were three or four inches in diameter and many feet in length. They were carefully broken off, and were laid down on the platform where they would remain frozen until wanted. Malcolm now felt secure against the attacks of thirst for some days to come. The stones of the parapet were next tried, and were without much trouble moved from their places, and were all carried to the side in which the door was situated, in readiness to hurl down upon any who might assault it. Some of the beams of the upper flooring were removed from their places, and being carried down, were wedged against the upper part of the door, securing it as firmly as did the stones below. These preparations being finished, Malcolm took a survey of the situation outside.

The group of peasants had increased largely, some thirty or forty men armed with pikes, bills, and scythes being gathered in a body, while many more could be seen across the country hurrying over the white plain towards the spot. The windows of the lower apartment had been barricaded with planks, partly to keep out missiles, partly for warmth. A good fire now blazed in the centre, and the soldiers, confident in themselves and their leader, cracked grim jokes as, their work being finished, they sat down around it and awaited the attack, one of their number being placed on the summit of the tower to give warning of the approach of the enemy.

"I would that we had a musket or two," Malcolm said; "for we might then keep them from the door. I have only some twenty charges for my pistols, and the most of these, at any rate, I must keep for the defence of the stairs."

Presently the sentry from above called out that the peasants were moving forward to the attack.

"Sergeant," Malcolm said, "do you fasten my green scarf to a

130

long strip of plank and fix it to the top of the tower. We cannot fight under a better banner. Now let us mount to the roof and give them a warm reception."

"Look out, sir," the sentry exclaimed as Malcolm ascended the stair, "three or four of them have got muskets."

"Then we must be careful," Malcolm said. "I don't suppose they are much of marksmen, but even a random shot will tell at times, and I want to take you all back safe with me; so keep low when you get on the roof, lads, and don't show your heads more than you can help."

Heralding their attack by a discharge from their muskets, whose balls whistled harmlessly round the tower, the peasants rushed forward to the door and commenced an assault upon it with hatchets and axes.

Malcolm and his men each lifted a heavy stone and rolled it over the parapet, the five loosing the missiles simultaneously. There was a dull crash, and with a terrible cry the peasants fled from the door. Looking over, Malcolm saw that six or seven men had been struck down. Five of these lay dead or senseless; two were endeavouring to drag themselves away.

"That is lesson number one," he said. "They will be more prudent next time."

The peasants, after holding a tumultuous council, scattered, most of them making for a wood a short distance off.

"They are going to cut down a tree and use it as a battering ram," Malcolm observed. "They know that these large stones are too heavy for us to cast many paces from the foot of the wall. We must get to work and break some of them up. That will not be difficult, for the wind and weather have rotted many of them half through."

The stones were for the most part from two to three feet long and nine or ten inches square. Two were laid down on the platform some eighteen inches apart and another placed across them. The four men then lifted another stone, and holding it perpendicularly brought it down with all their strength upon the unsupported centre of the stone, which broke in half at once. To break it again required greater efforts, but it yielded to the blows. Other stones were similarly treated, until a large pile was formed of blocks of some ten inches each way, besides a number of smaller fragments.

In half an hour the peasants reappeared with a slight well grown tree some forty feet long which had been robbed of its branches. It was laid down about fifty yards from the church, and then twenty men lifted it near the butt and advanced to use it as a

131

battering ram, with the small end forward; but before they were near enough to touch the door the bearers were arrested by a cry from the crowd as the defenders appeared on the tower, and poising their blocks of stone above their heads, hurled them down. Three of them flew over the heads of the peasants, but the others crashed down among them, slaying and terribly mutilating two of the bearers of the tree and striking several others to the ground. The battering ram was instantly dropped, and before the Scotchmen had time to lift another missile the peasants were beyond their reach.

"Lesson number two," Malcolm said. "What will our friends do next, I wonder?"

The peasants were clearly at a loss. A long consultation was held, but this was not followed by any renewal of the attack.

"I think they must have made up their minds to starve us out, sir," the sergeant remarked as the hours went slowly by without any renewal of the attack.

"Yes; either that, sergeant, or a night attack. In either case I consider that we are safe for a time, but sooner or later our fate is sealed unless aid comes to us, and therefore I propose that one of you should tonight try and bear a message to the Lech. We can lower him down by the bell rope from this window in the angle where the tower touches the church. Keeping round by the church he will be in deep shadow until he reaches the other end, and will then be close to the ruins of the village. Before morning he could reach our camp."

"I will undertake it myself, sir, if you will allow me," the sergeant said, while the other men also volunteered for the duty.

"You shall try first, sergeant," Malcolm said. "It will be dangerous work, for as the news of our being here spreads the peasants will be coming in from all quarters. Their numbers are already greatly increased since they commenced the attack, and there must be at least three or four hundred men around us. They will be sure to keep a sharp lookout against our escaping, and it will need all your care and caution to get through them."

"Never fear, sir," the man replied confidently. "I have stalked the deer scores of times, and it will be hard if I cannot crawl through a number of thick witted Bavarian peasants."

"Even beyond the village you will have to keep your eyes open, as you may meet parties of peasants on their way here. Fortunately you will have no difficulty in keeping the road, so well beaten is it by the march of the army. If by tomorrow night no rescue arrives I shall consider that you have been taken or killed, and shall try with

132

the others to make my way through. It would be better to die sword in hand while we have still the strength to wield our arms than to be cooped up here until too weak any longer to defend ourselves, and then to be slowly tortured to death."

As soon as it was dusk a sentry was placed on the top of the tower, with orders to report the slightest sound or stir. During the day this had not been necessary, for a view could be obtained from the windows, and the men with firearms, who had now considerably increased in numbers, kept up a constant fire at the tower.

An hour later the sentry reported that he could hear the sound of many feet in the darkness, with the occasional snapping as of dry twigs.

"They are going to burn down the door," Malcolm said. "That is what I expected. Now, sergeant, is your time. They are all busy and intent upon their purpose. You could not have a better time."

The rope was fastened round the sergeant's waist, and with some difficulty he squeezed himself through the narrow window, after listening attentively to discover if any were below.

All seemed perfectly still on this side, and he was gradually and steadily lowered down. Presently those above felt the rope slack. Another minute and it swung loosely. It was drawn up again, and Malcolm, placing one of the men at the loophole, with instructions to listen intently for any sound of alarm or conflict, turned his attention to the other side.

Soon he saw a number of dark figures bearing on their heads great bundles which he knew to be faggots approaching across the snow.

As they approached a brisk fire suddenly opened on the tower. Malcolm at once called the sentry down.

"It is of no use exposing yourself," he said, "and we could not do much harm to them did we take to stoning them again. We have nothing to do now but to wait."

Soon a series of dull heavy crashes were heard as the faggots were thrown down against the door. Malcolm descended the stairs until he reached the lowest loophole which lighted them, and which was a few feet above the top of the door. He took one of the men with him.

"Here are my flask and bullet pouch," he said. "Do you reload my pistols as I discharge them."

For some minutes the sound of the faggots being thrown down continued, then the footsteps were heard retreating, and all was quiet again.

"Now it is our turn again," Malcolm said. "It is one thing to prepare a fire and another to light it, my fine fellows. I expect that you have forgotten that there are firearms here."

Presently a light was seen in the distance, and two men with blazing brands approached. They advanced confidently until within twenty yards of the tower, then there was the sharp crack of a pistol, and one of them fell forward on his face, the other hesitated and stood irresolute, then, summoning up courage, he sprang forward.

As he did so another shot flashed out, and he, too, fell prostrate, the brand hissing and spluttering in the snow a few feet from the pile of brushwood. A loud yell of rage and disappointment arose on the night air, showing how large was the number of peasants who were watching the operations. Some time elapsed before any further move was made on the part of the assailants, then some twenty points of light were seen approaching.

"Donald," Malcolm said to the soldier, "go up to the top of the tower with your comrades. They are sure to light the pile this time, but if it is only fired in one place you may possibly dash out the light with a stone."

The lights rapidly approached, but when the bearers came within forty yards they stopped. They were a wild group, as, with their unkempt hair and beards, and their rough attire, they stood holding the lighted brands above their heads. A very tall and powerful man stood at their head.

"Come on," he said, "why do you hesitate? Let us finish with them." And he rushed forward.

Malcolm had his pistol lying on the sill of the loophole covering him, and when the peasant had run ten paces he fired, and the man fell headlong. The others stopped, and a second shot took effect among them. With a yell of terror they hurled the brands towards the pile and fled. Most of the brands fell short, others missed their aim, but from his loophole Malcolm saw that one had fallen on to the outside faggot of the pile.

Almost instantly a heavy stone fell in the snow close by, another, and another. Malcolm stood with his eyes fixed on the brand. The twigs against which it leaned were catching, and the flames began to shoot up. Higher and higher they rose, and a shout of triumph from the peasants told how keenly they were also watching. Still the heavy stones continued to fall. The flames rose higher, and half the faggot was now alight. Another minute and the fire would communicate with the pile. Then there was a crash. A shower of sparks leapt up as the faggot, struck by one of the heavy stones, was dashed from its place and lay blazing twenty feet distant from the pile. There it burnt itself out, and for a time the tower was safe.

For an hour the defenders watched the peasants, who had now lighted great fires just out of pistol shot from the tower, and were gathered thickly round them, the light flashing redly from pike head and scythe.

The uproar of voices was loud; but though the defenders guessed that they were discussing the next plan of attack they could catch no meaning from such words as reached them, for the patois of the Bavarian peasants was unintelligible. At last a large number seized brands, some approached as before towards the pile, the others scattered in various directions, while the men with muskets again opened fire at the top of the tower.

Malcolm took his post at the loophole awaiting attack, but the men in front of him did not advance. Suddenly a light sprang up beneath him. There was a sound of falling stones, but the light grew brighter and brighter, and he knew that this time the pile had been fired. As he ran upstairs he was met by one of the soldiers from above.

"They crept round by the back of the church, sir, and round at the foot of the tower, and they had fired the pile before we saw that they were there."

"It cannot be helped," Malcolm said, "they were sure to succeed sooner or later. Call the others down from the roof."

The door at the top of the stairs was now closed, and the crevices were stuffed tightly with strips torn from the men's clothes so as to prevent the smoke from entering when the door below gave way to the flames. A broad glare of light now lit up the scene, and showers of sparks, and an occasional tongue of flame were visible through the window.

"Shut down the trapdoor in the roof," Malcolm said, "that will check the draught through the windows."

The wood was dry, and what smoke made its way in through the window found its way out through the loopholes of the upper chamber without seriously incommoding those below.

"We can take it easy, now," Malcolm said as he set the example by sitting down against the wall. "It will be hours before the stonework below will be cool enough to permit them to attack."

"They are lighting a circle of fires all round the church," one of the soldiers said looking out.

"They think we shall be trying to escape, now that our door is

135

burned. They are too late; I trust our messenger is miles away by this time."

In half an hour the flames died away, but a deep red glow showed that the pile of embers was still giving out an intense heat. One of the men was now placed on the top of the tower again, as a measure of precaution, but it was certain that hours would elapse before an attack could be made. The peasants, indeed, secure of their prey, evinced no hurry to commence the attack, but spent the night in shouting and singing round their fires, occasionally yelling threats of the fate which awaited them against the defenders of the tower.

Towards daylight Malcolm commenced his preparations for defence. The door was taken off its hinges and was laid on the stone stairs. These were but two feet wide, the door itself being some three inches less. The rope was fastened round its upper end to prevent it from sliding down.

"I wish we had some grease to pour over it," Malcolm said, "but dry as it is it will be next to impossible for anyone to walk up that sharp incline, and we four should be able to hold it against the peasants till doomsday."

It was not until broad daylight that the peasants prepared for the attack. So long as the operation had been a distant one it had seemed easy enough, but as in a confused mass they approached the open doorway they realized that to ascend the narrow staircase, defended at the top by desperate men, was an enterprise of no common danger, and that the work which they had regarded as finished was in fact scarcely begun.

The greater part then hung back, but a band of men, who by their blackened garments and swarthy faces Malcolm judged to be charcoal burners, armed with heavy axes, advanced to the front, and with an air of dogged resolution approached the door. The defenders gave no sign of their presence, no pistol flashed out from window or loophole.

Striding through the still hot ashes the leader of the woodmen passed through the doorway and advanced up the stairs. These ran in short straight flights round the tower, lighted by narrow loopholes. No resistance was encountered until he reached the last turning, where a broader glare of light came from the open doorway, where two of the soldiers, pike in hand, stood ready to repel them. With a shout to his followers to come on, the peasant sprang forward. He ascended three steps, and then, as he placed his foot upon the sharply inclined plane of the door, which he had not

136

noticed, he stumbled forward. His companions, supposing he had been pierced with a spear, pressed on after him, but each fell when they trod upon the door until a heap of men cumbered the stair. These were not unharmed, for with their long pikes the Scottish spearmen ran them through and through as they lay.

Their bodies afforded a foothold to those who followed, but these could make but little way, for as but one could advance at a time, each as he came on was slain by the pikes. Finding that two were well able to hold the door, Malcolm with the other ran up to the top of the tower, and toppled over the stones of the parapet upon the mass gathered around the door. These at once scattered, and those on the stairs, finding themselves unable to get forward, for the narrow passage was now completely choked with the dead, made their way out again and rejoined their comrades.

"I expect they will send their musketeers first next time," Malcolm said as he rejoined those below, leaving the soldier on the watch. "Now let us get the door up again, and bring the dead here; we can form a barrier with them breast high."

The door was quickly shifted on one side, and then the troopers brought up the dead, who were eleven in number.

"Now replace the door," Malcolm ordered; "fill your iron caps with blood—there is plenty flowing from these fellows—and pour it over the door, it will be as good as oil."

This was done, and the bodies were then piled shoulder high across the door.

"They can fire as much as they like now," Malcolm said, "they will be no nearer, and I defy anyone to climb up that door now."

CHAPTER XV

A TIMELY RESCUE

Although unaware how much more formidable the task before them had become, the peasants were disheartened by their defeat, and even the boldest hesitated at the thought of again attacking foes so formidably posted. None of those who had returned were able to explain what was the obstacle which had checked their advance. All that they could tell was, that those before them had fallen, in some cases even before they were touched by the spears of the defenders. This mystery added to the dread which the assault of so difficult a position naturally inspired, and some hours were spent in discussing how the next attack should be made. Many indeed were strongly in favour of remaining quietly around the tower and starving its defenders into surrendering.

Others advocated an attempt to stifle them by heaping green wood and damp straw round the tower; but the more timid pointed out that many would be killed in carrying out the task by the firearms of the besieged, and that even were the combustibles placed in position and lighted the success of the experiment would be by no means certain, as the besieged might stuff up all the orifices, or at the worst might obtain sufficient fresh air on the top of the tower to enable them to breathe.

"You are forgetting," one of the peasants exclaimed, "the powder wagon which broke down as Count Tilly retreated from the Lech. Did we not carry off the powder barrels and hide them, partly to prevent them falling into the hands of these accursed Swedes, partly because the powder would last us for years for hunting the wolf and wild boar? We have only to stow these inside the tower to blow it into the air."

The idea was seized with shouts of acclamation. Most of the peasants who had assisted in carrying off the contents of the wagon were present, and these started instantly to dig up the barrels which they had taken as their share of the booty. The shouts of satisfaction and the departure of forty or fifty men at full speed in various directions did not pass unnoticed by the garrison of the tower.

"They have got a plan of some sort," Malcolm said; "what it is I have no idea, but they certainly seem confident about it. Look at those fellows throwing up their caps and waving their arms. I do not see how we can be attacked, but I do not like these signs of confidence on their part, for they know now how strong our position is. It seems to me that we are impregnable except against artillery."

Unable to repress his uneasiness Malcolm wandered from window to window watching attentively what was going on without, but keeping himself as far back as possible from the loopholes; for the men with muskets kept up a dropping fire at the openings, and although their aim was poor, bullets occasionally passed in and flattened themselves against the opposite walls.

"There is a man returning," he said in about half an hour; "he is carrying something on his shoulder, but I cannot see what it is."

In another ten minutes the man had reached the group of peasants standing two or three hundred yards from the church, and was greeted with cheers and waving of hats.

"Good heavens!" Malcolm exclaimed suddenly, "it is a barrel of powder. They must have stripped some broken down ammunition wagon. This is a danger indeed."

The men grasped their weapons and rose to their feet at the news, prepared to take any steps which their young officer might command, for his promptitude and ingenuity had inspired them with unbounded confidence in him.

"We must at all hazards," he said after a few minutes thought, "prevent them from storing these barrels below. Remove the barricade of bodies and then carry the door down the stairs. We must fix it again on the bottom steps. The bottom stair is but a foot or two inside the doorway; if you place it there it will hinder their rushing up to attack you, and your pikes, as you stand above it, will prevent any from placing their barrels inside.

"I will take my place at the loophole as before. We cannot prevent their crawling round from behind as they did to light the faggots; but if they pile them outside, they may blow in a hole in the wall of the tower, but it is possible that even then it may not fall. Two will be sufficient to hold the stairs, at any rate for the present. Do you, Cameron, take your place on the tower, and drop stones over on any who may try to make their way round from behind; even if you do no harm you will make them careful and delay the operation, and every hour now is of consequence."

Malcolm's instructions were carried out, and all was in readiness before the peasants, some of whom had to go considerable distances, had returned with the powder.

The lesson of the previous evening had evidently not been lost upon the peasants, for Malcolm saw a tall man who was acting as their leader wave his hand, and those who had brought the powder started to make a detour round the church. Malcolm, finding that no movement was being made towards the front, and that at present he could do nothing from his loophole, ran up to the top of the tower and took his place by the soldier who was lying down on the roof and looking over the edge.

Presently the first of the peasants appeared round the corner of the main building, and dashed rapidly across to the angle of the tower. Two heavy stones were dropped, but he had passed on long before they had reached the bottom. Man after man followed, and Malcolm, seeing that he could do nothing to stop them, again ran down. As he did so he heard a scream of agony. The leading peasants had reached the doorway, but as they dashed in to place their barrels of powder they were run through and through by the spears of the pikemen. They fell half in and half out of the doorway, and the barrels rolled some distance away. Those behind them stopped panic stricken at their sudden fall. Several of them dropped their barrels and fled, while others ran round the angle of the tower again, coming in violent contact with those following them; all then hurried round behind the church. Malcolm stamped his feet with vexation.

"What a fool I am," he muttered, "not to have thought of a sortie! If we had all held ourselves in readiness to spring out, we might have cut down the whole of them; at any rate none would have got off with their barrels."

This unexpected failure greatly damped the spirit of the peasants, and there was much consultation among them before any fresh move was made. As he saw that they were fully occupied, and paying no heed to the tower, Malcolm said to his men:

"I am going outside; prepare to help me up over the door again quickly if necessary."

Leaving his sword behind him, he took a leap from the step above the inclined plane and landed at the bottom, and at once threw himself down outside. With his dagger he removed the hoops of one of the barrels, and scattered the contents thickly along the front of the tower. None of the peasants perceived him, for there were many bodies lying round the foot of the tower; and even had any looked that way they would not have noticed that one prone figure had been added to the number.

Crawling cautiously along Malcolm pushed two other barrels before him, and opening them as before, spread the contents of one upon the ground near the side of the tower, and the other by the hinder face. The thick black layer on the snow would have told its tale instantly to a soldier, but Malcolm had little fear of the peasants in their haste paying attention to it. When his task was completed he crawled back again to the door and laid a train from the foot of the slide to the powder without.

"I will remain here," he said, "for the present. Do one of you take your place in the belfry. Tell Cameron to shout down to you what is passing behind, and do you run instantly down the stairs to tell me."

The peasants advanced next time accompanied by a strong force of their armed comrades. As before they came round from behind, intending to stack their barrels in the angle there. As the bearers of the first two or three powder barrels came round the corner Cameron shouted the news, and the soldier below ran down to Malcolm, who fired his pistol into the train. A broad flash of fire rose round the tower followed instantaneously by two heavy explosions. There was silence for an instant, and then a chorus of shrieks and yells.

The powder barrels borne by the two first men had exploded, their heads having been knocked in previously to admit of their ignition. Some thirty of the peasants were killed or terribly mutilated by the explosion, and the rest took to their heels in terror, leaving their wounded comrades on the ground.

The echoes of the explosion had scarce died away when a shout of terror broke from the main body of peasants, and Malcolm saw them flying in all directions. An instant afterwards the ringing sound of the Swedish trumpets was heard, and a squadron of horse galloped down full speed. The peasants attempted no resistance, but fled in all directions, hotly pursued by the Swedes, who broke up into small parties and followed the fugitives cross the country cutting down great numbers of them. The Swedish leader at once rode up to the foot of the tower, where Malcolm had already sallied out.

"I am glad indeed I am in time, Captain Graheme; we have ridden without drawing rein since your messenger arrived at four o'clock this morning."

"Thanks indeed, Captain Burgh," Malcolm replied. "Your coming is most welcome; though I think we have given the peasants so hot a lesson that they would not have attacked us again, and by tightening our waistbelts we could have held on for another three or four days."

"I see that you have punished them heavily," the Swedish

141

officer said, looking round at the bodies; "but what was the explosion I heard?"

"You will see its signs behind the tower," Malcolm said as he led the way there. "They tried to blow us up, but burnt their own fingers."

The scene behind the tower was ghastly. Some thirty peasants lay with their clothes completely burned from their bodies, the greater portion of them dead, but some still writhing in agony. Malcolm uttered an exclamation of horror.

"It were a kindness to put these wretches out of their misery," the Swede said, and dismounting he passed his sword through the bodies of the writhing men. "You know I am in favour of carrying on the war as mercifully as may be," he continued turning to Malcolm, "for we have talked the matter over before now; and God forbid that I should strike a fallen foe; but these poor wretches were beyond help, and it is true mercy to end their sufferings."

"They have had a heavy lesson," Malcolm said; "there are eleven more dead up in the belfry, which they tried to carry by storm, and a dozen at least crushed by stones.

"You and your three men have indeed given a good account of yourselves," Captain Burgh exclaimed; "but while I am talking you are fasting. Here is a bottle of wine, a cold chicken, and a manchet of bread which I put in my wallet on starting; let us breakfast, for though I do not pretend to have been fasting as you have, the morning ride has given me an appetite. I see your fellows are hard at work already on the viands which my orderly brought for them in his havresack; but first let us move away to the tree over yonder, for verily the scent of blood and of roasted flesh is enough to take away one's appetite, little squeamish as these wars have taught us to be."

Captain Burgh asked no questions until Malcolm had finished his meal. "I have plenty more food," he said, "for we have brought three led horses well laden; but it were better that you eat no more at present, tis ill overloading a fasting stomach. My men will not be back from the pursuit for a couple of hours yet, for they will not draw rein so long as their horses can gallop, so excited are they over the tales of the horrible cruelties which have been perpetrated on all our men who have fallen into the hands of the peasants, so now you can tell me in full the tale of your adventures. I had no time to ask any questions of your sergeant, for we were called up and sent off five minutes after he arrived with the news that you with three men were beleaguered here by a party of peasants."

Malcolm related the whole incidents which had befallen him

since he had been suddenly felled and made captive by the women in the hut in the village. The Swede laughed over this part of the adventure.

"To think," he said, "of you, a dashing captain of the Green Brigade, being made captive by a couple of old women. There is more than one gallant Scot, if reports be true, has fallen a captive to German maidens, but of another sort; to be taken prisoner and hid in a straw yard is too good."

"It was no laughing matter, I can tell you," Malcolm said, "though doubtless it will serve as a standing jest against me for a long time; however, I am so thankful I have got out of the scrape that those may laugh who will."

When Malcolm finished his story Captain Burgh said: "You have managed marvellously well indeed, Graheme, and can well afford to put up with a little laughter anent that matter of the women, for in truth there are few who would with three men have held a post against four or five hundred, as you have done—ay, and fairly defeated them before I came on the scene. That thought of yours of laying the door upon the stairs was a masterly one, and you rarely met and defeated every device of the enemy.

"Now, if you will, I will mount this stronghold of yours with you, and see exactly how it stands, for I shall have to tell the tale a score of times at least when I get back to camp, and I can do it all the better after I have seen for myself the various features of the place."

By the time they had mounted the top of the tower and Captain Burgh had fully satisfied himself as to the details of the defence the troopers began to return. Their horses were far too fatigued with the long ride from the camp and the subsequent pursuit to be able to travel farther. Fires were accordingly lit, rations distributed, and a halt ordered till the following morning, when, at daybreak, they returned to the Lech.

Two days later Malcolm and his men marched forward with a brigade which was advancing to reinforce the army under Gustavus, and reached Ingolstadt on the day when the king raised the siege, and accompanied him on his march to Munich.

Malcolm on rejoining was greeted with great pleasure by his comrades, who had made up their minds that he had in some way fallen a victim to the peasants. The noncommissioned officers and men of his party had been severely reprimanded for leaving the village without finding him. In their defence they declared that they had searched every house and shed, and, having found no sign of him, or of any struggle having taken place, they supposed that he must have returned alone. But their excuses were not held to be valid, the idea of Malcolm having left his men without orders being so preposterous that it was held it should never have been entertained for a moment by them.

"I shall never be anxious about you again," Nigel Graheme said, when Malcolm finished the narrative of his adventures to the officers of his regiment as they sat round the campfire on the evening when he rejoined them. "This is the third or fourth time that I have given you up for dead. Whatever happens in the future, I shall refuse to believe the possibility of any harm having come to you, and shall be sure that sooner or later you will walk quietly into camp with a fresh batch of adventures to tell us. Whoever of us may be doomed to lay our bones in this German soil, it will not be you. Some good fairy has distinctly taken charge of you, and there is no saying what brilliant destiny may await you."

"But he must keep clear of the petticoats, Graheme," Colonel Munro laughed; "evidently danger lurks for him there, and if he is caught napping again some Delilah will assuredly crop the hair of this young Samson of ours."

"There was not much of Delilah in that fury who felled me with a mallet, colonel," Malcolm laughed; "however, I will be careful in future, and will not give them a chance."

"Ah! it may come in another form next time, Malcolm," Munro said; "this time it was an old woman, next time it may be a young one. Beware, my boy! they are far the most dangerous, innocent though they may look."

A laugh ran round the circle.

"Forewarned forearmed, colonel," Malcolm said sturdily, "I will be on my guard against every female creature, young or old, in future. But I don't think that in this affair the woman has had much to boast about—she and her friends had best have left me alone."

"That is so, Malcolm," the colonel said warmly. "You have borne yourself well and bravely, and you have got an old head on those young shoulders of yours. You are as full of plans and stratagems as if you had been a campaigner for the last half century; and no man, even in the Green Brigade, no, not Hepburn himself, could have held that church tower more ably than you did. It will be a good tale to tell the king as we ride on the march tomorrow, for he loves a gallant deed, and the more so when there is prudence and good strategy as well as bravery. He has more than once asked if you have been getting into any new adventures, and seemed almost surprised when I told him that you were doing your duty with your company. He evidently regards it as your special mission to get into harebrained scrapes. He regards you, in fact, as a pedagogue might view the pickle of the school."

There was a general laugh at Malcolm's expense.

"I don't know how it is I am always getting into scrapes," the lad said half ruefully when the laugh subsided. "I am sure I don't want to get into them, colonel, and really I have never gone out of my way to do so, unless you call my march to help the Count of Mansfeld going out of my way. All the other things have come to me without any fault of my own."

"Quite so, Graheme," the colonel said smiling; "that's always the excuse of the boy who gets into scrapes. The question is, Why do these things always happen to you and to nobody else? If you can explain that your whole case is made out. But don't take it seriously, Malcolm," he continued, seeing that the lad looked really crestfallen.

"You know I am only laughing, and there is not a man here, including myself, who does not envy you a little for the numerous adventures which have fallen to your lot, and for the courage and wisdom which you have shown in extricating yourself from them."

"And now, please, will you tell me, colonel," Malcolm said more cheerfully, "why we are turning our backs upon Ingolstadt and are marching away without taking it? I have been away for ten days, you know, and it is a mystery to me why we are leaving the only enemy between us and Vienna, after having beaten him so heartily a fortnight since, without making an effort to rout him thoroughly."

"Maximilian's position is a very strong one, my lad, and covered as he is by the guns of Ingolstadt it would be even a harder task to dislodge him than it was to cross the Lech in his teeth. But you are wrong; his is not the only army which stands between us and Vienna. No sooner is old Tilly dead than a greater than Tilly appears to oppose us. Wallenstein is in the field again. It has been known that he has for some time been negotiating with the emperor, who has been imploring him to forgive the slight that was passed upon him before, and to again take the field.

"Wallenstein, knowing that the game was in his hands, and that the emperor must finally agree to any terms which he chose to dictate, has, while he has been negotiating, been collecting an army; and when the emperor finally agreed to his conditions, that he was at the conclusion of the peace to be assured a royal title and the fief of a sovereign state, he had an army ready to his hand, and is now on the point of entering Bohemia with 40,000 men."

"What his plans may be we cannot yet say, but at any rate it would not do to be delaying here and leaving Germany open to Wallenstein to operate as he will. It was a stern day at Leipzig, but, mark my words, it will be sterner still when we meet Wallenstein; for, great captain as Tilly undoubtedly was, Wallenstein is far greater, and Europe will hold its breath when Gustavus and he, the two greatest captains of the age, meet in a pitched battle."

At Munich the regiments of Munro and Spynie were quartered in the magnificent Electoral Palace, where they fared sumptuously and enjoyed not a little their comfortable quarters and the stores of old wines in the cellar. Sir John Hepburn was appointed military governor of Munich.

In the arsenal armour, arms, and clothing sufficient for 10,000 infantry were found, and a hundred and forty pieces of cannon were discovered buried beneath the floors of the palace. Their carriages were ready in the arsenal, and they were soon put in order for battle. For three weeks the army remained at Munich, Gustavus waiting to see what course Wallenstein was taking. The Imperialist general had entered Bohemia, had driven thence, with scarcely an effort, Arnheim and the Saxons, and formed a junction near Eger with the remnants of the army which had been beaten on the Lech; then, leaving a strong garrison in Ratisbon, he had marched on with an army of sixty thousand men.

He saw that his best plan to force Gustavus to loose his hold of Bavaria was to march on some important point lying between him and North Germany. He therefore selected a place which Gustavus could not abandon, and so would be obliged to leave Bavaria garrisoned only by a force insufficient to withstand the attacks of Pappenheim, who had collected a considerable army for the recovery of the territories of Maximilian. Such a point was Nuremberg, the greatest and strongest of the free cities, and which had been the first to open its gates to Gustavus. The Swedish king could hardly abandon this friendly city to the assaults of the Imperialists, and indeed its fall would have been followed by the general defection from his cause of all that part of Germany, and he would have found himself isolated and cut off from the North.

As soon as Gustavus perceived that Nuremberg was the point towards which Wallenstein was moving, he hastened at once from Munich to the assistance of the threatened city. The forces at his disposal had been weakened by the despatch of Marshal Horn to the Lower Palatinate, and by the garrisons left in the Bavarian cities, and he had but 17,000 men disposable to meet the 60,000 with whom Wallenstein was advancing. He did not hesitate, however, but sent off messengers at once to direct the corps in Swabia under General Banner, Prince William of Weimar, and General Ruthven, to join him, if possible, before Nuremberg.

Marching with all haste he arrived at Nuremberg before Wallenstein reached it, and prepared at once for the defence of the city. He first called together the principal citizens of Nuremberg and explained to them his position. He showed them that were he to fall back with his army he should be able to effect a junction with the troops under his generals, and would ere long be in a position to offer battle to Wallenstein upon more equal terms, but that were he to do so he would be forced to abandon the city to the vengeance of the Imperialists. He told them that did he remain before the city he must to a great extent be dependent upon them for food and supplies, as he would be beleaguered by Wallenstein, and should be unable to draw food and forage from the surrounding country; he could therefore only maintain himself by the aid of the cordial goodwill and assistance of the citizens.

The people of Nuremberg were true to the side they had chosen, and placed the whole of their resources at his disposal. Gustavus at once set his army to work to form a position in which he could confront the overwhelming forces of the enemy. Round the city, at a distance of about thirteen hundred yards from it, he dug a ditch, nowhere less than twelve feet wide and eight deep, but, where most exposed to an attack, eighteen feet wide and twelve deep. Within the circuit of this ditch he erected eight large forts and connected them with a long and thick earthen parapet strengthened with bastions. On the ramparts and forts three hundred cannon, for the most part supplied by the city of Nuremberg, were placed in position. As the camp between the ramparts and the town was traversed by the river Pegnitz numerous bridges were thrown across it, so that the whole force could concentrate on either side in case of attack. So vigorously did the army, assisted by the citizens, labour at these works, that they were completed in fourteen days after Gustavus reached Nuremberg.

It was on the 19th of June that the Swedish army arrived there, and on the 30th Wallenstein and Maximilian of Bavaria appeared before it with the intention of making an immediate assault. The works, however, although not yet quite completed, were so formidable that Wallenstein saw at once that the success of an assault upon them would be extremely doubtful, and, in spite of the earnest entreaties of Maximilian to lead his army to the assault, he decided to reduce the place by starvation. This method appeared at once easy and certain. The whole of the surrounding country belonged to the Bishop of Bamberg, who was devoted to the Imperialist cause, and he possessed all the towns, and strong places in the circle of country around Nuremberg. Wallenstein had brought with him vast stores of provisions, and could draw upon the surrounding country for the further maintenance of his army. It was only necessary then to place himself in a position where the Swedes could not attack him with a hope of success.

Such a position lay at a distance of three miles from Nuremberg, where there was a wooded hill known as the Alte Veste. Round this Wallenstein threw up a circle of defences, consisting of a ditch behind which was an interlacement of forest trees, baggage wagons, and gabions, forming an almost insurpassable obstacle to an attacking force. Within this circle he encamped his army, formed into eight divisions, each about seven thousand strong, while two considerable bodies of troops in the diocese of Bamberg and the Upper Palatinate prepared to oppose any forces approaching to the aid of Nuremberg, and the Croats, horse and foot, scoured the country day and night to prevent any supplies entering the city. Having thus adopted every means for starving out the beleaguered army and city, Wallenstein calmly awaited the result.

CHAPTER XVI

THE SIEGE OF NUREMBERG

Drearily passed the days in the beleaguered camp, varied only by an occasional raid by small parties to drive in cattle from the surrounding country, or to intercept convoys of provisions on their way to the Imperialists' camp. So active and watchful were the Croats that these enterprises seldom succeeded, although, to enable his men to move with celerity, Gustavus mounted bodies of infantry on horseback. Thus they were enabled to get over the ground quickly, and if attacked they dismounted and fought on foot.

To these mounted infantry the name of dragoons was given, and so useful were they found that the institution was adopted in other armies, and dragoons became a recognized portion of every military force. In time the custom of dismounting and fighting on foot was gradually abandoned, and dragoons became regular cavalry; but in modern times the utility of Gustavus's invention of mounted infantry has been again recognized, and in all the small wars in which England has been engaged bodies of mounted infantry have been organized. Ere long mounted infantry will again become a recognized arm of the service.

But these raids in search of provisions occupied but a small portion of the army. The rest passed their time in enforced idleness. There was nothing to be done save to clean and furbish their arms and armour; to stand on the ramparts and gaze on the distant heights of the Alte Veste, to watch the solid columns of the Imperial army, which from time to time Wallenstein marched down from his stronghold and paraded in order of battle, as a challenge to the Swedes to come out and fight, or to loiter through the narrow streets of Nuremberg, and to talk to the citizens, whose trade and commerce were now entirely at a standstill. Malcolm, with the restlessness of youth, seldom stayed many hours quiet in camp. He did not care either for drinking or gambling; nor could he imitate the passive tranquillity of the old soldiers, who were content to sleep away the greater part of their time. He therefore spent many hours every day in the city, where he speedily made many acquaintances.

In the city of Nuremberg time dragged as slowly as it did in the camp. At ordinary times the centre of a quiet and busy trade, the city was now cut off from the world. The shops were for the most part closed; the artisans stood idle in the streets, and the townsfolk had nought to do, save to gather in groups and discuss the times, or to take occasional excursions beyond the gates into the camp of their allies. The advances then of the young Scottish officer were willingly responded to, and he soon became intimate in the houses of all the principal citizens; and while the greater part of his comrades spent their evenings in drinking and gambling, he enjoyed the hours in conversation and music in the houses of the citizens of Nuremberg.

The long inaction brought its moral consequences, and the troops became demoralized and insubordinate from their enforced idleness. Plundering and acts of violence became so common that Gustavus was obliged to issue the most stringent ordinances to restore discipline; and an officer and many men had to be executed before the spirit of insubordination was quelled. In order to pass some of the hours of the days Malcolm obtained leave from one of the great clockmakers of the town—for Nuremberg was at that time the centre of the craft of clockmaking—to allow him to work in his shop, and to learn the mysteries of his trade.

Most of the establishments were closed, but Malcolm's acquaintance was one of the wealthiest of the citizens, and was able to keep his craftsmen at work, and to store the goods he manufactured until better times should return. Malcolm began the work purely to occupy his time, but he presently came to take a lively interest in it, and was soon able to take to pieces and put together again the cumbrous but simple machines which constituted the clocks of the period.

Workshops were not in those days factories. The master of a craft worked, surrounded by his craftsmen and apprentices. Every wheel and spring were made upon the premises, fashioned and finished with chisel and file; and there was an interest in the work far beyond any which it possesses in the present day, when watches are turned out wholesale, the separate parts being prepared by machinery, and the work of the artisan consisting solely in the finishing and putting them together.

Laying aside his armour and gay attire, and donning a workman's apron, Malcolm sat at the bench by the side of the master, shaping and filing, and listening to his stories connected with the trade and history of Nuremberg. He anticipated no advantage from the knowledge he was gaining, but regarded it simply as a pleasant way of getting through a portion of the day.

Thus for three months the armies confronted each other. Provisions were becoming terribly scarce, the magazines of the city

150

were emptying fast, and although working night and day, the mills of the place did not suffice to grind flour for the needs of so many mouths. The population of the city itself was greatly swollen by the crowds of Protestant fugitives who had fled there for refuge on the approach of the Imperialists, and the magazines of the city dwindled fast under the demands made upon them by this addition, and that of the Swedish army, to the normal population. Fever broke out in the city and camp. The waters of the Pegnitz were tainted by the carcasses of dead horses and other animals. The supplies of forage had long since been exhausted, and the baggage and troop animals died in vast numbers.

Still there was no sign of a change. Wallenstein would not attack, Gustavus could not. The Swedish king waited to take advantage of some false move on the part of the Imperial commander; but Wallenstein was as great a general as himself, and afforded him no opening, turning a deaf ear to the entreaties and importunities of Maximilian that he would end the tedious siege by an attack upon the small and enfeebled army around Nuremberg.

All this time Gustavus was in constant communication with his generals outside, his messengers making their way by speed or stratagem through the beleaguering Croats, and kept up the spirits of his men by daily reviews and by the cheerful countenance which he always wore.

The Swedish columns were gradually closing in towards Nuremberg. One was led by the chancellor Oxenstiern, to whom had been committed the care of the Middle Rhine and the Lower Palatinate, where he had been confronted by the Spanish troops under Don Philip de Sylva.

On the 11th July, leaving Horn with a small force to oppose the Spaniards, the chancellor set out to join his master. On the way he effected a junction with the forces of the Landgrave of Hesse-Cassel. This general had been opposed in Westphalia by Pappenheim, but he seized the opportunity when the latter had marched to relieve Maestricht, which was besieged by Frederic of Nassau, to march away and join Oxenstiern.

The Scotch officers Ballandine and Alexander Hamilton were with their regiment in the Duchy of Magdeburg. When the news of the king's danger reached them without waiting for instructions they marched to Halle and joining a portion of the division of the Duke of Saxe-Weimar, to which they were attached, pushed on to Zeitz, and were there joined by the duke himself, who had hurried on from the Lake of Constance, attended only by his guards, but, picking up five Saxon regiments in Franconia. Together they passed

151

on to Wurtzburg, where they joined Oxenstiern and the Landgrave of Hesse-Cassel. General Banner, with the fourth corps, was at Augsburg, opposed to Cratz, who was at the head of the remains of Tilly's old army.

Slipping away from his foes he marched to Windsheim, and was there joined by a body of troops under Bernhard of Weimar. The force from Wurtzburg soon afterwards came up, and the whole of the detached corps, amounting to 49,000 men, being now collected, they marched to Bruck, ten miles north of Nuremberg. Three days later, on the 16th of August, Gustavus rode into their camp, and on the 21st marched at their head into Nuremberg, unhindered by the Imperialists.

Gustavus probably calculated that the Imperialists would now move down and offer battle; but Wallenstein, who had detached 10,000 men to bring up supplies, could not place in the field a number equal to those of the reinforcements, and preferred to await an attack in the position which he had prepared with such care. He knew the straits to which Nuremberg and its defenders were reduced, and the impossibility there would be of feeding the new arrivals.

The country round for a vast distance had been long since stripped of provisions, and Gustavus had no course open to him but to march away with his army and leave the city to its fate, or to attack the Imperialists in their stronghold.

On the day after his arrival, the 21st of August, Gustavus marched out and opened a cannonade upon the Imperialists' position, in order to induce Wallenstein to come down and give battle. Wallenstein was not, however, to be tempted, but kept his whole army busy with the spade and axe further intrenching his position. The next day the king brought his guns nearer to the enemy's camp, and for twenty-four hours kept up a heavy fire. The only result, however, was that Wallenstein fell back a few hundred yards on to two ridges, on one of which was the ruined castle called the Alte Veste; the other was known as the Altenburg. The ascent to these was steep and craggy, and they were covered by a thick forest. Here Wallenstein formed in front of his position a threefold barrier of felled trees woven and interlaced with each other, each barrier rising in a semicircle one above the other. Before the Swedish cannon ceased to fire the new position of the Imperialists had been made impregnable.

Unfortunately for Gustavus he had at this moment lost the services of the best officer in his army, Sir John Hepburn, whom he had always regarded as his right hand. The quarrel had arisen from some trifling circumstance, and Gustavus in the heat of the moment made some disparaging allusion to the religion of Hepburn, who was a Catholic and also to that officer's love of dress and finery. The indignant Hepburn at once resigned his commission and swore never again to draw his sword in the service of the king—a resolution to which he adhered, although Gustavus, when his anger cooled, endeavoured in every way to appease the angry soldier.

As he persisted in his resolution Colonel Munro was appointed to the command of the Green Brigade. It is probable that the quarrel was the consummation of a long standing grievance. Hepburn as well as the other Scottish officers had shared the indignation of Sir John Hamilton when the latter resigned in consequence of the Swedish troop being placed in the post of honour at the storm of the castle of Marienburg after the Scots had done all the work. There had, too, been much discontent among them concerning the Marquis of Hamilton, whom they considered that Gustavus had treated ungenerously; and still more concerning Lieutenant Colonel Douglas, whom Gustavus had committed to a common prison for a slight breach of etiquette, a punishment at which the English ambassador, Sir Harry Vane, remonstrated, and which the whole Scottish officers considered an insult to them and their country.

There were probably faults on both sides. The Scottish troops were the backbone of the Swedish army, and to them were principally due almost the whole of the successes which Gustavus had gained. Doubtless they presumed upon the fact, and although Gustavus recognized his obligations, as is shown by the immense number of commands and governorships which he bestowed upon his Scottish officers, he may well have been angered and irritated by the insistance with which they asserted their claims and services. It was, however, a most unfortunate circumstance that just at this critical moment he should have lost the services of an officer whose prudence was equal to his daring, and who was unquestionably one of the greatest military leaders of his age.

It is probable that had Hepburn remained by his side the king would not have undertaken the attack upon the impregnable position of the Imperialists. Deprived of the counsellor upon whose advice he had hitherto invariably relied, Gustavus determined to attempt to drive Wallenstein from his position, the decision being finally induced by a ruse of the Imperialist commander, who desired nothing so much as that the Swedes should dash their forces against the terrible position he had prepared for them. Accordingly on the 24th of August he directed a considerable portion of his force to march away from the rear of his position as if, alarmed at the superior strength of the Swedes, he had determined to abandon the heights he had so long occupied and to march away.

Gustavus fell into the trap, and prepared at once to assault the position. Two hundred pieces of artillery heralded the advance, which was made by the whole body of the musketeers of the army, drafted from the several brigades and divided into battalions 500 strong, each commanded by a colonel. It was a terrible position which they were advancing to storm. Each of the lines of intrenchments was surmounted by rows of polished helmets, while pikes and arquebuses glittered in the sunshine; but it was not long that the scene was visible, for as the battalions approached the foot of the Altenburg 80 pieces of artillery opened from its summit and from the ridge of the Alte Veste, while the smoke of the arquebuses drifted up in a cloud from the lines of intrenchments.

Steadily and in good order the Scotch and Swedish infantry pressed forward, and forcing the lower ditch strove to climb the rocky heights; but in vain did they strive. Over and over again they reached the intrenchments, but were unable to force their way through the thickly bound fallen trees, while their lines were torn with a storm of iron and lead. Never did the Scottish soldiers of Gustavus fight with greater desperation and valour. Scores of them rolled lifeless down the slope, but fresh men took their places and strove to hack their way through the impenetrable screen through which the Imperialist bullets whistled like hail.

At last, when nigh half their number had fallen, the rest, exhausted, broken, and in disorder, fell suddenly back. Gustavus in person then led on his Finlanders, but these, after a struggle as obstinate and heroic as that of their predecessors, in their turn fell back baffled. The Livonians next made the attempt, but in vain.

In the meantime a sharp conflict had taken place between the Imperial cavalry and the Swedish left wing. Wallenstein's cuirassiers, hidden by the smoke, charged right through a column of Swedish infantry; but this success was counterbalanced by the rout of Cronenberg's Invincibles, a magnificent regiment of 1500 horsemen, by 200 Finland troopers. The troops of Duke Bernhard of Weimar, among whom were still the Scottish regiments of Hamilton and Douglas, marched against the heights which commanded the Alte Veste, and drove back the Imperialists with great loss. Five hundred musketeers of the Green Brigade under Colonel Munro then pushed gallantly forward and posted themselves far in advance, resisting all attempts of the Imperialists to drive them back, until Lieutenant Colonel Sinclair, who was now in command of Munro's own regiment, brought it forward to his assistance. Until the next morning this body of one thousand men maintained the ground they had won in spite of all the efforts of the Imperialists to dislodge them.

Colonel Munro was severely wounded in the left side. Lieutenant Colonel Maken, Capt. Innis, and Capt. Traill were killed, and an immense number of other Scottish officers were killed and wounded. The news was brought down to Gustavus of the advantage gained by Duke Bernhard, but he was unable to take advantage of it by moving his army round to that position, as he would have exposed himself to a counter attack of the enemy while doing so. He therefore launched a fresh column of attack against the Alte Veste.

This was followed by another and yet another, until every regiment in the army had in its turn attempted to storm the position, but still without success.

The battle had now raged for ten hours, and nightfall put an end to the struggle. Hepburn had all day ridden behind the king as a simple cavalier, and had twice carried messages through the thick of the fire when there were no others to bear them, so great had been the slaughter round the person of the king.

It was the first time that Gustavus had been repulsed, and he could hardly yet realize the fact; but as messenger after messenger came in from the different divisions he discovered how terrible had been his loss. Most of his generals and superior officers had been killed or wounded, 2000 men lay dead on the field, and there were nigh three times that number of wounded.

The Imperialists on their side lost 1000 killed and 1500 wounded; but the accounts of the losses on both sides differ greatly, some placing the Imperial loss higher than that of the Swedes, a palpably absurd estimate, as the Imperialists, fighting behind shelter, could not have suffered anything like so heavily as their assailants, who were exposed to their fire in the open.

Hepburn bore the order from the king for Munro's troops and those of Duke Bernhard to retire from the position they had won, as they were entirely cut off from the rest of the army, and would at daylight have had the whole of the Imperialists upon them. The service was one of great danger, and Hepburn had to cut his way sword in hand through the Croats who intervened between him and his comrades of the Green Brigade. He accomplished his task in safety, and before daylight Munro's men and the regiments of Duke Bernhard rejoined the army in the plain. But though repulsed

Gustavus was not defeated. He took up a new position just out of cannon shot of the Altenburg, and then offered battle to Wallenstein, the latter, however, well satisfied with his success, remained firm in his policy of starving out the enemy, and resisted every device of the king to turn him from his stronghold.

For fourteen days Gustavus remained in position. Then he could hold out no longer. The supplies were entirely exhausted. The summer had been unusually hot. The shrunken waters of the Pegnitz were putrid and stinking, the carcasses of dead horses poisoned the air, and fever and pestilence raged in the camp. Leaving, then, Kniphausen with eight thousand men to aid the citizens of Nuremberg to defend the city should Wallenstein besiege it, Gustavus marched on the 8th of September by way of Neustadt to Windsheim, and there halted to watch the further movements of the enemy.

Five days later Wallenstein quitted his camp and marched to Forsheim. So far the advantage of the campaign lay with him. His patience and iron resolution had given the first check to the victorious career of the Lion of the North.

Munro's regiment, as it was still called—for he was now its full colonel, although Lieutenant Colonel Sinclair commanded it in the field—had suffered terribly, but less, perhaps, than some of those who had in vain attempted to force their way up the slopes of the Alte Veste; and many an eye grew moist as at daybreak the regiment marched into its place in the ranks of the brigade and saw how terrible had been the slaughter among them. Munro's soldiers had had but little of that hand to hand fighting in which men's blood becomes heated and all thought of danger is lost in the fierce desire to kill. Their losses had been caused by the storm of cannonball and bullet which had swept through them, as, panting and breathless, they struggled up the steep slopes, incapable of answering the fire of the enemy. They had had their triumph, indeed, as the Imperial regiments broke and fled before their advance; but although proud that they at least had succeeded in a day when failure was general, there was not a man but regretted that he had not come within push of pike of the enemy.

Malcolm Graheme had passed scatheless through the fray—a good fortune that had attended but few of his brother officers. His uncle was badly wounded, and several of his friends had fallen. Of the men who had marched from Denmark but a year before scarce a third remained in the ranks, and although the regiment had been strengthened by the breaking up of two or three of the weaker battalions and their incorporation with the other Scottish regiments, it was now less than half its former strength. While Gustavus and Wallenstein had been facing each other at Nuremberg the war had continued without interruption in other parts, and the Swedes and their allies had gained advantages everywhere except in Westphalia and Lower Saxony, where Pappenheim had more than held his own against Baudissen, who commanded for Gustavus; and although Wallenstein had checked the king he had gained no material advantages and had wrested no single town or fortress from his hands. Gustavus was still in Bavaria, nearer to Munich than he was, his garrisons still holding Ulm, Nordlingen, and Donauworth, its strongest fortresses.

He felt sure, however, that it would be impossible for Gustavus to maintain at one spot the army which he had at Windsheim, and that with so many points to defend he would soon break it up into separate commands. He resolved then to wait until he did so, and then to sweep down upon Northern Germany, and so by threatening the king's line of retreat to force him to abandon Bavaria and the south and to march to meet him.

At present he was in no position to risk a battle, for he had already detached 4000 men to reinforce Holk, whom he had sent with 10,000 to threaten Dresden. The 13,000 Bavarians who were with him under Maximilian had separated from him on his way to Forsheim, and on arriving at that place his army numbered but 17,000 men, while Gustavus had more than 40,000 gathered at Windsheim.

Gustavus, on his part, determined to carry out his former projects, to march against Ingolstadt, which he had before failed to capture, and thence to penetrate into Upper Austria. But fearful lest Wallenstein, released from his presence, should attempt to recover the fortresses in Franconia, he despatched half his force under Duke Bernhard to prevent the Imperial general from crossing the Rhine. Could he succeed in doing this he would be in a position to dictate terms to the emperor in Vienna.

On the 12th of October he reached Neuberg, on the Danube, and halted there, awaiting the arrival of his siege train from Donauworth. While making the most vigorous exertions to press on the necessary arrangements for his march against Vienna he received the most urgent messages to return to Saxony. Not only, as he was told, had Wallenstein penetrated into that province, but he was employing all his influence to detach its elector from the Protestant cause, and there was great fear that the weak prince would yield to the solicitations of Wallenstein and to his own jealousy of the King of Sweden.

No sooner, in fact, had Gustavus crossed the Danube than Wallenstein moved towards Schweinfurt, and by so doing drew to that place the Swedish army under the command of Duke Bernhard. He then suddenly marched eastward at full speed, capturing Bamberg, Baireuth, and Culmbach, and pushed on to Colberg.

The town was captured, but the Swedish Colonel Dubatel, who was really a Scotchman, by name M'Dougal, a gallant and brilliant officer, threw himself with his dragoons into the castle, which commanded the town, and defended it so resolutely against the assaults of Wallenstein that Duke Bernhard had time to march to within twenty miles of the place. Wallenstein then raised the siege, marched east to Kronach, and then north to Weida, on the Elster. Thence he pressed on direct to Leipzig, which he besieged at once; and while the main body of his troops were engaged before the city, others took possession of the surrounding towns and fortresses.

Leipzig held out for only two days, and after its capture Wallenstein marched to Merseburg, where he was joined by the army under Pappenheim. Thus reinforced he was in a position to capture the whole of Saxony. The elector, timid and vacillating, was fully conscious of his danger and the solicitations of Wallenstein to break off from his alliance with the King of Sweden and to join the Imperialists were strongly seconded by Marshal Von Arnheim, his most trusted councillor, who was an intimate friend of the Imperialist general.

It was indeed a hard decision which Gustavus was called upon to make. On the one hand Vienna lay almost within his grasp, for Wallenstein was now too far north to interpose between him and the capital. On the other hand, should the Elector of Saxony join the Imperialists, his position after the capture of Vienna would be perilous in the extreme. The emperor would probably leave his capital before he arrived there, and the conquest would, therefore, be a barren one. Gustavus reluctantly determined to abandon his plan, and to march to the assistance of Saxony.

CHAPTER XVII

THE DEATH OF GUSTAVUS

The determination of Gustavus to march to the assistance of Saxony once taken, he lost not a moment in carrying it into effect. General Banner, whom he greatly trusted, was unfortunately suffering from a wound, and until he should recover he appointed the Prince Palatine of Burkenfeldt to command a corps 12,000 strong which he determined to leave on the Danube; then strengthening the garrisons of Augsburg, Rain, and Donauworth, he set out with the remainder of his army on his march to Saxony.

From Donauworth he marched to Nuremberg, stayed there forty-eight hours to recover the fortress of Lauf, and, having forced the garrison of that place to surrender at discretion, pushed on with all possible speed to Erfurt, which he had fixed upon as the point of junction for his several corps. The Green Brigade formed a portion of the force which Gustavus left behind him in Bavaria under the Prince Palatine. So terribly weakened were the Scottish regiments by the various battles of the campaign, in all of which they had borne the brunt of the fighting, that Gustavus determined reluctantly to leave them behind for rest and reorganization.

Hepburn, Sir James Hamilton, Sir James Ramsay, and the Marquis of Hamilton, who like Hepburn had quarrelled with Gustavus, left the Swedish army the day after they arrived at Neustadt, after marching away from Nuremberg. All the Scottish officers in the Swedish army accompanied Hepburn and his three companions along the road for a long German mile from Neustadt, and then parted with great grief from the gallant cavalier who had led them so often to victory.

Malcolm Graheme did not remain behind in Bavaria with his comrades of the Green Brigade. Gustavus, who had taken a great fancy to the young Scotch officer, whose spirit of adventure and daring were in strong harmony with his own character, appointed him to ride on his own personal staff. Although he parted with regret from his comrades, Malcolm was glad to accompany the king on his northward march, for there was no probability of any very active service in Bavaria, and it was certain that a desperate battle would be fought when Gustavus and Wallenstein met face to face in the open field.

At Erfurt Gustavus was joined by Duke Bernhard of Saxe-Weimar with his force, which raised his army to a strength of

20,000. The news of his approach had again revived the courage of the Elector of Saxony, who had occupied the only towns where the Elbe could be crossed, Dresden, Torgau, and Wittenberg—he himself, with his main army of 15,000 men, lying at Torgau. From him Gustavus learned that the Imperial army was divided into three chief corps—that of Wallenstein 12,000 strong, that of Pappenheim 10,000, those of Gallas and Holk united 16,000, making a total of 38,000 men.

So great was the speed with which Gustavus had marched to Erfurt that Wallenstein had received no notice of his approach; and believing that for some time to come he should meet with no serious opposition, he had on the very day after the Swedes reached Erfurt despatched Gallas with 12,000 men into Bohemia. A division of his troops was at the same time threatening Naumburg, whose possession would enable him to block the only easy road with which Gustavus could enter the country held by him.

But Gustavus at Erfurt learned that Naumburg had not yet fallen, and marching with great rapidity reached the neighbourhood of that town before the Imperialists were aware that he had quitted Erfurt, and cutting up a small detachment of the enemy who lay in his way, entered the town and at once began to intrench it. Wallenstein first learned from the fugitives of the beaten detachment that Gustavus had arrived at Naumburg, but as his own position lay almost centrally between Naumburg and Torgau, so long as he could prevent the Swedes and Saxons from uniting, he felt safe; for although together they would outnumber him, he was superior in strength to either if alone. The Imperialist general believed that Gustavus intended to pass the winter at Naumburg, and he had therefore no fear of an immediate attack.

In order to extend the area from which he could draw his supplies Wallenstein despatched Pappenheim to secure the fortress of Halle; for although that town had been captured the fortress held out, and barred the main road to the north. From Halle Pappenheim was to proceed to the relief of Cologne, which was menaced by the enemy.

Having done this, Wallenstein withdrew from the line of the Saale and prepared to distribute his army in winter quarters in the towns of the district, he himself with a portion of the force occupying the little town of Lutzen. But Gustavus had no idea of taking up his quarters for the winter at Naumburg; and he proposed to the Elector of Saxony that if he would march to Eilenberg, midway to Leipzig, he himself would make a detour to the south round Wallenstein's position and join him there. Without waiting to receive the answer of the elector, Gustavus, leaving a garrison in

Naumburg, set out at one o'clock in the morning on the 5th of November on his march; but before he had proceeded nine miles he learned from a number of gentlemen and peasants favourable to the cause that Pappenheim had started for Halle, that the remainder of the Imperial army lay dispersed among the towns and villages of the neighbourhood, and that Wallenstein himself was at Lutzen.

Gustavus called his generals together and informed them of the news. Learning that Lutzen was but five miles distant—as it turned out, a mistaken piece of information, as it was nearly twice as far—he ordered that the men should take some food, and then wheeling to the left, push on towards Lutzen.

It was not until some time later that Wallenstein learned from the Imperial scouts that Gustavus was upon him. It was then nearly five o'clock in the evening, and darkness was at hand. Considering the heavy state of the roads, and the fact that Gustavus would have in the last three miles of his march to traverse a morass crossed by a bridge over which only two persons could pass abreast, he felt confident that the attack could not be made until the following morning.

Mounted messengers were sent in all directions to bring up his troops from the villages in which they were posted, and in the meantime the troops stationed around Lutzen were employed in preparing obstacles to hinder the advance of the Swedes. On either side of the roads was a low swampy country intersected with ditches, and Wallenstein at once set his men to work to widen and deepen these ditches, which the troops as they arrived on the ground were to occupy. All night the troops laboured at this task.

In the meantime Gustavus had found the distance longer and the difficulties greater than he had anticipated; the roads were so heavy that it was with difficulty that the artillery and ammunition wagons could be dragged along them, and the delay caused by the passage of the morass was very great.

Indeed the passage would have been scarcely possible had the men of an Imperial regiment of cuirassiers and a battalion of Croats, who were posted in a village on the further side of the morass, defended it; but instead of doing so they fell back to an eminence in the rear of the village, and remained there quietly until, just as the sun set, the whole Swedish army got across. The cuirassiers and Croats were at once attacked and put to flight; but as darkness was now at hand it was impossible for Gustavus to make any further advance, and the army was ordered to bivouac as it stood. The state of the roads had defeated the plans of Gustavus. Instead of taking the enemy by surprise, as he had hoped, and falling upon them scattered and disunited, the delays which had occurred had given Wallenstein time to bring up all his forces, and at daybreak Gustavus would be confronted by a force nearly equal to his own, and occupying a position very strongly defended by natural obstacles.

Before the day was won, Pappenheim, for whom Wallenstein would have sent as soon as he heard of the Swedish advance, might be on the field, and in that case the Imperialists would not only have the advantage of position but also that of numbers. It was an anxious night, and Gustavus spent the greater part of it in conversation with his generals, especially Kniphausen and Duke Bernhard.

The former strongly urged that the army should repass the morass and march, as originally intended, to effect a junction with the Saxons. He pointed out that the troops were fatigued with their long and weary march during the day, and would have to fight without food, as it had been found impossible to bring up the wagons with the supplies; he particularly urged the point that Pappenheim would arrive on the field before the victory could be won. But Gustavus was of opinion that the disadvantages of retreat were greater than those of action. The troops, hungry, weary, and dispirited, would be attacked as they retired, and he believed that by beginning the action early the Imperialists could be defeated before Pappenheim could return from Halle.

Gustavus proposed to move forward at two o'clock in the morning; but fate was upon this occasion against the great Swedish leader. Just as on the previous day the expected length of the march and the heavy state of the roads had prevented him from crushing Wallenstein's scattered army, so now a thick fog springing up, making the night so dark that a soldier could not see the man standing next to him, prevented the possibility of movement, and instead of marching at two o'clock in the morning it was nine before the sun cleared away the fog sufficiently to enable the army to advance. Then, after addressing a few stirring words to his men, Gustavus ordered the advance towards Chursitz, the village in front of them.

The king himself led the right wing, consisting of six regiments of Swedes, supported by musketeers intermingled with cavalry. The left, composed of cavalry and infantry intermixed, was commanded by Duke Bernhard. The centre, consisting of four brigades of infantry supported by the Scottish regiments under Henderson, was commanded by Nicholas Brahe, Count of Weissenburg.

The reserves behind each of these divisions were formed entirely of cavalry, commanded on the right by Bulach, in the centre by Kniphausen, and on the left by Ernest, Prince of Anhalt. The field pieces, twenty in number, were disposed to the best advantage between the wings. Franz Albert of Lauenburg, who had joined the army the day before, rode by the king. A short halt was made at Chursitz, where the baggage was left behind, and the army then advanced against the Imperialists, who at once opened fire.

Wallenstein had posted his left so as to be covered by a canal, while his right was protected by the village of Lutzen. On some rising ground to the left of that village, where there were several windmills, he planted fourteen small pieces of cannon, while to support his front, which was composed of the musketeers in the ditches on either side of the road, he planted a battery of seven heavy pieces of artillery.

The main body of his infantry he formed into four massive brigades, which were flanked on both sides by musketeers intermixed with cavalry. Count Coloredo commanded on the left, Holk on the right, Terzky in the centre.

As the Swedish army advanced beyond Chursitz the seven heavy pieces of artillery on the side of the road opened upon them, doing much execution, while their own lighter guns could not reply effectively. The Swedes pressed forward to come to close quarters. The left wing, led by Duke Bernhard, was the first to arrive upon the scene of action. Gallantly led by the duke his men forced the ditches, cleared the road, charged the deadly battery, killed or drove away the gunners, and rushed with fury on the Imperialist right.

Holk, a resolute commander, tried in vain to stem the assault; the ardour of the Swedes was irresistible, and they scattered, one after the other, his three brigades. The battle seemed already lost when Wallenstein himself took his place at the head of the fourth brigade, and fell upon the Swedes, who were disordered by the rapidity and ardour of their charge, while at the same moment he launched three regiments of cavalry on their flanks.

The Swedes fought heroically but in vain; step by step they were driven back, the battery was recaptured, and the guns, which in the excitement of the advance the captors had omitted to spike, were retaken by the Imperialists.

In the meantime on the right the king had also forced the road, and had driven from the field the Croats and Poles opposed to him, and he was on the point of wheeling his troops to fall on the flank of the Imperialist centre when one of Duke Bernhard's aides-de-camp dashed up with the news that the left wing had fallen back broken and in disorder.

Leaving to Count Stalhaus to continue to press the enemy, Gustavus, accompanied by his staff, rode at full gallop to the left at the head of Steinboch's regiment of dragoons. Arrived on the spot he dashed to the front at a point where his men had not yet been forced back across the road, and riding among them roused them to fresh exertions. By his side were Franz Albert of Lauenberg and a few other followers. But his pace had been so furious that Steinboch's dragoons had not yet arrived. As he urged on his broken men Gustavus was struck in the shoulder by a musketball. He reeled in his saddle, but exclaimed, "It is nothing," and ordered them to charge the enemy with the dragoons. Malcolm Graheme and others on his staff hesitated, but the king exclaimed, "Ride all, the duke will see to me." The cavalry dashed forward, and the king, accompanied only by Franz Albert, Duke of Lauenberg, turned to leave the field, but he had scarcely moved a few paces when he received another shot in the back. Calling out to Franz Albert that it was all over with him, the mortally wounded king fell to the ground.

Franz Albert, believing the battle lost, galloped away; the king's page alone remained with the dying man. A minute later three Austrian cuirassiers rode up, and demanded the name of the dying man. The page Leubelfing refused to give it, and firing their pistols at him they stretched him mortally wounded beside the dying king. Gustavus then, but with difficulty, said who he was. The troopers leapt from their horses and stripped his rich armour from him, and then, as they saw Steinboch's dragoons returning from their charge, they placed their pistols close to the king's head and fired, and then leaping on their horses fled.

Great was the grief when Malcolm, happening to ride near the body, recognized it as that of the king. An instant later a regiment of Imperialist cavalry charged down, and a furious fight took place for some minutes over the king's body. It was, however, at last carried off by the Swedes, so disfigured by wounds and by the trampling of the horses in the fray as to be unrecognizable.

The news of the fall of their king, which spread rapidly through the ranks, so far from discouraging the Swedes, inspired them with a desperate determination to avenge his death, and burning with fury they advanced against the enemy, yet preserving the most perfect steadiness and order in their ranks.

In vain did Wallenstein and his officers strive to stem the attack of the left wing, their bravery and skill availed nothing to arrest that furious charge. Regiment after regiment who strove to bar their way were swept aside, the guns near the windmills were captured and turned against the enemy. Step by step the Imperial right wing was forced back, and the centre was assailed in flank by the guns from the rising ground, while Stalhaus with the right wing of the Swedes attacked them on their left.

Hopeless of victory the Imperialist centre was giving way, when the explosion of one of their powder wagons still further shook them. Attacked on both flanks and in front the Imperialist centre wavered, and in a few minutes would have been in full flight. The Swedish victory seemed assured, when a mighty trampling of horse was heard, and emerging from the smoke Pappenheim with eight regiments of Imperial cavalry dashed into the fray.

Pappenheim had already captured the citadel of Halle when Wallenstein's messenger reached him. To wait until his infantry, who were engaged in plundering, could be collected, and then to proceed at their pace to the field of battle, would be to arrive too late to be of service, and Pappenheim instantly placed himself at the head of his eight regiments of magnificent cavalry, and galloped at full speed to the battlefield eighteen miles distant. On the way he met large numbers of flying Poles and Croats, the remnants of the Austrian left, who had been driven from the field by Gustavus; these he rallied, and with them dashed upon the troops of Stalhaus who were pursuing them, and forced them backward. The relief afforded to the Imperialists by this opportune arrival was immense, and leaving Pappenheim to deal with the Swedish right, Wallenstein rallied his own right on the centre, and opposed a fresh front to the advancing troops of Duke Bernhard and Kniphausen. Inspirited by the arrival of the reinforcements, and burning to turn what had just appeared a defeat into a victory, the Imperialists advanced with such ardour that the Swedes were driven back, the guns on the hills recaptured, and it seemed that in this terrible battle victory was at last to declare itself in favour of the Imperialists.

It needed only the return of Pappenheim from the pursuit of the Swedish right to decide the day, but Pappenheim was not to come. Though driven back by the first impetuous charge of the Imperial cavalry, the Swedes under Stalhaus, reinforced by the Scottish regiments under Henderson, stubbornly opposed their further attacks.

While leading his men forward Pappenheim fell with two musketballs through his body. While lying there the rumour for the first time reached him that Gustavus had been killed. When upon inquiry the truth of the rumour was confirmed, the eyes of the dying man lighted up.

"Tell Wallenstein," he said to the officer nearest to him, "that I am lying here without hope of life, but I die gladly, knowing, as I now know, that the irreconcilable enemy of my faith has fallen on the same day."

The Imperialists, discouraged by the fall of their general, could not withstand the ardour with which the Swedes and Scottish infantry attacked them, and the cavalry rode from the field. Elsewhere the battle was still raging. Wallenstein's right and centre had driven Count Bernhard, the Duke of Brahe, and Kniphausen across that desperately contested road, but beyond this they could not force them, so stubbornly and desperately did they fight. But Stalhaus and his men, refreshed and invigorated by their victory over Pappenheim's force, again came up and took their part in the fight. Wallenstein had no longer a hope of victory, he fought now only to avoid defeat. The sun had already set, and if he could but maintain his position for another half hour darkness would save his army.

He fell back across the road again, fighting stubbornly and in good order, and extending his line to the left to prevent Stalhaus from turning his flank; and in this order the terrible struggle continued till nightfall. Both sides fought with splendid bravery. The Swedes, eager for the victory once again apparently within their grasp, pressed on with fury, while the Imperialists opposed them with the most stubborn obstinacy.

Seven times did Piccolomini charge with his cavalry upon the advancing Swedes. Seven times was his horse shot under him, but remounting each time, he drew off his men in good order, and in readiness to dash forward again at the first opportunity. The other Imperialist generals fought with equal courage and coolness, while Wallenstein, present wherever the danger was thickest, animated all by his courage and coolness. Though forced step by step to retire, the Imperialists never lost their formation, never turned their backs to the foe; and thus the fight went on till the darkness gathered thicker and thicker, the combatants could no longer see each other, and the desperate battle came to an end.

In the darkness, Wallenstein drew off his army and fell back to Leipzig, leaving behind him his colours and all his guns. In thus doing he threw away the opportunity of turning what his retreat acknowledged to be a defeat into a victory on the following morning, for scarcely had he left the field when the six regiments of Pappenheim's infantry arrived from Halle. Had he held his ground he could have renewed the battle in the morning, with the best prospects of success, for the struggle of the preceding day had been little more than a drawn battle, and the accessions of fresh troops should have given him a decided advantage over the weary Swedes. The newcomers, finding the field deserted, and learning from the wounded lying thickly over it that Wallenstein had retreated, at once marched away.

In the Swedish camp there was no assurance whatever that a victory had been gained, for nightfall had fallen on the Imperialists fighting as stubbornly as ever. The loss of the king, the master spirit of the war, dispirited and discouraged them, and Duke Bernhard and Kniphausen held in the darkness an anxious consultation as to whether the army should not at once retreat to Weissenburg. The plan was not carried out, only because it was considered that it was impracticable—as the army would be exposed to destruction should the Imperialists fall upon them while crossing the terrible morass in their rear.

The morning showed them that the Imperialists had disappeared, and that the mighty struggle had indeed been a victory for them—a victory won rather by the superior stubbornness with which the Swedish generals held their ground during the night, while Wallenstein fell back, than to the splendid courage with which the troops had fought on the preceding day. But better far would it have been for the cause which the Swedes championed, that they should have been driven a defeated host from the field of Lutzen, than that they should have gained a barren victory at the cost of the life of their gallant monarch—the soul of the struggle, the hope of Protestantism, the guiding spirit of the coalition against Catholicism as represented by Ferdinand of Austria.

The losses in the battle were about equal, no less than 9000 having fallen upon each side—a proportion without precedent in any battle of modern times, and testifying to the obstinacy and valour with which on both sides the struggle was maintained from early morning until night alone terminated it.

It is said, indeed, that every man, both of the yellow regiments of Swedish guards and of the blue regiments, composed entirely of English and Scotchmen, lay dead on the field. On both sides many men of high rank were killed. On the Swedish side, besides Gustavus himself, fell Count Milo, the Count of Brahe, General Uslar, Ernest Prince of Anhalt, and Colonels Gersdorf and Wildessein. On the Imperialist side Pappenheim, Schenk, Prince and Abbot of Fulda, Count Berthold Wallenstein, General Brenner, Issolani, general of the Croats, and six colonels were killed. Piccolomini received ten wounds, but none of them were mortal.

Holk was severely wounded, and, indeed, so close and desperate was the conflict, that it is said there was scarcely a man in the Imperial army who escaped altogether without a wound.

167

CHAPTER XVIII

WOUNDED

A controversy, which has never been cleared up, has long raged as to the death of Gustavus of Sweden; but the weight of evidence is strongly in favour of those who affirm that he received his fatal wound, that in the back, at the hand of Franz Albert of Lauenburg. The circumstantial evidence is, indeed, almost overwhelming. By birth the duke was the youngest of four sons of Franz II, Duke of Lauenburg. On his mother's side he was related to the Swedish royal family, and in his youth lived for some time at the court of Stockholm.

Owing to some impertinent remarks in reference to Gustavus he fell into disfavour with the queen, and had to leave Sweden. On attaining manhood he professed the Catholic faith, entered the Imperial army, obtained the command of a regiment, attached himself with much devotion to Wallenstein, and gained the confidence of that general. While the negotiations between the emperor and Wallenstein were pending Franz Albert was employed by the latter in endeavouring to bring about a secret understanding with the court of Dresden.

When Gustavus was blockaded in Nuremberg by Wallenstein Franz Albert left the camp of the latter and presented himself in that of Gustavus as a convert to the Reformed Religion and anxious to serve as a volunteer under him. No quarrel or disagreement had, so far as is known, taken place between him and Wallenstein, nor has any explanation ever been given for such an extraordinary change of sides, made, too, at a moment when it seemed that Gustavus was in a position almost desperate. By his profession of religious zeal he managed to win the king's heart, but Oxenstiern, when he saw him, entertained a profound distrust of him, and even warned the king against putting confidence in this sudden convert.

Gustavus, however, naturally frank and open in disposition, could not believe that treachery was intended, and continued to treat him with kindness. After the assault made by Gustavus upon Wallenstein's position Franz Albert quitted his camp, saying that he was desirous of raising some troops for his service in his father's territory. He rejoined him, however, with only his personal followers, on the very day before the battle of Lutzen, and was received by Gustavus with great cordiality, although the absence of his retainers increased the general doubts as to his sincerity.

He was by the king's side when Gustavus received his first wound. He was riding close behind him when the king received his second and fatal wound in the back, and the moment the king had fallen he rode away from the field, and it is asserted that it was he who brought the news of the king's death to Wallenstein.

Very soon after the battle he exchanged the Swedish service for the Saxon, and some eighteen months later he re-embraced the Roman Catholic faith and re-entered the Imperial army.

A stronger case of circumstantial evidence could hardly be put together, and it would certainly seem as if Lauenburg had entered the Swedish service with the intention of murdering the king. That he did not carry out his purpose during the attack on the Altenburg was perhaps due to the fact that Gustavus may not have been in such a position as to afford him an opportunity of doing so with safety to himself.

It is certainly curious that after that fight he should have absented himself, and only rejoined on the eve of the battle of Lutzen. The only piece of evidence in his favour is that of Truchsess, a chamberlain of the king, who, affirmed that he saw the fatal shot fired at a distance of ten paces from the king by an Imperial officer, Lieutenant General Falkenberg, who at once turned and fled, but was pursued and cut down by Luckau, master of horse of Franz Albert.

The general opinion of contemporary writers is certainly to the effect that the King of Sweden was murdered by Franz Albert; but the absolute facts must ever remain in doubt.

On the morning after the battle Wallenstein, having been joined by Pappenheim's infantry, sent a division of Croats back to the battlefield to take possession of it should they find that the Swedes had retired; but on their report that they still held the ground he retired at once from Leipzig, and, evacuating Saxony, marched into Bohemia, leaving the Swedes free to accomplish their junction with the army of the Elector, thus gaining the object for which they had fought at Lutzen.

After the death of the king, Malcolm Graheme, full of grief and rage at the loss of the monarch who was loved by all his troops, and had treated him with special kindness, joined the soldiers of Duke Bernhard, and took part in the charge which swept back the Imperialists and captured the cannon on the hill. At the very commencement of the struggle his horse fell dead under him, and he fought on foot among the Swedish infantry; but when the arrival of Pappenheim on the field enabled the Imperialists again to assume the offensive, Malcolm, having picked up a pike from the hands of a dead soldier, fought shoulder to shoulder in the ranks as the Swedes, contesting stubbornly every foot of the ground, were gradually driven back towards the road.

Suddenly a shot struck him; he reeled backwards a few feet, strove to steady himself and to level his pike, and then all consciousness left him, and he fell prostrate. Again and again, as the fortune of the desperate fray wavered one way or the other, did friend and foe pass over the place where he lay.

So thickly strewn was the field with dead that the combatants in their desperate struggle had long ceased to pick their way over the fallen, but trampled ruthlessly upon and over them as, hoarsely shouting their battle cry, they either pressed forward after the slowly retreating foe or with obstinate bravery strove to resist the charges of the enemy. When Malcolm recovered his consciousness all was still, save that here and there a faint moan was heard from others who like himself lay wounded on the battlefield. The night was intensely dark, and Malcolm's first sensation was that of bitter cold.

It was indeed freezing severely, and great numbers of the wounded who might otherwise have survived were frozen to death before morning; but a few, and among these were Malcolm, were saved by the frost. Although unconscious of the fact, he had been wounded in two places. The first ball had penetrated his breastpiece and had entered his body, and a few seconds later another ball had struck him in the arm. It was the first wound which had caused his insensibility; but from the second, which had severed one of the principal veins in the arm, he would have bled to death had it not been for the effects of the cold. For a time the life blood had flowed steadily away; but as the cold increased it froze and stiffened on his jerkin, and at last the wound was staunched.

It was none too soon, for before it ceased to flow Malcolm had lost a vast quantity of blood. It was hours before nature recovered from the drain. Gradually and slowly he awoke from his swoon. It was some time before he realized where he was and what had happened, then gradually his recollection of the fight returned to him.

"I remember now," he murmured to himself, "I was fighting with the Swedish infantry when a shot struck me in the body, I think, for I seemed to feel a sudden pain like a red hot iron. Who won the day, I wonder? How bitterly cold it is! I feel as if I were freezing to death."

So faint and stiff was he, partly from loss of blood, partly from being bruised from head to foot by being trampled on again and again as the ranks of the combatants swept over him, that it was some time before he was capable of making the slightest movement.

His left arm was, he found, entirely useless; it was indeed firmly frozen to the ground; but after some difficulty he succeeded in moving his right, and felt for the flask which had hung from his girdle.

So frozen and stiff were his fingers that he was unable to unbuckle the strap which fastened it; but, drawing his dagger, he at last cut through this, and removing the stopper of the flask, took a long draught of the wine with which it was filled. The relief which it afforded him was almost instantaneous, and he seemed to feel life again coursing in his veins.

After a while he was sufficiently restored to be enabled to get from his havresack some bread and meat which he had placed there after finishing his breakfast on the previous morning. He ate a few mouthfuls, took another long draught of wine, and then felt that he could hope to hold on until morning. He was unable to rise even into a sitting position, nor would it have availed him had he been able to walk, for he knew not where the armies were lying, nor could he have proceeded a yard in any direction without falling over the bodies which so thickly strewed the ground around him.

Though in fact it wanted but two hours of daylight when he recovered consciousness, the time appeared interminable; but at last, to his delight, a faint gleam of light spread across the sky. Stronger and stronger did it become until the day was fairly broken. It was another hour before he heard voices approaching. Almost holding his breath he listened as they approached, and his heart gave a throb of delight as he heard that they were speaking in Swedish. A victory had been won, then, for had it not been so, it would have been the Imperialists, not the Swedes, who would have been searching the field of battle.

"There are but few alive," one voice said, "the cold has finished the work which the enemy began."

Malcolm, unable to rise, lifted his arm and held it erect to call the attention of the searchers; it was quickly observed.

"There is some one still alive," the soldier exclaimed, "an officer, too; by his scarf and feathers he belongs to the Green Brigade."

"These Scotchmen are as hard as iron," another voice said; "come, bring a stretcher along."

They were soon by the side of Malcolm.

"Drink this, sir," one said, kneeling beside him and placing a flask of spirits to his lips; "that will warm your blood, I warrant, and you must be well nigh frozen."

Malcolm took a few gulps at the potent liquor, then he had strength to say:

"There is something the matter with my left arm, I can't move it, and I think I am hit in the body."

"You are hit in the body, sure enough," the man said, "for there is a bullet hole through your cuirass, and your jerkin below it is all stained with blood. You have been hit in the left arm too, and the blood is frozen to the ground; but we will soon free that for you. But before trying to do that we will cut open the sleeve of your jerkin and bandage your arm, or the movement may set it off bleeding again, and you have lost a pool of blood already."

Very carefully the soldiers did their work, and then placing Malcolm on the stretcher carried him away to the camp. Here the surgeons were all hard at work attending to the wounded who were brought in. They had already been busy all night, as those whose hurts had not actually disabled them found their way into the camp. As he was a Scotch officer he was carried to the lines occupied by Colonel Henderson with his Scotch brigade. He was known to many of the officers personally, and no time was lost in attending to him. He was nearly unconscious again by the time that he reached the camp, for the movement had caused the wound in his body to break out afresh.

His armour was at once unbuckled, and his clothes having been cut the surgeons proceeded to examine his wounds. They shook their heads as they did so. Passing a probe into the wound they found that the ball, breaking one of the ribs in its course, had gone straight on. They turned him gently over.

"Here it is," the surgeon said, producing a flattened bullet. The missile indeed had passed right through the body and had flattened against the back piece, which its force was too far spent to penetrate.

"Is the case hopeless, doctor?" one of the officers who was looking on asked.

"It is well nigh hopeless," the doctor said, "but it is just possible that it has not touched any vital part. The lad is young, and I judge that he has not ruined his constitution, as most of you have done, by hard drinking, so that there is just a chance for him. There is nothing for me to do but to put a piece of lint over the two holes, bandage it firmly, and leave it to nature. Now let me look at his arm.

"Ah!" he went on as he examined the wound, "he has had a narrow escape here. The ball has cut a vein and missed the principal artery by an eighth of an inch. If that had been cut he would have bled to death in five minutes. Evidently the lad has luck on his side, and I begin to think we may save him if we can only keep him quiet."

At the earnest request of the surgeons tents were brought up

172

and a hospital established on some rising ground near the field of battle for the serious cases among the wounded, and when the army marched away to join the Saxons at Leipzig a brigade was left encamped around the hospital.

Here for three weeks Malcolm lay between life and death. The quantity of blood he had lost was greatly in his favour, as it diminished the risk of inflammation, while his vigorous constitution and the life of fatigue and activity which he had led greatly strengthened his power. By a miracle the bullet in its passage had passed through without injuring any of the vital parts; and though his convalescence was slow it was steady, and even at the end of the first week the surgeons were able to pronounce a confident opinion that he would get over it.

But it was not until the end of the month that he was allowed to move from his recumbent position. A week later and he was able to sit up. On the following day, to his surprise, the Count of Mansfeld strode into his tent.

"Ah! my young friend," he exclaimed, "I am glad indeed to see you so far recovered. I came to Leipzig with the countess and my daughter; for Leipzig at present is the centre where all sorts of political combinations are seething as in a cooking pot. It is enough to make one sick of humanity and ashamed of one's country when one sees the greed which is displayed by every one, from the highest of the princes down to petty nobles who can scarce set twenty men in the field.

"Each and all are struggling to make terms by which he may better himself, and may add a province or an acre, as the case may be, to his patrimony at the expense of his neighbours. Truly I wonder that the noble Oxenstiern, who represents Sweden, does not call together the generals and troops of that country from all parts and march away northward, leaving these greedy princes and nobles to fight their own battles, and make the best terms they may with their Imperial master.

"But there, all that does not interest you at present; but I am so full of spleen and disgust that I could not help letting it out. We arrived there a week since, and of course one of our first inquiries was for you, and we heard to our grief that the Imperialists had shot one of their bullets through your body and another through your arm. This, of course, would have been sufficient for any ordinary carcass; but I knew my Scotchman, and was not surprised when they told me you were mending fast.

"I had speech yesterday with an officer who had ridden over from this camp, and he told me that the doctors said you were now convalescent, but would need repose and quiet for some time before you could again buckle on armour. The countess, when I told her, said at once, 'Then we will take him away back with us to Mansfeld.' Thekla clapped her hands and said, 'That will be capital! we will look after him, and he shall tell us stories about the wars.'

"So the thing was settled at once. I have brought over with me a horse litter, and have seen your surgeon, who says that although it will be some weeks before you can sit on a horse without the risk of your wound bursting out internally, there is no objection to your progression in a litter by easy stages; so that is settled, and the doctor will write to your colonel saying that it will be some months before you are fit for duty, and that he has therefore ordered you change and quiet.

"You need not be afraid of neglecting your duty or of getting out of the way of risking your life in harebrained ventures, for there will be no fighting till the spring. Everyone is negotiating at present, and you will be back with your regiment before fighting begins again. Well, what do you say?"

"I thank you, indeed," Malcolm replied. "It will of all things be the most pleasant; the doctor has told me that I shall not be fit for duty until the spring, and I have been wondering how ever I should be able to pass the time until then."

"Then we will be off without a minute's delay," the count said. "I sent off the litter last night and started myself at daybreak, promising the countess to be back with you ere nightfall, so we have no time to lose."

The news soon spread that Malcolm Graheme was about to leave the camp, and many of the Scottish officers came in to say adieu to him; but time pressed, and half an hour after the arrival of the count he started for Leipzig with Malcolm in a litter swung between two horses. As they travelled at a foot pace Malcolm did not find the journey uneasy, but the fresh air and motion soon made him drowsy, and he was fast asleep before he had left the camp an hour, and did not awake until the sound of the horses' hoofs on stone pavements told him that they were entering the town of Leipzig.

A few minutes later he was lying on a couch in the comfortable apartments occupied by the count, while the countess with her own hands was administering refreshments to him, and Thekla was looking timidly on, scarce able to believe that this pale and helpless invalid was the stalwart young Scottish soldier of whose adventures she was never weary of talking.

CHAPTER XIX

A PAUSE IN HOSTILITIES

Never had Malcolm Graheme spent a more pleasant time than the two months which he passed at Mansfeld. Travelling by very easy stages there he was so far convalescent upon his arrival that he was able to move about freely and could soon ride on horseback. For the time the neighbourhood of Mansfeld was undisturbed by the peasants or combatants on either side, and the count had acted with such vigour against any parties of brigands and marauders who might approach the vicinity of Mansfeld, or the country under his control, that a greater security of life and property existed than in most other parts of Germany. The ravages made by war were speedily effaced, and although the peasants carried on their operations in the fields without any surety as to who would gather the crops, they worked free from the harassing tyranny of the petty bands of robbers.

As soon as he was strong enough Malcolm rode with the count on his visits to the different parts of his estates, joined in several parties got up to hunt the boar in the hills, or to make war on a small scale against the wolves which, since the outbreak of the troubles, had vastly increased in number, committing great depredations upon the flocks and herds, and rendering it dangerous for the peasants to move between their villages except in strong parties.

The evenings were passed pleasantly and quietly. The countess would read aloud or would play on the zither, with which instrument she would accompany herself while she sang. Thekla would sit at her embroidery and would chat merrily to Malcolm, and ask many questions about Scotland and the life which the ladies led in that, as she asserted, "cold and desolate country." Sometimes the count's chaplain would be present and would gravely discuss theological questions with the count, wearying Malcolm and Thekla so excessively, that they would slip away from the others and play checkers or cards on a little table in a deep oriel window where their low talk and laughter did not disturb the discussions of their elders.

Once Malcolm was absent for two days on a visit to the village in the mountains he had so much aided in defending. Here he was joyfully received, and was glad to find that war had not penetrated to the quiet valley, and that prosperity still reigned there. Malcolm lingered at Mansfeld for some time after he felt that his strength was sufficiently restored to enable him to rejoin his regiment; but he knew that until the spring commenced no great movement of troops would take place, and he was so happy with his kind friends, who treated him completely as one of the family, that he was loath indeed to tear himself away. At last he felt that he could no longer delay, and neither the assurances of the count that the Protestant cause could dispense with his doughty services for a few weeks longer, or the tears of Thekla and her insistance that he could not care for them or he would not be in such a hurry to leave, could detain him longer, and mounting a horse with which the count had presented him he rode away to rejoin his regiment.

No military movements of importance had taken place subsequent to the battle of Lutzen. Oxenstiern had laboured night and day to repair as far as possible the effects of the death of Gustavus. He had been left by the will of the king regent of Sweden until the king's daughter, now a child of six years old, came of age, and he at once assumed the supreme direction of affairs. It was essential to revive the drooping courage of the weaker states, to meet the secret machinations of the enemy, to allay the jealousy of the more powerful allies, to arouse the friendly powers, France in particular, to active assistance, and above all to repair the ruined edifice of the German alliance and to reunite the scattered strength of the party by a close and permanent bond of union.

Had the emperor at this moment acted wisely Oxenstiern's efforts would have been in vain. Wallenstein, farseeing and broad minded, saw the proper course to pursue, and strongly urged upon the emperor the advisability of declaring a universal amnesty, and of offering favourable conditions to the Protestant princes, who, dismayed at the loss of their great champion, would gladly accept any proposals which would ensure the religious liberty for which they had fought; but the emperor, blinded by this unexpected turn of fortune and infatuated by Spanish counsels, now looked to a complete triumph and to enforce his absolute will upon the whole of Germany.

Instead, therefore, of listening to the wise counsels of Wallenstein he hastened to augment his forces. Spain sent him considerable supplies, negotiated for him with the ever vacillating Elector of Saxony, and levied troops for him in Italy. The Elector of Bavaria increased his army, and the Duke of Lorraine prepared again to take part in the struggle which now seemed to offer him an easy opportunity of increasing his dominions. For a time the Elector of Saxony, the Duke of Brunswick, and many others of the German princes wavered; but when they saw that Ferdinand, so far from being disposed to offer them favourable terms to detach them from the league, was preparing with greater vigour than ever to overwhelm them, they perceived that their interest was to remain faithful to their ally, and at a great meeting of princes and deputies held at Heilbronn the alliance was re-established on a firmer basis.

Before, however, the solemn compact was ratified scarce one of the German princes and nobles but required of Oxenstiern the gratification of private greed and ambition, and each bargained for some possession either already wrested or to be afterwards taken from the enemy. To the Landgrave of Hesse the abbacies of Paderborn, Corvey, Munster, and Fulda were promised, to Duke Bernhard of Weimar the Franconian bishoprics, to the Duke of Wurtemburg the ecclesiastical domains and the Austrian counties lying within his territories, all to be held as fiefs of Sweden.

Oxenstiern, an upright and conscientious man, was disgusted at the greed of these princes and nobles who professed to be warring solely in defence of their religious liberties, and he once exclaimed that he would have it entered in the Swedish archives as an everlasting memorial that a prince of the German empire made a request for such and such territory from a Swedish nobleman, and that the Swedish noble complied with the request by granting him German lands. However, the negotiations were at last completed, the Saxons marched towards Lusatia and Silesia to act in conjunction with Count Thurn against the Austrians in that quarter, a part of the Swedish army was led by the Duke of Weimar into Franconia, and the other by George, Duke of Brunswick, into Westphalia and Lower Saxony.

When Gustavus had marched south from Ingolstadt on the news of Wallenstein's entry into Saxony he had left the Count Palatine of Birkenfeld and General Banner to maintain the Swedish conquests in Bavaria. These generals had in the first instance pressed their conquests southward as far as Lake Constance; but towards the end of the year the Bavarian General Altringer pressed them with so powerful an army that Banner sent urgent requests to Horn to come to his assistance from Alsace, where he had been carrying all before him. Confiding his conquests to the Rhinegrave Otto Ludwig, Horn marched at the head of seven thousand men towards Swabia. Before he could join Banner, however, Altringer had forced the line of the Lech, and had received reinforcements strong enough to neutralize the aid brought to Banner by Horn. Deeming it necessary above all things to bar the future progress of the enemy, Horn sent orders to Otto Ludwig to join him with all the troops still remaining in Alsace; but finding himself still unable to resist the advance of Altringer, he despatched an urgent request to Duke Bernhard, who had captured Bamberg and the strong places of Kronach and Hochstadt in Franconia, to come to his assistance. The duke at once quitted Bamberg and marched southward, swept a strong detachment of the Bavarian army under John of Werth from his path, and pressing on reached Donauwurth in March 1633.

Malcolm had rejoined his regiment, which was with Duke Bernhard, just before it advanced from Bamberg and was received with a hearty welcome by his comrades, from whom he had been separated nine months, having quitted them three months before the battle of Lutzen.

The officers were full of hope that Duke Bernhard was going to strike a great blow. Altringer was away on the shore of Lake Constance facing Horn, Wallenstein was in Bohemia. Between Donauworth and Vienna were but the four strong places of Ingolstadt, Ratisbon, Passau, and Linz. Ingolstadt was, the duke knew, commanded by a traitor who was ready to surrender. Ratisbon had a Protestant population who were ready to open their gates. It seemed that the opportunity for ending the war by a march upon Vienna, which had been snatched by Wallenstein from Gustavus just when it appeared in his grasp, was now open to Duke Bernhard. But the duke was ambitious, his demands for Franconia had not yet been entirely complied with by Oxenstiern, and he saw an opportunity to obtain his own terms. The troops under his orders were discontented, owing to the fact that their pay was many months in arrear, and private agents of the duke fomented this feeling by assuring the men that their general was with them and would back their demands. Accordingly they refused to march further until their demands were fully satisfied. The Scotch regiments stood apart from the movement, though they too were equally in arrear with their pay. Munro and the officers of the Brigade chafed terribly at this untimely mutiny just when the way to Vienna appeared open to them. Duke Bernhard forwarded the demands of the soldiers to Oxenstiern, sending at the same time a demand on his own account, first that the territory of the Franconian bishoprics should at once be erected into a principality in his favour, and secondly, that he should be nominated commander-in-chief of all the armies fighting in Germany for the Protestant cause with the title of generalissimo.

Oxenstiern was alarmed by the receipt of the mutinous demands of the troops on the Danube, and was disgusted when he saw those demands virtually supported by their general. His first thought was to dismiss Duke Bernhard from the Swedish service; but he saw that if he did so the disaffection might spread, and that the duke might place himself at the head of the malcontents and bring ruin upon the cause. He therefore agreed to bestow at once the Franconian bishoprics upon him, and gave a pledge that Sweden would defend him in that position.

He declined to make him generalissimo of all the armies, but appointed him commander-in-chief of the forces south of the Maine. The duke accepted this modification, and had no difficulty in restoring order in the ranks of his army. But precious months had been wasted before this matter was brought to a conclusion, and the month of October arrived before the duke had completed all his preparations and was in a position to move forward.

While the delays had been going on Altringer, having been joined by the army of the Duke of Feria, quitted the line of the Danube, in spite of Wallenstein's absolute order not to do so, and, evading Horn and Birkenfeldt, marched into Alsace. The Swedish generals, however, pressed hotly upon him, and finally drove him out of Alsace. Ratisbon being left open by Altringer's disobedience to Wallenstein's orders, Duke Bernhard marched upon that city without opposition, and laid siege to it. Maximilian of Bavaria was himself there with a force sufficient to defend the city had he been supported by the inhabitants; but a large majority of the people were Protestants, and, moreover, bitterly hated the Bavarians, who had suppressed their rights as a free city.

Maximilian wrote urgently to the emperor and to Wallenstein, pledging himself to maintain Ratisbon if he could receive a reinforcement of 5000 men. The emperor was powerless; he had not the men to send, but he despatched to Wallenstein, one after another, seven messengers, urging him at all hazards to prevent the fall of so important a place. Wallenstein replied to the order that he would do all in his power, and in presence of the messengers ordered the Count of Gallas to march with 12,000 men on Ratisbon, but privately furnished the general with absolute orders, forbidding him on any account to do anything which might bring on an action with the duke.

Wallenstein's motives in so acting were, as he afterwards assured the emperor, that he was not strong enough to divide his army, and that he could best cover Vienna by maintaining a strong position in Bohemia, a policy which was afterwards justified by the event. Ratisbon resisted for a short time; but, finding that the promised relief did not arrive, it capitulated on the 5th of November, Maximilian having left the town before the surrender.

The duke now pushed on towards Vienna, and captured Straubing and Plattling. John of Werth, who was posted here, not being strong enough to dispute the passage of the Isar, fell back towards the Bohemian frontier, hoping to meet the troops which the emperor had urged Wallenstein to send to his aid, but which never came. Duke Bernhard crossed the Isar unopposed, and on the 12th came within sight of Passau.

So far Wallenstein had not moved; he had seemed to comply with the emperor's request to save Ratisbon, but had seemed only, and had not set a man in motion to reinforce John of Werth. He refused, in fact, to fritter away his army. Had he sent Gallas with 12,000 men to join John of Werth, and had their united forces been, as was probable, attacked and defeated by the Swedes, Wallenstein would have been too weak to save the empire. Keeping his army strong he had the key of the position in his hands.

He had fixed upon Passau as the point beyond which Duke Bernhard should not be allowed to advance, and felt that should he attack that city he and his army were lost. In front of him was the Inn, a broad and deep river protected by strongly fortified places; behind him John of Werth, a bitterly hostile country, and the river Isar. On his left would be Wallenstein himself marching across the Bohemian forest. When, therefore, he learned that Duke Bernhard was hastening on from the Isar towards Passau he put his army in motion and marched southward, so as to place himself in the left rear of the duke. This movement Duke Bernhard heard of just when he arrived in sight of Passau, and he instantly recognized the extreme danger of his position, and perceived with his usual quickness of glance that to be caught before Passau by Wallenstein and John of Werth would be absolute destruction. A moment's hesitation and the Swedish army would have been lost. Without an hour's delay he issued the necessary orders, and the army retraced its steps with all speed to Ratisbon, and not stopping even there marched northward into the Upper Palatinate, to defend that conquered country against Wallenstein even at the cost of a battle.

But Wallenstein declined to fight a battle there. He had but one army, and were that army destroyed, Duke Bernhard, with the prestige of victory upon him, could resume his march upon Vienna, which would then be open to him. Therefore, having secured the safety of the capital, he fell back again into winter quarters in Bohemia. Thus Ferdinand again owed his safety to Wallenstein, and should have been the more grateful since Wallenstein had saved him in defiance of his own orders.

At the time he fully admitted in his letters to Wallenstein that the general had acted wisely and prudently, nevertheless he was continually listening to the Spaniards, the Jesuits, and the many envious of Wallenstein's great position, and hoping to benefit by his disgrace, and, in spite of all the services his great general had rendered him, was preparing to repeat the humiliation which he had formerly laid upon him and again to deprive him of his command.

Wallenstein was not ignorant of the intrigue against him. Vast as were his possessions, his pride and ambition were even greater. A consciousness of splendid services rendered and of great intellectual power, a belief that the army which had been raised by him and was to a great extent paid out of his private funds, and which he had so often led to victory, was devoted to him, and to him alone, excited in his mind the determination to resist by force the intriguers who dominated the bigoted and narrow minded emperor, and, if necessary, to hurl the latter from his throne.

CHAPTER XX

FRIENDS IN TROUBLE

One day in the month of December, when Malcolm Graheme was with his regiment on outpost duty closely watching the Imperialists, a countryman approached.

"Can you direct me to Captain Malcolm Graheme, who, they tell me, belongs to this regiment?"

"You have come to the right man," Malcolm said. "I am Captain Graheme—what would you with me?"

"I am the bearer of a letter to you," the man said, and taking off his cap he pulled out the lining and brought out a letter hidden beneath it.

"I am to ask for some token from you by which it may be known that it has been safely delivered."

Malcolm cut with his dagger the silk with which the letter was fastened. It began:

"From the Lady Hilda, Countess of Mansfeld, to Captain Malcolm Graheme of Colonel Munro's Scottish regiment.—My dear friend,—I do not know whether you have heard the misfortune which has fallen upon us. The town and castle of Mansfeld were captured two months since by a sudden assault of the Imperialists, and my dear husband was grievously wounded in the defence. He was brought hither a prisoner, and Thekla and I also carried here. As the count still lies ill with his wounds he is not placed in a prison, but we are treated as captives and a close watch is kept upon us. The count is threatened with the forfeiture of all his possessions unless he will change sides and join the Imperialists, and some of his estates have been already conferred upon other nobles as a punishment for the part he has taken.

"Were my husband well and free he would treat the offers with scorn, believing that the tide will turn and that he will recover his possessions. Nor even were he certain of their perpetual forfeiture would he desert the cause of Protestantism. Moreover, the estates which I brought him in marriage lie in the north of Pomerania, and the income there from is more than ample for our needs. But the emperor has ordered that if the count remain contumacious Thekla shall be taken from us and placed in a convent, where she will be forced to embrace Catholicism, and will,

182

when she comes of age, be given in marriage to some adherent of the emperor, who will with her receive the greater portion of her father's lands.

"She is now sixteen years old, and in another year will be deemed marriageable. My heart is broken at the thought, and I can scarce see the paper on which I write for weeping. I know not why I send to you, nor does the count know that I am writing, nor does it seem possible that any aid can come to us, seeing that we are here in the heart of Bohemia, and that Wallenstein's army lies between us and you. But somehow in my heart I have a hope that you may aid us, and at any rate I know that you will sympathize with us greatly. I feel sure that if there be any mode in which we may be aided it will be seized by your ready wit. And now adieu! This letter will be brought to you by a messenger who will be hired by a woman who attends us, and who has a kind heart as well as an eye to her own interests. Send back by the messenger some token which she may pass on to me, that I may know that you have received it. Send no written answer, for the danger is too great."

Malcolm twisted off two or three links of the chain which had long before been presented to him by the count, and then, until relieved from duty, paced up and down, slowly revolving in his mind what could best be done to aid his friends. His mind was at last made up, and when his company was called in he went to his colonel and asked for leave of absence, stating his reasons for wishing to absent himself from the regiment.

"It is a perilous business, Malcolm," Colonel Munro said. "I have scarce a handful of the friends with whom I joined Gustavus but three years and a half ago remaining, and I can ill spare another; nevertheless I will not stay you in your enterprise. The Count of Mansfeld has been a steady ally of ours, and is one of the few who has appeared to have at heart the cause of Protestantism rather than of personal gain.

"Moreover, he is as you say a friend of yours, and has shown you real kindness in time of need. Therefore go, my boy, and Heaven be with you! It is not likely that there will be any more serious fighting this year. Wallenstein lies inactive, negotiating now with Saxony, now with Oxenstiern. What are his aims and plans Heaven only knows; but at any rate we have no right to grumble at the great schemer, for ever since Lutzen he has kept the emperor's best army inactive. Make it a point, Malcolm, to find out, so far as you can, what is the public opinion in Bohemia as to his real intentions. If you can bring back any information as to his plans you will have done good service to the cause, however long your absence from the camp may be."

That evening Malcolm packed up his armour, arms, court suits, and valuables, and sent them away to the care of his friend the syndic of the clockmakers of Nuremberg, with a letter requesting him to keep them in trust for him until he returned; and in the event of his not arriving to claim them in the course of six months, to sell them, and to devote the proceeds to the assistance of sick or wounded Scottish soldiers. Then he purchased garments suitable for a respectable craftsman, and having attired himself in these, with a stout sword banging from his leathern belt, a wallet containing a change of garments and a number of light tools used in clockmaking, with a long staff in his hand, and fifty ducats sewed in the lining of the doublet, he set out on foot on his journey.

It was nigh three weeks from the time when he started before he arrived at Prague, for not only had he to make a very long detour to avoid the contending armies, but he was forced to wait at each considerable town until he could join a company of travellers going in the same direction, for the whole country so swarmed with disbanded soldiers, plunderers, and marauding bands that none thought of traversing the roads save in parties sufficiently strong to defend themselves and their property. None of those with whom he journeyed suspected Malcolm to be aught but what he professed himself—a craftsman who had served his time at a clockmaker's in Nuremberg, and who was on his way to seek for employment in Vienna.

During his three years and a half residence in Germany he had come to speak the language like a native, and, indeed, the dialect of the different provinces varied so widely, that, even had he spoken the language with less fluency, no suspicion would have arisen of his being a foreigner. Arrived at Prague, his first care was to hire a modest lodging, and he then set to work to discover the house in which the Count of Mansfeld was lying as a prisoner.

This he had no difficulty in doing without exciting suspicion, for the count was a well known personage, and he soon found that he and his family had apartments in a large house, the rest of which was occupied by Imperialist officers and their families. There was a separate entrance to the portion occupied by the count, and a sentry stood always at the door.

The day after his arrival Malcolm watched the door from a distance throughout the whole day, but none entered or came out. The next morning he resumed his watch at a much earlier hour, and presently had the satisfaction of seeing a woman in the attire of a domestic issue from the door. She was carrying a basket, and was evidently bent upon purchasing the supplies for the day. He followed her to the market, and, after watching her make her purchases, he followed her until, on her return, she entered a street where but few people were about. There he quickened his pace and overtook her.

"You are the attendant of the Countess of Mansfeld, are you not?" he said.

"I am," she replied; "but what is that to you?"

"I will tell you presently," Malcolm replied, "but in the first place please inform me whether you are her only attendant, and in the next place how long you have been in her service. I can assure you," he went on, as the woman, indignant at thus being questioned by a craftsman who was a stranger to her, tossed her head indignantly, and was about to move on, "that I ask not from any impertinent curiosity. Here is a ducat as a proof that I am interested in my questions."

The woman gave him a quick and searching glance; she took the piece of money, and replied more civilly. "I am the only attendant on the countess. I cannot be said to be in her service, since I have been placed there by the commandant of the prison, whither the count will be moved in a few days, but I have been with them since their arrival there, nigh three months since."

"Then you are the person whom I seek. I am he to whom a certain letter which you wot of was sent, and who returned by the messenger as token that he received it two links of this chain."

The woman started as he spoke, and looked round anxiously to see that they were not observed; then she said hurriedly:

"For goodness sake, sir, if you be he, put aside that grave and earnest look, and chat with me lightly and laughingly, so that if any observe us speaking they will think that you are trying to persuade me that my face has taken your admiration. Not so very difficult a task, methinks," she added coquettishly, acting the part she had indicated.

"By no means," Malcolm replied laughing, for the girl was really good looking, "and were it not that other thoughts occupy me at present you might well have another captive to look after; and now tell me, how is it possible for me to obtain an interview with the count?"

"And the countess, and the Fraulein Thekla," the girl said laughing, "for I suppose you are the young Scottish officer of whom the young countess is always talking. I don't see that it is possible."

"Twenty ducats are worth earning," Malcolm said quietly.

"Very well worth earning," the woman replied, "but a costly day's work if they lead to a prison and flogging, if not to the gallows."

"But we must take care that you run no risk," Malcolm said. "Surely such a clever head as I see you have can contrive some way for me to get in."

"Yes; it might be managed," the girl said thoughtfully. "The orders were strict just at first, but seeing that the count cannot move from his couch, and that the countess and the fraulein have no motive in seeking to leave him, the strictness has been relaxed. The orders of the sentry are stringent that neither of the ladies shall be allowed to set foot outside the door, but I do not think they have any orders to prevent others from going in and out had they some good excuse for their visit."

"Then it is not so impossible after all," Malcolm said with a smile, "for I have an excellent excuse.

"What is that?" the woman asked.

"The clock in the count's chamber has stopped, and it wearies him to lie there and not know how the time passes, so he has requested you to fetch in a craftsman to set it going again."

"A very good plan," the girl said. "There is a clock, and it shall stop this afternoon. I will find out from the sentry as I go in whether he has any orders touching the admission of strangers. If he has I will go across to the prison and try and get a pass for you. I shall come to market in the morning."

So saying, with a wave of her hand she tripped on towards the house, which was now near at hand, leaving Malcolm to arrange his plans for next day. His first care was to purchase a suit of clothes such as would be worn by a boy of the class to which he appeared to belong. Then he went to one of the small inns patronized by the peasants who brought their goods into market, and without difficulty bargained with one of them for the purchase of a cart with two oxen, which were to remain at the inn until he called for them. Then he bought a suit of peasant's clothes, after which, well satisfied with the day's work, he returned to his lodging. In the morning he again met the servant.

"It was well I asked," she said, "for the sentry had orders to prevent any, save nobles and officers, from passing in. However, I went to the prison, and saw one of the governor's deputies, and told him that the count was fretting because his clock had stopped, and, as while I said so I slipped five ducats the countess had given me for the purpose into his hand, he made no difficulty about giving me the pass. Here it is. Now," she said, "I have earned my twenty ducats."

"You have earned them well," Malcolm replied, handing them to her.

"Now mind," she said, "you must not count on me farther. I don't know what you are going to do, and I don't want to know. I have run quite a risk enough as it is, and mean, directly the count is lodged in the prison, to make my way home, having collected a dowry which will enable me to buy a farm and marry my bachelor, who has been waiting for me for the last three years. His father is an old curmudgeon, who has declared that his son shall never marry except a maid who can bring as much money as he will give him. I told Fritz that if he would trust to my wits and wait I would in five years produce the dowry. Now I have treble the sum, and shall go off and make Fritz happy."

"He is a lucky fellow," Malcolm said laughing. "It is not every one who gets beauty, wit, and wealth all together in a wife."

"You are a flatterer," the girl laughed; "but for all that I think myself that Fritz is not unfortunate."

"And now tell me," Malcolm asked, "at what time is the sentry generally changed?"

"At sunrise, at noon, at sunset, and at midnight," the girl replied; "but what is that to you?"

"Never mind;" Malcolm laughed; "you know you don't want to be told what I'm going to do. I will tell you if you like."

"No, no," the girl replied hurriedly. "I would rather be able to always take my oath on the holy relics that I know nothing about it."

"Very well," Malcolm replied; "then this afternoon I will call."

Having hidden away under his doublet the suit of boy's clothes, and with the tools of his trade in a small basket in his hand, Malcolm presented himself at three o'clock in the afternoon to the sentry at the door leading to the count's apartments. The soldier glanced at the pass and permitted him to enter without remark.

The waiting maid met him inside and conducted him upstairs, and ushered him into a spacious apartment, in which the count was lying on a couch, while the countess and Thekla sat at work beside him. She then retired and closed the door after her. The count and Thekla looked with surprise at the young artisan, but the countess ran to meet him, and threw her arms round his neck as if she had been his mother, while Thekla gave a cry of delight as she recognized him.

"Welcome a thousand times! Welcome, my brave friend!" the

countess exclaimed. "What dangers must you not have encountered on your way hither to us! The count and Thekla knew not that I had written to you, for I feared a failure; and when I learned yesterday that you had arrived I still kept silence, partly to give a joyful surprise to my lord today, partly because, if the governor called, I was sure that this child's telltale face would excite his suspicion that something unusual had happened."

"How imprudent!" the count said, holding out his hand to Malcolm. "Had I known that my wife was sending to you I would not have suffered her to do so, for the risk is altogether too great, and yet, indeed, I am truly glad to see you again."

Thekla gave Malcolm her hand, but said nothing. She had now reached an age when girls feel a strange shyness in expressing their feelings; but her hand trembled with pleasure as she placed it in Malcolm's, and her cheek flushed hotly as, in accordance with the custom of the times, she presented it to his kiss.

"Now," the count said, "do not let us waste time; tell us quickly by what miracle you have arrived here, and have penetrated to what is really my prison. You must be quick, for we have much to say, and your visit must be a short one for every third day the governor of the prison pays me a visit to see how I am getting on, and I expect that he will be here ere long."

"Then," Malcolm said, "I had best prepare for his coming, for assuredly I am not going to hurry away."

So saying, he lifted down the great clock which stood on a bracket on the wall, and placed it on a side table. "I am a clockmaker," he said, "and am come to put this machine, whose stopping has annoyed you sadly, into order."

So saying, he took some tools from his basket, removed the works of the clock, and, taking them in pieces, laid them on the table.

"I spent much of my time at Nuremberg," he said, in answer to the surprised exclamations of the count, "in learning the mysteries of horology, and can take a clock to pieces and can put it together again with fair skill. There, now, I am ready, and if the governor comes he will find me hard at work. And now I will briefly tell you how I got here; then I will hear what plans you may have formed, and I will tell you mine."

"For myself, I have no plans," the count said. "I am helpless, and must for the present submit to whatever may befall me. That I will not renounce the cause of my religion you may be sure; as for my wife, we know not yet whether, when they remove me to the

188

fortress, they will allow her to accompany me or not. If they do, she will stay with me, but it is more likely that they will not. The emperor is merciless to those who oppose him. They will more likely keep her under their eye here or in Vienna. But for ourselves we care little; our anxiety is for Thekla. It is through her that they are striking us. You know what they have threatened if I do not abandon the cause of Protestantism. Thekla is to be placed in a convent, forced to become a Catholic, and married to the man on whom the emperor may please to bestow my estates."

"I would rather die, father, than become a Catholic," Thekla exclaimed firmly.

"Yes, dear!" the count said gently, "but it is not death you have to face; with a fresh and unbroken spirit, it were comparatively easy to die, but it needs an energy and a spirit almost superhuman to resist the pressure which may be placed on those who are committed to a convent. The hopelessness, the silence, the gloom, to say nothing of threats, menaces, and constant and unremitting pressure, are sufficient to break down the firmest resolution. The body becomes enfeebled, the nerves shattered, and the power of resistance enfeebled. No, my darling, brave as you are in your young strength, you could not resist the influence which would be brought to bear upon you."

"Then it is clear," Malcolm said cheerfully, "that we must get your daughter out of the clutches of the emperor and the nuns."

"That is what I have thought over again and again as I have lain here helpless, but I can see no means of doing so. We have no friends in the city, and, could the child be got safely out of this place, there is nowhere whither she could go."

"And it is for that I have sent for you," the countess said. "I knew that if it were in any way possible you would contrive her escape and aid her to carry it out."

"Assuredly I will, my dear countess," Malcolm said. "You only wanted a friend outside, and now you have got one. I see no difficulty about it."

At this moment the door suddenly opened; the waiting maid put in her head and exclaimed, "The governor is alighting at the door." Malcolm at once seated himself at the side table and began oiling the wheels of the clock, while the countess and Thekla took up their work again and seated themselves, as before, by the couch of the count. A moment later the attendant opened the door and in a loud voice announced the Baron of Steinburg.

The governor as he entered cast a keen glance at Malcolm,

and then bowing ceremoniously approached the count and inquired after his health, and paid the usual compliments to the countess. The count replied languidly that he gained strength slowly, while the countess said quietly that he had slept but badly and that his wound troubled him much. It was well for Thekla that she was not obliged to take part in the conversation, for she would have found it impossible to speak quietly and indifferently, for every nerve was tingling with joy at Malcolm's last words. The prospect had seemed so hopeless that her spirits had sunk to the lowest ebb. Her mother had done her best to cheer her, but the count, weakened by pain and illness, had all along taken the most gloomy view. He had told himself that it was better for the girl to submit to her fate than to break her heart like a wild bird beating out its life against the bars of its cage, and he wished to show her that neither he nor the world would blame her for yielding to the tremendous pressure which would be put upon her.

For himself, he would have died a thousand times rather than renounce his faith; but he told himself that Thekla was but a child, that women cared little for dogmas, and that she would learn to pray as sincerely in a Catholic as in a Protestant church, without troubling her mind as to whether there were gross abuses in the government of the church, in the sale of absolutions, or errors in abstruse doctrines. But to Thekla it had seemed impossible that she could become a Catholic.

The two religions stood in arms against each other; Catholics and Protestants differed not only in faith but in politics. In all things they were actively and openly opposed to each other, and the thought that she might be compelled to abjure her faith was most terrible to the girl; and she was firmly resolved that, so long as her strength lasted and her mind was unimpaired, she would resist whatever pressure might be placed upon her, and would yield neither to menaces, to solitary confinement, or even to active cruelty. The prospect, however; had weighed heavily upon her mind. Her father had appeared to consider any escape impossible; her mother had said nothing of her hopes; and the words which Malcolm had spoken, indicating something like a surety of freeing her from her terrible position, filled her with surprise and delight.

"Whom have you here?" the governor asked, indicating Malcolm by a motion of the head.

"It is a craftsman from Nuremberg. The clock had stopped, and the count, with whom the hours pass but slowly, fretted himself at not being able to count them; so I asked our attendant to bring hither a craftsman to put it in order, first sending her with a note to you asking for permission for him to come; as you were out your deputy signed the order."

"He should not have done so," the baron said shortly, "for the orders are strict touching the entry of any here. However, as he has taken the clock to pieces, he can put it together again." So saying he went over to the table where Malcolm was at work and stood for a minute or two watching him. The manner in which Malcolm fitted the wheels into their places, filing and oiling them wherever they did not run smoothly, satisfied him that the youth was what he seemed.

"You are young to have completed your apprenticeship," he said.

"It is expired but two months, sir," Malcolm said, standing up respectfully.

"Under whom did you learn your trade?" the governor asked; "for I have been in Nuremberg and know most of the guild of clockmakers by name."

"Under Jans Boerhoff, the syndic of the guild," Malcolm replied.

"Ah!" the baron said shortly; "and his shop is in—"

"The Cron Strasse," Malcolm said promptly in answer to the implied question.

Quite satisfied now, the baron turned away and conversed a few minutes with the count, telling him that as the surgeon said he could now be safely removed he would in three days be transferred to an apartment in the fortress.

"Will the countess be permitted to accompany me?" the count asked.

"That I cannot tell you," the baron replied. "We are expecting a messenger with his majesty's orders on the subject tomorrow or next day. I have already informed you that, in his solicitude for her welfare, his majesty has been good enough to order that the young countess shall be placed in the care of the lady superior of the Convent of St. Catherine."

A few minutes later he left the room. Not a word was spoken in the room until the sound of horse's hoofs without told that he had ridden off.

As the door closed the countess and Thekla had dropped their work and sat anxiously awaiting the continuance of the conversation. The count was the first to speak.

"How mean you, Malcolm? How think you it possible that Thekla can escape, and where could she go?"

"I like not to make the proposal," Malcolm said gravely, "nor under any other circumstances should I think of doing so; but in a desperate position desperate measures must be adopted. It is impossible that in your present state you can escape hence, and the countess will not leave you; but what is absolutely urgent is that your daughter should be freed from the strait. Save myself you have no friends here; and therefore, count, if she is to escape it must be through my agency and she must be committed wholly to my care. I know it is a great responsibility; but if you and the countess can bring yourselves to commit her to me I swear to you, as a Scottish gentleman and a Protestant soldier, that I will watch over her as a brother until I place her in all honour in safe hands."

The count looked at the countess and at Thekla, who sat pale and still.

"We can trust you, Malcolm Graheme," he said after a pause. "There are few, indeed, into whose hands we would thus confide our daughter; but we know you to be indeed, as you say, a Scottish gentleman and a Protestant soldier. Moreover, we know you to be faithful, honourable, and true. Therefore we will, seeing that there is no other mode of escape from the fate which awaits her, confide her wholly to you. And now tell us what are your plans?"

CHAPTER XXI

FLIGHT

"I THANK you, count, and you, dear lady," Malcolm said gratefully, "for the confidence you place in me, and will carry out my trust were it to cost me my life. My plan is a simple one. The guard will be changed in half an hour's time. I have brought hither a suit of boy's garments, which I must pray the Countess Thekla to don, seeing that it will be impossible for her to sally out in her own garb. I show my pass to the sentry, who will deem that my companion entered with me, and is my apprentice, and will suppose that, since the sentry who preceded him suffered him to enter with me he may well pass him out without question. In the town I have a wagon in readiness, and shall, disguised as a peasant, start with it this evening. Thekla will be in the bottom covered with straw. We shall travel all night.

"Tomorrow, when your attendant discovers that your daughter has escaped, she will at once take the news to the governor. The sentries will all be questioned, and it will be found that, whereas but one clockmaker came in two went out. The city will be searched and the country round scoured but if the horsemen overtake me they will be looking for a craftsman and his apprentice, and will not suspect a solitary peasant with a wagon.

"The first danger over I must be guided by circumstances; but in any case Thekla must travel as a boy to the end of the journey, for in such troubled times as these it were unsafe indeed for a young girl to travel through Germany except under a strong escort of men-at-arms. I design to make my way to Nuremberg, and shall then place her in the hands of my good friend Jans Boerhoff, whose wife and daughters will, I am sure, gladly receive and care for her until the time, which I hope is not far off, that peace be made and you can again rejoin her."

"The plan is a good one," the count said when Malcolm had concluded, "and offers every prospect of success. 'Tis hazardous, but there is no escape from such a strait as ours without risk. What say you, wife?"

"Assuredly I can think of nothing better. But what say you, Thekla? Are you ready to run the risks, the danger, and the hardships of such a journey under the protection only of this brave Scottish gentleman?"

193

"I am ready, mother," Thekla said quickly, "but I wish—I wish"—and she hesitated.

"You wish you could go in your own garments, Thekla, with jewels on your fingers and a white horse to carry you on a pillion behind your protector," the count said with a smile, for his spirits had risen with the hope of his daughter's escape from the peril in which she was placed. "It cannot be, Thekla. Malcolm's plan must be carried out to the letter, and I doubt not that you will pass well as a 'prentice boy. But your mother must cut off that long hair of yours; I will keep it, my child, and will stroke it often and often in my prison as I have done when it has been on your head; your hair may be long again before I next see you."

His eyes filled with tears as he spoke, and Thekla and the countess both broke into a fit of crying. Leaving them by themselves, Malcolm returned to his work, and in half an hour had replaced the machinery of the clock and had set it in motion, while a tender conversation went on between the count and countess and their daughter. By this time the sun had set, and the attendant entered and lighted the candles in the apartment, saying, as she placed one on the table by Malcolm, "You must need a light for your work." No sooner had she left the room than Malcolm said:

"I would not hurry your parting, countess, but the sooner we are off now the better."

Without a word the countess rose, and, taking the clothes which Malcolm produced from his doublet, retired to her chamber, followed by Thekla.

"Malcolm Graheme," the count said, "it may be that we shall not meet again. The emperor is not tender with obstinate prisoners, and I have no strength to support long hardships. Should aught happen to me I beseech you to watch over the happiness of my child. Had she been a year older, and had you been willing, I would now have solemnly betrothed her to you, and should then have felt secure of her future whatever may befall me. Methinks she will make a good wife, and though my estates may be forfeited by the emperor her mother's lands will make a dowry such as many a German noble would gladly accept with his wife.

"I might betroth her to you now, for many girls are betrothed at a far younger age, but I would rather leave it as it is. You are young yet, and she in most matters is but a child, and it would be better in every way did she start on this adventure with you regarding you as a brother than in any other light. Only remember that if we should not meet again, and you in future years should seek the woman who is now a child as your wife, you have my fullest approval and consent—nay, more, that it is my dearest wish."

"I thank you most deeply for what you have said, count," Malcolm replied gravely. "As I have seen your daughter growing up from a child I have thought how sweet a wife she would make, but I have put the thought from me, seeing that she is heiress to broad lands and I a Scottish soldier of fortune, whose lands, though wide enough for me to live in comfort at home, are yet but a mere farm in comparison with your broad estates. I have even told myself that as she grew up I must no longer make long stays in your castle, for it would be dishonourable indeed did I reward your kindness and hospitality by winning the heart of your daughter; but after what you have so generously said I need no longer fear my heart, and will, when the time comes, proudly remind you of your promise. For this journey I will put all such thoughts aside, and will regard Thekla as my merry playfellow of the last three years. But after I have once placed her in safety I shall thenceforward think of her as my wife who is to be, and will watch over her safety as over my greatest treasure, trusting that in some happy change of times and circumstances you yourself and the dear countess, whom I already regard almost as my parents, will give her to me."

"So be it," the count said solemnly. "My blessing on you both should I ne'er see you again. I can meet whatever fate may be before me with constancy and comfort now that her future is assured—but here they come."

The door opened, and the countess appeared, followed by Thekla, shrinking behind her mother's skirts in her boyish attire.

"You will pass well," the count said gravely, for he knew that jest now would jar upon her. "Keep that cap well down over your eyes, and try and assume a little more of the jaunty and impudent air of a boy. Fortunately it will be dark below, and the sentry will not be able to mark how fair is your skin and how delicate your hands. And now farewell, my child. Let us not stand talking, for the quicker a parting is over the better. May God in heaven bless you and keep you! Malcolm knows all my wishes concerning you, and when I am not with you trust yourself to his advice and guidance as you would to mine. There, my darling, do not break down. You must be brave for all our sakes. Should the emperor hold me in durance your mother will try and join you ere long at Nuremberg."

While the count was embracing Thekla, as she bravely but in vain tried to suppress her tears, the countess opened the door, and glanced into the anteroom to see that all was clear and the attendant in her own apartment. Then she returned, kissed her daughter fondly, and placed her hand in Malcolm's, saying to the latter, "God bless you, dear friend! Take her quickly away for her sake and ours."

One last adieu and Malcolm and Thekla stood alone in the anteroom.

"Now, Thekla," he said firmly, "be brave, the danger is at hand, and your safety and escape from your fate, and my life, depend upon your calmness. Do you carry this basket of tools and play your part as my apprentice. Just as we open the door drop the basket and I will rate you soundly for your carelessness. Keep your head down, and do not let the light which swings over the door fall upon your face."

For a minute or two Thekla stood struggling to master her emotions. Then she said, in a quiet voice, "I am ready now," and taking up the basket of tools she followed Malcolm down the stairs. Malcolm opened the door, and as he did so Thekla dropped the basket.

"How stupid you are!" Malcolm exclaimed sharply. "How often have I told you to be careful! You don't suppose that those fine tools can stand being knocked about in that way without injury? Another time an' you are so careless I will give you a taste of the strap, you little rascal."

"What is all this?" the sentry asked, barring the way with his pike, "and who are you who are issuing from this house with so much noise? My orders are that none pass out here without an order from the governor."

"And such an order have I," Malcolm said, producing the document. "There's the governor's seal. I have been sent for to repair the clock in the Count of Mansfeld's apartment, and a rare job it has been."

The sentry was unable to read, but he looked at the seal which he had been taught to recognize.

"But there is only one seal," he said, "and there are two of you."

"Pooh!" Malcolm said scornfully. "Dost think that when ten persons are admitted to pass in together the governor puts ten seals on the pass? You see for yourself that it is but a young boy, my apprentice. Why, the governor himself left scarce an hour ago, and was in the apartment with me while I was at work. Had it not been all right he would have hauled me to the prison quickly enough."

As the sentry knew that the governor had left but a short time before he came on guard this convinced him, and, standing aside, he allowed Malcolm and his companion to pass. Malcolm made his way first to the apartment he had occupied, where he had already settled for his lodging.

Leaving Thekla below he ran upstairs, and hastily donned the suit of peasant's clothes, and then making the others into a bundle

196

descended again, and with Thekla made his way to the quiet spot outside the city gates where the wagon was standing ready for a start. He had already paid the peasant half the sum agreed, and now handed him the remainder.

"I should scarce have known you," the peasant said, examining Malcolm by the light of his pinewood torch. "Why, you look like one of us instead of a city craftsman."

"I am going to astonish them when I get home," Malcolm said, "and shall make the old folks a present of the wagon. So I am going to arrive just as I was when I left them."

The peasant asked no farther questions, but, handing the torch to Malcolm, and telling him that he would find half a dozen more in the wagon, he took his way back to the town, where he intended to sleep in the stables and to start at daybreak for his home.

He thought that the transaction was a curious one; but, as he had been paid handsomely for his wagon, he troubled not his head about any mystery there might be in the matter. As soon as he had gone Malcolm arranged the straw in the bottom of the wagon so as to form a bed; but Thekla said that for the present she would rather walk with him.

"It is weeks since I have been out, and I shall enjoy walking for a time; besides, it is all so strange that I should have no chance to sleep were I to lie down."

Malcolm at once consented, and taking his place at the head of the oxen, he started them, walking ahead to light the way and leading them by cords passed through their nostrils. He had not the least fear of pursuit for the present, for it had been arranged that the countess should inform their attendant that Thekla was feeling unwell, and had retired to bed, and the woman, whatever she might suspect, would take care not to verify the statement, and it would be well on in the following morning before her absence was discovered.

Malcolm tried his best to distract Thekla's thoughts from her parents, and from the strange situation in which she was placed, and chatted to her of the events of the war since he had last seen her, of the route which he intended to adopt, and the prospects of peace. In two hours' time the girl, unaccustomed to exercise, acknowledged that she was tired; she therefore took her place in the wagon.

Malcolm covered her up with straw and threw some sacks lightly over her, and then continued his journey. He travelled all night, and in the morning stopped at a wayside inn, where his arrival at that hour excited no surprise, as the peasants often travelled at night, because there was then less chance of their carts

197

being seized and requisitioned by the troops. He only stopped a short time to water and feed the oxen, and to purchase some black bread and cheese. This he did, not because he required it, for he had an ample supply of provisions in the cart far more suited for Thekla's appetite than the peasant's fare, but to act in the usual manner, and so avoid any comment. Thekla was still asleep under the covering, which completely concealed her. Malcolm journeyed on until two miles further he came to a wood, then, drawing aside from the road, he unyoked the oxen and allowed them to lie down, for they had already made a long journey. Then he woke Thekla, who leaped up gaily on finding that it was broad daylight. Breakfast was eaten, and after a four hours' halt they resumed their way, Thekla taking her place in the wagon again, and being carefully covered up in such a manner that a passerby would not suspect that anyone was lying under the straw and sacks at one end of the wagon. Just at midday Malcolm heard the trampling of horses behind him and saw a party of cavalry coming along at full gallop. The leader drew rein when he overtook the wagon.

"Have you seen anything," he asked Malcolm, "of two seeming craftsmen, a man and a boy, journeying along the road?"

Malcolm shook his head. "I have seen no one on foot since I started an hour since."

Without a word the soldiers went on. They had no reason, indeed, for believing that those for whom they were in search had taken that particular road. As soon as Thekla's disappearance had been discovered by the waiting woman she had hurried to the governor, and with much perturbation and many tears informed him that the young countess was missing, and that her couch had not been slept on. The governor had at once hurried to the spot. The count and countess resolutely refused to state what had become of their daughter.

The sentries had all been strictly questioned, and it was found that the mender of clocks had, when he left, been accompanied by an apprentice whom the sentry previously on duty asserted had not entered with him. The woman was then closely questioned; she asserted stoutly that she knew nothing whatever of the affair. The count had commissioned her to obtain a craftsman to set the clock in order, and she had bethought her of a young man whose acquaintance she had made some time previously, and who had informed her in the course of conversation that he had come from Nuremberg, and was a clockmaker by trade, and was at present out of work. She had met him, she said, on several occasions, and as he was a pleasant youth and comely, when he had spoken to her of marriage she had not been averse, now it was plain he had deceived her; and here she began to cry bitterly and loudly.

Her story seemed probable enough, for any friend of the count who had intended to carry off his daughter would naturally have begun by ingratiating himself with her attendant. She was, however, placed in confinement for a time. The count and countess were at once removed to the fortress. Orders were given that the town should be searched thoroughly, and any person answering to the description which the governor was able to give of the supposed clockmaker should be arrested, while parties of horse were despatched along all the roads with orders to arrest and bring to Prague any craftsman or other person accompanied by a young boy whom they might overtake by the way. Several innocent peasants with their sons were pounced upon on the roads and hauled to Prague; but no news was obtained of the real fugitives, who quietly pursued their way undisturbed further by the active search which was being made for them. The anger of the emperor when he heard of the escape of the prize he had destined for one of his favourite officers was extreme. He ordered the count to be treated with the greatest rigour, and declared all his estates and those of his wife forfeited, the latter part of the sentence being at present inoperative, her estates being in a part of the country far beyond the range of the Imperialist troops. The waiting maid was after some weeks' detention released, as there was no evidence whatever of her complicity in the affair.

Malcolm continued his journey quietly towards the frontier of Bavaria; but, on arriving at a small town within a few miles of Pilsen, he learned that Wallenstein had fallen back with his army to that place. Much alarmed at the news he determined to turn off by a cross road and endeavour to avoid the Imperialists. He had not, however, left the place before a party of Imperialist horse rode in.

Malcolm was at once stopped, and was told that he must accompany the troops to Pilsen, as they had orders to requisition all carts for the supply of provisions for the army. Malcolm knew that it was of no use to remonstrate, but, with many loud grumblings at his hard lot, he moved to the marketplace, where he remained until all the wagons in the place and in the surrounding country had been collected.

Loud and bitter were the curses which the peasants uttered at finding themselves taken from their homes and compelled to perform service for which the pay, if received at all, would be scanty in the extreme. There was, however, no help for it; and when all were collected they started in a long procession guarded by the cavalry for Pilsen. On arriving there they were ordered to take up their station with the great train of wagons collected for the supply of the army.

Thekla had from her hiding place heard the conversation, and was greatly alarmed at finding that they were again in the power of the Imperialists. No one, however, approached the wagon, and it was not until darkness had set in that she heard Malcolm's voice whispering to her to arise quietly.

"We must leave the wagon; it will be impossible for you to remain concealed here longer, for tomorrow I may be sent out to bring in supplies. For the present we must remain in Pilsen. The whole country will be scoured by the troops, and it will not be safe to traverse the roads. Here in Pilsen no one will think of looking for us.

"Wallenstein's headquarters are the last place where we should be suspected of hiding, and you may be sure that, however close the search may be elsewhere, the governor of Prague will not have thought of informing Wallenstein of an affair so foreign to the business of war as the escape from the emperor's clutches of a young lady. I have donned my craftsman dress again, and we will boldly seek for lodgings."

They soon entered the town, which was crowded with troops, searching about in the poorer quarters.

Malcolm presently found a woman who agreed to let him two rooms. He accounted for his need for the second room by saying that his young brother was ill and needed perfect rest and quiet, and that the filing and hammering which was necessary in his craft prevented the lad from sleeping. As Malcolm agreed at once to the terms she asked for the rooms, the woman accepted his statement without doubt. They were soon lodged in two attics at the top of the house, furnished only with a table, two chairs, and a truckle bed in each; but Malcolm was well contented with the shelter he had found.

Seeing that it would be extremely difficult at present to journey further, he determined to remain some little time in the town, thinking that he might be able to carry out the instructions which he had received from Colonel Munro, and to obtain information as to the plans of Wallenstein and the feelings of the army.

"You will have to remain a prisoner here, Thekla, I am afraid, almost as strictly as at Prague, for it would not do to risk the discovery that you are a girl by your appearing in the streets in daylight, and after dark the streets of the town, occupied by Wallenstein's soldiers, are no place for any peaceful persons.

"I may as well be here as at Nuremberg," Thekla said, "and as

200

I shall have you with me instead of being with strangers, the longer we stay here the better."

The next morning Malcolm sallied out into the town to see if he could find employment. There was, however, but one clockmaker in Pilsen, and the war had so injured his trade that he had discharged all his journeymen, for clocks were still comparatively rare luxuries, and were only to be seen in the houses of nobles and rich citizens. Knowing that Wallenstein was devoted to luxury and magnificence, always taking with him, except when making the most rapid marches, a long train of baggage and furniture, Malcolm thought it possible that he might obtain some employment in his apartments. He accordingly went boldly to the castle where the duke had established himself, and, asking for his steward, stated that he was a clockmaker from the workshop of the celebrated horologist, Master Jans Boerhoff, and could repair any clocks or watches that might be out of order.

"Then you are the very man we need," the steward said. "My master, the duke, is curious in such matters, and ever carries with him some half dozen clocks with his other furniture; and, use what care I will in packing them, the shaking of the wagons is constantly putting them out of repair. It was but this morning the duke told me to bring a craftsman, if one capable of the work could be found in the town, and to get the clocks put in order, for it displeases him if they do not all keep the time to the same minute. Follow me."

He led the way into the private apartments of the duke. These were magnificently furnished, the walls being covered with rich velvet hangings. Thick carpets brought from the East covered the floors. Indeed, in point of luxury and magnificence, Wallenstein kept up a state far surpassing that of his Imperial master.

There were several clocks standing on tables and on brackets, for Wallenstein, although in most respects of a clear and commanding intellect, was a slave to superstition. He was always accompanied by an astrologer, who read for him the course of events from the movements of the stars, who indicated the lucky and unlucky days, and the hours at which it was not propitious to transact important business. Hence it was that he placed so great an importance on the exact observance of the hour by his numerous time pieces.

"Here are some of the clocks," the steward said, indicating them. "Of course you cannot work here, and they are too heavy to be removed, besides being too costly to intrust out of my charge, I will have a room prepared in the castle where you can work. Come again at noon with your tools, and all shall be in readiness."

At the hour appointed Malcolm again presented himself.

"The duke has given personal instructions," he said, "that a closet close by shall be fitted up for you, in order that he himself if he chooses may see you at work."

Malcolm was conducted to a small room near at hand. Here one of the clocks which had stopped had been placed on the table, and he at once set to work. He soon discovered that one of the wheels had been shaken from its place by the jolting of the wagons, and that the clock could be set going by a few minutes work. As, however, his object was to prolong his visit to the castle as long as possible, he set to work and took it entirely to pieces. Two hours later the door opened and a tall handsome man of commanding presence entered. Malcolm rose and bowed respectfully, feeling that he was in the presence of the great general.

"You come from Nuremberg," Wallenstein said, "as I am told, and have learned your craft in the workshop of Master Jans Boerhoff, who is well known as being the greatest master of his craft."

Malcolm bowed silently.

"It is strange," Wallenstein muttered to himself, "that this young man's destiny should be connected with mine; and yet the astrologer said that he who should present himself at the castle nearest to the stroke of nine this morning would be a factor in my future, and, as my steward tells me, the clock sounded nine as this young man addressed him." He then asked Malcolm several questions as to the work upon which he was engaged, and then said abruptly: "Dost know the day and hour on which you were born?"

Malcolm was somewhat surprised at the question, for he had not heard the muttered words of Wallenstein, but he at once replied that he had heard that he was born at the stroke of midnight on the last day in the year.

The duke said no more, but left the closet and proceeded at once to an apartment near his own bed chamber, which, although he had arrived but a few hours previously, had already been fitted up for the use of his astrologer. The walls were hidden by a plain hanging of scarlet cloth; a large telescope stood at the window, a chart of the heavens was spread out on the table, and piles of books stood beside it. On the ceiling the signs of the zodiac had been painted, and some mystical circles had been marked out on the floor. A tall spare old man with a long white beard was seated at the table. He rose when Wallenstein entered.

"I cannot but think," the duke said, "that your calculations must for once have been mistaken, and that there must have been an error in the hour, for I see not how the destiny of this craftsman, who seems to be a simple lad, can in any way be connected with mine."

"I have made the calculation three times, your grace," the old man replied, "and am sure there is no error."

"He was born," Wallenstein said, "at midnight on December 31st, 1613. Work out his nativity, and see what stars were in the ascendant, and whether there are any affinities between us."

"I will do so at once," the astrologer said; "by tonight I shall be able to give your grace the information you require."

"Tonight," the duke said, "we will go over your calculations together as to our great enterprise. It is all important that there should be no mistake. I have for a whole year remained inactive because you told me that the time had not yet come, and now that you say the propitious moment is approaching would fain be sure that no error has been committed. All seems well, the troops are devoted to me, and will fight against whomsoever I bid them. By lavish gifts and favours I have attached all my generals firmly to me, and soon this ungrateful emperor shall feel how rash and foolish he has been to insult the man to whom alone he owes it that he was not long ago a fugitive and an exile, with the Swedes victorious masters of his capital and kingdom.

"Have not I alone saved him? Did not I at my own cost raise an army and stand between him and the victorious Gustavus? Have not I alone of all his generals checked the triumphant progress of the invaders? And yet he evades all his promises, he procrastinates and falters. Not one step does he take to give me the sovereignty of Bohemia which he so solemnly promised me, and seems to think that it is honour and reward enough for me to have spent my treasure and blood in his service. But my turn is at hand, and when the hand which saved his throne shall cast him from it he will learn how rash he has been to have deceived and slighted me. And you say that the stars last night all pointed to a favourable conjunction, and that the time for striking the great blow is at hand?"

"Nothing could be better," the astrologer said; "Jupiter, your own planet, and Mars are in the ascendant. Saturn is still too near them to encourage instant action, but he will shortly remove to another house and then your time will have come."

"So be it," Wallenstein said, "and the sooner the better. Now I will leave you to your studies, and will ride out to inspect the troops, and to see that they have all that they need, for they must be kept in the best of humours at present."

CHAPTER XXII

THE CONSPIRACY

The next day Wallenstein again entered Malcolm's workroom and said abruptly to him: "What deeds of bravery have you performed?"

Malcolm looked astonished.

"In an idle moment," the duke said, "having an interest in nativities and seeing that you were born between two years, I asked my astrologer to work out the calculations. He tells me that it was fated that you should perform deeds of notable bravery while still young. It seemed the horoscope of a soldier rather than of a craftsman, and so I told the sage; but he will have it that he has made no mistake."

Malcolm hesitated for a moment; the blind faith which the otherwise intelligent and capable general placed in the science of astrology was well known to the world. Should he deny that he had accomplished any feats, the duke, believing implicitly the statement which his astrologer had made him, would suspect that he was not what he seemed; he therefore replied modestly, "I have done no deeds worthy relating to your excellency, but I once swam across a swollen river to direct some travellers who would otherwise have perished, and my neighbours were good enough to say that none in those parts save myself would have attempted such a feat."

"Ah!" the duke exclaimed in a tone of satisfaction, "as usual the stars have spoken correctly. Doubtless as great courage is required to swim a river in flood as to charge into the ranks of the enemy."

So saying Wallenstein left the room, filled with a desire to attach to himself the young man whom his adviser had assured him was in some way connected with his destiny. Wallenstein a day or two later offered Malcolm to take him into his permanent service, saying that he was frequently plagued by the stoppages of his clocks, and desired to have a craftsman capable of attending to them on his establishment. He even told the young man that he might expect promotion altogether beyond his present station.

Malcolm could not refuse so flattering an offer, and was at once installed as a member of Wallenstein's household, declining however the use of the apartment which the steward offered him, saying that he had a sick brother lodging with him in the town. Mingling with the soldiers in the evenings Malcolm learned that there were rumours that negotiations for peace were going on with Saxony and Sweden. This was indeed the case, but Wallenstein was negotiating on his own behalf, and not on that of the emperor. So far but little had come of these negotiations, for Oxenstiern had the strongest doubts of Wallenstein's sincerity, and believed that he was only trying to gain time and delay operations by pretended proposals for peace. He could not believe that the great Imperialist general, the right hand of the emperor, had any real intention of turning against his master. Towards the end of January there was some excitement in Pilsen owing to the arrival there of all the generals of the Imperialist army save only Gallas, Coloredo, and Altringer.

Malcolm was sure that such a gathering could only have been summoned by Wallenstein upon some matter of the most vital importance, and he determined at all hazards to learn what was taking place, in order that he might enlighten Oxenstiern as to the real sentiments of the duke. Learning that the principal chamber in the castle had been cleared, and that a meeting of the officers would take place there in the evening, he told Thekla when he went home to his meal at midday that she must not be surprised if he did not return until a late hour. He continued his work until nearly six o'clock, the time at which the meeting was to begin, and then extinguishing his light, he made his way through the passages of the castle until he reached the council chamber, meeting with no interruption from the domestics, who were by this time familiar with his person, and who regarded him as one rising in favour with their master. He waited in the vicinity of the chamber until he saw an opportunity for entering unobserved, then he stole into the room and secreted himself behind the arras beneath a table standing against the wall, and where, being in shadow, the bulge in the hanging would not attract attention.

In a few minutes he heard heavy steps with the clanking of swords and jingling of spurs, and knew that the council was beginning to assemble. The hum of conversation rose louder and louder for a quarter of an hour; then he heard the door of the apartment closed, and knew that the council was about to commence. The buzz of conversation ceased, and then a voice, which was that of Field Marshal Illo, one of the three men in Wallenstein's confidence, rose in the silence. He began by laying before the army the orders which the emperor had sent for its dispersal to various parts of the country, and by the turn he gave to these he found it easy to excite the indignation of the assembly.

He then expatiated with much eloquence upon the merits of the army and its generals, and upon the ingratitude with which the emperor had treated them after their noble efforts in his behalf. The court, he said, was governed by Spanish influence. The ministry were in the pay of Spain. Wallenstein alone had hitherto opposed this tyranny, and had thus drawn upon himself the deadly enmity of the Spaniards. To remove him from the command, or to make away with him entirely, had, he asserted, been long the end of their desires, and until they could succeed they endeavoured to abridge his power in the field. The supreme command was to be placed in the hands of the King of Hungary solely to promote the Spanish power in Germany, as this prince was merely the passive instrument of Spain.

It was only with the view of weakening the army that six thousand troops were ordered to be detached from it, and solely to harass it by a winter campaign that they were now called upon at this inhospitable season to undertake the recovery of Ratisbon. The Jesuits and the ministry enriched themselves with the treasure wrung from the provinces, and squandered the money intended for the pay of the troops.

The general, then, abandoned by the court, was forced to acknowledge his inability to keep his engagements to the army. For all the services which for two-and-twenty years he had rendered to the house of Austria, in return for all the difficulties with which he had struggled, for all the treasures of his own which he had expended in the Imperial service, a second disgraceful dismissal awaited him. But he was resolved the matter should not come to this; he was determined voluntarily to resign the command before it should be wrested from his hands, "and this," continued the speaker, "is what he has summoned you here to make known to you, and what he has commissioned me to inform you."

It was now for them to say whether they would permit him to leave them; it was for each man present to consider who was to repay him the sums he had expended in the emperor's service; how he was ever to reap the rewards for his bravery and devotion, when the chief who alone was cognizant of their efforts, who was their sole advocate and champion, was removed from them.

When the speaker concluded a loud cry broke from all the officers that they would not permit Wallenstein to be taken from them. Then a babel of talk arose, and after much discussion four of the officers were appointed as a deputation to wait upon the duke to assure him of the devotion of the army, and to beg him not to withdraw himself from them. The four officers intrusted with the commission left the room and repaired to the private chamber of the general. They returned in a short time, saying that the duke refused to yield.

Another deputation was sent to pray him in even stronger terms to remain with them. These returned with the news that Wallenstein had reluctantly yielded to their request; but upon the condition that each of them should give a written promise to truly and firmly adhere to him, neither to separate or to allow himself to be separated from him, and to shed his last drop of blood in his defence. Whoever should break this covenant, so long as Wallenstein should employ the army in the emperor's service, was to be regarded as a perfidious traitor and to be treated by the rest as a common enemy.

As these last words appeared to indicate clearly that Wallenstein had no thought of assuming a position hostile to the emperor, or of defying his authority, save in the point of refusing to be separated from his army, all present agreed with acclamations to sign the documents required.

"Then, gentlemen," Marshal Illo said, "I will have the document for your signatures at once drawn up. A banquet has been prepared in the next room, of which I invite you now all to partake, and at its conclusion the document shall be ready."

Malcolm from his hiding place heard the general movement as the officers left the apartment, and looking cautiously out from beneath the arras, saw that the chamber was entirely empty. He determined, however, to remain and to hear the conclusion of the conference. He accordingly remained quiet for upwards of an hour. During this time the attendants had entered and extinguished the lights, as the guests would not return to the council chamber.

He now left his hiding place and made his way to the door which separated him from the banqueting hall. Listening intently at the keyhole, he heard the clinking of glasses and the sound of voices loudly raised, and he guessed that the revelry was at its height. More and more noisy did it become, for Marshal Illo was plying his guests with wine in order that they might sign without examination the document which he had prepared for their signatures. Feeling confident that none would hear him in the state at which they had now arrived, Malcolm cautiously opened the door an inch or two, and was able to hear and see all that passed.

It was another hour before Marshal Illo produced the document and passed it round for signature. Many of those to whom it was handed signed it at once without reading the engagement; but one more sober than the rest insisted on reading it through, and at once rising to his feet, announced to the others that the important words "as long as Wallenstein shall employ the army for the emperor's service," which had been inserted in the first draft agreed to by Wallenstein and the deputation, had been omitted.

A scene of noisy confusion ensued. Several of the officers declared that they would not sign the document as it stood. General Piccolomini, who had only attended the meeting in order that he might inform the emperor, to whom he was devoted, of what took place there, had drunk so much wine that he forgot the part he was playing, and rose to his feet and with drunken gravity proposed the health of the emperor.

Louder and louder grew the din of tongues until Count Terzky, who was alone with Illo and Colonel Kinsky in Wallenstein's confidence, arose, and in a thundering voice declared that all were perjured villains who should recede from their engagement, and would, according to their agreements be treated as enemies by the rest. His menaces and the evident danger which any who might now draw back would run, overcame the scruples of the recalcitrants, and all signed the paper. This done the meeting broke up, and Malcolm, stealing away from his post of observation, made his way back to his lodgings.

He slept little that night. What he had seen convinced him that Wallenstein was really in earnest in the propositions which he had made to Oxenstiern and the Elector of Saxony, and that he meditated an open rebellion against the emperor. It was of extreme importance that Oxenstiern should be made acquainted with these facts; but it would be next to impossible to escape from Pilsen, burdened as he was with Thekla, and to cross the country which intervened between the two armies and which was constantly traversed by cavalry parties and scouts of both sides.

After much deliberation, therefore, he determined upon the bold course of frankly informing Wallenstein who he was and what he had heard, and to beg of him to furnish him with an escort to pass through the lines in order that he might make his way with all speed to Oxenstiern in order to assure him of the good faith of the duke and of the importance of his frankly and speedily accepting his proposals. It was possible, of course, that he might fall a victim to Wallenstein's first anger when he found out that he had been duped, and the plot in which he was engaged discovered; but he resolved to run the risk, believing that the duke would see the advantage to be gained by complying with his proposal.

It was necessary, however, to prepare Thekla for the worst.

"Thekla," he said in the morning, "an end has come to our stay here. Circumstances have occurred which will either enable us to continue our journey at once and in safety or which may place me in a prison."

Thekla gave a cry of surprise and terror. "I do not think, my dear girl," Malcolm went on, "that there is much fear of the second alternative, but we must be prepared for it. You must obey my instructions implicitly. Should I not return by nightfall you will know that for a time at least I have been detained. You will tell the woman of the house, who is aware that I am employed by Wallenstein, that I have been sent by him to examine and set in order the clocks in his palace in Vienna in readiness for his return there, but that as you were too unwell to travel I have bade you remain here until I return to fetch you.

"You have an ample supply of money even without the purse of gold which the duke presented to me yesterday. You must remain here quietly until the spring, when the tide of war is sure to roll away to some other quarter, and I trust that, long ere that, even should I be detained, I shall be free to come to you again; but if not, do you then despatch this letter which I have written for you to Jans Boerhoff. In this I tell him where you are, in order that, if your mother comes to him asking for you, or your parents are able to write to him to inquire for you, he may inform them of your hiding place. I have also written you a letter to the commander of any Swedish force which may enter this town, telling him who you are, and praying him to forward you under an escort to Nuremberg."

"But what shall I do without you?" Thekla sobbed.

"I trust, my dear, that you will not have to do without me, and feel convinced that tomorrow we shall be upon our way to the Swedish outposts. I only give you instructions in case of the worst. It troubles me terribly that I am forced to do anything which may possibly deprive you of my protection, but my duty to the country I serve compels me to take this step, which is one of supreme importance to our cause."

It was long before Thekla was pacified, and Malcolm himself was deeply troubled at the thought that the girl might be left alone and unprotected in a strange place. Still there appeared every probability that she would be able to remain there in safety until an opportunity should occur for her to make her way to Nuremberg. It was with a heavy heart, caused far more by the thought of Thekla's position than of danger to himself, that he took his way to the castle; but he felt that his duty was imperative, and was at heart convinced that Wallenstein would eagerly embrace his offer.

It was not until midday that he was able to see the duke. Wallenstein had been greatly angered as well as alarmed at the resistance which his scheme had met with on the previous evening. He had believed that his favours and liberality had so thoroughly attached his generals to his person that they would have followed him willingly and without hesitation, even in a war against the emperor, and the discovery that, although willing to support him against deprivation from his command, they shrunk alarmed at the idea of disloyalty to the emperor, showed that his position was dangerous in the extreme.

He found that the signatures to the document had for the most part been scrawled so illegibly that the writers would be able to repudiate them if necessary, and that deceit was evidently intended. In the morning he called together the whole of the generals, and personally received them. After pouring out the bitterest reproaches and abuse against the court, he reminded them of their opposition to the proposition set before them on the previous evening, and declared that this circumstance had induced him to retract his own promise, and that he should at once resign his command.

The generals, in confusion and dismay, withdrew to the antechamber, and after a short consultation returned to offer their apologies for their conduct on the previous evening and to offer to sign anew the engagement which bound them to him. This was done, and it now remained only for Wallenstein to obtain the adhesion of Gallas, Altringer, and Coloredo, which, as they held important separate commands, was necessary for the success of his plan. Messengers were accordingly sent out at once to request them to come instantly to Pilsen.

After this business was despatched and Wallenstein was disengaged he was informed that Malcolm desired earnestly to speak to him on particular business. Greatly surprised at the request, he ordered that he should be shown in to him.

"Your excellency," Malcolm began when they were alone, "what I am about to say may anger you, but as I trust that much advantage may arise from my communication, I implore you to restrain your anger until you hear me to the end, after which it will be for you to do with me as you will."

Still more surprised at this commencement, Wallenstein signed to him to continue.

"I am, sir," Malcolm went on, "no clockmaker, although, indeed, having worked for some time in the shop of Master Jans Boerhoff at the time of the siege of Nuremberg, I am able to set clocks and watches in repair, as I have done to those which have been placed in my hands here. In reality, sir, I am a Scottish officer, a captain in the service of Sweden."

Wallenstein gave a short exclamation of angry surprise. "You must not think, sir, that I have come hither in disguise to be a spy upon the movements of your army. I came here unwillingly, being captured by your troops, and forced to accompany them.

"I left the Swedish camp on a private mission, having received there a missive from the Countess of Mansfeld, who, with her husband, was a kind friend of mine, telling me that they were prisoners of the emperor at Prague, and begging me to come to their assistance. Bethinking me of the occupation which had amused my leisure hours during the weary months when we were shut up by you in Nuremberg, I obtained leave of absence, attired myself as a craftsman, and made my way to Prague. There I found the count confined to his couch by a wound and unable to move. The countess had no thought of quitting him. Her anxiety was wholly for her daughter, a girl of fifteen, whom the emperor purposed to shut up in a convent and force to change her religion, and then to bestow her hand upon one of his favourites, with her father's confiscated estates as her dowry.

"I succeeded in effecting her escape, disguised as a boy; I myself travelling in the disguise of a peasant with a wagon. We were making our way towards the Swedish lines when we came across your army, which had, unknown to me, suddenly moved hither. I and my cart were requisitioned for the service of the army. On the night of my arrival here I resumed my disguise as a craftsman, left my wagon, and with my young companion took up my lodging here, intending to remain quietly working at the craft I assumed until an opportunity offered for continuing our journey. Accident obtained me employment here, and as rumour said that overtures for peace were passing between yourself and the Swedish chancellor, I may frankly say that I determined to use the position in which I accidentally found myself for the benefit of the country I served, by ascertaining, if I could, how far your excellency was in earnest as to the offers you were making. In pursuance of that plan I yesterday concealed myself and overheard all that passed in the council chamber with the officers, and at the banquet subsequently."

211

Wallenstein leapt to his feet with an angry exclamation.

"Your excellency will please to remember," Malcolm went on quietly, "that I could have kept all this to myself and used it to the benefit or detriment of your excellency, but it seemed to me that I should benefit at once your designs and the cause I serve by frankly acquainting you with what I have discovered. It would be a work of time for me to make my way with my companion through the lines of your army and to gain those of the Swedes. I might be slain in so doing and the important information I have acquired lost.

"It is of all things important to you that the Swedish chancellor, whose nature is cautious and suspicious, should be thoroughly convinced that it is your intention to make common cause with him and to join him heart and soul in forcing the emperor to accept the conditions which you and he united may impose upon him. This the information I have acquired will assuredly suffice to do, and he will, without doubt, at once set his army in motion to act in concert with yours."

Wallenstein paced the room for a minute or two in silence.

"The stars truly said that you are a brave man and that your destiny is connected with mine," he said at length, "for assuredly none but a brave man would venture to tell me that he had spied into my councils. I see, however, that what you say is reasonable and cogent, and that the news you have to tell may well induce Oxenstiern to lay aside the doubts which have so long kept us asunder and at once to embrace my offer. What, then, do you propose?"

"I would ask, sir," Malcolm replied, "that you would at once order a squadron of horse to escort me and my companion through the debatable land between your army and that of the Swedes, with orders for us to pass freely on as soon as we are beyond your outposts and in the neighbourhood of those of the Swedes."

"It shall be done," Wallenstein said. "In half an hour a squadron of horse shall be drawn up in the courtyard here, and a horse and pillion in readiness for yourself and the maiden. In the meantime I will myself prepare a letter for you to present to the Swedish chancellor with fresh proposals for common action."

CHAPTER XXIII

THE MURDER OF WALLENSTEIN

Malcolm hurried back to his lodging, where he was received with a cry of delight from Thekla, who had passed the time since he had left her on her knees praying for his safety. He told her at once that she was about to be restored to safety among friends, that her troubles were at an end, and she was again to resume her proper garments which she had brought with her in the basket containing his tools at the time of her flight.

A few minutes sufficed to make the change, and then she accompanied Malcolm to the castle. Wallenstein's orders had been rapidly carried out; a squadron of cavalry were formed up in the courtyard, and in front of them an attendant held a horse with a pillion behind the saddle. Malcolm lifted Thekla on to the pillion and sprang into the saddle in front of her. One of Wallenstein's household handed a letter to him and then gave him into the charge of the officer commanding the squadron, who had already received his orders. The officer at once gave the word and rode from the castle followed by the cavalry.

As soon as they were out of the town the pace was quickened, and the cavalcade proceeded at a trot which was kept up with few intermissions until nightfall, by which time twenty miles had been covered. They halted for the night in a small town where the soldiers were billeted on the inhabitants, comfortable apartments being assigned to Malcolm and his charge.

Soon after daybreak the journey was continued. A sharp watch was now kept up, as at any moment parties of the Swedish cavalry making a raid far in advance of their lines might be met with. No such adventure happened, and late in the afternoon the troop halted on the crest of a low hill.

"Here," the officer said, "we part. That town which you see across the river is held by the Swedes, and you will certainly meet with no molestation from any of our side as you ride down to it."

Malcolm thanked the officer for the courtesy he had shown him on the journey, and then rode forward towards the town. It was getting dusk as he neared the bridge, but as he came close Malcolm's heart gave a bound as he recognized the green scarves and plumes worn by the sentries at the bridge. These seeing only a single horseman with a female behind him did not attempt to question him as he passed; but he reined in his horse.

"Whose regiment do you belong to?" he asked.

The men looked up in surprise at being addressed in their own language by one whose attire was that of a simple craftsman, but whom they now saw rode a horse of great strength and beauty.

"We belong to Hamilton's regiment," they replied.

"And where shall I find that of Munro?"

"It is lying in quarters fifteen miles away," one of the soldiers answered.

"Then we cannot get on there tonight," Malcolm said. "Where are your officers quartered?"

A soldier standing near at once volunteered to act as guide, and in a few minutes Malcolm arrived at the house occupied by them. He was of course personally known to all the officers, and as soon as their surprise at his disguise and at seeing him accompanied by a young lady had subsided, they received him most heartily.

Thekla was at once taken to the house of the burgomaster, which was close at hand, and handed over to the wife of that functionary for the night, and Malcolm spent a merry evening with the Scottish officers, to whom he related the adventures which had so satisfactorily terminated—making, however, no allusion to the political secrets which he had discovered or the mission with which he was charged. He was soon furnished from the wardrobes of the officers with a suit of clothes, and although his craftsman attire had served him well he was glad to don again the uniform of the Scottish brigade.

"You have cut your narrative strangely short at the end, Graheme," Colonel Hamilton said when Malcolm brought his story to a conclusion. "How did you get away from Pilsen at last, and from whom did you steal that splendid charger on whom you rode up to the door?"

"That is not my own secret, colonel, and I can only tell you at present that Wallenstein himself gave it to me."

A roar of incredulous laughter broke from the officers round the table.

"A likely story indeed, Graheme; the duke was so fascinated with your talents as a watchmaker that he bestowed a charger fit for his own riding upon you to carry you across into our lines."

"It does not sound likely, I grant you," Malcolm said, "but it is true, as you will acknowledge when the time comes that there will be no longer any occasion for me to keep the circumstances secret. I

214

only repeat, Wallenstein gave me the honour of an escort which conducted me to the crest of the hill two miles away, where, if your sentries and outposts had been keeping their eyes open, they might have seen them."

It was late before the party broke up, but soon after daylight Malcolm was again in the saddle, and with Thekla as before on the pillion he continued his journey, and in three hours reached the town where his regiment was quartered.

Alighting at the door of the colonel's quarters, he led Thekla to his apartments. The colonel received him with the greatest cordiality and welcomed Thekla with a kindness which soon put her at her ease, for now that the danger was past she was beginning to feel keenly the strangeness of her position.

She remembered Colonel Munro perfectly, as he and the other officers of the regiment had been frequently at her father's during the stay of the regiment at Maintz. The colonel placed her at once in charge of the wife of one of the principal citizens, who upon hearing that she was the daughter of the Count of Mansfeld, well known for his attachment to the Protestant cause, willingly received her, and offered to retain her as her guest until an opportunity should occur for sending her on to Nuremberg, should Malcolm not be able at once to continue his journey to that city.

"That," Colonel Munro said as soon as Malcolm informed him of the extremely important information he had gained, "is out of the question. Your news is of supreme importance, it alters the whole course of events, and offers hopes of an early termination of the struggle. There is no doubt that Wallenstein is in earnest now, for he has committed himself beyond reparation. The only question is whether he can carry the army with him. However, it is clear that you must ride with all haste to Oxenstiern with your tidings; not a moment must be lost. He is in the Palatinate, and it will take you four days of hard riding at the least to reach him.

"In the meantime, your little maid, who by the way is already nearly a woman, had best remain here—I will see that she is comfortable and well cared for, and after all she is as well here as at Nuremberg, as there is no fear now of an advance of the Imperialists. In case of anything extraordinary occurring which might render this town an unsafe abiding place, I will forward her in safety to Nuremberg, even I if I have to detach a score of my men as her escort."

Before mounting again Malcolm paid a hurried visit to Thekla, who expressed her contentment with her new abode, and her readiness to stay there until he should return to take her to Nuremberg, even should it be weeks before he could do so.

"I quite feel among friends now," she said, "and Colonel Munro and your Scotch officers will, I am sure, take good care of me till you return."

Glad to feel that his charge was left in good hands Malcolm mounted his horse with a light heart and galloped away. Four days later he was closeted with the Swedish chancellor, and relating to him the scene in the castle at Pilsen. When he had finished his narrative Oxenstiern, who had, before Malcolm began, read the letter which Wallenstein had sent him, said:

"After what you tell me there can be no longer the slightest doubts of Wallenstein's intention. Ever since the death of the king he has been negotiating privately with me, but I could not believe that he was in earnest or that such monstrous treachery was possible. How could I suppose that he who has been raised from the rank of a simple gentleman to that of a duke and prince, and who, save the fortunes which he obtained with his wives, owes everything to the bounty of the emperor, could be preparing to turn his arms against him?"

"It is true that he has done great things for Ferdinand, but his ambition is even greater than his military talent. Any other man would have been content with the enormous possessions and splendid dignity which he has attained, and which in fact render him far richer than his Imperial master; but to be a prince does not suffice for him. He has been promised a kingdom, but even that is insufficient for his ambition. It is clear that he aims to dethrone the emperor and to set himself up in his place; however, his ingratitude does not concern me, it suffices now that at any rate he is sincere, and that a happy issue out of the struggle opens before us henceforth.

"I can trust him thoroughly; but though he has the will to join us has he the power? Wallenstein, with his generals and his army fighting for the emperor, is a mighty personage, but Wallenstein a rebel is another altogether. By what you tell me it seems more than doubtful whether his officers will follow him; and although his army is attached to him, and might follow him could he put himself at its head, it is scattered in its cantonments, and each section will obey the orders which the general in its command may give.

"Probably some of those who signed the document, pledging their fidelity to Wallenstein, have already sent news to the emperor of what is being done. It is a strange situation and needs great care;

the elements are all uncertain. Wallenstein writes to me as if he were assured of the allegiance of the whole of his army, and speaks unquestionably of his power to overthrow the emperor; but the man is clearly blinded by his ambition and infatuated by his fixed belief in the stars. However, one thing is certain, he and as much of his army as he can hold in hand are now our allies, and I must lose no time in moving such troops as are most easily disposable to his assistance.

"I will send to Saxony and urge the elector to put in motion a force to support him, and Duke Bernhard shall move with a division of our troops. I will at once pen a despatch to Wallenstein, accepting his alliance and promising him active aid as soon as possible.

"What say you, young sir? You have shown the greatest circumspection and ability in this affair. Will you undertake to carry my despatch? You must not travel as a Scottish officer, for if there are any traitors among the officers of Wallenstein they will assuredly endeavour to intercept any despatches which may be passing between us in order to send them to the emperor as proofs of the duke's guilt."

"I will undertake the task willingly, sir," Malcolm replied, "and doubt not that I shall be able to penetrate to him in the same disguise which I before wore. When I once reach him is your wish that I should remain near him, or that I should at once return?"

"It were best that you should remain for a time," the chancellor said. "You may be able to send me news from time to time of what is passing around the duke. Before you start, you shall be supplied with an ample amount of money to pay messengers to bring your reports to me. Wallenstein hardly appears to see the danger of his situation; but you will be more clear sighted. It is a strange drama which is being played, and may well terminate in a tragedy. At any rate the next month will decide what is to come of these strange combinations."

The horse on which Malcolm had ridden was knocked up from the speed at which he had travelled, and, ordering it to be carefully tended till his return, he obtained a fresh horse and again set out. He made the journey at the same speed at which he had before passed over the ground, and paused for a few hours only at Amberg, where he found Thekla well and comfortable, and quite recovered from the effects of her journeys and anxiety. She received him with delight; but her joy was dashed when she found that, instead of returning to remain with his regiment, as she had hoped, he was only passing through on another mission.

At Amberg he again laid aside his uniform and donned his costume as a craftsman. Colonel Munro gave him an escort of twenty troopers; with these he crossed the river at nightfall, and, making a detour to avoid the Imperialist outposts, rode some fifteen miles on his way. He then dismounted and handed over his horse to his escort, who at once started on their way back to Amberg, while he pursued his journey on foot towards Pilsen. It was late the next evening before he reached the town; and on arriving he learned that Wallenstein was still there.

The Imperialist general, immediately upon obtaining the signature of his officers, had sent to urge Altringer and Gallas, who had been absent from the meeting, to come to him with all speed. Altringer, on pretence of sickness, did not comply with the invitation. Gallas made his appearance, but merely with the intention of finding out all Wallenstein's plans and of keeping the emperor informed of them. Piccolomini had, immediately the meeting broke up, sent full details of its proceedings to the court, and Gallas was furnished with a secret commission containing the emperor's orders to the colonels and officers, granting an amnesty for their adhesion to Wallenstein at Pilsen, and ordering them to make known to the army that it was released from its obedience to Wallenstein, and was placed under the command of Gallas himself, who received orders, if possible, to arrest Wallenstein.

Gallas on his arrival perceived the impossibility of executing his commission, for Wallenstein's troops and officers were devoted to him, and not even the crime of high treason could overcome their veneration and respect for him. Finding that he could do nothing, and fearful that Wallenstein should discover the commission with which he was charged, Gallas sought for a pretence to escape from Pilsen, and offered to go to Altringer and to persuade him to return with him.

Wallenstein had no doubts of the fidelity of the general, and allowed him to depart. As he did not return at once Piccolomini, who was also most anxious to get out of the grasp of Wallenstein, offered to go and fetch both Gallas and Altringer. Wallenstein consented, and conveyed Piccolomini in his own carriage to Lintz. No sooner had Piccolomini left him than he hurried to his own command, denounced Wallenstein as a traitor, and prepared to surprise the duke in Pilsen. Gallas at the same time sent round copies of his commission to all the Imperial camps.

Upon his arrival Malcolm at once proceeded to the castle, and, finding the steward, requested him to inform the duke that he had returned. In a few minutes he was ushered into his presence, and handed to him the letter from Oxenstiern. Wallenstein tore it open without a word and gave an exclamation of satisfaction as he glanced it through.

"This is opportune indeed," he said, "and I thank you for bringing me the news so rapidly. Well did the astrologer say that my destiny to some extent depended on you; this is a proof that he was right. The chancellor tells me that the Duke of Saxe-Lauenberg will march instantly with four thousand men to join me, and that Duke Bernhard will move down at once with six thousand of the best Swedish troops. I may yet be even with the traitors."

Although the defection of Gallas and Piccolomini and the news of the issue of the Imperial proclamation had fallen with stunning force upon Wallenstein, he had still faith in the fidelity of the army at large, and he had already despatched Marshal Terzky to Prague, where all the troops faithful to him were to assemble, intending to follow himself with the regiments at Pilsen as soon as carriage could be obtained from the country round. His astrologer still assured him that the stars were favourable, and Wallenstein's faith in his own destiny was unshaken.

Upon finding that Malcolm had orders to remain with him until he was joined by Duke Bernhard, he ordered handsome apartments to be prepared for him, and as there was no longer any reason why the fact that a Swedish officer was in the castle should be concealed, he commanded that Malcolm should be furnished with handsome raiment of all sorts and a suit of superb armour. Upon the following morning Wallenstein sent for him.

"I have bad news," he said. "General Suys with an army arrived at Prague before Terzky got there, and I fear that the influence of Piccolomini, Gallas, and Altringer have withdrawn from me the corps which they command. Terzky will return tomorrow morning, and I shall then march with him and the troops here to Egra. There I shall effect a junction with Duke Bernhard, who is instructed to march upon that town."

The duke, though anxious, still appeared confident; but the outlook seemed to Malcolm extremely gloomy. The whole army save the regiments around Pilsen had fallen away from Wallenstein. His princely generosity to the generals and officers and his popularity among the troops had failed to attach them to him now that he had declared against the emperor, and it appeared to Malcolm that he would be able to bring over to the Swedish cause only the corps which he immediately commanded.

Still his defection could not but cause a vast gap in the Imperial defences, and the loss of the services of the greatest of their leaders would in itself be a heavy blow to the Imperialist cause, which had been almost solely supported by his commanding talents and his vast private income. Terzky arrived on the following morning, and the same afternoon Wallenstein with the whole of the troops at Pilsen marched towards Egra.

Among the officers attached to Wallenstein's person was a Scotchman named Leslie, to whom and a few other confidants Wallenstein had confided his designs. Wallenstein had at once introduced Malcolm to him, and the two rode in company during the march to Egra. Malcolm did not find him a cheerful companion. They chatted at times of the engagements in which both had taken part although on opposite sides; but Malcolm saw that his companion was absent and preoccupied, and that he avoided any conversation as to the turn which events had taken.

At the end of the first day's ride Malcolm came to the decided conclusion that he did not like his companion, and, moreover, that his heart was far from being in the enterprise on which they were engaged. The following day he avoided joining him, and rode with some of the other officers. Upon their arrival at Egra the gates were opened at their approach, and Colonel Butler, an Irishman who commanded the garrison, met Wallenstein as he entered, and saluted him with all honour. Wallenstein was pleased to find that the disaffection which had spread so rapidly through the army had not reached Egra.

A few hours after he had entered the town Wallenstein received the news that an Imperial edict had been issued proclaiming him a traitor and an outlaw; he also learned that the corps under the Duke of Saxe-Lauenburg was within a day's march of Egra. As soon as the duke retired to his apartments Leslie sought out Colonel Butler, and revealed to him the purposes of Wallenstein, and informed him of the Imperial order absolving the army from their allegiance to him. The two men, with Lieutenant Colonel Gordon, another Imperialist officer, at once determined to capture Wallenstein and to hand him over as a prisoner to the emperor.

In the afternoon Leslie had an interview with Wallenstein, who told him of the near approach of the Dukes of Saxe-Lauenburg and Saxe-Weimar, and informed him of his plans for advancing from Egra direct into the heart of Bohemia.

The treacherous officer at once hurried away with the news to his two associates, and it was agreed that the near approach of the Saxons rendered it impossible for them to carry out their first plan, but that instant and more urgent steps must be taken. That evening a banquet was given by Butler to Wallenstein and his officers. The duke, however, was too anxious to appear at it, and remained in his own apartment, the rest of the officers, among them Wallenstein's chief confidants, Illo, Terzky, and Kinsky, together with Captain Neumann, an intimate adviser of Terzky, were among the guests. Malcolm was also present.

The banquet passed off gaily, Wallenstein's health was drunk in full bumpers, and his friends boasted freely that in a few days he would find himself at the head of as powerful an army as he had ever before commanded. Malcolm had naturally been placed at the table near his compatriots, and it seemed to him that their gaiety was forced and unnatural, and a sense of danger came over him.

The danger indeed was great, although he knew it not. The drawbridge of the castle had been drawn up, the avenues leading to it guarded, and twenty infantry soldiers and six of Butler's dragoons were in hiding in the apartment next to the banqueting hall.

Dessert was placed on the table; Leslie gave the signal, and in an instant the hall was filled with armed men, who placed themselves behind the chairs of Wallenstein's trusted officers with shouts of "Long live Ferdinand!" The three officers instantly sprang to their feet, but Terzky and Kinsky were slain before they had time to draw their swords.

Neumann in the confusion escaped into the court, where he too was cut down. Illo burst through his assailants, and placing his back against a window stood on his defence. As he kept his assailants at bay he poured the bitterest reproaches upon Gordon for his treachery, and challenged him to fight him fairly and honourably. After a gallant resistance, in which he slew two of his assailants, he fell to the ground overpowered by numbers, and pierced with ten wounds.

Malcolm had sprung to his feet at the commencement of the tumult, but was pressed down again into his chair by two soldiers, while Leslie exclaimed, "Keep yourself quiet, sir, I would fain save you as a fellow countryman, and as one who is simply here in the execution of his duty; but if you draw sword to defend these traitors, you must share their fate."

No sooner had the murder of the four officers been accomplished than Leslie, Butler, and Gordon issued into the town. Butler's cavalry paraded the streets, and that officer quieted the garrison by telling them that Wallenstein had been proclaimed a traitor and an outlaw, and that all who were faithful to the emperor must obey their orders. The regiments most attached to Wallenstein had not entered the city, and the garrison listened to the voice of their commander.

Wallenstein knew nothing of what had taken place in the castle, and had just retired to bed when a band of Butler's soldiers, led by Captain Devereux, an Irishman, burst into his apartment. The duke leaped from his bed, but before he could snatch up a sword he was pierced through and through by the murderers' halberts.

So fell one of the greatest men of his age. Even to the present day there are differences of opinion as to the extent of his guilt, but none as to the treachery with which he was murdered by his most trusted officers. That Wallenstein owed much gratitude to the emperor is unquestionable, but upon the other hand he had even a greater title to the gratitude of Ferdinand, whose crown and empire he had repeatedly saved. Wallenstein was no bigot, his views were broad and enlightened, and he was therefore viewed with the greatest hostility by the violent Catholics around the king, by Maximilian of Bavaria, by the Spaniards, and by the Jesuits, who were all powerful at court. These had once before brought about his dismissal from the command, after he had rendered supreme services, and their intrigues against him were again at the point of success when Wallenstein determined to defy and dethrone the emperor. The coldness with which he was treated at court, the marked inattention to all his requests, the consciousness that while he was winning victories in the field his enemies were successfully plotting at court, angered the proud and haughty spirit of Wallenstein almost to madness, and it may truly be said that he was goaded into rebellion. The verdict of posterity has certainly been favourable to him, and the dastardly murder which requited a lifetime of brilliant services has been held to more than counterbalance the faults which he committed.

CHAPTER XXIV

MALCOLM'S ESCAPE

After the fall of Wallenstein's colonels Malcolm was led away a prisoner, and was conducted to a dungeon in the castle. It was not until the door closed behind him that he could fairly realize what had taken place, so sudden and unexpected had been the scene in the banqueting hall. Five minutes before he had been feasting and drinking the health of Wallenstein, now he was a prisoner of the Imperialists. Wallenstein's adherents had been murdered, and it was but too probable that a like fate would befall the general himself. The alliance from which so much had been hoped, which seemed to offer a prospect of a termination of the long and bloody struggle, was cut short at a blow.

As to his own fate it seemed dark enough, and his captivity might last for years, for the Imperialists' treatment of their prisoners was harsh in the extreme. The system of exchange, which was usual then as now, was in abeyance during the religious war in Germany. There was an almost personal hatred between the combatants, and, as Malcolm knew, many of his compatriots who had fallen into the hands of the Imperialists had been treated with such harshness in prison that they had died there. Some, indeed, were more than suspected of having been deliberately starved to death.

However, Malcolm had gone through so many adventures that even the scene which he had witnessed and his own captivity and uncertain fate were insufficient to banish sleep from his eyes, and he reposed as soundly on the heap of straw in the corner of his cell as he would have done in the carved and gilded bed in the apartment which had been assigned to him in the castle.

The sun was shining through the loophole of his dungeon when he awoke. For an hour he occupied himself in polishing carefully the magnificently inlaid armour which Wallenstein had presented him, and which, with the exception of his helmet, he had not laid aside when he sat down to the banquet, for it was very light and in no way hampered his movements, and except when quartered in towns far removed from an enemy officers seldom laid aside their arms. He still retained his sword and dagger, for his captors, in their haste to finish the first act of the tragedy, and to resist any rising which might take place among the soldiery, had omitted to take them from him when they hurried him away.

On examination he found that with his dagger he could shove back the lock of the door, but this was firmly held by bolts without. Thinking that on some future occasion the blade might be useful to him, he pushed the dagger well into the lock, and with a sharp jerk snapped it off at the hilt. Then he concealed the steel within his long boot and cast the hilt through the loophole.

Presently a soldier brought him his breakfast—a manchet of bread and a stoup of wine. He was visited again at dinner and supper. Before the soldier came in the first time Malcolm concealed his sword in the straw, thinking that the soldier would be sure to remove it if he noticed it. The man who brought his breakfast and dinner was taciturn, and made no reply to his questions, but another man brought his supper, and he turned out of a more communicative disposition.

"What has happened?" he repeated in reply to Malcolm's question. "Well, I don't know much about it myself, but I do know that Wallenstein is dead, for the trooper who rides next to me helped to kill him. Everyone is content that the traitor has been punished, and as the troops have all pronounced for the emperor every thing is quiet. We had a good laugh this afternoon. The colonel sent out one of our men dressed up in Wallenstein's livery to meet the Duke of Saxe-Lauenburg and invite him to come on at once and join him here. The duke suspected no danger, and rode on ahead of his troops, with a few attendants, and you should have seen his face, when, after passing through the gates, he suddenly found himself surrounded by our men and a prisoner. Bernhard of Saxe-Weimar will be here tomorrow, as they say, and we shall catch him in the same way. It's a rare trap this, I can tell you."

The news heightened Malcolm's uneasiness. The capture of Duke Bernhard, the most brilliant of the German generals on the Protestant side, would be a heavy blow indeed to the cause, and leaving his supper untasted Malcolm walked up and down his cell in a fever of rage at his impotence to prevent so serious a disaster.

At last he ate his supper, and then threw himself upon the straw, but he was unable to sleep. The death of Wallenstein had made a deep impression upon him. The Imperialist general was greatly respected by his foes. Not only was he admired for his immense military talents, but he carried on the war with a chivalry and humanity which contrasted strongly with the ferocity of Tilly, Pappenheim, and Piccolomini. Prisoners who fell into his hands were always treated with courtesy, and although, from motives of policy, he placed but little check upon the excesses of his soldiery, no massacres, such as those which had caused the names of Tilly and Pappenheim to be held in abhorrence by the Protestants of Germany, were associated with that of Wallenstein. Then, too, the princely dignity and noble presence of the duke had greatly impressed the young soldier, and the courtesy with which he had treated him personally had attracted his liking as well as respect. To think that this great general, this princely noble, the man who alone had baffled the Lion of the North, had been foully murdered by those he had trusted and favoured, filled him with grief and indignation, the more so since two of the principal assassins were Scotchmen.

The thought that on the morrow Duke Bernhard of Weimar—a leader in importance second only to the Chancellor of Sweden—would fall unsuspiciously into the trap set for him goaded him almost to madness, and he tossed restlessly on the straw through the long hours of the night. Towards morning he heard a faint creaking of bolts, then there was a sound of the locks of the door being turned. He grasped his sword and sprang to his feet. He heard the door close again, and then a man produced a lantern from beneath a long cloak, and he saw Wallenstein's steward before him. The old man's eyes were bloodshot with weeping, and his face betokened the anguish which the death of his master had caused him.

"You have heard the news?" he asked.

"Alas!" Malcolm replied, "I have heard it indeed."

"I am determined," the old man said, "to thwart the projects of these murderers and to have vengeance upon them. None have thought of me. I was an old man, too insignificant for notice, and I have passed the day in my chamber lamenting the kindest of lords, the best of masters. Last evening I heard the soldiers boasting that today they would capture the Duke of Saxe-Weimar, and I determined to foil them. They have been feasting and drinking all night, and it is but now that the troopers have fallen into a drunken slumber and I was able to possess myself of the key of your dungeon.

"Here is your helmet. I will lead you to the stable, where I have saddled the best and fastest of my master's horses. You must remain there quietly until you deem that the gates are open, then leap upon the horse, and ride for your life. Few will know you, and you will probably pass out of the gate unquestioned. If not, you have your sword to cut your way. Once beyond the town ride to meet the duke. Tell him my master has been murdered, that Egra is in the hands of the Imperialists, and that Saxe-Lauenburg is a prisoner. Bid him march on this place with his force, take it by assault, and leave not one of the assassins of my lord living within its walls."

"You will run no risk, I hope, for your share in this adventure," Malcolm said.

"It matters little to me," the old man replied. "My life is worthless, and I would gladly die in the thought that I have brought retribution on the head of the murderers of my master. But they will not suspect me. I shall lock the door behind us, and place the key again in the girdle of the drunken guard, and then return to my own chamber."

Quietly Malcolm and his conductor made their way through the castle and out into the courtyard. Then they entered the stables.

"This is the horse," the steward said, again uncovering his lantern. "Is he not a splendid animal? He was my master's favourite, and sooner than that his murderers should ride him I would cut the throat of the noble beast with my dagger; but he has a better mission in carrying the avenger of his master's blood. And now farewell. The rest is in your own hands. May Heaven give you good fortune." So saying, the old man set down his lantern and left Malcolm alone.

The latter, after examining the saddle and bridle, and seeing that every buckle was firm and in its place, extinguished the light, and waited patiently for morning. In two hours a faint light began to show itself. Stronger and stronger it grew until it was broad day. Still there were but few sounds of life and movement in the castle. Presently, however, the noise of footsteps and voices was heard in the courtyard.

Although apprehensive that at any moment the stable door might open, Malcolm still delayed his start, as it would be fatal were he to set out before the opening of the gates. At last he felt sure that they must be opened to admit the country people coming in with supplies for the market. He had donned his helmet before leaving his cell, and he now quietly opened the stable door, sprang into the saddle, and rode boldly out.

Several soldiers were loitering about the courtyard. Some were washing at the trough and bathing their heads beneath the fountain to get rid of the fumes of the wine they had indulged in overnight. Others were cleaning their arms.

The sudden appearance of a mounted officer armed from

head to foot caused a general pause in their occupation, although none had any suspicion that the splendidly attired officer was a fugitive; but, believing that he was one of Leslie's friends who was setting out on some mission, they paid no further heed to him, as quietly and without any sign of haste he rode through the gateway of the castle into the town. The inhabitants were already in the streets, country women with baskets were vending their produce, and the market was full of people. Malcolm rode on at a foot pace until he was within sight of the open gate of the town. When within fifty yards of the gate he suddenly came upon Colonel Leslie, who had thus early been making a tour of the walls to see that the sentries were upon the alert, for Duke Bernhard's force was within a few miles. He instantly recognized Malcolm.

"Ah!" he exclaimed, "Captain Graheme—treachery! treachery! shut the gate there," and drawing his sword, threw himself in Malcolm's way.

Malcolm touched the horse with his spur and it bounded forward; he parried the blow which Leslie struck at him, and, with a sweeping cut full on the traitor's helmet, struck him to the ground and then dashed onward. A sentry was beginning to shut the gate, and his comrades were running out from the guardhouse as Malcolm galloped up.

The steward had fastened the holsters on to the saddle, and Malcolm, before starting, had seen to the priming of the pistols in them. Drawing one he shot the man who was closing the gate, and before his comrades could run up he dashed through it and over the drawbridge.

Several bullets whizzed around him, but he was soon out of range, and galloping at full speed in the direction in which the steward had told him that Duke Bernhard was encamped. In half an hour he reached the Swedish lines, and rode at once to the tent of the duke who was upon the point of mounting; beside him stood a man in the livery of Wallenstein. As he rode up Malcolm drew his pistol, and said to the man:

"If you move a foot I will send a bullet through your head."

"What is this?" exclaimed the duke in astonishment, "and who are you, sir, who with such scant courtesy ride into my camp?"

Malcolm raised his vizor. "I am Captain Graheme of Munro's regiment," he said, "and I have ridden here to warn your excellency of treachery. Wallenstein has been foully murdered. Egra is in the hands of the Imperialists, the Duke of Saxe-Lauenburg has been beguiled into a trap and taken prisoner, and this fellow, who is one of Butler's troopers, has been sent here to lead you into a like snare."

"Wallenstein murdered!" the duke exclaimed in tones of horror. "Murdered, say you? Impossible!"

"It is but too true, sir," Malcolm replied; "I myself saw his friends Illo, Terzky, and Kinsky assassinated before my eyes at a banquet. Wallenstein was murdered by his favourites Leslie and Gordon and the Irishman Butler. I was seized and thrown into a dungeon, but have escaped by a miracle to warn you of your danger."

"This is a blow indeed," the duke said mournfully. Turning to his attendants he ordered them to hang the false messenger to the nearest tree, and then begged Malcolm to follow him into his tent and give him full details of this terrible transaction.

"This upsets all our schemes indeed," the duke said when he had concluded. "What is the strength of the garrison at Egra?"

"There were Butler's dragoons and an infantry regiment in garrison there when we arrived; six regiments accompanied us on the march, and I fear that all these must now be considered as having gone over to the Imperialists."

"Then their force is superior to my own," the duke said, "for I have but six thousand men with me, and have no artillery heavy enough to make any impression upon the walls of the town. Much as I should like to meet these traitors and to deal out to them the punishment they deserve, I cannot adventure on the siege of Egra until I have communicated this terrible news to the Swedish chancellor. Egra was all important to us as affording an entrance into Bohemia so long as Wallenstein was with us, but now that he has been murdered and our schemes thus suddenly destroyed I cannot risk the destruction of my force by an assault upon the city, which is no longer of use to us."

Much as Malcolm would have liked to have seen the punishment of Wallenstein's treacherous followers, he could not but feel that the duke's view was, under the circumstances, the correct one. The tents were speedily struck, and the force fell back with all speed towards Bavaria, and after accompanying them for a march or two, Malcolm left them and rode to join his regiment, the duke having already sent off a messenger to Oxenstiern with a full account of the murder of Wallenstein.

As none could say what events were likely to follow the changed position of things, Malcolm determined at once to carry out the original intention of placing Thekla under the care of his friends at Nuremberg, in which direction it was not probable that the tide of war would for the present flow. After staying therefore a day or two with his regiment, where his relation of the events he had witnessed caused the greatest excitement and interest, Malcolm obtained leave from his colonel to escort Thekla to Nuremberg.

In order that they might pass in perfect safety across the intervening country Munro gave him an escort of twelve troopers, and with these he journeyed by easy stages to Nuremberg, where the worthy syndic of the clockmakers and his wife gladly received Thekla, and promised to treat her as one of their own daughters.

Here Malcolm took possession of his arms and valises, which he had sent, upon starting for Prague, to the care of Jans Boerhoff; not indeed that he needed the armour, for the suit which Wallenstein had given him was the admiration and envy of his comrades, and Munro had laughingly said that since Hepburn had left them no such gallantly attired cavalier had ridden in the ranks of the Scottish brigade.

There were many tears on Thekla's part as her young protector bade her adieu, for there was no saying how long a time might elapse before she might again see him, and Malcolm was sorely tempted to tell her that he had her father's consent to wooing her as his wife. He thought it, however, better to abstain from speaking, for should he fall in the campaign her grief would be all the greater had she come to think of him as her destined husband, for her hearty affection for him already assured him that she would make no objection to carrying out her father's wishes.

Shortly after rejoining his regiment Malcolm received a communication from the Swedish chancellor expressing in high terms his approbation of the manner in which he had carried out his instructions with regard to Wallenstein, and especially for the great service he had rendered the cause by warning the Duke of Saxe-Weimar of the trap which the Imperialists had set for him.

The death of Wallenstein was followed by a short pause in the war. It had entirely frustrated all the plans and hopes of the Protestants, and it caused a delay in the movement of the Imperialists. The emperor, when he heard of Wallenstein's death, heaped favours and honours upon the three men who had plotted and carried out his murder, and then appointed his son Ferdinand, King of Hungary, to the chief command of the army, with General Gallas as his principal adviser.

The Duke of Lorraine marched with an army to join the Imperialists, who were also strengthened by the arrival of 10,000

Spanish veterans, and early in May the new Imperial general entered the Palatinate and marched to lay siege to Ratisbon. To oppose the Imperial army, which numbered 35,000 men, Duke Bernhard, after having drawn together all the troops scattered in the neighbourhood, could only put 15,000 in the field. With so great a disparity of force he could not offer battle, but in every way he harassed and interrupted the advance of the Imperialists, while he sent pressing messages to Oxenstiern for men and money, and to Marshal Horn, who commanded in Alsace, to beg him march with all haste to his assistance.

Unfortunately Horn and Duke Bernhard were men of extremely different temperaments. The latter was vivacious, enterprising, and daring even to rashness, ready to undertake any enterprise which offered the smallest hope of success. Marshal Horn, on the other hand, although a good general, was slow, over cautious and hesitating, and would never move until his plans appeared to promise almost a certainty of success. Besides this, Horn, a Swede, was a little jealous that Duke Bernhard, a German, should be placed in the position of general-in-chief, and this feeling no doubt tended to increase his caution and to delay his action.

Consequently he was so long a time before he obeyed the pressing messages sent by the duke, that Ratisbon, after a valiant defence, surrendered on the 29th of July, before he had effected a junction with the duke's army. The Imperialists then marched upon Donauworth, and this place, after a feeble defence, also capitulated. The duke, heartbroken at seeing the conquests, which had been effected at so great a loss of life and treasure, wrested from his hands while he was unable to strike a blow to save them, in despair marched away to Swabia to meet the slowly advancing army of Marshal Horn.

No sooner was the junction effected than he turned quickly back and reached the vicinity of Nordlingen, only to find the enemy already there before him, and posted on the more advanced of the two heights which dominate the plain. By a skillful manoeuvre, however, he was enabled to throw within its walls a reinforcement to the garrison of eight hundred men.

Nordlingen, an important free town, stands on the south bank of the Ries, some 18 miles to the northeast of Donauworth. It was surrounded by a wall, interspersed with numerous towers, sufficiently strong to guard it against any surprise, but not to defend it against a regular siege by a numerous army. The vast plain on which the town stands is broken near its centre by two heights rising at a distance of three thousand yards from each other.

230

The height nearest to the town, which is very steep and craggy, is known as the Weinberg, the other is called Allersheim; a village stands some three hundred yards in advance of the valley between the heights, and is nearer to the town than either of the two eminences.

The Scotch brigade formed part of Duke Bernhard's command. It was now nearly two years since a pitched battle had been fought, for although there had been many skirmishes and assaults in the preceding year no great encounter had taken place between the armies since Gustavus fell at Lutzen, in October, 1632, and the Scotch brigade had not been present at that battle. In the time which had elapsed many recruits had arrived from Scotland, and Munro's regiment had been again raised to the strength at which it had landed at Rugen four years before. Not half a dozen of the officers who had then, full of life and spirit, marched in its ranks were now present. Death had indeed been busy among them. On the evening of their arrival in sight of the Imperialist army the two Grahemes supped with their colonel. Munro had but just arrived from the duke's quarters.

"I suppose we shall fight tomorrow, Munro," Major Graheme said.

"It is not settled," the colonel replied; "between ourselves the duke and Horn are not of one mind. The duke wants to fight; he urges that were we to allow Nordlingen to fall, as we have allowed Ratisbon and Donauworth, without striking a blow to save it, it would be an evidence of caution and even cowardice which would have the worst possible effect through Germany. Nordlingen has ever been staunch to the cause, and the Protestants would everywhere fall away from us did they find that we had so little care for their safety as to stand by and see them fall into the hands of the Imperialists without an effort. It is better, in the duke's opinion, to fight and to be beaten than to tamely yield Nordlingen to the Imperialists. In the one case honour would be satisfied and the reformers throughout Germany would feel that we had done our utmost to save their co-religionists, on the other hand there would be shame and disgrace."

"There is much in what the duke says," Nigel Graheme remarked.

"There is much," Munro rejoined; "but there is much also in the arguments of Horn. He reasons that we are outnumbered, the enemy is superior to us by at least a third, and to save the town we must attack them in an immensely strong position, which it will cost us great numbers to capture.

231

"The chances against our winning a victory are fully five to one. Granted the fall of Nordlingen will injure us in the eyes of the princes and people of Germany; but with good management on our part the feeling thus aroused will be but temporary, for we should soon wipe out the reverse. Of the 35,000 men of which the Imperial army is composed, 8000 at least are Spaniards who are on their way to Flanders, and who will very shortly leave it.

"On the other hand the Rhinegrave Otto Ludwig is with 7000 men within a few marches of us; in a short time therefore we shall actually outnumber the enemy, and shall be able to recover our prestige, just as we recovered it at Leipzig after suffering Magdeburg to fall. We shall recapture the towns which he has taken, and if the enemy should dare to accept battle we shall beat him, and shall be in a position to march upon Vienna."

"Horn's arguments are the strongest," Nigel Graheme said gravely; "the course he advises is the most prudent one."

"Undoubtedly," Munro replied; "but I think that it will not be followed. The duke is of a fiery spirit, and he would feel it, as most of us would feel it, a disgrace to fall back without striking a blow for Nordlingen. He has, too, been goaded nearly to madness during the last few days by messengers and letters which have reached him from the reformed princes and the free towns in all parts of Germany, reproaching him bitterly for having suffered Ratisbon and Donauworth to fall into the hands of the enemy without a blow, and he feels that his honour is concerned. I have little doubt that we shall fight a great battle to save Nordlingen."

CHAPTER XXV

NORDLINGEN

While Colonel Munro and his companions were discussing the matter a council of war was being held, and Duke Bernhard's view was adopted by all his generals, who felt with him that their honour was involved in the question, and that it would be disgraceful to march away without striking a blow to save the besieged city. Horn, therefore, being outvoted, was forced to give way. Up to nightfall the Imperialists had showed no signs of an intention to occupy the Weinberg, their forces being massed on and around the Allersheim Hill. It was determined therefore to seize the Weinberg at once, and the execution of this step was committed to Horn.

The choice was most unfortunate. The service was one upon the prompt carrying out of which victory depended, and Horn, though a brave and capable commander, was slow and cautious, and particularly unfitted for executing a service which had to be performed in a dark night across a country with which he was not familiar. Taking with him four thousand chosen musketeers and pikemen and twelve guns he set out at nine o'clock, but the rough road, the dikes, and ditches which intercepted the country impeded him, and the fact that he was unacquainted with the general position of the country made him doubly cautious, and it was not until midnight that he reached the foot of the hill.

Here, unfortunately, he came to the conclusion that since he had encountered such difficulties in crossing the flat country he should meet with even greater obstacles and delays in ascending the hill in the dark; he therefore took the fatal resolution of remaining where he was until daylight, and accordingly ordered the column to halt. Had he continued his march he would have reached the summit of the Weinberg unopposed, and the fate of the battle on the following day would have been changed. But the Imperialist leaders, Gallas and Cardinal Infanta Don Fernando, had not been unmindful of the commanding position of the hill upon which Horn was marching, and had given orders that it should be occupied before daylight by four hundred Spaniards.

The commander of this force was as over prompt in the execution of his orders as Horn was over cautious. He reached the top of the Weinberg before midnight, and at once set his men to work to intrench themselves strongly. As soon as daybreak enabled Horn to see the fatal consequences which had arisen from his delay he ordered his men to advance. With their usual gallantry the Swedes mounted the hill and rushed at the intrenchment. It was defended with the greatest obstinacy and courage by the Spaniards; but after desperate fighting the Swedes forced their way into the work at two points, and were upon the point of capturing the position when an ammunition wagon accidentally exploded in their midst, killing great numbers and throwing the rest into a temporary disorder, which enabled the Spaniards to drive them out and again occupy the intrenchments.

Before the Swedes had fully recovered themselves the Spanish cavalry, which at the first sound of the conflict the cardinal had ordered to the spot, charged them in flank and forced them to a precipitate retreat down the hillside. Bitterly regretting his delay at midnight, Horn brought up fresh troops, and after addressing encouraging words to those who had been already repulsed, led the united body to the assault.

But the Weinberg, which had been occupied in the early morning by only four hundred men, was now defended by the whole of the Spanish infantry. Vain now was the energy of Horn, and ineffectual the valour of his troops. Time after time did the Swedes climb the hill and strive to obtain a footing on its crest, each assault was repulsed with prodigious slaughter. Duke Bernhard was now fully engaged with the Imperialists on the Allersheim, and was gradually gaining ground. Seeing, however, how fruitless were the efforts of Horn to capture the Weinberg, he despatched as many of his infantry as he could spare to reinforce the marshal. Among these was Munro's regiment.

"Now, my brave lads," Colonel Munro shouted, as he led his regiment against the hill, "show them what Scottish hearts can do." With a cheer the regiment advanced. Pressing forward unflinchingly under a hail of bullets they won their way up the hill, and then gathering, hurled themselves with a shout upon the heavy masses of Spanish veterans. For a moment the latter recoiled before the onset; then they closed in around the Scotch, who had already lost a third of their number in ascending the hill.

Never did the famous regiment fight with greater courage and fury; but they were outnumbered ten to one, and their opponents were soldiers of European reputation. In vain the Scotchmen strove to break through the serried line of pikes which surrounded them. Here and there a knot of desperate men would win a way through; but ere others could follow them the Spanish line closed in again and cut them off from their comrades, and they died fighting to the last.

Fighting desperately in the front rank Munro and his officers encouraged their men with shouts and example; but it was all in vain, and he at last shouted to the remains of his followers to form in a solid body and cut their way back through the enemy who surrounded them. Hemmed in as they were by enemies the Scottish spearmen obeyed, and, headed by their colonel, flung themselves with a sudden rush upon the enemy. Before the weight and fury of the charge the veterans of Spain gave way, and the Scots found themselves on the crest of the hill which they had lately ascended. No sooner were they free from the Spanish ranks than the musketeers of the latter opened fire upon them, and numbers fell in the retreat. When they reached the foot of the fatal hill, and bleeding and breathless gathered round their commander, Munro burst into tears on finding that of the noble regiment he had led up the hill scarce enough remained to form a single company. Seven times now had Horn striven to carry the hill, seven times had he been repulsed with terrible slaughter, and he now began to fall back to join the force of Duke Bernhard. The latter, recognizing that the battle was lost, and that Horn, if not speedily succoured, was doomed, for the Imperialists, flushed with victory, were striving to cut him off, made a desperate attack upon the enemy hoping to draw their whole forces upon himself, and so enable Horn to retire. For the moment he succeeded, but he was too weak in numbers to bear the assault he had thus provoked. John of Werth, who commanded the Imperial cavalry, charged down upon the Swedish horsemen and overthrew them so completely that these, forced back upon their infantry, threw them also into complete disorder.

The instant Horn had given the orders to retreat, Colonel Munro, seeing the danger of the force being surrounded, formed up the little remnant of his regiment and set off at the double to rejoin the force of the duke. It was well that he did so, for just when he had passed over the intervening ground the Imperialist cavalry, fresh from the defeat of the Swedes, swept across the ground, completely cutting off Horn's division from that of the duke. A few minutes later Marshal Horn, surrounded on all sides by the enemy, and feeling the impossibility of further resistance with his weakened and diminished force, was forced to surrender with all his command.

Duke Bernhard narrowly escaped the same fate; but in the end he managed to rally some nine thousand men and retreated towards the Maine. The defeat was a terrible one; ten thousand men were killed and wounded, and four thousand under Horn taken prisoners; all the guns, equipage, and baggage fell into the hands of the enemy.

Nordlingen was the most decisive battle of the war; its effect was to change a war which had hitherto been really only a civil war—a war of religion—into one with a foreign enemy. Hitherto France had contented herself with subsidizing Sweden, who had played the principal part. Henceforward Sweden was to occupy but a secondary position. Cardinal Richelieu saw the danger of allowing Austria to aggrandize itself at the expense of all Germany, and now took the field in earnest.

Upon the other hand Nordlingen dissolved the confederacy of the Protestant German princes against Ferdinand the Second. The Elector of Saxony, who had ever been vacillating and irresolute in his policy, was the first to set the example by making peace with the emperor. The Elector of Brandenburg, Duke William of Weimar, the Prince of Anhalt, the Duke of Brunswick-Luneburg, the Duke of Mecklenburg, Pomerania, and the cities of Augsburg, Wurzburg, and Coburg, and many others hastened to follow the example of all the leading members of the Protestant Union.

Dukes Bernhard of Weimar and William of Cassel were almost alone in supporting the cause to maintain which Gustavus Adolphus had invaded Germany. The Swedish army, whose exploits had made the court of Vienna tremble, seemed annihilated, and well might the emperor deem that his final triumph over Protestantism was complete when he heard of the battle of Nordlingen, for as yet he dreamed not that its result would bring France into the field against him.

Malcolm Graheme was one of the few officers of Munro's regiment who burst his way through the Spanish lines on the top of the Weinberg. He was bleeding from several wounds, but none of them were serious. Nigel was beside him as they began to descend the hill; but scarcely had he gone a step when he fell headlong, struck by a ball from an arquebus. Malcolm and one of the sergeants raised him, and between them carried him to the foot of the hill; then, when the remains of the regiments started to rejoin Duke Bernhard, they were forced to leave him. Although Malcolm kept up with his regiment in the retreat he was so utterly exhausted by loss of blood that he could no longer accompany them. By the death of so many of his seniors he was now one of the majors of the regiment, if that could be called a regiment which was scarce a company in strength. A few days after the battle Colonel Munro received orders to march with his shattered remnant, scarce one of whom but was from wounds unfit for present service, by easy stages to North Germany, there to await the arrival of reinforcements from Scotland, which might raise the regiment to a strength which would enable it again to take the field.

Malcolm remained behind until his strength slowly returned. The colonel, before leaving, had bade him take his time before rejoining, as months would probably elapse before the regiment would again be fit for service. As soon as he was able to travel he journeyed to Nuremberg. On arriving at the abode of Jans Boerhoff he learned that Thekla was no longer an inmate of the family. The Count of Mansfeld had died in prison, and the countess had arrived at Nuremberg and had taken up her abode there. Malcolm made his way to the house she occupied. The meeting was an affecting one. Malcolm was greatly grieved over the death of his staunch friend, and joined in the sorrow of the countess and her daughter. A few days after his arrival the countess said to him:

"I am of course aware, Malcolm, of the conversation which the count had with you concerning Thekla, and my wishes fully agreed with his on the subject. In other times one would not speak of marriage when Thekla's father had been but two months dead; but it is no time for conventionalities now. All Southern Germany is falling away from the Protestant cause, and ere long we may see the Imperialists at the gate of Nuremberg, and it may be that in a few months the whole of Germany will be in their power. Therefore, I would that there should be no delay. Thekla is nearly seventeen; you are twenty-one—over young both to enter upon the path of matrimony; but the events of the last few months have made a woman of her, while you have long since proved yourself both in thoughtfulness and in valour to be a man. Thekla is no longer a great heiress. Since Nordlingen we may consider that her father's estates have gone for ever, mine may follow in a few months. Therefore I must ask you, are you ready to take her without dowry?"

"I am," Malcolm said earnestly, "and that right gladly, for I love her with all my heart."

"It needs no questioning on my part," the countess said, "to know that she loves you as truly, and that her happiness depends wholly on you. I saw her anguish when the news came of the terrible defeat at Nordlingen and of the annihilation of some of the Scottish regiments. My heart was wrung by her silent despair, her white and rigid face, until the news came that you were among the few who had survived the battle, and, in the outburst of joy and thankfulness at the news, she owned to me that she loved you, her only fear being that you cared for her only as a sister, since no word of love had ever passed your lips. I reassured her on that score by telling her of your conversation with her father, and that a feeling of duty alone had kept you silent while she remained under your protection.

"However, Malcolm, she will not come to you penniless, for, seeing that it was possible that the war would terminate adversely, and determined to quit the country should he be forbidden to worship according to his own religion here, the count has from time to time despatched considerable sums to the care of a banker at Hamburg, and there are now 10,000 gold crowns in his hands.

"There are, moreover, my estates at Silesia, but these I have for sometime foreseen would follow those of my husband and fall into the hands of the emperor. Before the death of the count I talked over the whole matter with him, and he urged me in any case, even should you fall before becoming the husband of Thekla, to leave this unhappy country and to take refuge abroad.

"Before his death I had an interview with my nearest kinsman, who has taken sides with the Imperialists, and to him I offered to resign Thekla's rights as heiress to the estate for the sum of 10,000 crowns. As this was but three years revenue of the estates, and it secured their possession to him whether the Imperialists or Swedes were victorious in the struggle, he consented, after having obtained the emperor's consent to the step, and I have this morning received a letter from him saying that the money has been lodged in the hands of the banker at Hamburg, and Thekla and I have this morning signed a deed renouncing in his favour all claim to the estate. Thus Thekla has a dowry of 20,000 gold crowns—a sum not unworthy of a dowry even for the daughter of a Count of Mansfeld; but with it you must take me also, for I would fain leave the country and end my days with her."

"Do you keep the dowry so long as you live, countess," Malcolm said earnestly. "It is more than the richest noble in Scotland could give with his daughter. My own estate, though small, is sufficient to keep Thekla and myself in ease, and my pleasure in having you with us will be equal to hers. You would wish, of course, that I should quit the army and return home, and, indeed, I am ready to do so. I have had more than enough of wars and fighting. I have been preserved well nigh by a miracle, when my comrades have fallen around me like grass. I cannot hope that such fortune would always attend me. The cause for which I have fought seems lost, and since the Protestant princes of Germany are hastening to desert it, neither honour nor common sense demand that I, a soldier of fortune and a foreigner, should struggle any longer for it; therefore I am ready at once to resign my commission and to return to Scotland."

"So be it," the countess said; "but regarding Thekla's dowry I shall insist on having my way. I should wish to see her in a position similar to that in which she was born, and with this sum you can largely increase your estates and take rank among the nobles of your country. Now I will call Thekla in and leave you to ask her to agree to the arrangements we have made.

"My child," she went on, as Thekla in obedience to her

summons entered the apartment, "Malcolm Graheme has asked your hand of me. He tells me that he loves you truly, and is willing to take you as a penniless bride, and to carry you and me away with him far from these terrible wars to his native Scotland—what say you, my love?"

Thekla affected neither shyness or confusion, her colour hardly heightened as in her sombre mourning she advanced to Malcolm, and laying her hand in his, said:

"He cannot doubt my answer, mother; he must know that I love him with my whole heart."

"Then, my daughter," the countess said, "I will leave you to yourselves; there is much to arrange, for time presses, and your betrothal must be quickly followed by marriage."

It was but a few days later that Malcolm led Thekla to the altar in St. Sebald's Church, Nuremberg. The marriage was a quiet one, seeing that the bride had been so lately orphaned, and only Jans Boerhoff and his family, and two or three Scottish comrades of Malcolm's, who were recovering from their wounds at Nuremberg, were present at the quiet ceremony. The following day the little party started for the north. Malcolm had already received a letter from Oxenstiern accepting his resignation, thanking him heartily for the good services he had rendered, and congratulating him on his approaching wedding.

Without adventure they reached Hamburg, and there, arranging with the banker for the transmission of the sum in his hands to Edinburgh, they took ship and crossed to Scotland.

Three months later Malcolm was delighted by the appearance of his uncle Nigel. The latter was indeed in dilapidated condition, having lost an arm, and suffering from other wounds. He had been retained a prisoner by the Imperialists only until he was cured, when they had freed him in exchange for an Imperial officer who had been captured by the Swedes.

Thekla's dowry enabled her husband largely to increase his estates. A new and handsome mansion was erected at a short distance from the old castle, and here Malcolm Graheme lived quietly for very many years with his beautiful wife, and saw a numerous progeny rise around them.

To the gratification of both, five years after her coming to Scotland, the Countess of Mansfeld married Nigel Graheme and the pair took up their abode in the old castle, which was thoroughly repaired and set in order by Malcolm for their use, while he and Thekla insisted that the fortune he had received as a dowry with his wife should be shared by the countess and Nigel.